Indebted to the Bratva

AN AGE GAP, ALPHA MALE, DARK RUSSIAN MAFIA ROMANCE

ELLIE DANIELS

AF420124

Indebted to the Bratva

Copyright © 2024 Ellie Daniels & Street Cat

Publishing

All rights reserved.

No part of this book may be reproduced, distributed, or transmitted in any form or by any means, including photocopying, recording, or other electronic or mechanical methods, without the prior written permission of the publisher, except in the case of brief quotations embodied in critical reviews and certain other noncommercial uses permitted by copyright law.

Other Titles by
Ellie Daniels:

Volkov Bratva Series:
Claimed by the Bratva King
Promised to the Bratva
Knocked Up by the Bratva Enforcer
Indebted to the Bratva
Desired by the Bratva Lieutenant

Taboo Relationships

My Professor's Secret

Moonlit Desires

Bound by Betrayal

Table of Contents

Chapter 1

The cargo ship groaned beneath the weight of its freight, the sound of shifting metal grating on Katya's nerves as the vessel rocked gently in the dark waters. The air was thick with the stench of sweat and salt, mingling with the acrid scent of rusting steel. She could feel the dampness seeping into her bones, the cold biting at her skin as she sat huddled against a grimy wall. It had been days since she'd boarded, though it felt like years—each hour stretching into an eternity as fear gnawed at her insides. Her body ached from the cramped space, her muscles stiff from holding herself together, both physically and emotionally.

Katya Sokolov was twenty years old, with long, dark brown hair that hung in loose waves past her shoulders, framing her pale face. Her dark brown eyes, usually filled with quiet fire, were now dulled by exhaustion and fear. Petite but curvaceous, her figure often drew unwanted attention, but she'd learned long ago how to navigate the unwanted stares—though now, in this cold and harsh reality, her physical appearance offered her no advantages. The chill of the ship's hold made her shiver, the thin layers of her clothes doing little to protect her from the cold. She pulled her knees up to her chest, wrapping her arms around herself in an effort to stay warm.

She hadn't expected the journey to be pleasant, but nothing had prepared her for the reality of it. They had been packed into the cargo hold like livestock, herded onto the ship with little more than a barked command and a shove. The space was dimly lit, with only a few weak bulbs casting flickering shadows along the walls. The others—two young women and two men, all in varying states of despair—huddled near her, their faces pale with exhaustion and fear. No one spoke much. What was there to say? They were all in the same situation, dragged here by forces beyond their control, each of them carrying the weight of debts they hadn't incurred.

Katya clenched her jaw, trying to suppress the anger that bubbled inside her. It was easier to be angry than afraid. Anger made her feel alive, reminded her that she was still fighting, even if it was only in her mind. Fear, on the other hand, was an enemy she couldn't seem to shake. It clung to her like a second skin, tightening around her chest until every breath felt like a battle.

She glanced at the others. The men sat with their heads down, too weary to look up, while one of the women quietly cried, her thin shoulders shaking with each sob. Katya wanted to comfort her, but what could she say? They were all prisoners here, bound by invisible chains. A part of her envied the woman's ability to cry. Katya hadn't cried once since she boarded the ship. Her tears had dried up long ago, back when her father had first betrayed her.

Her father. The thought of him sent a fresh wave of anger coursing through her. She could still see his face, the hollow eyes, the way his lips had tightened into a thin line when he'd told her about the deal he'd made with the Bratva. He hadn't even had the decency to look her in the eye. Her stomach twisted with the memory. How could he? How could he sell her out like that, offer her up to pay for his sins like she was nothing more than a bargaining chip?

She pressed the heels of her hands into her eyes, willing the image of him away. But the anger remained, simmering just below the surface. Her life had been ripped apart because of him. The small, quiet life she'd built for herself back in Russia, gone in the blink of an eye. Her job, her friends, her freedom—everything had been stolen from her, all because of her father's greed.

Now, here she was, on a cargo ship headed to Los Angeles, a city she'd only ever seen in movies. The reality of it felt distant, surreal. What would happen to her when she arrived? Would they force her into a life of degradation, like she had heard whispered among those who owed debts to the Bratva? The rumors had haunted her, gnawing at her insides during the long nights on the ship. She knew what happened to women like her—those who were sent to work off their fathers' mistakes.

Katya wasn't naive. She knew she had been lucky so far. The men aboard the ship hadn't touched her, though she had caught their hungry glances more than once. She could feel their eyes on her, and it made her skin crawl. She kept her head down, avoided any unnecessary attention, and prayed that her ordeal wouldn't get worse.

The ship gave another lurch as it neared the docks. The sound of chains rattling against the deck reverberated through the hold. Katya tensed, knowing that they were close now. Her heart began to pound in her chest, the adrenaline kicking in as reality settled over her. This was it. The moment she had been dreading and preparing for since the day she boarded the ship. She was about to be thrown into a world she didn't understand, into the hands of men who saw her as nothing more than a tool—a means to an end.

Her body ached from exhaustion, but her mind was racing, trying to calculate her next move. But what could she do? Run? Hide? There was no escape. Not from the Bratva.

The door to the cargo hold creaked open, and a shaft of light pierced the darkness. Katya shielded her eyes against the sudden brightness, her heart hammering in her chest. Footsteps echoed against the metal floor as a group of men entered. Their faces were hard, expressionless, guns strapped to their belts. The one in charge—a large, burly man with a thick beard and cold eyes—barked out orders in Russian. They were to disembark now. No questions, no arguments.

Katya stood, her legs shaky from disuse. She glanced around at the others, her heart sinking as she saw the fear in their faces. They were all just as lost as she was, caught up in a dangerous game they couldn't hope to win. She swallowed hard, trying to keep her composure as they were led off the ship.

The docks were bustling with activity—workers unloading crates, forklifts beeping as they maneuvered heavy pallets across the concrete. But Katya had no time to take it all in. Armed men were waiting for them, their eyes scanning the group with cold detachment. It was clear that they were nothing more than merchandise here, commodities to be sorted and used.

Katya felt her throat tighten, but she forced herself to keep her head up. She wouldn't let them see her fear. She wouldn't give them that satisfaction. As they were herded into a waiting van, Katya glanced back at the ship one last time. The sea stretched out behind it, endless and unforgiving, a reminder of the life she had left behind.

She didn't know what awaited her in Los Angeles, but one thing was certain: she was in the Bratva's world now, and there was no turning back.

The van ride was silent except for the hum of the engine and the occasional sharp turn that made Katya's stomach churn. Her nerves were stretched thin, fraying with each passing second. She tried to focus on the world outside the small, fogged-up windows, but there wasn't much to see. The streets they drove through were dark and desolate, a sharp contrast to the glitzy image of Los Angeles she had seen in movies. This part of the city was industrial, cold, and unwelcoming—just like the men who had herded them into the van.

The other women sat huddled beside her, their bodies tense and their eyes cast down. Katya could feel the weight of their fear, as palpable as her own, but she refused to let it show. She clenched her fists in her lap, willing herself to stay strong, even as her heart pounded in her chest. There was a quiet determination in her—no matter how powerless she felt, she wouldn't let them break her. Not yet.

The van came to a halt with a sudden jerk, and the men outside barked orders. Katya's pulse quickened as she heard the heavy sound of doors being wrenched open. It was time. They had arrived. The sliding door was yanked back, revealing a dull, gray warehouse. The air was heavy with the scent of oil and metal, the sharp tang filling her nostrils and making her already uneasy stomach twist further.

"Get out," one of the men growled, motioning them forward with a nod of his head. His hand rested on the grip of his gun, a casual yet menacing reminder of where the power lay.

Katya climbed out, her legs stiff from the hours of sitting, and glanced around. The warehouse was massive, with towering shelves stacked with crates and pallets. The dull buzz of forklifts and machinery echoed in the distance, adding to the sense of cold efficiency. It was a world that operated with precision, where human lives were just another commodity, traded and moved around like the crates on the shelves.

The office they were led into was no different. It was small and stark, the walls made of unpainted concrete, with a single overhead light casting a harsh glow. The furniture was sparse—a few metal chairs, a table, and nothing else to soften the edges of the room. The air inside was thick, suffocating, with the faint metallic scent that seemed to cling to everything.

Katya glanced at the other women. They kept their heads down, their shoulders hunched, as if trying to make themselves smaller, less noticeable. She could feel the tension radiating from them—the same fear that had been her companion on the ship was now a living, breathing presence in the room. Every breath felt labored, as if the weight of their circumstances pressed down on them from all sides.

But Katya wouldn't let herself crumble. She couldn't. Her father's betrayal had already cost her so much—her life, her freedom, her future. She wouldn't give the Bratva the satisfaction of seeing her break under the pressure. She straightened her spine, forcing her chin up, even though the fear gnawed at her insides like a ravenous beast.

Her eyes darted around the room, taking in every detail as if cataloging her new reality. The flickering fluorescent light overhead cast a sickly glow over the scene, and the sound of distant machinery continued to hum in the background, a constant reminder that they were far from any place of comfort or safety. There was no luxury here, no pretense of warmth—just the cold, hard reality of the world she had been thrust into.

Her breath hitched as she thought about what might come next. She had heard the rumors—the whispered stories of what happened to women who owed their lives to the Bratva. Some were sent to strip clubs, others into worse fates. The fear of being reduced to a mere object for their use tightened in her chest, but she pushed it down, clinging to the small flicker of resolve that still burned inside her.

The door to the office opened, and the sound of heavy footsteps filled the room. Katya's body tensed instinctively as several men entered. They were large, imposing figures, each with a cold, calculating expression that sent shivers down her spine. Their eyes scanned the room like predators assessing their prey. One of them stood out—a man in his mid-forties, broad-shouldered and gruff, his eyes sharp and watchful. He carried himself with the confidence of someone who was used to having control, someone who didn't need to raise his voice to command attention.

"Line up," one of the men ordered, his voice a harsh rasp that brooked no argument.

Katya moved forward along with the others, her heart pounding so loudly in her chest she was sure they could hear it. The other women kept their heads bowed, their eyes fixed on the floor, but Katya couldn't bring herself to look down. She stood tall, her chin slightly lifted, though her mind raced with a thousand fears. What would they do with her? Where would they send her? Every rumor she'd ever heard about the Bratva played on repeat in her mind.

The men didn't speak right away. They simply looked at them, appraising them like livestock at auction. The air felt thick with tension, and each passing second seemed to stretch into eternity.

Katya's anxiety spiked as her senses sharpened, every noise in the warehouse outside magnified in her mind. The distant clanging of metal, the low murmur of voices—it all made her feel like she was standing on the edge of a precipice, about to fall into something dark and dangerous. She glanced at the other women, noting the way they trembled, their fear almost tangible in the stale air. But she kept her head held high, refusing to let the men see the fear that gnawed at her insides.

The office felt like a cage, its concrete walls pressing in on her, making it hard to breathe. Every step the men took echoed, heavy and deliberate. Katya's heart pounded, her muscles tense, ready for whatever was coming next. She tried to calm herself, to remind herself that she'd survived worse than this. But a part of her, the part that knew how ruthless these men could be, couldn't stop imagining what might lie ahead.

She had to stay strong. No matter what happened, she had to survive. It was all she had left.

The door opened again, and another man entered. Katya's breath caught as she saw him—the one they were here to meet. He was older, powerful, and undeniably dangerous.

Ivan Volkov.

His mere presence shifted the energy in the room. The other men stiffened slightly, their gazes darting toward him in acknowledgment of the authority he held. Katya's heartbeat quickened as she tried to steady herself. This was it—the moment her new reality was about to be defined.

Ivan Volkov stepped forward into the dimly lit office, his presence impossible to ignore. Katya stood frozen, her heart racing in her chest as his cold, calculating eyes locked onto her. The room suddenly felt smaller, the air thicker as Ivan took his place behind the desk, commanding the space as if he owned not just the room, but everyone in it.

Katya swallowed hard, forcing herself to breathe evenly, though the tension in her body betrayed the calm she tried to project.

Even in the low light, Ivan Volkov's presence dominated the space. Around him stood several other Bratva men, their gazes cold and dispassionate as they surveyed the newcomers. Katya had heard his name whispered on the ship, in hushed tones of fear and respect. Ivan Volkov, the head of the Volkov family's operations in Los Angeles, and cousin to the powerful Nikolai Volkov, who ruled the Bratva's New York operations. To cross Ivan was to sign your own death warrant.

He was older, mid-forties, with an air of authority that made her stomach twist in both fear and, to her horror, something else. His broad shoulders filled out his tailored suit, the fabric stretching slightly across the expanse of his chest as he leaned back in his chair. Dark tattoos snaked their way up his neck and, from what little she could see, beneath the collar of his shirt, hinting at a body marked by years in the Bratva's world.

Katya's throat tightened as her eyes traveled over him. He wasn't like the other men in the room. His power was different—it wasn't just about physical strength, though he clearly possessed that in spades. No, Ivan exuded control. His presence was magnetic, drawing attention to him without so much as a word.

The light from the single lamp on the desk cast shadows over his face, but she could still make out his sharp, chiseled features. His jawline was strong, and his dark hair was cropped short, with a hint of gray just starting to show at his temples. His eyes, though, were what truly held her. Piercing and dark, they locked onto her the moment she entered the room, pinning her in place as though he could see straight through her. It felt like an unspoken challenge, one she wasn't sure she could win.

The longer Ivan stared at her, the more difficult it became for Katya to keep her breathing steady. It was as if he could see straight through her, through all the fear, anger, and uncertainty she had fought so hard to bury deep within herself. The other men in the room faded into the background, their presence irrelevant in the face of Ivan's focused intensity.

Katya knew she should look away, should lower her gaze like the others, but something inside her wouldn't let her. A fierce wave of defiance surged up, almost instinctively. If she was going to be indebted to this man for five years—if her life was going to be tied to his—then she would not enter this arrangement like a cowering dog. She would meet his eyes, even if it meant provoking whatever dangerous energy simmered beneath his calm exterior.

She lifted her chin slightly, her gaze unwavering as she stared back at him. It was a silent rebellion, but it was all she had. Her heart continued to hammer in her chest, each beat drumming louder in her ears as the tension between them thickened.

Ivan's expression remained impassive, but there was a flicker of something in his eyes—curiosity, perhaps, or amusement. Katya couldn't be sure. He didn't look away either, didn't dismiss her the way he had with the others. The challenge between them was palpable, hanging in the air like an unspoken threat.

Ivan's expression remained impassive, but there was a flicker of something in his eyes—curiosity, perhaps, or amusement. Katya couldn't be sure. He didn't look away either, didn't dismiss her the way he had with the others. The challenge between them was palpable, hanging in the air like an unspoken threat.

Before she could dwell on what that flicker meant, the room shifted as Ivan's attention turned toward the others. The sharp sound of a chair scraping against the concrete floor jolted Katya, her focus snapping back to the present. The two young men who had traveled with her from Russia stood stiffly to the side, their eyes fixed firmly on the floor, shoulders hunched in submission. The two young women, barely older than Katya herself, looked equally terrified, their faces pale, their bodies tense as they awaited their fate.

Ivan's gaze slid over them with the same cold detachment he had used on her, but without the curiosity. These people were nothing more than cogs in his well-oiled machine. He gestured with a flick of his wrist to one of the men standing by his side, a silent command for them to be dealt with. His authority radiated from him in waves—there was no need for words.

"These two," the man beside Ivan said, pointing to the young men, "will go down to the shipping yard. They'll be working the docks. Long hours, put them in the bunkhouse with the other men." His tone was casual, as if he were discussing the weather rather than dictating the future of these two men.

The young men didn't flinch. Katya imagined they had been expecting something like this—manual labor, endless shifts unloading cargo and working under the harsh sun. It wasn't glamorous, but it was safer than what the other women would face. A knot of anxiety tightened in her stomach as she glanced toward the other two women.

"And these two," the man continued, his voice taking on an edge of boredom, "send them to the clubs. We need fresh faces there."

The two women froze, their faces drained of all color. Katya's heart skipped a beat as her fear for them—and for herself—intensified. They had been expecting this, hadn't they? Just like she had? Still, the cold indifference with which they were dismissed, sent to lives that would likely be filled with exploitation and degradation, chilled her to the core. The Bratva didn't care about them. They were just bodies to be used, nothing more.

Katya's heart pounded in her chest, and the icy dread that had been slowly creeping over her now took full hold. Would she be next? Her breath quickened as she mentally prepared herself for the same fate. She could already see the scenario playing out in her mind—Ivan's dismissive gesture, the man's bored tone as he ordered her off to some seedy club where she'd be nothing more than a tool for the men who frequented those places.

She tried to control the panic rising in her throat. She had known this was coming since the day she left Russia, hadn't she? The second her father had betrayed the Bratva, her future had been sealed. She'd tried to tell herself that it might not be this bad, that maybe, just maybe, she'd be given something less degrading. But now, standing in the cold, sterile office, her fate looming over her, the reality hit hard.

This was it. Her life wasn't hers anymore. It belonged to Ivan Volkov, and he could send her anywhere he pleased. A strip club. Worse. Her stomach twisted painfully at the thought.

She could already hear the man's voice in her mind, telling Ivan to send her away with the others, his words dripping with that same indifference. She would be just another girl sent to work off a debt that wasn't hers, another face in the crowd of women forced into a world they had no control over.

A thin sheen of sweat broke out across her forehead as her fear reached its peak. She forced herself to breathe slowly, to calm the frantic beating of her heart, but it was no use. The room felt colder now, as if the very walls were closing in on her, suffocating her with their weight. She had never felt so helpless, so powerless.

Katya's mind raced, desperate for an escape, but there was none. She was trapped, bound to the Bratva's will, to Ivan's will.

Her fingers twitched at her sides, and she resisted the urge to clench her fists in frustration. She couldn't show fear. Not now, not in front of him. But no matter how hard she tried to suppress it, the terror gnawed at her, biting into her resolve like a wild animal that refused to be tamed.

The two women were quietly escorted out of the office, their eyes blank with resignation. The door shut behind them with a soft click, sealing their fate. Katya swallowed hard, the bile rising in her throat.

Now, it was her turn.

She straightened her spine, forcing herself to remain calm, but her thoughts spiraled as she waited for Ivan's verdict.

Ivan's gaze slid back to her, his eyes locking onto hers with a cold, unrelenting intensity. The weight of his attention bore down on her like an invisible hand around her throat. The room seemed to shrink, and suddenly it felt as though the very air had thickened. Katya's skin prickled as the silence deepened, everyone waiting for Ivan to speak.

Her heart hammered in her chest, loud enough that she feared the others might hear it. She stood frozen under his scrutiny, her muscles tense, ready to flinch at whatever verdict he was about to deliver. She expected the worst—perhaps she'd be sent to a club after all, despite the brief flicker of hope that she'd escape such a fate.

Ivan didn't speak immediately. His dark eyes traced her face, then moved down the length of her body, slowly, deliberately. It wasn't lust she saw in his gaze—it was something far more dangerous. He was sizing her up, evaluating her, as if determining how useful she would be to him. The room was still, as if the world itself held its breath, waiting for Ivan's word.

"Katya," he said at last, her name rolling off his tongue with a weight that made her stomach twist. The low timbre of his voice resonated through the room, demanding attention. He leaned forward slightly in his chair, resting his forearms on the desk, and for a brief moment, Katya wished she had looked away earlier, had lowered her gaze like the others. But it was too late for that now.

"You're here because of your father's betrayal," Ivan began, his voice cold and authoritative. There was no trace of emotion in it, no sign that he cared one way or another about her fate—only the brutal facts. "He was a thief. A coward who thought he could steal from the Bratva and get away with it."

Katya's stomach churned. She had known it would come to this, but hearing Ivan say the words out loud felt like being struck. Her father's crime, his betrayal, had cost her everything. And now, she was paying the price.

Ivan's eyes narrowed slightly as he continued. "Because of him, you now belong to me. You are indebted to the Volkov family for five years."

The words hit her like a punch to the gut, knocking the wind from her lungs. Five years. Five years of her life that she would never get back. Five years where she had no control, no freedom. She would be bound to him, forced to serve in whatever capacity he saw fit, all because of her father's selfishness.

Her jaw clenched, but she didn't look away. She refused to let him see how much his words affected her. She couldn't give him that satisfaction.

"And I don't tolerate thievery," Ivan added, his voice dropping to a menacing growl. "Your father's sins are now yours to bear. But let me make one thing clear—you will not repeat his mistakes. Not in my house."

The room felt colder now, and Katya had to fight to keep her expression neutral. Inside, her blood boiled. How could he speak to her like this? As if she were the one who had stolen from him, as if she had any control over the situation she was in? She was here because of her father, yes, but she had done nothing to deserve this.

"Your role," Ivan said, leaning back slightly, "is to work as a nanny. My children will be your responsibility, and you will see to their needs." His voice was sharp, each word delivered like a command. "Do your job well, and you'll avoid the fate of the others."

Katya's heart skipped a beat. A nanny? She wasn't
being sent to the clubs? Relief flooded her, so
intense that she had to force herself not to sag in
place. She had been bracing for something much
worse, something far more degrading, but this—this
she could do. She could take care of children.

But Ivan wasn't finished. His eyes darkened, and
his voice took on a harsher edge. "If you fail—if you
disappoint me—there will be consequences." He let
the words hang in the air, heavy with menace. "And
I'm sure you know what those consequences will
be."

Katya felt her stomach drop again. She didn't need
him to spell it out. She knew exactly what he was
threatening. If she failed in her duties, if she
displeased him in any way, he would send her to
one of those clubs, or worse. He was giving her
one chance—just one—and if she blew it, her fate
would be sealed.

Her mouth was dry, but she managed a nod. Her
throat felt tight, her pulse hammering in her ears.
Relief and fear warred inside her—relief that she
hadn't been immediately condemned to the life she
had feared most, and fear that Ivan still held her
fate in his hands.

She could feel his gaze still on her, weighing her,
testing her resolve. He was expecting obedience,
submission. He had made it clear that she had no
other choice. She was his now, bound to him for

five years, and he wanted her to know just how precarious her position was.

But even as the weight of it all settled over her, even as the fear tightened its grip around her chest, Katya felt something else stir inside her—something sharp and defiant. She hated this man. Hated him for the power he held over her, for the way he spoke to her as though she were nothing more than a tool to be used. Hated the way her body reacted to his presence, betraying her with its unwanted attraction.

But more than anything, she hated the feeling of helplessness that threatened to swallow her whole.

She wouldn't let him break her. She couldn't.

Katya straightened her spine, her chin lifting slightly as she met Ivan's gaze once more. She could feel the heat of his dominance pressing down on her, could see the cold authority in his eyes, but she wouldn't cower. Not here. Not now. She might be indebted to him, but that didn't mean she had to surrender her sense of self.

Ivan's eyes flickered again, a small, barely perceptible movement, as if he had noticed the shift in her posture. For a brief second, there was a tension in the air between them, an unspoken understanding. She wasn't backing down.

His lips curled into the faintest hint of a smirk, and Katya's heart stuttered in her chest.

"Good," Ivan said softly, almost as if he were speaking to himself. "Let's see if that fire burns bright enough to survive."

And with that, he dismissed her with a simple wave of his hand, turning his attention back to the papers on his desk.

Katya turned and walked out of the office, her mind swirling with emotions. She had survived the first hurdle, but the battle was far from over. She was now trapped in Ivan's world, bound to him by a debt that wasn't hers.

But she was still Katya, and she would not break. Not yet.

As the door to the office clicked shut behind her, one of the men from Ivan's crew appeared beside her, gesturing for her to follow. Katya forced herself to keep her steps steady as they walked through the cold, dimly lit hallway, her heart still racing from the encounter. She had no idea where they were taking her next, but she knew it didn't matter. No matter where she went, she was under Ivan's control now.

She clenched her fists at her sides as she walked down the narrow corridor, her footsteps echoing off the concrete walls. The other men and women who had traveled with her were already gone, whisked away to their respective fates. She imagined them now—those young men working at the docks, their lives filled with backbreaking labor, and those women, shipped off to the clubs, their futures carved out by Ivan's cold decisions.

Katya knew she had been spared, but it didn't feel like salvation. She had avoided one fate, only to be handed over to another. As she left the building, stepping out into the humid Los Angeles air, the reality of her situation settled over her with suffocating clarity.

She was indebted to Ivan Volkov for five years. Five long years. And he hadn't hesitated to remind her that he didn't tolerate thieves. Her father's betrayal was now hers to bear, and the threat of what would happen if she failed hung over her like a guillotine blade, ready to drop at any moment.

She could feel the weight of it—his control, his power. It followed her even now, outside of his office, as though the cold shadow of his dominance clung to her skin. She had no illusions about the life she was entering. She had seen the way he looked at her, how he calculated every move, sizing her up like a piece of property. To him, she wasn't a person. She was a tool. A means to an end.

The anger that had been simmering deep within her began to flare again, sharp and hot. Her father had done this to her. Her father had sold her out, traded her life for his own cowardice and selfishness. And now she was paying the price for his sins, bound to a man she didn't know, a man she despised even as she was inexplicably drawn to him. How had it come to this?

Her thoughts tumbled and twisted in her mind as she walked through the warehouse, her steps quick and uneven. She was relieved, yes—relieved that she wouldn't be forced into the clubs, forced to sell her body like so many other women had been. But that relief was fleeting, overwhelmed by the burning resentment that now fueled her every step.

She hated Ivan. Hated his power. Hated the way he had looked at her like he owned her. Hated that he *did* own her. But more than anything, she hated her father for putting her in this position, for abandoning her to the mercy of men like Ivan Volkov. It was his betrayal that had led her here, trapped in a life that was no longer her own. He had traded her for his own survival, and the bitterness of that truth tasted like bile in her throat.

But underneath the anger, beneath the resentment and fear, there was something else. A flicker of something she didn't want to acknowledge, but that refused to be ignored.

Katya could still feel the tension that had sparked between her and Ivan in that office. The way his gaze had lingered on her, the way her body had responded against her will. It disgusted her, the way she had felt a pull toward him, a dangerous magnetism that made her stomach twist. How could she feel even the slightest attraction to a man like him? A man who held her life in his hands, who could destroy her with a word?

But it was there, buried deep, and no matter how much she tried to ignore it, she couldn't deny the way her pulse had quickened when he had spoken her name, the way her skin had burned under his gaze. It was infuriating.

Outside, a black van idled by the warehouse entrance. Without a word, the man opened the door for her, and Katya climbed inside, her body tense as the door slid shut behind her with a heavy thud. She settled into her seat, staring out of the window as the van pulled away from the warehouse. The city lights blurred into streaks of neon and shadow as they drove, and Katya felt the weight of her situation press down on her once again.

She had to stay focused. She had five years ahead of her—five long years of servitude to a man who saw her as nothing more than a pawn. But she wouldn't let that break her. She couldn't.

Ivan might hold the power now, but Katya had no intention of simply giving in. There was a spark of rebellion inside her, one that had kept her alive during the journey from Russia, one that had refused to bow to the Bratva's cold grip. It was that spark she would hold onto, that defiance that would see her through the next five years.

She might be indebted to Ivan, but she wasn't going to lose herself. She wasn't going to submit, not easily, not without a fight.

As the van wound through the dark streets of Los Angeles, Katya stared out into the night, her heart hardening with resolve. She had a long road ahead of her, one filled with danger and uncertainty. But she wasn't going to break.

No matter what Ivan Volkov or the Bratva threw at her, she would survive.

And one day, when her five years were up, she would be free again.

Chapter 2

Ivan exited the dimly lit office, the weight of the door closing behind him barely registering over the churn of thoughts in his mind. The moment the door latched, the murmur of the warehouse buzzed back into focus—the low hum of machinery, the distant clatter of footsteps on concrete, and the muted conversation of men discussing business. But all of that faded into the background as his mind replayed the meeting. Specifically, the part where he had met her.

Katya Sokolov.

He had entered that room with a plan. The moment he laid eyes on the young women sent to settle their debts, he already knew their fates. They were just another part of the machine, cogs in the complex world of the Bratva. The clubs and brothels under his control could always use more faces—ones that would attract attention and money. His operation ran like a well-oiled machine, and there was no room for sentimentality, no time for second thoughts. They were there to work, and he was there to direct their futures.

But Katya had thrown a wrench in his carefully laid plans.

He hadn't expected her to be any different from the others. She had the same look of fear in her eyes as the other women when she first entered, the same uncertainty as the weight of their situation pressed down on them. And yet, there was something else too—something he hadn't seen in a long time. Defiance. A spark of rebellion that shouldn't have been there. She hadn't averted her eyes like the other women did. She hadn't shrunk under the gravity of the situation. She'd stared straight at him, and though fear had danced behind her dark eyes, there was something else there too. A challenge.

Ivan's jaw tightened as he descended the staircase from his office, each step echoing in the cavernous warehouse. He was a man who prided himself on control, and there was nothing about Katya that suggested control. She was defiant, proud even, despite the fact that her very life was in his hands. It made no sense. In his world, defiance was dangerous. It needed to be quashed. But the more he thought about it, the more that spark intrigued him. He knew, logically, that she needed to be broken, that this defiance would cause trouble if not handled properly. But deep down, another part of him was curious to see how far that spark would burn before it flickered out.

The thought unsettled him, but it didn't stop his mind from returning to that look in her eyes. It wasn't just fear or obedience—it was more complex than that. A mixture of anger and survival instinct. He had seen it in men before—never in women. Most of the women who crossed his path either surrendered immediately to his power or attempted to manipulate it for their own gain. But Katya had stood there, meeting his gaze head-on, as if silently daring him to do his worst.

He hated it. But at the same time, he couldn't stop thinking about it.

Power was what had brought him to this point in his life. Control over his men, control over his operations, control over every inch of the empire he had built here on the West Coast. He had risen through the ranks not just because of his ruthlessness but because of his ability to outthink and outmaneuver everyone around him. Nothing happened in his world without his knowledge or approval, and no one defied him without consequences.

And yet, Katya's defiance wasn't an overt challenge. It was something quieter, something more internal. She wasn't foolish enough to speak out or openly resist him, but there was a fire there. One he had to control.

He hadn't expected to feel anything about her beyond the usual calculations—debt, power, control. But she was different. And the more he thought about it, the more he realized that sending her to one of his clubs had been too simple a solution. There was no challenge in it, no satisfaction in controlling her from afar. He needed her closer.

Ivan's grip tightened as he walked, his boots thudding against the concrete floor. This wasn't about desire, he told himself. This was about power, about strategy. He was head of the Volkov family's LA operations for a reason—he knew how to read people, how to exploit their weaknesses, how to manipulate situations to his advantage. And Katya... she was a variable he hadn't accounted for.

Keeping her as a nanny for his children was the best decision. He convinced himself of that. She needed to be broken, and that couldn't happen if she was working in some club, surrounded by people who might encourage her defiance. No, she needed to be under his roof, under his control, where he could bend her will to his own. It was the only way to ensure that she didn't become a problem. He would break her spirit personally, watch as that fire in her eyes slowly extinguished, leaving behind only submission.

He told himself it was tactical. Logical. Nothing more than an extension of the control he wielded over every aspect of his life.

But even as he walked through the warehouse, his mind kept returning to her. The way she had looked at him, her dark eyes meeting his without flinching. That moment had stayed with him. Her defiance wasn't like anything he had encountered before. Other women—those who came through the Bratva's fold—were either terrified or calculating, trying to use whatever leverage they had to survive. But Katya? She had something else. A fire, a spirit that made him want to crush it, to dominate it completely.

Dangerous thoughts flickered at the edge of his mind, thoughts he wasn't used to having about women like her. He'd had his share of women—women who had come willingly, some who hadn't. But none of them lingered in his thoughts the way Katya was now. It unsettled him. He had made a decision to keep her close, but the reasons were becoming more tangled the more he thought about it. Was it really about control? Or was there something else?

Ivan's jaw tightened as he stepped into the main section of the warehouse, glancing at the men loading crates into a truck. The noise of the operation grounded him, pulling him back from his thoughts. He reminded himself that this was about strategy. Keeping her close was the right decision—she needed to learn her place. And the easiest way to ensure that happened was by watching her every move. He couldn't afford to have someone like Katya become a threat. She needed to be contained, tamed.

The thought of breaking her spirit sent a surge of satisfaction through him, though he wasn't sure if it was the idea of control or something darker that stirred within him.

His thoughts briefly wandered to the other nannies who had come and gone in recent months. None of them had lasted long, either too weak to handle the responsibility or too frightened to stay in his presence. And none had left any kind of impression on him. They had been replaceable, like the furniture in his house, useful until they weren't.

But Katya?

He could already feel her presence clinging to his thoughts. It was irrational, and that irritated him. He prided himself on being a man of control, of discipline. He didn't let emotion cloud his judgment. And yet... there was something about her that lingered.

His hand clenched into a fist as he crossed the warehouse floor, the memory of her dark eyes flashing in his mind again.

This wasn't about desire, he reminded himself. It was about dominance. Breaking her would be a test, a challenge. She wouldn't bend easily, but that made it all the more satisfying. It was a game of power, and Ivan Volkov never lost when it came to power.

The Volkov family had built its reputation on strength, control, and ruthlessness. His cousin Nikolai held New York in a similar grip, and Ivan had made sure the West Coast was no different. He would not be outdone. No one in his world dared defy him—Katya's father had learned that lesson the hard way.

Ivan paused for a moment, leaning against one of the crates stacked near the loading dock. Katya was her father's daughter, and that made her a risk. Thievery, betrayal—it ran in her blood, and he couldn't afford to tolerate it in his home.

But there was something else too. The idea of bending her to his will, of watching that defiance fade into submission, excited him in a way he hadn't anticipated. The thought of her fire bending—not breaking, but bending—under his control stirred something primal in him.

He wasn't just thinking about her as an employee, someone to keep in line. It was more than that. It was a power play, a test of wills. And Ivan had every intention of winning.

He stood upright again, straightening his jacket as his eyes swept over the warehouse floor. He would handle Katya like he handled everything else in his life—with precision, with control. She would learn her place, and he would ensure that her fire was extinguished, or at least, brought under his command.

Because in Ivan's world, there was no room for anything—or anyone—that he couldn't control.

He made his way back to his office door and paused for a moment, his hand resting on the cool metal of the handle. He had been ready—more than ready—to send her to one of his clubs. It was the easiest solution. She was indebted to him for five years, and he could have made more money off her in the clubs than in any other role. It was a decision he had made hundreds of times before, with women who had entered his world with no options left. It was efficient. It made sense.

But Katya didn't fit the mold.

Sending her to a club felt like a mistake, and the more he thought about it, the more he knew that mistake could come back to haunt him. That fire in her spirit would burn brighter if left unchecked, and in the environment of his clubs, she could find allies—or worse, she could become a problem. No, she needed to be closer. She needed to be under his thumb, where he could snuff out that fire personally.

The realization settled in his chest like a stone, heavy and final. He wouldn't send her away. Not yet. She was a risk, but she was also a challenge. And Ivan Volkov never backed down from a challenge.

Katya Sokolov would be broken. He would see to that personally.

He opened the door to his office and stepped inside, the familiar hum of the warehouse fading as the door clicked shut behind him. Ivan knew that Katya would be arriving at his house soon. He would make sure she understood her place, understood the consequences of her father's actions and what they meant for her future.

Five years. That was how long she owed him.

It wouldn't take nearly that long to break her.

Chapter 3

The van rumbled to a halt in front of towering wrought iron gates, the sound of the engine cutting through the eerie silence of the night. Katya glanced up from her seat, her eyes widening as she caught her first glimpse of Ivan Volkov's estate. The sheer size of the mansion beyond the gates was staggering, a sprawling structure that seemed to stretch endlessly across the perfectly manicured grounds. It was unlike anything she had ever seen before, a stark contrast to the world she had left behind in Russia. The van doors creaked open, and Katya stepped out onto the gravel drive, her boots crunching beneath her as she stared in awe at the house before her.

The gates swung open with a slow, deliberate groan, revealing the estate in its full glory. Towering stone walls framed the mansion, which stood like a fortress in the midst of the lush, green lawns. The building's façade was a blend of modern elegance and old-world charm, its tall windows reflecting the glow of the moonlight. Ornate stonework framed the front entrance, and ivy crawled up the sides of the walls, giving the mansion an almost regal appearance. The air smelled of fresh-cut grass, flowers, and wealth—a scent Katya had never associated with anything in her life.

She swallowed hard, her throat dry as her heart raced in her chest. It was impossible to ignore the stark divide between this world and the one she had come from. She thought of the small apartment she had shared with her mother in Russia, a cramped space filled with second-hand furniture and the scent of cheap food. It had been a modest, simple life—one she had taken for granted. Now, standing in front of this opulent estate, Katya felt a wave of resentment surge through her. None of this was her choice. She didn't want to be here, indebted to a man like Ivan Volkov, thrust into a life that wasn't hers.

But here she was, standing before the gates of wealth and power, and there was no escape.

The van door slammed shut behind her, jolting her from her thoughts. She looked over her shoulder to see the driver already pulling away, leaving her standing alone in the driveway. The mansion loomed ahead of her like a beast waiting to swallow her whole. Katya felt a chill creep down her spine. She wasn't sure if it was from the cool night air or the sense of dread settling in her stomach.

This is your life now, she reminded herself. Whether you like it or not.

As she took a hesitant step forward, her legs felt heavy, as if the weight of her new reality was physically pressing down on her. Only weeks ago, she had been in Russia, dealing with the fallout of her father's betrayal. It all felt like a blur now—the rushed departure, the journey on the cargo ship, and the suffocating fear that had followed her every step. And now, she was here, standing in front of a mansion that felt more like a prison than a home.

Her heart pounded in her chest as she approached the front door. Every step felt like a journey deeper into a world she didn't belong to. Katya couldn't shake the feeling of being out of place, like an intruder in someone else's life. The luxury around her was overwhelming—the meticulously trimmed hedges, the sparkling fountain at the center of the driveway, and the soft glow of the mansion's outdoor lights casting everything in a warm, golden hue. It all screamed wealth and privilege, two things she had never known.

She steeled herself as she reached the massive wooden door, her hand trembling slightly as she raised it to knock. Before she could make contact, the door swung open with a quiet creak, revealing an older woman standing on the threshold. The woman was tall and thin, with silver hair pulled back into a tight bun. She wore a crisp, black dress with a white apron tied neatly around her waist, her sharp blue eyes taking in Katya with a quick, assessing glance.

"You must be Katya," the woman said, her voice brisk but not unkind. "I'm Sofia, the housekeeper."

Katya nodded, unsure of what to say. Sofia's presence immediately set the tone of the household—controlled, orderly, and disciplined. There was no warmth in her greeting, no attempt at small talk or reassurance. Everything about her demeanor spoke of efficiency and structure, the kind of environment where mistakes were not tolerated.

"Come in," Sofia said, stepping aside to allow Katya to enter.

Katya hesitated for a moment, her gaze flicking back to the van that had already disappeared down the long driveway. There was no going back now. She took a deep breath and stepped inside.

The interior of the mansion was even more imposing than the exterior. The floors were made of gleaming marble, the walls adorned with expensive paintings and ornate sconces casting soft light across the space. A grand staircase curved elegantly upward, its bannister polished to a high shine. The air inside was cool and smelled faintly of lavender, a stark contrast to the stifling heat and grime of the cargo ship she had been on only hours ago.

Sofia led her through the foyer without a word, her footsteps echoing loudly in the vast, empty space. Katya followed in silence, her eyes darting around the mansion as they passed through one lavish room after another. The opulence was dizzying. It felt like every inch of the house was designed to display wealth and power, and it made her feel small in comparison.

As they headed through an archway, Sofia stopped and turned to face her. "I'll show you around the house," she said, her tone still formal. "You'll meet the children later. They're already asleep for the night."

Katya nodded, biting her lip to keep from asking any questions. She had so many—about the house, about Ivan, about what her role here would truly entail—but she wasn't sure if Sofia was the right person to ask.

As they started walking, Katya's mind raced with a hundred different thoughts. She couldn't believe how much her life had changed in such a short amount of time. Only days ago, she had been in Russia, living a modest life, never imagining that she would end up in a place like this. Now, she was here, in this enormous mansion, bound to a man like Ivan Volkov. The weight of it all pressed down on her, and for a moment, she felt like she might collapse under the pressure.

But she couldn't. She had to stay strong.

Katya followed Sofia through the expansive halls of the mansion, her footsteps echoing softly against the polished marble floors. The grandeur of the place was overwhelming, every inch of it gleaming with wealth and power. Towering ceilings stretched high above, and each chandelier that hung from them glittered with crystal light, casting a soft glow across the room. The walls were adorned with expensive artwork, the kind that looked as though they belonged in a museum rather than someone's home. Every turn, every corner, screamed of opulence, and it made Katya feel smaller with each passing second.

She tried to stand tall, her back straight and her head held high, but the weight of the luxury around her pressed down on her. This was a world she had never been a part of—a world she had only ever seen from the outside, in movies or magazines. And now, she was walking through it, being led deeper into its heart.

Sofia moved ahead with purpose, her heels clicking sharply against the marble, but Katya's gaze darted around the mansion, her eyes wide as she took everything in. There was a chill in the air, the kind that only comes from a house this large, where heat seems to disappear into the vastness. The furniture was all dark wood and leather, meticulously placed in every room as if each piece had been selected to exude a sense of authority.

Katya's stomach twisted in knots. She had never been anywhere like this. The stark contrast between the small, cramped apartment she had shared with her father and this sprawling estate felt like a slap in the face. She remembered the worn-out couch they used to sit on, the tiny kitchen where her father would cook simple meals—nothing at all like the gourmet kitchen she had glimpsed as they passed by. Her mind flitted back to those moments, to the simplicity of her former life, and how everything had changed in a matter of days.

Would she ever feel comfortable here? Or would this mansion always remind her of how out of place she was? It was one thing to be indebted to Ivan Volkov, but to live in his house, to be surrounded by this constant reminder of the world she wasn't a part of—it was too much. It felt like an invisible barrier, separating her from the people who belonged in this life and reminding her that she was merely passing through.

Sofia led her down a long hallway, the walls lined with ornate sconces that gave off a soft, amber light. Katya glanced at the portraits hanging on the walls, all stern-faced men and women, their eyes seeming to follow her as she walked. The unease that had settled in her stomach grew heavier. She wondered how many people had walked these halls before her, and how many had been discarded by Ivan once their use was over.

As they passed a closed door, Sofia's voice broke the silence. "That's Mr. Volkov's office," she said, her tone clipped. "You'll need to stay out of there unless he specifically calls for you."

Katya nodded, though the idea of being summoned to Ivan's office made her pulse quicken. She could feel the weight of his presence, even when he wasn't around. It was as though his power lingered in the air, seeping into every corner of the mansion.

Sofia's tone was polite but distant, as though she were reciting facts rather than engaging in conversation. "The children have their own playroom down the hall," she continued. "You'll be spending most of your time there with them. The library is just past it, though it's rarely used these days." There was a note of something—regret, perhaps?—in Sofia's voice, but Katya wasn't sure. It could have been nothing, or it could have been the first glimpse of the undercurrents in this household.

She glanced at the closed doors as they passed, wondering what secrets lay behind them. There was an almost oppressive silence in the house, broken only by the occasional creak of the floorboards under Sofia's steps. It made the mansion feel empty, despite its grandeur, like a hollow shell dressed in finery.

"The house is large, but you'll find that it's mostly quiet," Sofia added as they turned another corner. "The children... well, they keep to themselves more often than not." She paused briefly, her lips pressing into a thin line. "There haven't been many nannies who've stayed long."

Katya's eyebrows lifted at that, but she didn't press for more information. She had a sinking feeling that she was about to find out why for herself.

As they walked, the halls seemed to stretch on forever, each turn revealing another room that Katya would never have thought to exist in one home. She wondered how someone could even live in a place this large, how it could ever feel like a home rather than a museum. But then again, she reminded herself, this wasn't just a house. This was Ivan Volkov's fortress, a testament to his power and dominance. Everything about it screamed control and precision, and she was now a part of it, whether she liked it or not.

By the time they circled back to the grand staircase leading to the upper levels, Katya's mind was swirling with thoughts. She couldn't shake the feeling that the house was watching her, testing her. And even though Sofia had said little, there was a sense of foreboding in her words, an unspoken warning that Katya couldn't quite put her finger on.

As they climbed the stairs, Sofia's voice softened just slightly. "Mr. Volkov's room is just ahead. I'll show you where the children sleep as well, but they're already in bed for the night. Your room is farther down the hall."

Katya nodded, grateful for the quiet as they continued down the hall. The house may have been beautiful, but it felt like a gilded cage. And now, she was trapped inside it.

At the end of the hallway, Sofia stopped in front of a door and opened it. "This is your room," she said, stepping aside to allow Katya to enter.

Katya crossed the threshold and took in her new living space. It was modest compared to the rest of the house, but still far nicer than anything she'd ever had. The bed was large, with a thick comforter neatly folded on top. A small dresser sat against the wall, and there was a window that overlooked the back of the property, where Katya could see the expansive lawn stretching out to a line of trees in the distance. The air in the room smelled faintly of lavender, a scent Katya found oddly calming despite the weight of everything that had happened today.

"It's... nice," Katya said, trying to sound grateful, though her mind was racing with everything else.

Sofia gave a brief nod, her face still impassive. "You'll have privacy here. The children's rooms are just down the hall," she said, pointing to a closed door further along the corridor. "Your responsibilities begin in the morning."

Katya turned toward Sofia, noting the way the older woman's gaze seemed to soften slightly, as if a more personal conversation was coming. It made her curious—this entire place seemed to operate with such strict formality that any break in that made her feel like there was something more beneath the surface.

"What are they like?" Katya asked, her voice quieter now. "The children, I mean."

Sofia's face faltered for a moment, a brief crack in her composed demeanor, before she carefully set Katya's small bag on the dresser and began folding the few clothes Katya had. "There are two of them," she said. "A boy and a girl. Kirill is four, and Dasha is six. They are... challenging, to say the least."

Challenging. The word hung in the air like a warning. Katya felt her stomach twist. She had never been around children before, not like this. She hadn't even had siblings growing up, and now she was supposed to care for two young ones? The weight of the responsibility pressed down on her.

Sofia hesitated again, and Katya sensed the shift in her tone. She glanced at the housekeeper, noticing the subtle way her hands stilled as she arranged Katya's things. "Their mother died six months ago," Sofia said softly, the words carrying an unexpected heaviness. "In a car accident."

Katya swallowed hard, unsure of what to say. "I'm sorry," she finally managed, her voice coming out smaller than she'd intended.

Sofia gave a slight nod, her expression softening just a little. "It's been hard on them. They miss her, and they don't take well to strangers. We've had several nannies come through since her passing, but none have stayed long. The children..." She trailed off, a slight sigh escaping her lips before she continued. "They haven't handled the loss well."

Katya felt the knot in her stomach tighten. She had no experience with children, let alone ones who were grieving. The weight of her new role felt even heavier now. How was she supposed to connect with these kids when she didn't even know how to care for herself in this new life?

"They've been through a lot," Sofia continued, folding the last of Katya's few belongings and placing them in the drawer. "It won't be easy. They are resistant to new faces, and they don't trust easily."

Katya's mind raced with doubt. What had she gotten herself into? The idea of trying to bond with these children, especially under such tragic circumstances, felt impossible. How could she help them when she didn't even know what she was doing?

"What happened with the other nannies?" Katya asked, trying to keep her voice steady.

Sofia's lips thinned slightly. "Some left on their own. Some were... encouraged to leave," she said cryptically. "The children can be overwhelming at times. And Mr. Volkov... has his expectations."

Of course, Ivan had expectations. That much was clear. He demanded obedience, discipline, and control from everyone around him, and it was evident that extended to the care of his children. But Katya wondered just how far those expectations went.

Her thoughts spiraled with doubt. She had never been responsible for anyone but herself. She had no idea how to care for children, especially ones who had been through so much. But she knew one thing—failing wasn't an option. Ivan had made that much clear. There would be consequences if she didn't fulfill her duties, and the threat of being sent somewhere far worse loomed in the back of her mind.

As Sofia finished up and turned to leave, Katya's heart sank. She felt more lost than ever, overwhelmed by the weight of what lay ahead. She was alone in this mansion, surrounded by wealth she couldn't comprehend, responsible for two children she didn't know how to reach.

But there was no way out. Not for five long years.

"I'll call for you in the morning," Sofia said, giving Katya a brief nod before exiting the room.

Katya was left standing in the quiet, the walls of the mansion closing in around her.

***

The next morning, the sun filtered weakly through the thick curtains of Katya's room, casting a dull light over the space. She had barely slept, tossing and turning in the oversized bed, her mind racing with thoughts of the day ahead. The enormity of her situation—of everything she'd been thrust into—pressed heavily on her chest. Her body was stiff from the uncomfortable night, and every time she closed her eyes, she found herself replaying yesterday's events, from the coldness of the Bratva to Ivan's penetrating gaze.

Katya sat on the edge of the bed, staring at the small mirror on the dresser. Her reflection looked back at her, pale and tired, the dark circles under her eyes betraying her lack of sleep. She ran a hand through her dark hair, smoothing it down, trying to make herself look somewhat presentable.

She had never been responsible for anyone but herself, and today she was supposed to meet the children—two small strangers who had already been through so much. Her stomach twisted with anxiety. How could she care for them when she didn't even know how to take care of herself in this new life?

A soft knock at the door startled her. Sofia entered, her face as impassive as it had been the day before. "It's time to meet the children," she said simply, gesturing for Katya to follow.

Katya stood, smoothing her clothes and taking a deep breath. Her nerves felt like they were on fire, every muscle tense with anticipation. As she followed Sofia down the hall, her mind raced with questions. What would the children be like? Would they be cold and distant like Ivan? Or were they too young to be shaped by the harshness of their father's world?

They reached the end of the corridor, and Sofia opened a door that led into a spacious playroom. The room was bright, filled with toys and books, a stark contrast to the rest of the mansion's cold, formal atmosphere. Two small figures sat at a table in the middle of the room, quietly coloring with crayons. The boy, Kirill, was six, his hair a dark shade like his father's, his little face serious as he focused on his drawing. Dasha, the younger girl, sat beside him, her curly hair spilling down her back, her small hands clumsily holding a crayon.

Sofia stepped aside, motioning for Katya to enter the room. "Children," she said in a soft yet firm tone, "this is Katya. She's going to be helping take care of you."

Neither child looked up. Kirill continued drawing, his brow furrowed in concentration, while Dasha glanced briefly at the new presence in the room before returning to her paper. There was no greeting, no curiosity in their eyes. The silence in the room felt thick and heavy, filled with the weight of unspoken grief.

Katya stood awkwardly in the doorway, unsure of what to say or do. She had expected the children to at least acknowledge her, but their aloofness took her by surprise. She could feel the distance between them, an invisible wall that had been built long before she arrived, and it left her feeling more out of place than ever.

Her gaze flickered to Sofia, hoping for some guidance, but the older woman simply watched the children with a resigned expression. "They've been quiet like this for a while now," Sofia said in a low voice. "Since their mother passed, they haven't been the same. It's been hard to get them to connect with anyone."

Katya's heart clenched at the mention of their mother. Of course, it made sense now—the sadness that hung around the children, the way they kept to themselves. They were still grieving, their young hearts weighed down by a loss too heavy for them to bear. It wasn't that they didn't care about her arrival; they simply didn't have the energy to engage with anyone new.

Katya shifted uncomfortably. What was she supposed to do in the face of that kind of pain? She didn't know how to comfort children, especially ones who had lost so much. Her thoughts felt jumbled, panic slowly creeping in. She was supposed to be their nanny, but how could she do this when she didn't know where to begin?

She took a tentative step forward, her eyes scanning the room for something, anything that might help her connect with them. But the children remained engrossed in their drawings, paying her no attention.

Katya opened her mouth to say something, but no words came out. What could she say that wouldn't sound hollow? She stood there for a moment, feeling utterly lost, until Sofia gently cleared her throat.

"Don't take it personally," Sofia said quietly, as though reading Katya's thoughts. "They've been like this with everyone. They don't trust easily, not anymore."

Katya swallowed hard. She wanted to ask more, to understand what had happened in this house before her arrival, but she didn't want to pry. Instead, she nodded, feeling the weight of the children's grief settle heavily on her shoulders.

Sofia gave Katya a small, reassuring smile before stepping back toward the door. "I'll leave you to get acquainted," she said, her voice soft. "Just give them time."

And with that, Sofia was gone, leaving Katya alone with the two small figures at the table. The room felt unbearably quiet now, the ticking of the clock on the wall the only sound breaking the silence.

Katya stood there for a few moments longer, watching the children as they continued to draw. She felt a surge of helplessness. How was she supposed to do this? They were like tiny strangers, and she didn't know how to bridge the gap between them. She had never been around children before, never been responsible for anyone but herself. And now she was expected to care for these two, to somehow make up for the loss of a mother they clearly still mourned.

Her gaze shifted to Kirill. His small hand moved methodically over the paper, his drawing slow and careful. There was a seriousness to him, a weight that seemed far too heavy for a child his age. Dasha, on the other hand, seemed more distant, her little face blank as she scribbled aimlessly with a crayon.

As Sofia quietly excused herself from the playroom, Katya felt a wave of unease wash over her. The door clicked shut behind the housekeeper, leaving her alone with Kirill and Dasha. For a moment, the room was filled with an uncomfortable silence, broken only by the soft scratch of crayons against paper. Katya hesitated, unsure of what to do next. She'd never cared for children, let alone two who had suffered such a great loss. They seemed so fragile yet distant, as though they had built walls she wasn't sure how to break down.

After a few more moments of standing awkwardly by the door, Katya decided to sit down on the floor, not far from where the children were drawing. She watched them out of the corner of her eye, their small hands methodically moving crayons across paper. The soft colors they chose—blues, purples, and yellows—seemed to clash with the heavy atmosphere in the room.

Katya let out a quiet sigh, feeling a sharp pang of empathy for the little ones. They seemed so sad, so withdrawn, and in that moment, she realized that she was feeling the same way. She was scared. She was lonely. Just like them, she had been thrust into a new and unfamiliar world, surrounded by strangers. She wasn't sure if she belonged here, or if she could make this work. She had no idea how to reach these children, but maybe... maybe they were feeling just as lost as she was.

Steeling herself, she spoke softly, not wanting to startle them. "I know this might sound strange, but... I'm new here." Her voice felt small in the quiet room. "I don't know anyone, and... it's a little scary for me."

Kirill didn't react, his focus seemingly unshakable as he continued to draw long, careful lines on his paper. Dasha, however, paused for just a moment. Katya glanced at the little girl, her heart pounding with the hope that maybe she had heard her.

The silence stretched between them, and Katya wondered if she had said the wrong thing, or maybe too much. But before she could overthink it, Dasha lifted her head ever so slightly and looked at Katya. Her big brown eyes blinked once, and then she wordlessly extended a small piece of paper and a handful of crayons toward her.

Katya blinked in surprise, her breath catching in her throat. For a moment, she wasn't sure what to do. The gesture was so simple, yet it felt monumental, as though a bridge had been extended between them, fragile but real. Slowly, Katya reached out and took the paper and crayons from Dasha's outstretched hand. "Thank you," she whispered, trying to keep the emotion from her voice.

Dasha said nothing, simply going back to her drawing as though the moment had never happened. But to Katya, it felt like the first small crack in the wall the children had built around themselves.

Katya stared down at the blank paper in front of her, feeling a strange mixture of gratitude and disbelief. She didn't know what to draw, but she didn't want to squander the tiny connection Dasha had just offered her. So, she picked up a crayon and began to draw. Simple lines, shapes—anything to keep the silence from stretching too long. The coloring was quiet, unassuming, but somehow, it felt like a significant step.

As the minutes passed, Katya found herself relaxing, at least a little. The tension in her shoulders eased as the room settled into a comfortable quiet, the three of them coloring in silence. It wasn't much, but it was a start. And for now, that was enough.

Chapter 4

It had been a week. Seven long days in Ivan Volkov's mansion, and Katya still felt like a stranger, an outsider looking in on a world that wasn't hers. As she stood in the kitchen, her hands busy preparing breakfast for the children, her mind buzzed with a growing sense of frustration and resentment. The house was quiet—too quiet—and the weight of it pressed down on her, making her feel trapped, suffocated by the walls of luxury that surrounded her.

She whisked eggs in a glass bowl, the rhythm of her movements oddly soothing despite the whirlwind of thoughts swirling in her mind. This wasn't how she imagined her life. Not even close. Being forced to serve in a house that wasn't hers, for children that weren't hers, under the control of a man who saw her as nothing more than an object to be controlled. A pawn in his larger game.

Katya's jaw tightened as she thought of Ivan, the way he moved through the house with quiet authority, barely sparing her a glance unless it was to give an order. She hated how invisible she felt when he was around, like she was just part of the scenery—another tool in his grand, cold machine. The fact that he never even bothered to acknowledge her unless it was to issue a command grated on her nerves. It was as if he thought her beneath him, unworthy of his attention.

And yet, it was his presence that unsettled her the most. Every time Ivan was near, Katya felt a strange pull, something dark and primal that gnawed at the edges of her resentment. She despised him—his control, his power, the way he made her feel like a captive in his home. But despite all of that, she couldn't ignore the way her body betrayed her whenever he was close. The heat that rose in her chest, the flutter in her stomach that she tried desperately to push down. It was infuriating, and she hated herself for it.

The kitchen was filled with the soft clatter of dishes and the sizzle of eggs hitting the pan. The children were still upstairs, probably just waking up. Katya glanced at the clock on the wall, knowing it was only a matter of time before she'd have to rouse them for breakfast. Her heart ached a little at the thought. Kirill and Dasha had been difficult to connect with, their aloofness a constant reminder of how much they missed their mother. Katya understood that, but it didn't make the task any easier.

No matter how hard she tried, the children remained distant, their little hearts too broken to trust someone new in their lives. It hurt more than she liked to admit. Every day, she pushed herself to try a little harder, to smile a little more, hoping that one day they might respond. But they didn't. Not really. And it made her feel like a failure in her role, adding another layer of frustration to the pile that had been building up all week.

A deep sigh escaped her lips as she stirred the eggs, her thoughts once again drifting back to Ivan. It wasn't just the children's aloofness that got under her skin—it was him. The way he moved through the house like he owned not just the property, but everything in it, including her. He was a constant presence, silent and watchful, and yet he made her feel as though she didn't exist.

Except, of course, in those moments when their eyes met. Those brief seconds where she could feel the air change, thickening with something unspoken and dangerous. She hated the way he looked at her, as though he could see through the walls she put up, as though he knew how much she loathed him and yet was amused by it. And worse, the way her own body reacted to that look, the spark of awareness that ignited inside her whenever he was near. It was maddening.

How could she feel anything for a man like Ivan? A man who represented everything she despised—power, control, dominance. He had taken her life, or what little remained of it, and reshaped it to fit his needs. She was here, in his home, because of her father's betrayal. Because her father, in his selfishness, had handed her over like a bargaining chip, leaving her to pay the price for his sins.

Katya clenched the handle of the pan tighter, her knuckles whitening with the force of her grip. She wanted to scream, to rail against the injustice of it all, but she knew it would be useless. She was stuck here, under Ivan's thumb, with no way out for the next five years. Five long years of servitude, of following his rules, of living in this cold, oppressive house with him looming over her.

She wasn't even sure what she hated more—the fact that she was here, or the fact that despite all of that, she couldn't stop thinking about him. Ivan Volkov was a force of nature, a man who exuded power and danger in every movement. He was older than her by at least twenty years, a fact that only made the pull she felt toward him more baffling. He was cold, calculating, and utterly ruthless. And yet, every time their eyes met, she felt the heat rise in her body, a warmth that contrasted with the cold rage simmering inside her.

It was wrong. All of it. She shouldn't be thinking about him this way. She shouldn't be feeling this way. But she couldn't help it. No matter how much she tried to focus on her work, on the children, on getting through each day, Ivan always found a way to creep into her thoughts. The way he moved, the sound of his voice, the weight of his gaze when it lingered on her for just a moment too long.

Katya scowled as she flipped the eggs, trying to push the thoughts away. She wasn't here for him. She was here to pay off her father's debt, to get through the next five years and then be free. That was all that mattered. Whatever strange, unwanted attraction she felt for Ivan was just a distraction—one she couldn't afford. She had to stay focused, had to stay strong. No matter how much he got under her skin, no matter how much her body betrayed her, she couldn't let him win.

Not now. Not ever.

The eggs were done, and Katya plated them with a sense of finality, as though putting food on the table was the only thing she had control over in this house. She stared at the plate for a moment, her hands trembling slightly as she let out another slow breath.

It was going to be a long five years.

Katya sat cross-legged on the floor of the children's playroom, her attention focused on Kirill and Dasha as they worked on a puzzle together. It had been a small victory to get them this far—both of them sitting quietly, participating in something that wasn't sulking or retreating into their own little worlds.

Katya had learned early on that patience was key with them, that pushing too hard would only cause them to pull away. So she tried her best to let them come to her, offering gentle encouragement when needed but otherwise allowing them space to be themselves.

Kirill, the older of the two, was more receptive, though his aloofness remained. He would glance up at her occasionally, those serious blue eyes betraying flickers of curiosity, as though he were still trying to decide whether or not he trusted her. Dasha, on the other hand, barely acknowledged her presence most days, preferring instead to cling to her older brother. But today, Katya had managed to coax a small smile out of her when she handed the girl a piece of the puzzle that fit perfectly. It wasn't much, but it felt like progress.

She watched them now, her own heart softening as she observed their quiet concentration. They were so young, so fragile in their grief. It was hard not to feel a pang of sympathy for them, knowing they had lost their mother and were now being raised in this cold, imposing house. And yet, there was a part of her that couldn't help but relate to them. She, too, felt lost in a world that wasn't hers, trying to navigate the darkness and uncertainty that surrounded her.

The soft sound of footsteps made her tense, her senses immediately sharpening. She didn't need to look up to know who it was. The air in the room seemed to shift, growing heavier, more oppressive. Ivan.

Katya's spine straightened instinctively, her body becoming acutely aware of his presence even before he spoke. She hated how attuned she had become to him, how his mere presence could affect her so deeply. It was infuriating, and yet, there was something in the pit of her stomach that stirred whenever he was near. Something she didn't want to acknowledge.

Ivan stood in the doorway, his broad frame casting a shadow across the playroom. He didn't say anything, didn't make a move to join them. He just watched. Silently. His dark eyes locked on Katya, observing her every move. The weight of his gaze was like a physical touch, and she could feel it crawling over her skin, making her all too aware of herself.

Katya's fingers tightened around the puzzle piece she was holding, her annoyance flaring. What was it with him? Always watching, always judging, but never saying anything. She hated the way he made her feel—like she was constantly under scrutiny, like she had to prove herself at every turn. And yet, he barely acknowledged her existence unless it was to issue a command.

Kirill and Dasha had both noticed their father's presence too. Kirill had straightened up, his small hands stilling on the puzzle, while Dasha's gaze flickered nervously toward Ivan before quickly darting away. Neither of them said a word, the tension in the room palpable. They were as wary of him as Katya was, though for entirely different reasons.

She could feel Ivan's eyes on her, a silent challenge hanging in the air between them. Katya tried to ignore him, focusing instead on the children, but it was impossible. His presence loomed too large, too imposing to ignore. Finally, unable to take it any longer, she glanced up at him, meeting his gaze head-on.

There it was again—that unspoken tension, the push and pull between them that had been simmering since the day they met. Katya could see the faintest glimmer of amusement in Ivan's eyes, as if her defiance somehow entertained him. It only fueled her irritation.

"Do you just stand there all day watching people work for you?" she asked, her voice sharp and biting.

The words were out before she could stop them, and she immediately regretted it. She knew better than to provoke him, to challenge the man who held her future in his hands. But the irritation bubbling inside her had gotten the better of her. She couldn't help herself.

Ivan's expression didn't change, but his gaze darkened slightly. There was a pause, a beat of silence that stretched between them like a taut string about to snap. Katya's heart raced, her pulse quickening as she wondered if she had gone too far.

But then Ivan's lips curled into a small, almost imperceptible smirk.

"I like to know who's under my roof," he replied, his voice low and smooth, laced with that same undercurrent of control that always seemed to follow him.

There was something in the way he said it, something that made Katya's skin prickle with heat. He hadn't raised his voice, hadn't even shown any real anger, but the power in his words was undeniable. It was a reminder that she was here because of him, that he controlled her life now. And yet, there was something else in his tone—a hint of amusement, of challenge, as though he enjoyed this little game of defiance she played.

Katya swallowed hard, her defiance faltering for a moment under the intensity of his gaze. Her stomach twisted with conflicting emotions—anger, resentment, and that cursed attraction that gnawed at her insides every time he was near. She hated how he made her feel, hated the way her body seemed to betray her whenever their eyes met.

But she wouldn't back down. Not this time.

"Well," she said, her voice steadier now, "I'm not going anywhere. So you'll have plenty of time to watch."

The challenge in her voice was unmistakable, and for a moment, Katya thought she saw something flicker in Ivan's eyes. Something darker, something that made her pulse quicken in a way she didn't want to acknowledge.

As soon as Ivan turned and walked out of the room, the heavy atmosphere seemed to lift, but not entirely. His presence lingered, like a shadow that refused to dissipate, and Katya felt the weight of it pressing on her chest. Her heartbeat, which had quickened during their exchange, was still pounding in her ears.

She had challenged him, spoken out in a way that no one else around him dared to. There had been a part of her, deep down, that feared the consequences, that expected him to lash out or put her in her place. But he hadn't. He had smirked, amused by her defiance, and then left her standing there, as if this little game between them was far from over.

Katya's hands trembled slightly as she returned her gaze to the children. Kirill and Dasha were still watching her with wide, curious eyes, as if trying to figure out what had just happened. She could see the confusion on their faces, the way they looked between her and the empty doorway, unsure of how to react. The tension in the room hadn't just affected her—it had unsettled them, too.

Katya forced a smile, though it felt thin and fragile. "Let's get back to your puzzle, okay?" she said softly, her voice betraying none of the turmoil swirling inside her.

Kirill nodded slowly, his small hands reaching for another puzzle piece, while Dasha remained quiet, her eyes flickering up to the door one last time before she hesitantly resumed her drawing. The children were fragile, just like she was—both of them, in their own way, trying to find a sense of stability in a world that felt anything but safe. And in that moment, Katya felt a pang of empathy for them. She was supposed to be their caregiver, the one to help them through the loss of their mother, but she felt just as lost as they did.

Her mind, however, was far from focused on the task at hand. The confrontation with Ivan replayed itself over and over, the heat of his gaze, the low, commanding tone of his voice. She hated how much it affected her, hated that she couldn't push him out of her thoughts. He was the last person she wanted to be thinking about, yet her mind kept drifting back to him, drawn in by the undercurrent of something dark and magnetic that simmered between them.

What was it about him? Why did he make her feel this way?

She glanced down at her hands, still trembling slightly as she fumbled with the puzzle pieces. Her emotions were a tangled mess—frustration, anger, resentment... and something else. Something she didn't want to name. It burned low in her belly, the unbidden attraction she felt for him. She scolded herself for it, told herself it was wrong, but the pull was there, undeniable.

The children worked quietly beside her, but Katya could feel their unease. Dasha kept glancing up at her, as if trying to read her face, and Kirill seemed more withdrawn than usual. She could sense that Ivan's brief appearance had unsettled them, reminding them of his looming presence in the house.

And in a way, that mirrored how she felt—always aware of Ivan, always conscious of the fact that he was nearby, watching, judging. It infuriated her, but it also left her restless in a way she didn't fully understand. She wasn't supposed to care what he thought of her, wasn't supposed to feel the weight of his gaze every time he entered a room, but she did.

And the worst part was that her body seemed to react to him without her consent. That simmering tension, the strange, twisted attraction—it made her feel like she was losing control of herself, like Ivan had some invisible hold on her, even though he barely spoke to her.

Katya took a slow, deep breath, trying to push the thoughts away. She needed to focus on the children, not Ivan. She had a job to do, a role to fulfill. She couldn't afford to get distracted by the powerful man who lurked in the background, no matter how much his presence rattled her.

But as much as she tried to convince herself, the truth was that Ivan had gotten under her skin. His dominance, his control—it all reminded her of the precarious situation she was in. She was indebted to him, bound to this house for the next five years, and she couldn't afford to forget that.

Yet, that sense of helplessness, that feeling of being trapped—it was part of what fueled her defiance. Katya wasn't the type to cower in the face of power, even if it was dangerous to push back. She had fought for every ounce of strength she had, and she wasn't going to let Ivan break her.

Her hands stilled on the puzzle pieces as her resolve hardened. She would survive this, just as she had survived everything else. She would endure Ivan's silent challenges, his heavy presence, and she would come out the other side stronger. He might have control over her life right now, but that didn't mean she had to submit.

Katya looked up, her gaze steady, as if silently reminding herself of her own strength. She had to believe that, no matter what, she wouldn't let Ivan—no, she wouldn't let anyone—break her spirit.

And yet, as the quiet resumed in the room, a part of her knew that her battle with Ivan was just beginning. The silent war of wills between them had only just started, and she could already feel the stakes rising. The question wasn't whether she could hold her own—it was whether she could resist the magnetic pull he had over her long enough to keep her sense of self intact.

With that thought weighing on her, Katya continued to work on the puzzle with the children, her mind elsewhere, focused on the storm brewing between her and the man who now controlled her fate.

Chapter 5

Ivan leaned back in his leather chair, his gaze fixed on the darkened windows of his office. The quiet hum of the mansion surrounded him, but his mind was elsewhere, still lingering in the playroom hours after the incident with Katya. Her defiance had been unexpected, a spark that flickered against the cold, controlled environment he had so carefully crafted. He wasn't used to being challenged, especially not by someone in her position—someone under his control. And yet, instead of feeling the satisfaction of putting her in her place, he found himself unsettled.

That sharp retort, the way she had spoken back to him with fire in her eyes, played over and over in his mind. She hadn't cowered like the others. She hadn't looked away, hadn't bent to his authority the way most women did when faced with his silent intimidation. Katya had stood strong, met his gaze, and thrown his own words back at him. It should have angered him, and on some level, it did. But there was something else there, something he hadn't expected.

It intrigued him.

Ivan had always prided himself on control. Control over his business, control over his men, control over his household. He had earned his place as the head of the Volkov family's LA operations by maintaining that control, by ensuring that everything around him bent to his will. His world was built on dominance, and he thrived in that space. But something about Katya's resistance... it made him feel off-balance, and that was not a feeling Ivan welcomed. Still, no matter how much her defiance unsettled him, it also made his blood hum in a way he hadn't felt in a long time. There was something dangerous about her strength. It made him want to push back, to break through that wall of defiance just to see how far she could go before she shattered.

A smirk tugged at the corner of his lips. There was a fire in Katya, a quiet, simmering rage that burned just beneath the surface. She tried to hide it, but he had seen it in her eyes when she thought no one was looking. That fire was rare, especially in a woman who knew the kind of power he wielded. Most of them bent under the pressure, eager to please, afraid of what would happen if they didn't. But not her.

She was different.

Ivan drummed his fingers on the desk, staring at the polished wood surface as he considered his next move. He could crush her. It wouldn't take much. A few harsh words, a reminder of who held the power in this arrangement, and she'd fall in line.

Most did. It was the simplest way to maintain control, and he was a master at it. He could break her spirit if he wanted to, snuff out that spark of defiance and bend her to his will. But something in him hesitated.

He wanted to see how far she would go before she broke.

The tension between them had been building since the moment she stepped into his office on her first day. He'd seen the fear in her eyes then, but it hadn't been the same kind of fear he was used to seeing. It hadn't been paralyzing. No, her fear had been wrapped in something else—anger, determination. It was as though she had already decided that no matter what he did, she wouldn't let him break her. And that was a challenge Ivan hadn't been able to ignore.

He leaned forward in his chair, resting his elbows on the desk as he replayed her words in his mind. The sharpness in her voice, the way she had thrown his own authority back at him, the look in her eyes that dared him to push her further. She didn't know it yet, but she was playing a dangerous game. A game he always won.

His fingers tapped the edge of the desk as his mind raced through the possibilities. He could make her submit, crush that spark of rebellion, and remind her who was in control. But then what? She'd become like the others—compliant, eager to please, no longer a challenge. No, there was more to this than just breaking her will. He wanted to see how far she could go, how long she could keep up this act of defiance before she finally surrendered.

But it wasn't just about power. Not entirely. There was something about the way she carried herself, the way her eyes flared with that quiet rage, that made him want to see her break not just in fear, but in desire. He wanted her to fight him, to resist him, and then to give in—completely. It was a dangerous thought, one he should push aside, but Ivan wasn't in the habit of denying himself what he wanted.

The smirk faded from his lips as his thoughts grew darker, more focused. Katya was a fire waiting to be extinguished, but he didn't want to snuff out that flame too soon. He wanted to feel its heat, to see how brightly it could burn before it consumed them both. And when the time came, he would take what he wanted. He always did.

But for now, he would wait.

He would let her believe that she had won this round, that her defiance had gone unnoticed or unpunished. He'd watch her, observe her, and when the time was right, he'd strike. Ivan always enjoyed the hunt, and with Katya, it was clear he had found a worthy opponent.

The question was, how long could she hold out before she realized there was no escaping him?

With a deep breath, Ivan leaned back in his chair, his gaze shifting to the closed door of his office. Somewhere down the hall, Katya was with his children, fulfilling her role as their nanny, unaware of the thoughts swirling in his mind. For now, he would let her play her part. But soon, very soon, she would learn just how dangerous it was to challenge a man like him.

And when she did, there would be no turning back.

The next morning, Ivan stood in the hallway, his arms crossed over his broad chest as he watched Katya with the children from the shadows. She had no idea he was there, and he preferred it that way. It gave him a chance to observe her without the weight of his presence pressing down on her. She was focused entirely on Kirill and Dasha, trying to engage them in some kind of game. It was a simple scene, one he had witnessed countless times with previous nannies. Yet, something about the way she moved, the way she persisted with the children, caught his attention.

Kirill and Dasha sat at a small table, quietly coloring as Katya crouched beside them, offering gentle suggestions. Her patience surprised Ivan. The children had been distant with every nanny since their mother's death, and he hadn't expected them to warm up to Katya any faster. But there was something different in her approach. She didn't force them to respond, didn't demand their attention. Instead, she stayed close, giving them space while still making herself available.

Ivan could see the tension in her shoulders, the subtle frustration she hid behind her soft words. The children hadn't responded much to her efforts, but she didn't give up. Her persistence intrigued him. Most of the women who had come through his house had either been too soft or too harsh with the children, either coddling them to the point of smothering or snapping at them when their silence dragged on. Katya, however, had found a balance. She was determined, and that determination stirred something inside Ivan that he hadn't anticipated.

He shifted his weight, his eyes narrowing as he continued to observe. He wasn't sure what he expected from her when he'd assigned her this role. In truth, he had anticipated her failure, just like the others. But now, watching her with his children, he couldn't help but wonder if she would succeed where the others had failed. There was a fire in her, a quiet resilience that had caught his attention from the moment she walked into his office. And now, it was beginning to show in her interactions with Kirill and Dasha.

Katya leaned closer to Kirill, pointing out something on the page he was coloring. The boy glanced at her, his dark eyes briefly meeting hers before flicking back down to his paper. It was a small gesture, barely noticeable, but Ivan caught it. Kirill had acknowledged her, even if it was only for a moment. Ivan's jaw tightened as he processed the significance of it. The boy was slow to trust, even slower to open up, but that brief glance was a step forward.

He wasn't sure why it mattered to him, why he felt the need to watch over these interactions so closely. Perhaps it was because of how important the children were to him, though he wasn't the kind of father to hover. He valued their safety and their future, but he had always kept a certain emotional distance. Now, though, he found himself strangely invested in how Katya interacted with them.

As he watched her coaxing Dasha to join in the activity, he felt a pang of something unfamiliar—something dangerously close to admiration. She was doing more than just following orders. There was genuine effort in her actions, a desire to connect with his children that went beyond the cold duty she was assigned. And that made him uncomfortable. It made him question his motives, his reasons for keeping her here instead of sending her to one of his clubs.

Ivan leaned against the wall, his thoughts darkening as he continued to watch. Katya was supposed to be indebted to him, nothing more. She was a pawn, paying off her father's betrayal with her service to his family. But despite his desire for control, there was an undeniable pull between them. He had sensed it the first time she looked him in the eye, the defiance that simmered just beneath the surface.

It wasn't just about power anymore. Not with her.

His mind wandered, recalling the brief encounter in the playroom the day before. The way she had snapped back at him, her words sharp, her gaze unyielding. Most people wouldn't dare speak to him that way, especially not someone in her position. But she had. And instead of anger, it had sparked something far more dangerous. He wanted to push her, to see how far that defiance would go before she broke. But there was more to it than that. He wasn't just looking to break her—he wanted to own her.

Ivan clenched his fists at his sides, his nails digging into his palms as he struggled to reign in the conflicting emotions that stirred within him. He couldn't afford to let his desire for her cloud his judgment. Katya was here to work off a debt, nothing more. She was a means to an end, a tool to ensure her father's sins were repaid. But every time he watched her, every time she challenged him, he felt that line blur. He had control, but how long could he maintain it before she began to control him?

His thoughts were interrupted as Kirill finally spoke, his voice soft but clear. "Can I have the blue crayon?"

Katya smiled, handing him the crayon without hesitation. "Of course."

Ivan's chest tightened at the small interaction. It wasn't much, but it was progress. And that progress made him wonder, for the first time, if she could be more than just another temporary fixture in his life. If her fire could be channeled into something greater.

But no. She was still a risk. And Ivan Volkov didn't take risks lightly.

With a final glance at the scene before him, Ivan turned and walked away, leaving Katya and the children to their quiet moment. There was time yet to decide her fate, but for now, he would watch. And when the time came, he would act.

After all, control was what he did best.

Ivan leaned back in his office chair later that evening, swirling a glass of whiskey as the memory of Katya's defiance replayed in his mind. It wasn't just her sharp words in the playroom that had caught his attention—it was the way she had looked him in the eyes, unflinching, challenging him. There had been no fear in her gaze, only fire. It was a rare thing to find in someone who stood in front of him, especially in her position. Most people, especially women, would lower their gaze, desperate to avoid provoking him. But not Katya. She had met him head-on, and that intrigued him.

He had been prepared to break her, to force her into submission just like anyone else who dared to challenge his authority. But something about her defiance stirred something deeper inside him. It wasn't just the usual hunger he felt for women—this was different. She wasn't like the others. She didn't seek his approval or fear his power. Instead, she pushed back, daring him to respond.

Ivan took a slow sip of his drink, his eyes narrowing as he considered the dangerous game Katya was playing. She didn't realize it yet, but she was walking a fine line. He could easily break her if he wanted to—he had done it to others before her, crushed any trace of resistance until all that remained was submission. And yet, he hadn't. He found himself holding back, watching, waiting to see what she would do next. It was a strange sensation, this urge to let the tension between them build.

His mind drifted back to their first encounter, the way her chin had lifted slightly when she realized she wouldn't be sent to one of his clubs like the other women. Even then, she had shown strength, an inner fire that had set her apart. Most women would have been relieved, grateful to escape the fate he could have easily condemned them to. But Katya hadn't thanked him. Instead, she had held her head high, silently challenging him even in that moment.

And that was what gnawed at him now. Katya didn't seek his approval like so many others. She didn't try to win him over, didn't bend to his will in the ways he was used to. It was as though she resented him, and that resentment only fueled his desire to dominate her. To own her. It wasn't just about control anymore—it was about watching her defiance crumble under his touch. There was something exhilarating in knowing that he could break her if he wanted to, that he could make her submit, not through fear, but through the sheer force of his power over her.

Ivan's grip tightened around the glass as he thought about Katya's defiance. It wasn't just physical attraction that had him intrigued, though he couldn't deny the pull of her body. It was more than that. He found himself drawn to her spirit, the way she pushed back against him even when she had no power to do so. It was maddening, but at the same time, he couldn't get enough of it. It made him want to test her limits, to see how far she would go before she finally broke.

He had seen women crumble beneath his control before—seen them transform from strong, independent individuals into pliant, submissive shadows of their former selves. But Katya... she was different. The thought of bending her to his will made his pulse quicken, but it wasn't just the usual desire for dominance that drove him. There was something else, something he couldn't quite name. It was deeper than the physical, more primal than his usual need for control.

It frustrated him, this growing obsession. Ivan was not a man who let his desires rule him. Control was everything—control over his business, his men, his world. And yet, when it came to Katya, he found that control slipping, just a little. She had gotten under his skin in a way no one else had, and that made her dangerous. He knew it, even if he didn't want to admit it. He was supposed to be the one with all the power, the one calling the shots. But with Katya, it felt like the power dynamics were shifting, if only slightly.

Ivan clenched his jaw, determined not to let her win this silent battle. She might think she could challenge him, but he would show her who held the real power in this situation. She was indebted to him, and she would learn what that meant. He would break her if he had to, but for now, he would let the tension build, let her defiance grow until the moment he decided to crush it.

But the truth was more complicated than that, and he knew it. Deep down, beneath the layers of dominance and control, there was a part of him that didn't want to break her—not completely. He wanted to see how far she could go, how much fire she could withstand before she finally bent to his will. It was a dangerous game, but one he was eager to play.

Ivan set the glass down with a sharp clink, his mind still filled with thoughts of Katya. She was a puzzle, one he was determined to solve. And when the time came, he would make sure she knew exactly who held the power in their dynamic. She would submit to him—eventually.

But until then, he would enjoy watching the fire in her eyes burn brighter with each passing day.

Chapter 6

Katya stood in the dimly lit bedroom, gazing down at Kirill and Dasha as they slept. Their small faces were peaceful, free from the burdens they carried while awake. The weight of the past week settled heavily on her chest, making it difficult to breathe. She had tried so hard to reach them, to give them some sense of comfort, but their sadness was a constant, oppressive force. It clung to them like a shadow, and no matter what she did, she couldn't seem to break through.

She knelt by Kirill's bed, gently brushing a stray lock of hair from his forehead. He stirred slightly but didn't wake. It was moments like this that made her heart ache the most. These children had been through so much, losing their mother in such a tragic way. But it wasn't just the loss of their mother that hurt them. They were slowly losing their father too, and that thought sparked a flame of anger deep inside her.

Ivan. His name alone made her blood boil. How could he be so distant, so cold? The children needed him—desperately. And yet, he acted as though they were an afterthought, a responsibility he could push onto others. She had been in this house for a week, and in that time, she had barely seen him interact with them. He was too busy, too preoccupied with his world of power and control to notice how much his children were suffering.

Katya rose from Kirill's bed and turned toward the door, pausing for a moment to look back at the two sleeping figures. Dasha was curled up tightly under her blanket, her thumb in her mouth. Katya's heart twisted. This wasn't fair. None of it was fair. These children deserved better. They deserved a father who cared for them, who showed them love and attention. Instead, they had Ivan—a man who seemed more like a statue than a parent.

The anger that had simmered inside her for days bubbled up, threatening to spill over. She clenched her fists, her nails biting into the palms of her hands. She wanted to scream, to shake Ivan and demand to know how he could be so heartless. But what good would that do? He was untouchable, distant, locked away in his study while his children fell further into sadness and silence.

As she stood there, her emotions whirling, Katya's thoughts drifted to Ivan's cold, piercing eyes. She hated how much control he had over everything—over her, over his children, over her very thoughts. And yet, there was something else. Something she refused to acknowledge, but couldn't shake.

It wasn't just anger driving her toward Ivan. As much as she hated to admit it, there was an undeniable tension between them, something that simmered beneath the surface every time they were near each other. She had felt it from the moment they met, when his eyes had locked onto hers in that dimly lit office. It infuriated her, this attraction she couldn't control. She resented him for it, resented herself for it even more.

How could she feel anything other than hatred for a man like him? A man who controlled her life, who held her future in his hands? And yet, her body responded to him in ways she couldn't understand, in ways she didn't want to understand. Every time he was near, she could feel the heat between them, the unspoken desire that neither of them would admit. It was maddening, confusing, and it made her feel weak in a way she despised.

Katya bit her lip, the frustration and confusion swirling inside her like a storm. She had no control, not over Ivan, not over her situation, and not even over her own feelings. It was infuriating. But the children... the children were suffering, and she couldn't stand by and watch them continue to be ignored by the one person who should be there for them.

She made up her mind in an instant. She would confront Ivan. He needed to hear what she had to say, needed to understand that he was failing his children. They deserved better than this cold, distant version of him. Katya knew she was risking a lot by going to him like this, but she didn't care.

The children's well-being mattered more than whatever consequences she might face. She wasn't just doing this for them, though. Deep down, she knew she was doing it for herself too.

As she quietly slipped out of the children's room and made her way down the long hallway toward Ivan's study, her heart pounded in her chest. Her footsteps were light, but each one felt heavy with the weight of her decision. She didn't know what she was going to say when she got there, but she knew she couldn't hold it in any longer. Ivan needed to know how much damage he was doing by staying so detached.

Her emotions bubbled up again—anger, resentment, and that unspoken attraction she tried so hard to ignore. She pushed it all down as best as she could, but the closer she got to Ivan's study, the more the tension grew. It was more than just the children. She couldn't deny it any longer. There was something between her and Ivan, something dangerous and electric, and it terrified her how much she was drawn to it.

Katya's hand hovered over the door to Ivan's study, hesitating for just a moment. Was she really going to do this? Confront him like this, when she wasn't even sure what she was going to say? She took a deep breath, trying to steady herself. She had to do this. For the children. For herself.

Without thinking any further, she knocked lightly on the door and then pushed it open, her heart pounding with adrenaline and frustration. The heavy wood creaked as it swung inward, and for a split second, she hesitated on the threshold. The room before her was dim, cloaked in shadows, with only a soft, amber glow from a single desk lamp casting long shapes across the space. The deep, dark mahogany walls seemed to close in, and the quiet hum of the outside world disappeared, leaving only the oppressive silence between her and Ivan.

He sat behind his large, imposing desk, hunched over papers that appeared to be contracts or documents, his expression unreadable in the dim light. The steady scratch of his pen was the only sound in the room until the creaking door announced her presence. Katya's breath hitched as his gaze slowly rose to meet hers, his cold eyes locking onto hers with an intensity that nearly made her backpedal.

Immediately, the air in the room changed. The once solid wall of her anger began to crack under the weight of his gaze. Her determination wavered as a sudden surge of something deeper—a mix of fear and an unwelcome desire—rushed through her veins. She had come here to confront him, to demand answers, to release the fury she'd been harboring all week, but now, as she stood in his study, Ivan's brooding presence filled the room and threatened to suffocate her resolve.

Her fingers trembled, but she clenched them into fists at her sides, grounding herself. *You came here for a reason,* she reminded herself. *Don't back down now.*

With her pulse drumming loudly in her ears, Katya finally stepped inside, forcing her feet to move. "You need to spend more time with your children," she said, her voice sharper and louder than she had intended. It felt almost too harsh in the stillness of the room. Ivan didn't respond immediately, and that just added fuel to her fire. She watched his expression, searching for any sign of emotion, but all she could see was that infuriating calmness. His eyes flickered with something—amusement, perhaps? Disinterest?—but they quickly returned to their icy stillness.

"They've lost their mother," she pressed on, her anger boiling over. She hadn't come here to be dismissed or ignored. "They barely see you. They need you, Ivan."

The weight of her words hung in the air, but Ivan didn't flinch. His gaze never wavered, and Katya felt a new surge of frustration rising in her chest. *How can he just sit there, so calm, so detached? Doesn't he care at all?*

Her heart pounded louder as she felt the edges of her control slipping. There was more than anger now; it was everything she had been holding in since she arrived—the fear, the resentment, and the tension that clung to every interaction she had with Ivan. Her pulse quickened, not just from anger, but from the unspoken desire that she refused to acknowledge. It simmered beneath the surface, a magnetic pull toward him that she hated herself for feeling.

Ivan remained silent for a long moment, his cold gaze boring into her with a focus that made her feel both exposed and challenged. He leaned back in his chair, his large frame still as a predator waiting to pounce. The silence stretched, and the quiet only served to stoke Katya's frustration further.

"You don't even care about them, do you?" she spat, her voice trembling with a mix of anger and something else she couldn't name. "You're just hiding in here while they suffer, while they—"

Ivan's pen paused mid-stroke. He set it down with deliberate calmness and slowly rose to his feet. The movement was unhurried, controlled, and yet it sent a shiver down Katya's spine. He wasn't reacting in the way she had expected. No anger, no raised voice. Instead, his silence felt like the eye of a storm—calm, yet promising devastation.

He moved around the desk with the slow, calculated grace of someone who knew the power they wielded. His presence filled the room, and with each step he took toward her, Katya's bravado faltered just a little more. She stood her ground, but inside, her heart was racing, her skin tingling with the awareness of him closing the distance between them.

"You presume to tell me how to take care of my children?" Ivan's voice was low, dangerous, and laced with the authority of someone used to being in control. He stopped just inches from her, towering over her petite frame, and the tension between them crackled like electricity.

Katya's breath caught in her throat. His words were a warning, a reminder of who he was and what he was capable of, but instead of retreating, her anger flared again. She couldn't back down now. She wouldn't.

"They're not just your children," she retorted, her voice sharp but unsteady. "They're people. They need you."

Ivan's eyes narrowed, and the flicker of something dark crossed his face—surprise, perhaps, or maybe amusement. But whatever it was, it only lasted for a split second before his usual mask of calm indifference returned. The space between them felt suffocating now, charged with both the tension of their argument and something else, something primal that neither of them could deny.

His gaze dropped to her lips, and Katya felt her pulse quicken in response. She hated how much her body responded to him, how her anger seemed to fuel the desire that had been simmering between them since the day they met. But here, standing so close to him, the lines between anger and attraction blurred.

The intensity of his presence held her in place, and all the words she had come here to say evaporated in the heat of the moment.

"You think you know me, Katya?" His voice was soft now, almost a whisper, but it was laced with danger. "You don't know anything."

Katya swallowed hard, her heart hammering in her chest. She tried to respond, to throw something back at him, but the words were stuck in her throat. The desire she had fought to suppress was now undeniable, and she could see it reflected in Ivan's dark, hungry gaze.

The space between them was shrinking, the air thick with unspoken tension. She could feel the heat radiating from his body, could smell the faint scent of his cologne mixed with something darker, something primal. Her breath came faster, her anger fading into something else entirely.

But she wasn't ready to give in. Not yet.

Katya's breath hitched as Ivan's voice sharpened, the cool indifference from before melting away into something far more dangerous. The shift in his demeanor was palpable, his calm slipping as he advanced on her with an intensity that made the air around them seem thicker, heavier.

"You think you can walk into my house and tell me how to run my life?" His words were like a whip, each syllable cutting through the air with a force that made Katya's stomach twist. He stepped closer, his tall frame casting a shadow that seemed to swallow the space between them. The controlled power he exuded made her feel small, but she forced herself to stand her ground, even as her pulse quickened.

Katya could feel the heat of him, the overwhelming presence that seemed to suck the oxygen from the room. She knew she was playing a dangerous game, but something inside her refused to back down. Even as her heart pounded in her chest and her body reacted to him in ways she couldn't control, she stood her ground, her defiance a shield she clung to desperately.

"Someone has to say it," she spat, her voice trembling but steady. She would not let him see her falter. "They need their father. You can't just ignore them, Ivan."

For a split second, something flickered in Ivan's eyes—something dark, something that sent a shiver down her spine. His jaw clenched, and for a moment, she thought she might have pushed him too far. But even as the fear danced at the edges of her consciousness, there was something else, something that terrified her even more: the way her body responded to him, the way her skin tingled under his intense gaze, the heat that pooled in her core despite the anger raging in her chest.

Katya clenched her fists, biting back the urge to lash out again. But what was the point? It was clear Ivan wouldn't change—he wouldn't listen to reason. Her words meant nothing to him. The futility of the situation washed over her, and with a frustrated sigh, she turned sharply on her heel, ready to walk away, to leave him behind before her emotions got the better of her. She needed to regain control, to put as much distance between them as possible, because being near him made it impossible to think straight.

Ivan's movements were swift and deliberate. Before she could react, his hand shot out, grabbing her wrist in a tight grip. The force of it sent a jolt through her, but the gasp that escaped her lips wasn't one of fear—it was something else entirely, something that made her stomach twist in knots of anticipation.

His grip tightened as he pulled her closer, and suddenly, the world seemed to tilt on its axis. Katya's heart raced, her breath coming in quick, shallow bursts as Ivan closed the remaining distance between them. His face was mere inches from hers now, the heat of his body pressing against her, enveloping her in a way that made it impossible to think straight.

"You don't get to walk away when I'm not done with you," he growled, his voice low and menacing, filled with a primal dominance that made her knees weak. His other hand reached up, grabbing her chin with a rough, possessive grip, tilting her head back so that she was forced to meet his gaze.

The world seemed to narrow to just the two of them—the anger, the tension, the undeniable pull that had been simmering between them since the moment they met. It all came crashing to the surface in an instant, and Katya's heart pounded so loudly she was sure Ivan could hear it.

Her breath hitched again as his eyes bore into hers, dark and unreadable. She should have been afraid. She *was* afraid, but not in the way she expected. It wasn't fear of Ivan's power or his control that made her chest tighten—it was the fear of her own reaction to him, the way her body betrayed her despite the anger simmering beneath the surface.

Katya's pulse raced as she felt the roughness of his hand against her chin, the strength in his grip as he held her in place. She should push him away. She should say something, do something, anything to break the spell that seemed to have settled over them. But instead, she stood frozen, her body responding to his in ways she didn't understand and couldn't control.

Her breath came in quick, shallow gasps as she felt
the tension between them rise to a boiling point.
Ivan's grip tightened, and she could feel the raw
power radiating from him, the unspoken command
in his touch. He was in control—he had always
been in control—but now, standing so close to him,
Katya realized just how little power she had in this
moment.

And yet, despite the anger that still burned in her
chest, despite the fear that coursed through her
veins, there was something else—something dark
and thrilling that pulsed beneath the surface of her
skin. She could feel it, the magnetic pull that drew
her toward him, the undeniable force that made her
want to surrender, to give in to the desire that she
had tried so hard to ignore.

Ivan's breath was hot against her skin as he leaned
in closer, his eyes never leaving hers. "You're going
to learn, Katya," he whispered, his voice rough and
dangerous. "You're going to learn that I'm the one
in control here. You don't get to tell me how to live
my life."

Her chest heaved as she tried to form a response,
but the words caught in her throat. She hated him
for this, for the way he made her feel, for the way
her body seemed to betray her at every turn. But
even more than that, she hated the part of her that
wanted this, that craved the control he exerted over
her, that longed for the dominance in his touch.

Katya's skin tingled under his gaze, her heart pounding harder with every second that passed. She could feel the heat rising between them, the tension thick and suffocating, and yet, there was a part of her that didn't want it to end.

She knew she should resist, she *needed* to resist, but as Ivan's grip on her wrist tightened and his face drew closer to hers, the line between anger and desire blurred beyond recognition.

Without warning, Ivan's mouth crashed down on hers, fierce and demanding. Katya gasped against his lips, her hands instinctively pushing against his broad chest in a desperate attempt to gain some control, but it was no use. His grip was strong, commanding, and unyielding. Despite herself, her body responded in ways she couldn't control, betraying the anger she'd walked in with moments ago. A sudden flood of heat coursed through her, drowning out any logical thoughts. Before she could stop herself, she was kissing him back, her fingers curling into the fabric of his shirt, clinging to him.

The kiss was intense, filled with an urgency that left no room for hesitation or doubt. Ivan was in control, and for reasons she couldn't comprehend, she didn't pull away. She hated herself for how easily her body succumbed to his touch, hated the way her heart raced when he deepened the kiss, but she couldn't stop. The taste of him overwhelmed her senses, clouding her mind with desire she had spent weeks trying to deny.

Ivan's hands moved over her body, rough and possessive. One slid around her waist, pulling her closer to him, while the other gripped the back of her neck, holding her in place as his lips devoured hers. Every brush of his mouth, every rough touch of his fingers sent jolts of heat through her, and it became harder and harder to remember why she was angry in the first place. He was everywhere, consuming her, his strength and dominance evident in every move.

Her body betrayed her, yielding to him even as her mind screamed for her to stop. She shouldn't want this. She should push him away, remind herself of who he was and what he represented, but it was too late. She was lost in the moment, lost in him.

Ivan deepened the kiss, his mouth hot and demanding against hers, his hands roaming freely now, as if he owned her. Katya's heart pounded in her chest, her skin tingling with every touch, every caress. She hated that she couldn't stop the way her body responded to him. He was overwhelming, all-consuming, and the more she fought it, the more intense the desire became.

She tried to resist, tried to remind herself of the reasons she had stormed into his study, but every time his hands gripped her tighter, pulling her closer, the anger faded, replaced by a burning need. His mouth moved down her neck, leaving a trail of heat in its wake, his stubble grazing her sensitive skin. Her breath hitched, a soft moan escaping her lips before she could stop it.

Ivan's hands found the hem of her shirt, yanking it over her head with a swift, practiced motion. The air between them crackled with tension as her bra fell away, leaving her exposed to his intense gaze.

For a brief moment, she felt vulnerable, but the way his eyes darkened with desire made her shiver in anticipation.

Her breath hitched as he stepped back for a moment, his gaze raking over her bare skin before his hands moved to his own shirt. Katya's pulse quickened as she watched him tear it off, revealing the broad expanse of his chest, his powerful muscles covered in intricate tattoos. His chiseled abs flexed as he moved, and despite everything, Katya felt a surge of desire at the sight of him.

Her hands instinctively reached out, running over his hard chest, feeling the strength beneath her fingers. He was dangerous, powerful, and she knew she should stop, but instead, her hands moved to his belt, tugging it open as his mouth descended on her neck.

He didn't waste time. His mouth was on her breast immediately, teasing her hard nipple with his tongue.

His hands gripped her hips tightly, pulling her closer, as his mouth worked over her sensitive skin. Each flick of his tongue was deliberate, and when he bit down again, a sharper gasp escaped her lips, the pain blending seamlessly with pleasure. The tension in the room thickened, and Katya's body reacted on instinct, her fingers curling into his hair, holding him to her as if afraid the pleasure might stop.

Her breath came in shallow bursts as his mouth moved from one breast to the other, his stubble grazing her skin and adding to the overwhelming sensation. She could feel the heat radiating from him, his body pressed so close to hers that it was impossible to ignore how hard he was beneath his clothes. His every movement was confident, controlled, yet filled with an urgency that matched the wild rhythm of her heartbeat.

Katya's mind raced, torn between the part of her that screamed this was wrong and the undeniable need coursing through her veins. The way he dominated her senses left her craving more—more of his touch, more of his control. She had never felt anything like this before, and the overwhelming sensation of his body against hers was intoxicating, blurring the lines of what she knew she should want and what she couldn't resist any longer.

Katya gasped, her back arching toward him. The sensation was too much, too intense, and yet she craved more. Her nipples hardened under his skilled touch, and she could feel the wetness pooling between her legs, undeniable proof of how much she wanted him. She cursed herself for it, but the desire was overwhelming, and there was no turning back now.

Without warning, Ivan's hand gripped her hips and spun her around, bending her roughly over the desk. Her palms slapped against the smooth surface as she gasped for breath, her mind spinning with the force of what was happening. Her skirt rode up around her hips, and before she could protest, she felt his hands on her, sliding her panties down her legs in one swift movement.

Ivan's hand slid between her legs, his touch possessive and demanding as his fingers parted her slick folds. The moment his fingers found her wetness, his low, guttural growl sent a shiver down her spine.

"You want this," he growled, his voice thick with authority, with a sense of control that made her knees weaken. His fingers teased her, sliding over her sensitive clit, making her gasp, before thrusting deep inside her without hesitation.

Katya bit her lip, a small whimper escaping her as she tried to process what was happening. Her mind was spinning, battling between the urge to fight him and the undeniable pull of desire coursing through her. She wanted to deny it, to say that this wasn't what she wanted, that she hadn't stormed into his study to end up like this—but the truth was, her body craved him, craved his touch. She couldn't lie to herself any longer.

Her body pushed back against his hand, desperate for more, each thrust of his fingers sending jolts of pleasure straight through her. She could feel herself surrendering, her resistance crumbling as his fingers moved inside her with ruthless intensity, unrelenting as his thumb circled her clit in slow, tantalizing motions.

Katya moaned, her breath coming in ragged gasps as her body trembled with the force of the need building inside her. Her hands gripped the edge of the desk tightly, knuckles white, as waves of pleasure crashed through her, pulling her closer and closer to the edge. She could feel herself teetering on the brink of release, every nerve in her body alive, burning with anticipation, but Ivan wasn't finished with her yet.

He leaned down, his breath hot against her ear, his lips grazing her skin as he growled, "Beg for it."

The words sent a jolt of fury through her, even as her body betrayed her once more. Katya gasped, her mind spinning, fighting the war between hating him for the control he held over her and the desperate need clawing at her insides. She hated him for making her want this, for pushing her to the point where she would do anything to find release—but she couldn't stop herself.

"Please," she whispered, her voice barely audible, shaking with a mixture of humiliation and raw desire.

"That's not good enough," he said, his voice rough with control. "Tell me what you want."

Katya's breath caught in her throat, the shame and desire battling inside her. She wanted to scream at him, to push him away, but every nerve in her body was on fire, demanding more of his touch. She could feel herself teetering on the edge of something dangerous, something she couldn't come back from, but it was too late to stop now.

"Please!" she cried, louder now, her voice trembling with need. "Please, I want you—please!" Her body trembled as the words left her lips, her heart pounding with the weight of the admission.

The words were barely out of her mouth when Ivan's fingers thrust harder, faster, pushing her body to the very edge. She cried out, her body arching against him as the tension built, threatening to snap at any moment. The sensation was overwhelming, drowning her in a tidal wave of pleasure that left her breathless, trembling with need.

She was no longer in control—he was, and she hated how much she loved it.

But just as she felt herself tipping over the edge, Ivan pulled his fingers away, leaving her gasping, trembling, her body aching with unfulfilled need. The sudden absence of his touch left her reeling, her mind blank as her body screamed for more.

Katya whimpered, her frustration mingling with her desire, but before she could form another thought, she heard the unmistakable sound of his zipper being undone. Her heart raced, her breath catching in her throat as she felt the hard press of his cock against her slick entrance, hot and demanding.

"I told you," Ivan growled, his voice low and rough, sending another wave of anticipation coursing through her. "I wasn't done with you."

And with one rough, powerful thrust, he buried himself inside her, filling her completely.

Katya's breath hitched, her body arching against the desk as she tried to adjust to the overwhelming sensation of him inside her. Every inch of him stretched her, filling her in ways she had never experienced before. The force of his thrust left her gasping, a mixture of pain and pleasure blurring together in a heady, intoxicating mix.

He didn't give her time to think, to process, as he began to move, each thrust harder and deeper than the last. His hands gripped her hips, pulling her back against him with a strength that left her powerless to do anything but submit to the raw, primal need driving him.

The sound of their bodies colliding echoed through the room, each thrust sending a new wave of pleasure crashing through her. Katya's mind was lost to the sensation, every nerve in her body alive with the intensity of it. She could feel him everywhere—his hands, his cock, his breath hot against her skin—and the intensity of it all left her teetering on the brink once again.

Her cries filled the air, mingling with his grunts of satisfaction as he pounded into her relentlessly. Her fingers gripped the desk for support, her body trembling as the pleasure built and built, her climax nearing with every hard, deep thrust.

She had never experienced anything like this—never been with a man this powerful, this commanding. Ivan knew exactly what he wanted, and he took it without hesitation, without apology. And Katya, despite everything, found herself wanting it too, wanting him in ways that scared her, ways she couldn't deny.

With one final, fierce thrust, the tension inside her snapped, her body shuddering as her climax ripped through her, her moans turning into cries of pleasure. Her muscles clenched around him, pulling him deeper, and with a low growl, Ivan followed, his body tensing as he found his release inside her.

They stayed like that for a moment, both of them breathing heavily, the weight of the encounter hanging in the air around them. Ivan's hands slowly loosened their grip on her hips, his breath hot against her back as he slowly pulled out of her, leaving her feeling both sated and raw, her body still trembling from the intensity of it all.

Katya's heart raced as she sat up, her body still humming with the aftershocks of what had just happened. Shame clawed at her chest, a sharp contrast to the desire that still pulsed through her veins. She hated how much she had wanted it, hated how quickly her body had given in to him. The anger she had felt walking into the room was gone, replaced by confusion and a raw vulnerability she hadn't been prepared for.

Ivan stood in front of her, his breathing heavy, his chest rising and falling with the remnants of his release. For a moment, his gaze softened as he looked at her, and Katya caught a glimpse of something deeper in his eyes—something more than just the raw, possessive lust that had consumed them both.

There was a flicker of an emotion she couldn't quite place—something that seemed almost human in its intensity, vulnerable even. It was as if, for that brief moment, the layers of dominance and control peeled back to reveal a man underneath the hardness. The intensity of the moment shook her, making her stomach twist with uncertainty. What was that she had seen? Guilt? Longing?

But just as quickly as it appeared, it was gone. His expression hardened, his jaw tightening as he turned away from her, running a hand through his tousled hair. The vulnerability that had briefly passed between them vanished, replaced with the cold, commanding demeanor that Katya had grown to despise.

"You can leave now," he said, his voice low but devoid of the passion that had burned between them moments ago. There was no warmth, no acknowledgment of what they had just shared. It was as if the entire encounter had meant nothing to him.

Katya's heart sank, the weight of his words hitting her like a physical blow. She had expected something—anything—to make sense of the chaos that had erupted between them. But there was nothing. No explanation, no comfort. Just cold dismissal.

With trembling hands, Katya gathered her clothes, slipping them back on as quickly as she could. Her skin felt exposed, raw, as if the intensity of their encounter had stripped away more than just her clothes. She avoided Ivan's gaze, too ashamed to look at him, too confused by the mess of emotions swirling inside her.

As she adjusted her skirt and ran a hand through her disheveled hair, she felt a wave of nausea wash over her. What had she done? How had she let this happen? She had walked into that study with anger in her heart, but somewhere along the way, her body had betrayed her, giving in to the very man she had sworn to hate.

Ivan remained silent, his back to her now, as if the entire thing had already been forgotten. Katya swallowed hard, her throat tight with unshed tears. She couldn't cry, not here. Not in front of him. She had to get out. She had to escape the suffocating mix of desire, shame, and confusion that pressed down on her chest like a weight she couldn't bear.

Without another word, Katya turned on her heel and walked out of the study, her footsteps quick and unsteady as she fled the room. The heavy door closed behind her with a soft click, but the sound reverberated in her mind, echoing in the hollow space where her pride had once been.

As she walked down the hallway, her mind raced with conflicting thoughts. Shame burned at her core, but beneath it, there was something darker, something that scared her more than the shame: a lingering desire. Despite everything, despite how wrong it had felt, a part of her wanted more. A part

of her craved the intensity, the power he had over
her.

Katya's stomach twisted in knots as she reached
her room, her hands shaking as she closed the
door behind her. She leaned against it, sliding down
until she was sitting on the floor, her knees drawn
to her chest. The silence of the room pressed in
around her, the weight of what had just happened
settling heavily on her shoulders.

She hated herself for giving in, for letting Ivan
control her like that. But the worst part, the part that
made her chest tighten with fear, was the
knowledge that she would never forget it. And deep
down, she knew this was only the beginning.

Chapter 7

Katya woke up with a start, her heart pounding as memories from the night before surged back into her mind. She lay there, staring at the ceiling, trying to make sense of the whirlwind of emotions that had taken hold of her. Anger, frustration, confusion—it all twisted inside her, but so did something else, something darker and more unsettling. Desire.

Her body ached in places she didn't want to admit, the lingering sensation of Ivan's hands on her skin burning into her memory. She should hate him for what had happened, and a part of her did. The way he had controlled her, dominated her, it made her furious. But another part of her, a part she wanted to bury deep inside, craved more. That was what terrified her the most—the way her body had responded, the way she had wanted him in ways that went beyond the anger. She clenched her fists, trying to push the thoughts away, but they clung to her like an unwelcome shadow. How could she have let it happen? How could she have wanted it?

Her chest tightened as she swung her legs over the side of the bed, forcing herself to focus on the day ahead. The children would be waking up soon, and they needed her. The routine would help her clear her head, help her forget the heat of Ivan's touch, at least for a while. She didn't have time to dwell on her own feelings. There were two little lives that depended on her.

She moved to the small mirror in her room, catching sight of herself. Her long dark hair hung loosely around her shoulders, and her brown eyes looked troubled, unsettled. There was a flush to her cheeks she didn't like, a reminder of the desire she had felt. She shook her head, straightened her posture, and left the room to tend to the children.

As she stepped into Kirill and Dasha's bedroom, the innocence of their sleepy faces was like a balm to her frayed nerves. Kirill was already stirring, his eyes blinking open, while Dasha was still curled up in her blankets, her thumb resting near her mouth. They looked so small, so fragile, and for a moment, Katya felt the weight of their loss press down on her. They had already lost their mother, and now they had a father who barely acknowledged them. She couldn't imagine how lonely that must feel for them.

"Good morning," she said softly, smiling as she approached Kirill's bed. He sat up, rubbing his eyes with his little fists, and Katya's heart ached. "Did you sleep well?"

Kirill nodded sleepily, his dark hair sticking up in all directions. Katya helped him out of bed and patted down his rumpled pajamas before turning her attention to Dasha. Gently, she stroked the little girl's hair, murmuring for her to wake up. Dasha stirred, blinking up at Katya with wide eyes, and a small smile tugged at the corners of her lips.

The children's trust in her was growing, slowly but surely, and that brought a sense of warmth to Katya's heart. They were her responsibility now, more so than ever, and she wouldn't fail them. But as she helped them get dressed and prepared for the day, her mind drifted back to Ivan. His absence in their lives infuriated her. How could he just stand back and watch them grow up from a distance? Didn't he care?

Yet, despite the anger she felt toward him, she couldn't shake the memory of the night before—the intensity, the rawness of it. It left her feeling disoriented, as if part of her resented him deeply, but another part—one she didn't want to admit—was drawn to him. She scolded herself for even entertaining those thoughts. He was the man responsible for her father's downfall, the man who now owned her for the next five years. There was nothing redeeming about him, and yet, the way his hands had moved over her body, the way his lips had claimed hers… she shivered at the memory.

Sofia's sudden entrance into the room broke her from her thoughts. The older woman bustled in, her expression as brisk and no-nonsense as ever. She gave Katya a nod of acknowledgment before turning her attention to the children.

"Ivan has decided the children will have their breakfast in the dining room each morning now," Sofia said, her voice even but with a hint of surprise, as if the decision had caught her off guard too.

Katya blinked, her thoughts racing. That was a change. Up until now, the children had eaten in the kitchen while Ivan remained distant, holed up in his study or conducting business elsewhere. What had made him decide this? Was it something she had said last night? Could their heated argument have actually gotten through to him?

Her stomach tightened at the thought. Had he actually listened to her, or was this just a coincidence? She wasn't sure what to make of it, but the idea of seeing Ivan this morning, sitting at the same table with his children, sent a ripple of anxiety through her. After everything that had happened between them, the prospect of being near him again was almost too much to bear. Her body still remembered the way he had touched her, and her mind was already at war with itself over how she should feel about it.

"Are you alright, dear?" Sofia asked, noticing the slight hesitation in Katya's movements.

Katya quickly plastered on a smile, nodding as she gathered her thoughts. "Yes, I'm fine. I'll get the children ready for breakfast."

But as she led Kirill and Dasha toward the dining room, her heart pounded in her chest. Would Ivan be there, waiting for them? Would she be able to keep her composure after everything that had transpired the night before? The memory of his hands on her, the heat of his body pressed against hers, lingered in her mind, and no matter how hard she tried, she couldn't shake it.

Katya's heart thudded in her chest as she guided the children into the dining room, her hand gently resting on Dasha's shoulder while Kirill walked ahead. She had been preparing herself to leave them at the table as usual, expecting Sofia to take over, but the sight that greeted her stopped her in her tracks.

Ivan was already seated at the head of the table, a cup of coffee in hand. The steam curled lazily from the surface of the dark liquid, but it wasn't the coffee that made Katya pause. It was Ivan himself, sitting there as if nothing had changed, as if the night before hadn't happened. His presence shifted the entire atmosphere of the room. She could feel it immediately, a tension that made the air thick and heavy. Her heart skipped a beat when his eyes lifted from his coffee and locked onto hers for a brief moment.

"Daddy!" Dasha's small voice broke the silence, and Katya glanced down to see the little girl's face light up with a shy smile. Kirill, too, looked surprised but pleased, his eyes wide as he stood frozen for a second before rushing over to the table.

"Good morning," Ivan said, his voice quieter than Katya had expected. There was no trace of the harshness or command that usually laced his words. His tone had softened, almost as if the children's presence melted away some of the cold exterior he kept up so fiercely.

Katya stood frozen, watching the scene unfold with a strange mix of emotions swirling inside her. A part of her was relieved, even happy, to see Ivan interacting with his children like this. It was something she hadn't expected—his attention focused on them, his expression more relaxed. And yet, there was that other part of her, the one that couldn't stop replaying the events of the night before. Her skin tingled at the memory of his touch, the way he had dominated her so completely. She swallowed hard, forcing the thoughts away.

"Sit down," Ivan said to the children, his voice still carrying that undercurrent of command, though now directed at his son and daughter. Kirill eagerly took his place at the table, and Dasha followed, her eyes flickering back to her father as if still unsure of his sudden presence.

Katya's chest tightened. She wanted to be glad that Ivan was finally spending time with them, but she couldn't shake the unease that had settled deep in her stomach. Had their confrontation last night truly reached him? Or was this just another layer to the control he held over everyone in this house, including her?

She busied herself helping Dasha into her chair, her hands trembling slightly as she adjusted the child's seat. Kirill was already talking, his voice animated as he recounted a story from yesterday's playtime. Ivan listened, his expression calm, nodding along as Kirill's words tumbled out. It was a stark contrast to the man Katya had seen the night before—the man who had taken her with a raw, almost brutal intensity.

As she stepped back, Katya caught Ivan's gaze again. His eyes lingered on her for just a moment, but there was no warmth in them, no acknowledgment of what had transpired between them. His face was unreadable, the mask of control firmly back in place.

"You can go now," Ivan said, his voice cutting through the air with a crisp finality. He dismissed her without so much as a second glance, turning his attention back to his children as if she no longer existed in the room.

The words stung more than Katya had expected. She had known he wouldn't acknowledge their encounter, but the cold dismissal twisted something inside her. She felt a pang of rejection, despite the fact that she had anticipated being brushed off. She stood there for a second, unsure if she should say something, but Ivan had already turned away, pouring his attention into Dasha, who was now telling him about the dollhouse she had been playing with yesterday.

Katya swallowed her emotions and nodded, though no one was looking at her anymore. "Enjoy your breakfast," she said softly to the children, her voice barely above a whisper, but they were too focused on their father to respond. With that, she turned and made her way toward the door, her mind spinning with a thousand thoughts.

As she walked down the hallway, her steps echoed in the quiet house, and the memory of last night came rushing back in vivid detail. She could still feel the heat of his touch, the way his hands had claimed her, the way she had responded to him. She hated herself for it—hated how much she had wanted him in that moment, how she had lost herself completely in the raw, overpowering desire that had overtaken them both.

And now here he was, acting as if none of it had ever happened.

Her fists clenched at her sides as she made her way back toward the kitchen, her thoughts a whirlwind of confusion and frustration. What had that meant for him? Was it just another display of power, another way to control her? Or had it been something more? For a brief second, back in his study, she had seen something in his eyes—something vulnerable, something real. But just as quickly as it had appeared, it had vanished, replaced by the cold, distant man she had come to know.

Katya leaned against the kitchen counter, staring out the window but not really seeing the view. The tight knot of emotions inside her refused to unravel. She had no idea what to make of this new dynamic between them. Last night had been a turning point—whether for better or worse, she couldn't tell. And now, watching Ivan with his children, seeing the way they lit up in his presence, she wondered if she had actually gotten through to him. Had she made him see what they needed?

The way he had touched her, the way he had kissed her—it had been more than just lust. She knew it, even if he wouldn't admit it. There had been something else there, something deeper. But now, standing here in the cold light of morning, Katya wasn't sure what any of it meant.

As she stood in the kitchen, her heart still racing from the tension of the dining room, she couldn't help but wonder what the day would bring. She had challenged Ivan last night, and though he had dismissed her this morning, she couldn't shake the feeling that something had shifted between them. Whether it was for better or worse remained to be seen.

Katya's hands trembled slightly as she gathered the children after breakfast. Her heart pounded with a mixture of apprehension and uncertainty. The encounter with Ivan at the dining table had been civil enough on the surface, but there had been an underlying tension that still lingered in the air, crackling like an invisible force between them. It made her hesitate now as she walked toward Ivan's study, the children trailing quietly behind her.

She knew she had to ask his permission to take the children anywhere outside of their normal routine, but the very idea of approaching him again after what had happened the night before filled her with nerves. Her mind raced, replaying the intensity of their encounter over and over, trying to make sense of it, trying to push it away, yet it clung to her like a shadow she couldn't shake.

Taking a deep breath, she reached the doorway of his study and paused, gathering her courage. The door was slightly ajar, and through the gap, she could see Ivan seated at his desk, reviewing documents with his usual air of calm authority. The sight of him, so composed and in control, sent a ripple of anxiety through her. She wanted to leave, to avoid the confrontation altogether, but the children needed this. They needed to get out, to have a moment of joy away from the heaviness that seemed to linger in the house.

She pushed the door open fully and stepped inside, her voice betraying none of the nerves bubbling within her. "I'd like to take the children to the park today," she said, her tone carefully neutral, though her stomach tightened with every word. "I think they could use some fresh air."

For a moment, Ivan didn't respond, and the silence hung thick in the air. He didn't even look up from his paperwork immediately, which made the tension in Katya's chest grow. She could feel his quiet power radiating from where he sat, his presence filling the room even without a word. Finally, he lifted his gaze to meet hers, his eyes narrowing slightly as if weighing her request.

The intensity of his gaze made Katya's pulse quicken. She felt like he could see straight through her, as though the question itself wasn't just about the children, but about the dynamic between them that had changed so drastically. She couldn't read his expression—was he angry with her? Displeased by her request? The memory of how he had commanded her last night made her bristle with a mix of defiance and a lingering attraction she hated to acknowledge.

Kirill and Dasha stood quietly by her side, their small faces turned up toward their father, waiting for his response. Katya wondered if they could sense the unspoken tension in the room, the way the air felt heavier when Ivan was near.

After what felt like an eternity, Ivan finally nodded, though the gesture was slow, deliberate. "Fine," he said, his voice cool and measured. "But you'll take a driver. I don't want you taking them anywhere alone."

His tone was authoritative, and though Katya felt a surge of relief that he had allowed them to go, there was a sting in his words. He still didn't trust her. The thought of being watched, of needing a chaperone, grated on her nerves. But she pushed the irritation down, reminding herself that this wasn't about her—it was about the children. They needed this. They needed to get outside, to be free, even for a little while.

"Thank you," she said, her voice even, though she struggled to keep the sharp edge from creeping into her tone.

Ivan's eyes lingered on her for a moment longer, his gaze unreadable. Katya felt the weight of his attention, her heart beating faster beneath the intensity of it. She wasn't sure if he was thinking about their conversation or the night they had shared, but she could feel the unspoken tension between them crackling just beneath the surface.

She turned to lead the children out, but not before Dasha tugged on Ivan's pant leg, looking up at him with wide eyes. "Bye, Daddy," she whispered shyly.

Katya watched from the corner of her eye as Ivan's expression softened for a brief second, the coldness in his face melting just a little. He reached down and patted Dasha's head, his large hand gentle as it rested there for a moment. Katya's heart squeezed in her chest as she witnessed the small but poignant interaction. The flicker of emotion in his eyes—a tenderness that was so rarely shown—made her wonder again if, perhaps, there was something deeper beneath his hard exterior. But just as quickly as it had appeared, the softness vanished, replaced by the stoic mask she had grown used to.

Kirill, too, said goodbye, though his voice was more energetic than his sister's. "Bye, Daddy," he called out, smiling.

Ivan nodded to his son, but his attention was already shifting back to his work, as if the moment had passed and he had moved on. Katya gave the children a gentle nudge toward the hallway, and they followed her out of the room quietly, their small hands in hers.

As they walked down the hall, Katya's mind buzzed with conflicting thoughts. On one hand, she was grateful that Ivan had allowed them to go, but the way he had dismissed her still stung. Did he truly see her as nothing more than the children's nanny, someone to be ordered around and controlled? Or had their encounter last night shifted something between them? She couldn't tell. The way he had looked at her, the way his touch had ignited something inside her, was impossible to forget.

She sighed softly, glancing down at Kirill and Dasha as they skipped along, their excitement bubbling just beneath the surface. Whatever her issues with Ivan, the children were her priority. She had to focus on them, on their happiness. Even if her own emotions were a tangled mess, she couldn't let that affect how she cared for them.

As they neared the front door, Katya spotted the driver waiting by the car. He nodded to her as she approached, opening the door for the children with a polite smile. She helped them climb inside, making sure they were settled before sliding in next to them.

The tension in her chest eased slightly as the car pulled away from the house, the quiet hum of the engine lulling her thoughts into a momentary calm. Today wasn't about Ivan. Today was about the children. And as they drove toward the park, she reminded herself of that again and again.

The sun shone brightly as the car rolled to a stop at the entrance of the park. Katya stepped out first, her gaze drifting across the open space—the well-maintained lawns, the large trees offering generous shade, and the quiet playground nestled at one corner. It was a peaceful contrast to the tension she felt earlier at the house, a reprieve she hoped would give the children a much-needed break from their usual routine.

She helped Kirill and Dasha out of the car, the driver giving her a polite nod as he remained by the vehicle. The park was fairly quiet, with only a few other families scattered about. Katya took a deep breath, trying to center herself. The fresh air helped clear her mind, though not entirely. The memory of Ivan lingered, his touch still vivid against her skin, and the way she had reacted to him—how much she wanted him—gnawed at her. She hated that she couldn't stop thinking about him, that even now, standing in the bright sun, her body remembered the feel of his hands.

But she pushed those thoughts aside as she looked down at the two children standing by her, their small faces tilted toward the playground. They hadn't said much on the ride over, and Katya was learning that silence was normal for them. But there was something in the way they held themselves today—perhaps it was the glimmer of curiosity in their eyes or the slight bounce in Kirill's step—that gave her hope.

"Shall we head to the playground?" she asked gently, her voice warm.

Kirill and Dasha nodded, and together they made their way toward the swings and slides. The playground wasn't busy, only a few other children were playing quietly. Katya guided them to a shaded bench nearby, where she sat down, giving them space but keeping a watchful eye.

At first, they were cautious, exploring the swings and slides with measured steps. Kirill went down the slide once, landing with a soft thud before quickly retreating back to the swings, while Dasha followed behind her brother, mimicking his movements. It was still a quiet play, no laughter, no racing around with unbridled joy like other children, but Katya noticed they weren't as stiff as they had been before. They were beginning to let their guard down, even if just a little.

Katya sat on the bench, the warmth of the sun on her face doing little to ease the storm of emotions swirling inside her. She watched the children playing quietly, but her mind was far from the peaceful park. Her thoughts drifted back to the previous night, to the moment in Ivan's study when everything had shifted between them. The raw intensity of it—the way his hands had claimed her, the force behind his touch—still lingered on her skin. It had been overwhelming, but what disturbed her most was how much she had craved it. Every part of her had responded to him, her body betraying her anger and frustration.

As much as she hated to admit it, she had never felt anything like it. The way he had dominated her, the power he exuded—it had ignited something inside her that she couldn't easily extinguish. And now, sitting here in the quiet park, her mind kept wandering back to that moment, replaying it over and over again. The more she thought about it, the more conflicted she felt. How could she be drawn to a man she resented so much? The man who controlled her life, dictated her every move, and yet... the man who had made her feel things she couldn't explain.

Katya sighed, her eyes drifting to Kirill and Dasha, who were quietly swinging side by side. They were always so close, always together, as if they were their own little world, untouched by the chaos that surrounded them. She admired their bond, the way they seemed to protect each other without words. It was a bond she had never known herself, being an only child. Watching them now, she wished she could give them more—more than the cold, distant father they had, more than the fragmented life they were living.

It was in that moment, as she was lost in thought, that an idea came to her. Maybe a change of scenery would lift their spirits even more. Katya stood from the bench, her legs stiff from sitting too long, and walked over to them.

"Would you like to go for a walk?" she asked softly, her voice gentle as she approached them.

Dasha looked up first, her eyes curious but quiet as always. Kirill's gaze followed, a flicker of interest lighting his expression. Slowly, they nodded, and without a word, Kirill took Dasha's hand, leading her toward the path that wound through the park. Katya smiled softly as she followed behind them, her heart warming at the sight of their tiny hands clasped together. There was something so pure about the way they stuck together, as if they were each other's lifeline. It was as though they had forged their own little bubble, one that kept them safe from the outside world.

As they walked, the children remained quiet, but their steps were lighter, their movements more relaxed than before. Katya noticed how they stayed close, always side by side, their bond unbreakable. It was heartwarming and heartbreaking all at once. She could only imagine how lost they must feel without their mother, and with Ivan being so emotionally distant. It was as if the two of them had learned to rely solely on each other, filling the void left by the adults in their lives.

After a few minutes of walking in companionable silence, the sound of quacking echoed in the distance, drawing Katya's attention to a small pond just up ahead. She smiled softly. Maybe this would be a nice moment for them to enjoy. "Shall we go see the pond?" she suggested, her tone light.

The children didn't respond immediately, but there was a shift in their demeanor. They kept walking toward the pond, hand in hand, their quiet forms moving with a purpose now. Katya followed a few steps behind, watching them closely. She could see the glimmers of excitement growing in Kirill's expression, though he was trying to hide it. It wasn't until they got closer to the water that he finally let his excitement show.

"Look Kat! Ducks!" Kirill shouted, his voice ringing out with such enthusiasm that it startled her. He pointed eagerly toward the water where a small group of ducks paddled near the shore. His face lit up, a wide smile spreading across his usually serious features.

Katya's heart stuttered in her chest at the sound of him calling her "Kat." It was such a small thing, but it felt like a breakthrough—a sign that maybe, just maybe, she was beginning to reach him. Up until now, he had always called her by her full name, keeping a polite distance between them. But now, this one small change felt like the first crack in the walls he had built around himself.

She blinked back the sudden rush of emotion and smiled at him. "Do you want to feed them?" she asked, her voice soft but filled with warmth.

Kirill nodded eagerly, still holding Dasha's hand as they both hurried toward the edge of the pond. Katya trailed behind, watching with a full heart as they crouched down together, their faces filled with wonder as they watched the ducks swim closer.

For the first time since she'd arrived, the children seemed genuinely happy. It was a small moment, but it was enough to make Katya's chest tighten with emotion. She knelt beside them, digging through her bag until she found some crackers. "Here," she said, handing a few pieces to each of them. "You can feed them these."

Kirill and Dasha's faces lit up with delight as they carefully tossed the crackers toward the ducks. The birds eagerly waddled closer, snatching the food from the water's surface with soft quacks of gratitude. The children giggled, their quiet joy filling the air around them, and Katya couldn't help but smile. It was the first time she had heard them laugh like that, the first time she had seen them truly relax.

She sat back on her heels, watching them with a soft, contented expression. Maybe, just maybe, she was starting to make a difference. Even if it was only in small moments like this, she was beginning to feel like she belonged in their lives. She had never expected to feel this way, not after everything that had happened, but now, as she watched the children's happiness bloom before her, she realized that she wanted to be here for them. She wanted to give them these small moments of joy.

After a while, the ducks swam away, and Katya knew it was time to head back. "Come on," she said gently, standing up and brushing off her knees. "Let's head back to the car."

Kirill and Dasha stood up too, their little faces flushed with happiness. They took each other's hands once again, their bond unshakable as always. But then, something happened that Katya hadn't expected. As they began walking back toward the car, Dasha, without saying a word, reached out her free hand to Katya.

For a moment, Katya just stared at the small hand extended toward her, her heart swelling with unexpected emotion. It was such a simple gesture, but it meant everything. She took Dasha's hand, squeezing it gently, and together, the three of them walked back to the car, hand in hand.

As they reached the car and climbed in, Katya felt a sense of peace settle over her. It wasn't perfect, and there was still so much she didn't understand about her place in this strange new life, but for the first time, she felt like she was beginning to find her footing. She glanced at the children, their small hands still holding onto each other, and she knew that no matter what happened next, she would fight for them. She would be here for them, in whatever way they needed her.

As the car pulled away from the park, Katya's thoughts drifted once again to Ivan, and the strange tension that still lingered between them. But for now, she pushed those thoughts aside. Today had been about the children, about giving them a moment of happiness, and that was enough. For now, that was more than enough.

Chapter 8

Ivan leaned back in his leather chair, the glass of whiskey cool in his hand as he swirled it absently. His office was dimly lit, the soft glow from a single lamp casting long shadows across the room. The usual sounds of the warehouse—the low hum of machines, distant voices of his men—faded into the background as his mind drifted back to the night before.

He took a slow sip of the whiskey, the burn traveling down his throat, but it did little to distract him from the thoughts that gnawed at him. Katya. It had all been meant as a power play. That's what he told himself. A way to put her in her place, to remind her of who was in control. But now, no matter how hard he tried, he couldn't shake the memory of her. Her body pressed against his, the way she had looked at him with that mix of defiance and something else, something he hadn't been able to place.

She had spoken to him like no one else dared. Challenged him. Questioned him as a father. He had never allowed anyone to speak to him like that—not his men, not his enemies, not even his wife when she was alive. And yet, Katya had. It had made his blood boil in the moment, but now, hours later, he found himself reflecting on her words.

The truth was, she had a point. His grip on the whiskey tightened. He didn't want to admit it, but as much as it angered him, she wasn't wrong. His children needed him, and deep down, he knew he hadn't been there for them, not the way they needed.

His gaze shifted to the window, where the lights from the city twinkled in the distance. Six months. That's how long it had been since his wife died. Six months since everything changed.

He hadn't loved her, not in the way a man loves a wife. Their marriage had been one of convenience, a strategic move that benefited both families. She had understood that, and over time, they had developed a mutual respect. But when she died, it had left a void, one that Ivan had been unwilling, or perhaps unable, to face. He had buried himself in his work, throwing himself deeper into the Bratva's operations, ignoring the grief that gnawed at him, the pain that lingered beneath the surface.

And the children... Ivan exhaled slowly, his chest tightening as guilt settled in. They had lost their mother, and in many ways, they had lost him too. He hadn't known how to handle it. He still didn't. Their mother had always been the one to care for them, to shield them from the brutal realities of his world while he focused on business. But now, with her gone, they were left with a father who didn't know how to relate to them, how to comfort them in their pain.

Katya's words echoed in his mind, her accusation sharp and cutting. "They need you."

His jaw clenched, a bitter taste filling his mouth. No one ever questioned him, yet she had, and worse, he couldn't dismiss it. Breakfast with the children this morning had been... different. It wasn't just about sitting with them at the table—it was about seeing the way their faces lit up when he walked in. The small smile on Kirill's face, the way Dasha shyly clung to his leg as they said goodbye. It was something he hadn't expected. Something that unsettled him.

And then there was Katya.

The desire from the night before still lingered, simmering beneath the surface. But it wasn't just lust. There was something more. The way she had stood her ground with him, the fire in her eyes as she defied him—it had ignited something inside him. He was used to women who fell in line, who submitted to his will without question. But Katya was different. She wasn't afraid to push back, to challenge him, and that intrigued him. It made him want her more, not just physically, but in a way that he hadn't anticipated.

He hated how much she had gotten under his skin. She was supposed to be a pawn, a means to an end, a way to settle her father's debt. But she was becoming more than that. More than just someone he could control. She had managed to stir something in him that he hadn't felt in a long time.

Ivan's gaze shifted back to his desk, where a stack of papers waited for his attention. Bratva business. Deals to be made, enemies to be dealt with. But his mind kept drifting back to Katya and the way she had made him feel—angry, yes, but alive. Challenged in a way he hadn't been in years.

She was dangerous, not just because of the way she defied him, but because of the way she made him question himself. And he didn't like questioning himself. He liked control. Power. Dominance.

But Katya... she was slipping through his grasp, in more ways than one.

He downed the rest of the whiskey in one gulp, the burn doing little to ease the turmoil inside him. She was making him feel things he didn't want to feel, forcing him to confront truths he had been avoiding for too long. And the more time she spent with his children, the more she became a part of his life—whether he liked it or not.

With a growl of frustration, Ivan set the glass down with a hard thud, the sound reverberating through the quiet office. He needed to get his mind back on track, back to business. But as much as he tried to push thoughts of Katya away, she lingered. In the corners of his mind, in the quiet moments when he was alone, she was there, making him question everything.

Ivan's lips curled into a grim smile. She had no idea what she had started. And neither did he.

A knock on the door pulled Ivan from his thoughts. His grip on the empty glass tightened momentarily before he set it down on the polished surface of his desk. It was as if the sharp rap on the wood had shattered the trance he'd been in, pulling him back into the harsh realities of his world. He shifted in his chair, straightening his posture as his gaze flicked toward the door.

"Come in," Ivan called, his voice steady, masking the inner turmoil still simmering beneath the surface.

The door swung open, and Eriks stepped inside, his expression as grim as usual. Eriks was a man of few words but sharp instincts, someone Ivan had trusted for years as his second-in-command. His presence alone was enough to signal that whatever news he was bringing was important—and likely not good.

"Boss," Eriks greeted, inclining his head in respect before shutting the door behind him. He moved toward the chair opposite Ivan's desk, his heavy boots echoing on the hardwood floor. Without waiting for permission, he sat down, a folder tucked under his arm. Ivan gestured toward the folder with a slight nod, his brow furrowing as he braced himself for the update.

"Let's hear it," Ivan said, his voice a low growl as he leaned forward, elbows resting on the edge of his desk.

Eriks placed the folder on the desk, flipping it open to reveal a stack of papers. His eyes met Ivan's briefly before he began. "It's the West Coast operations," he started, his tone clipped. "We've got disruptions coming from the Morozov Bratva. They've been testing us for months, but it's escalated. A shipment went missing two days ago—heavy weapons cache. Was supposed to come in at the docks, but it never made it."

Ivan's eyes darkened at the mention of the Morozov Bratva. The rival organization had been a thorn in their side for a while now, but this? This was a direct challenge. The Morozovs were making a move, and it wasn't something Ivan could ignore. He could feel his blood beginning to boil again, this time not from the lingering thoughts of Katya but from the blatant audacity of his enemies.

"They're pushing their luck," Ivan muttered, his voice laced with frustration. His mind was already calculating the cost of the missing shipment and the potential ramifications if they didn't act quickly.

Eriks nodded, his jaw tightening. "The situation's worse than just the missing shipment," he continued. "There's been a power shift within the Morozovs. They've got a new leader running things out of New York—a real bastard by the name of Alexei Morozov. Younger, more ambitious. He's not content with just New York, and he's spreading his influence out here."

Ivan leaned back in his chair, his fingers tapping rhythmically against the armrest as he absorbed the information. Alexei Morozov. The name was familiar, though Ivan had never crossed paths with him personally. He had heard the rumors—about how the younger Morozov had seized power after his uncle's assassination in a bloody coup, eliminating anyone who stood in his way, even those within his own family. Ruthless, ambitious, dangerous. The kind of man Ivan understood all too well because he had once been that man, clawing his way to the top of the Volkov Bratva, eliminating every threat to his reign.

"How much of our territory has he encroached on?" Ivan asked, his voice deadly calm.

Eriks shifted, pulling out a map from the folder and laying it flat on the desk. Red markings indicated the areas where the Morozovs had begun to make their move. "We've lost control of a few key spots along the coast, particularly near the docks and the border towns. They've been subtle so far, keeping their movements quiet, but this missing shipment? It's no coincidence. They're testing us, boss."

Ivan's gaze narrowed as he studied the map. His territories, carefully built over years of calculated moves and alliances, were now being challenged by this upstart Morozov. It wasn't just the weapons shipment that angered him—it was the audacity of it. Alexei Morozov was pushing, probing for weakness, and Ivan knew that in the Bratva world, any sign of vulnerability could be fatal.

"He's trying to see how far he can go before we push back," Ivan said, his voice low but filled with menace. "He's making a play for our territory, trying to destabilize us before we even realize what's happening."

Eriks nodded, his expression grim. "That's what it looks like. And it's not just weapons, either. We've had a couple of our informants go silent in the last week—guys we had embedded in some of the Morozov-run docks. We haven't been able to contact them."

"Dead or turned," Ivan muttered, knowing the brutal reality of their business.

"Could be either. We're looking into it, but it's not looking good," Eriks confirmed.

Ivan's jaw tightened as he sat back in his chair, his mind already running through the options.

Retaliation was inevitable, but it had to be calculated. They couldn't afford to act rashly, not when the Morozovs were clearly baiting them into making the first move. But Ivan also knew that if they didn't respond, it would be seen as weakness. And weakness was something the Volkov Bratva could never afford.

"We need to send a message," Ivan said after a long silence. His voice was cold, his expression hardening with resolve. "A reminder of who controls the West Coast. I want the men on high alert. No one makes a move without my approval. And find out what happened to that shipment."

Eriks nodded. "Understood, boss."

Ivan's mind churned with plans as he glanced back down at the map. The Morozovs were making a play for power, and Alexei Morozov was clearly willing to risk war to expand his influence. It wouldn't be long before this situation escalated, and Ivan knew that he needed to be prepared for what was coming.

But beneath the layers of strategy and retaliation, something else tugged at his thoughts—something that had nothing to do with the Morozovs and everything to do with the woman currently sleeping under his roof.

His gaze shifted toward the window for a moment, and the image of Katya's defiant stare from the night before flashed in his mind. The fire in her eyes, the way she had challenged him—it lingered, refusing to be pushed aside. As much as he tried to focus on the Bratva business at hand, his mind kept returning to her.

She was becoming a distraction, one he couldn't afford in the midst of a brewing war.

Eriks' voice pulled him back to the present. "I'll have the men tighten security around the docks and get more intel on Alexei's movements."

"Good," Ivan replied, his tone sharp. "And keep an eye on everything. I don't want any surprises."

As Eriks gathered his papers and prepared to leave, Ivan's thoughts lingered on the brewing war between the Volkov and Morozov Bratvas. But in the back of his mind, Katya remained, her presence a constant pull that he couldn't quite shake.

And that, perhaps, was the most dangerous threat of all.

Ivan leaned back in his chair, the weight of the upcoming retaliation pressing heavily on his shoulders. The consequences of striking back against the Morozov Bratva swirled through his mind, an intricate web of bloodshed and power plays that could spiral out of control faster than any of them anticipated. Every action, every decision he made would ripple through his organization and into the streets, and he had no doubt the Morozovs would retaliate. It would be brutal, it would be bloody, and it would be a direct challenge to the foundation of the Volkov family's dominance on the West Coast.

His grip on the glass in his hand tightened, the faint creak of the crystal barely audible over the pounding thoughts in his head. The Morozov Bratva had been a nuisance for months, testing the boundaries of their power, but with this latest move—taking the weapons shipment—it had become clear they were pushing for war. And Ivan knew that once that line was crossed, there would be no going back.

War wasn't new to Ivan. He had risen to power through blood and violence, and he'd maintained that power with a brutal efficiency that few could match. His reputation had been built on the back of swift, decisive action, and he knew that now was the time to strike. He couldn't afford to appear weak. But the thought of the chaos that would follow—of the blood that would inevitably be spilled—gnawed at the edges of his resolve.

It wasn't just his empire that was at stake anymore.

His thoughts shifted uncomfortably to his children. Kirill and Dasha were innocent in all of this, but Ivan knew all too well that innocence meant little in their world. If things escalated, there was no guarantee they'd be safe, even under his roof. His enemies wouldn't hesitate to strike where it hurt most, and his children would be easy targets.

A cold chill slithered down his spine at the thought, but Ivan forced it down, swallowing the knot of fear that threatened to rise. He couldn't allow himself to think like that. Fear was a weakness, and he'd spent his entire life cutting weaknesses out of himself. His children were safe, as safe as he could make them. He would ensure that, no matter the cost.

And yet, Katya.

Her name echoed in his mind, louder than it should. She had become more than a simple pawn in this game, more than just the woman forced into his life because of her father's debt. The fire in her eyes, the way she stood up to him, the way she connected with his children—it had complicated everything. Her presence in his home was a double-edged sword. She was getting too close to his children, too close to him.

Ivan knew that by bringing her in, by keeping her under his roof, he had exposed her to the dangers of his world. It hadn't been his intention. She was supposed to work off her father's debt and then be gone. But now she was entangled in his life, in his family, and it was becoming harder to imagine his household without her. It was a dangerous complication, one he hadn't foreseen.

His fingers drummed against the armrest as his mind drifted back to the night in his study. The way her defiance had both angered and excited him. He'd wanted to dominate her, to make her understand her place, but now he found himself questioning why he couldn't stop thinking about her. It wasn't just the physical desire that had him restless—it was her. Her strength, her determination, her vulnerability. All of it tangled together in a way that unsettled him.

He had never allowed himself to be vulnerable, not with anyone. Not even with his wife. His marriage had been an arrangement, a calculated move to solidify power within the Bratva. Love hadn't factored into the equation, but there had been a level of trust, a partnership that had worked well enough. But now, with Katya, things felt different. Unpredictable. And Ivan didn't like unpredictability.

He let out a slow breath, pushing the thoughts of her aside as best he could. This wasn't the time to dwell on feelings he didn't fully understand. There were more pressing matters at hand. The Morozov Bratva was encroaching on his territory, and he needed to focus on that. The retaliation had to be swift, decisive, and calculated. One wrong move could cost him everything.

But no matter how hard he tried to push Katya out of his mind, she lingered there, an irritating presence he couldn't shake. Her defiance had intrigued him, yes, but it was more than that. She was having an impact on his children, softening them, connecting with them in ways he couldn't. The breakfast that morning had been the first time he'd seen his children light up around him in months, and he knew that it was because of her.

She was dangerous in a way that had nothing to do with the Bratva and everything to do with the way she was changing the dynamic in his home. The children were beginning to rely on her, and Ivan knew that by allowing her to stay, he was making himself vulnerable. Vulnerable to emotions he didn't want to feel, to connections he didn't want to form.

Yet, he couldn't let her go. Not now.

With a frustrated sigh, Ivan stood from his chair and walked to the window, looking out at the bustling activity in the warehouse below. His men were moving with purpose, preparing for whatever retaliation he would soon order. The tension in the air was palpable, the calm before the storm. And Ivan knew that storm was coming.

The Morozovs had thrown down the gauntlet, and it was only a matter of time before blood was spilled. His fingers tightened around the glass he was still holding as he stared down at the scene below. He had built this empire with his own hands, and he would do whatever it took to protect it.

But now, he had more to protect than just his business.

His children. His legacy. And, whether he wanted to admit it or not, Katya.

It was a dangerous game he was playing, balancing the cutthroat world of the Bratva with the growing attachment he was developing toward the woman living under his roof. And Ivan knew that if he wasn't careful, everything could come crashing down.

With a steely resolve, he turned away from the window, setting his glass down on the desk with a sharp clink. He would handle the Morozovs. He would handle Katya. He would handle it all.

Because in his world, there was no room for vulnerability. There was only power, control, and survival.

And Ivan Volkov had no intention of losing any of it.

Chapter 9

Katya stood at the kitchen counter, the sharp scent of freshly sliced fruit filling the air as she worked quietly, preparing snacks for the children for the next day. It had become part of her routine, these quiet, late-night moments when the house was still and she could think. She hadn't expected to find any kind of solace in her role as their nanny, but in those small, silent spaces, when the children were asleep, she found a strange sense of peace. It was a fragile peace, though—always interrupted by thoughts of him.

As she sliced through an apple, her mind wandered to the children, Kirill and Dasha. It had been only a few days, but already she had started to see small changes in them—small moments of connection that hadn't been there when she first arrived. Kirill had called her "Kat" for the first time at the park that day, a simple word that had filled her heart with an unexpected warmth. And Dasha, with her quiet ways, had reached out to hold her hand as they walked. These tiny gestures were proof that she was making progress with them, and for the first time since she had been thrust into this new life, Katya felt like she was doing something that mattered.

But then there was Ivan.

Her knife slipped for a moment, and she had to catch herself, shaking her head as if to push the thought of him away. It was impossible, though. He was everywhere—in the walls of this house, in the silent stares of his children, and most of all, in her own mind. She should hate him. He had control over every part of her life for the next five years, a punishment for her father's sins. He was cold, ruthless, and he made no attempt to hide the fact that she was nothing more than a pawn to him.

And yet…

Katya's hand stilled on the counter, her breath catching as she remembered the feel of his hands on her, the way he had looked at her the night before in his study. It had been a power play, she knew that, but it was more than that. There had been something in the way he kissed her, something raw and possessive, something that made her body respond despite her every instinct to resist. She hated how much she had wanted him in that moment, how much her body still craved his touch even now.

But what terrified her most wasn't the attraction itself—it was the fact that, for all his dominance, for all his control, she had glimpsed something else in him. A flicker of vulnerability, a crack in the cold, impenetrable wall he surrounded himself with. She didn't know what it meant, but she couldn't stop thinking about it.

The sharp click of the door opening pulled her from her thoughts, and Katya's entire body tensed. She didn't have to turn around to know who it was. She could feel him—feel his presence, the weight of it filling the room before he even said a word.

Ivan.

He walked in with the same quiet, commanding stride that always made her nerves hum with tension. She kept her back to him, trying to ignore the way her pulse quickened just from knowing he was standing there. He wasn't supposed to be here, not now, not tonight. She had thought she'd have at least a few more hours of peace before having to face him again.

As if sensing her tension, Ivan moved closer. She could hear the soft sound of his footsteps on the floor, could feel the warmth of his body as he came to stand just behind her. He was so close she could practically feel the heat radiating off him, and it made her stomach twist with a mixture of frustration and something much more dangerous.

She continued slicing the fruit, refusing to turn around, refusing to acknowledge him. Her heart raced in her chest, the memory of the night before suddenly too vivid, too real. She knew he was watching her, his eyes on her back, and it took every ounce of strength she had to keep her movements steady, to pretend she wasn't affected by his presence.

Ivan didn't say anything at first. Instead, he reached over her shoulder, his large hand brushing against hers as he picked up a piece of fruit from the counter. Katya's grip tightened on the knife as a surge of irritation shot through her.

"I needed that," she snapped, her voice sharp, almost harsher than she intended. "You could have asked."

Her heart pounded as the words left her mouth. She didn't know what possessed her to speak to him that way—maybe it was the constant tension between them, maybe it was her own frustration at being trapped in this situation. Or maybe it was the fact that every time he was near, her body betrayed her, craving his touch in ways she couldn't understand.

Ivan's voice came, low and smooth, tinged with amusement. "Do you always speak to your employer like that, Katya?"

The sound of her name on his lips sent a shiver down her spine, but she refused to back down. Her fingers tightened around the knife, and she forced herself to turn around, finally meeting his gaze.

He was standing close, too close, and when her eyes met his, her breath hitched. He was dressed casually—just a simple t-shirt and jeans—but the way he filled the space made him seem just as imposing as he had in his suit the night before. His gaze was sharp, intense, and filled with something she didn't want to name.

Her pulse raced, but she didn't flinch. She lifted her chin, narrowing her eyes at him. "Maybe I just don't like the way you look at me," she shot back, her voice laced with defiance.

Ivan's expression shifted. The playful amusement that had been in his eyes just moments ago disappeared, replaced by something darker, more dangerous. He stepped closer, forcing her back against the counter, his towering frame making her feel small, yet somehow even more defiant.

"And how do I look at you?" he growled, his voice a low, dangerous murmur that sent a shiver of something entirely different down her spine.

Katya refused to look away, her eyes locked on Ivan's as the tension between them coiled tighter, almost suffocating in its intensity. Her breath caught in her throat, but she forced herself to stand firm, not allowing him to see how deeply he was affecting her. "Like you think you own me," she replied, her voice sharp, though a slight tremor betrayed her underlying uncertainty.

Ivan's lips twitched, but it wasn't a smile. It was something far more dangerous, more predatory, like a wolf toying with its prey. "Maybe I do," he murmured, his voice soft but menacing, the threat laced with something darker. His words hit her like a physical blow, sending a jolt through her body. Anger rose hot and sharp in her chest, but mixed with it was something else—a heat she couldn't control, a pull she couldn't deny.

"You don't," Katya snapped back, but even she could hear the wavering in her voice. It lacked conviction, and Ivan, of course, picked up on it. He always did. His eyes narrowed slightly, the darkness in them deepening as he stepped even closer, closing the small distance that remained between them.

Her heart pounded in her chest, each beat loud and erratic, betraying her resolve. She knew she should step away, put some space between them, but her feet felt rooted to the spot, her body refusing to follow the commands of her mind. The heat radiating from him was overwhelming, wrapping around her like a suffocating blanket of desire. Every nerve in her body was acutely aware of his presence, every inch of her skin tingling with the anticipation of his touch.

"You don't own me," she repeated, but the words sounded hollow even to her ears. The air between them was thick, charged with unspoken tension, desire simmering just beneath the surface.

Ivan's hand lifted slowly, almost lazily, as if he had all the time in the world. His fingers brushed against her cheek, gently tucking a stray lock of hair behind her ear. The touch was light, barely there, but it sent a wave of heat cascading through her body, making her knees feel weak. His fingers lingered, trailing down the side of her neck, the possessiveness in the gesture unmistakable.

Katya's breath hitched, her pulse racing beneath her skin as she fought to keep her emotions in check. Her hands trembled slightly at her sides, and she clenched them into fists, trying to keep her control from slipping completely. She hated him for this—for the way he made her feel, for the way her body responded to him even when her mind screamed at her to resist. She hated the power he held over her, not just physically, but emotionally. He was in her head, and she couldn't seem to get him out.

"Playing a dangerous game, Katya," Ivan warned, his voice a low, rough growl that sent shivers down her spine. He stepped even closer, his body now mere inches from hers, the heat between them palpable. She could feel the weight of him, the power, and it only stoked the fire that had been building inside her since the moment he walked into the kitchen.

Katya's eyes narrowed, her heart pounding, but she refused to let him see how much he was affecting her. She wouldn't give him the satisfaction of knowing how badly she was unraveling. "Maybe I'm not the one playing," she bit back, her voice steady, though the storm of emotions raging inside her was anything but. Her words were filled with defiance, but inside, she was a mess—torn between wanting to lash out and wanting to give in to the undeniable pull between them.

Ivan's eyes darkened further at her words, his gaze intense, focused solely on her. His hand slid down from her neck, his fingers grazing the curve of her collarbone before resting on her hip. The touch was light, almost teasing, but it was enough to set her entire body on fire. She could feel his breath on her skin, his body so close that it made her dizzy with the weight of what was happening. Every rational thought told her to push him away, to step back and create distance, but she couldn't. She was frozen, trapped in the electric connection between them.

"You don't know what you're asking for," Ivan murmured, his voice low, dangerous, and filled with promise. His hand tightened on her hip, pulling her closer, and Katya's breath caught in her throat as their bodies brushed against each other. His other hand moved to cup her jaw, tilting her head up so she had no choice but to meet his gaze.

The intensity of his stare was almost unbearable, like he was seeing right through her, stripping her down to her very core. Her pulse pounded in her ears, her heart racing as she struggled to maintain control, but the pull between them was undeniable. She could feel the air crackling with tension, the unspoken challenge hanging in the space between them.

"Then stop looking at me like that," Katya whispered, her voice breathless, though she hated how weak it sounded.

Ivan's lips curled slightly, but there was no amusement in the expression—only heat, only want. "Like what?" he asked, his voice a soft, dangerous growl. His thumb brushed against her bottom lip, the gesture both tender and possessive, sending a shockwave of sensation through her. Katya's breath hitched, and she felt her knees wobble slightly as his other hand slid around her waist, pulling her flush against him.

"Like you want to control me," she shot back, her voice trembling slightly.

His grip tightened, his body pressing against hers in a way that made her breathless. "Maybe I do."

The air between them sizzled with tension, and Katya could feel herself teetering on the edge of something dangerous, something she knew she should pull away from—but she didn't.

Without another word, Ivan's mouth crashed down on hers, fierce and demanding. The kiss was rough, overwhelming, and Katya gasped against his lips, her hands instinctively pushing against his chest. His grip, however, was unrelenting, his hands pulling her closer as he deepened the kiss, his lips pressing harder against hers. Despite the fury that had boiled inside her just moments ago, Katya's body betrayed her. The heat of his kiss, the intensity with which he claimed her mouth, drowned out every ounce of anger she had felt.

Katya's hands pushed weakly against his broad chest, her fingers curling into the fabric of his shirt. She wanted to resist, to maintain the last shred of control she had over herself, but her resolve wavered. Ivan was like a storm, overpowering her with his presence, and try as she might, she couldn't deny the heat rushing through her. The kiss wasn't gentle—it was possessive, dominant, and all-consuming, and it stoked a fire deep inside her she hadn't known existed.

His hands moved over her body, rough and possessive, one gripping her waist while the other slid up her back, pulling her even tighter against him. The sheer force of his touch sent waves of electricity through her, each one eroding her resistance. His strength was undeniable, every movement purposeful, and Katya felt herself being swept up in it, her mind clouded with desire. A small voice in the back of her head screamed for her to stop, to break away, but her body refused to listen.

Ivan deepened the kiss, his tongue invading her mouth, taking everything. And Katya, to her surprise, kissed him back. Her fingers tangled in the fabric of his shirt, clinging to him as if holding on for dear life. The feel of his body against hers, the heat radiating from him, overwhelmed her senses, drowning out every rational thought. She hated how much she wanted this, hated how easily she was giving in to him, but she couldn't stop. The pull was too strong, the fire too intense.

Without breaking the kiss, Ivan's hands became more insistent, his fingers finding the hem of her shirt and yanking it over her head in one swift motion. The cool air of the kitchen hit her bare skin, but it was nothing compared to the heat that radiated from him. Her bra was gone in seconds, tossed carelessly aside, and before she could protest, his mouth descended on her breast.

Katya gasped, her back arching toward him as his tongue flicked over her nipple, teasing and tormenting her in equal measure. His mouth was hot, his teeth grazing her sensitive skin, sending sharp jolts of pleasure through her. Her nipples hardened under his touch, and Katya's head fell back, a moan escaping her lips before she could stop it. The sensation was too much, too intense, and she felt her knees weaken. She was losing herself in him, in the way his mouth moved over her body, the way his hands gripped her so tightly, as if he was afraid she might slip away.

Her hands found his shoulders, fingers digging into the hard muscles beneath his shirt, trying to anchor herself to something solid. But even as she clung to him, she could feel the heat pooling between her legs, undeniable proof of just how much she wanted him. She cursed herself for it, for wanting a man who embodied everything she despised, but the desire was overwhelming, impossible to ignore.

Ivan stepped back briefly, his hands dropping away from her just long enough to yank his shirt over his head. Katya's breath caught in her throat as she took him in—his broad chest, covered in intricate tattoos that seemed to ripple over the hard planes of his muscles. His shoulders were wide, his arms thick with strength, and the sight of him like this, half-naked and commanding, sent another surge of heat through her.

Her hands reached out instinctively, running over his chest, feeling the heat of his skin beneath her fingers. He was everything she had imagined—dangerous, powerful, untouchable. And yet, here he was, standing before her, desire darkening his gaze. But before she could fully take him in, Ivan was back on her, his mouth claiming hers with renewed intensity.

With a swift motion, Ivan's hands found the waistband of her pants. He tugged them down her legs, taking her panties with them, leaving her fully exposed to him. The cool air hit her skin, heightening her awareness of every touch, every breath. Katya's heart raced as his hands gripped her bare hips, pulling her flush against him once more. His fingers dug into her skin possessively, sending a shiver of anticipation through her as his mouth found hers again, more demanding than before.

With a swift, practiced motion, Ivan pushed her against the wall, his body pressing firmly against hers as his lips devoured hers. There was nothing gentle about it—this was a man taking what he wanted, and Katya couldn't deny the thrill it sent through her. Her hands fumbled with his belt, her fingers trembling as she tried to free him from the confines of his pants. Ivan groaned against her mouth, his body pressing harder against hers as she finally released him.

He was hard and throbbing beneath the fabric, and when she finally freed him, Katya's breath hitched at the sight of him. He was large, engorged, and commanding, his cock standing proudly between them. Another wave of desire crashed over her, stronger this time, and Katya's hand instinctively reached out, wrapping around him, feeling the heat and hardness beneath her fingers.

Ivan growled low in his throat, his hand shooting out to grab her wrists, pinning her hands above her head with one of his large hands. "Not yet," he muttered, his voice a rough whisper in her ear. His other hand moved between her legs, his fingers finding her wet and ready.

"You want this," he growled, his fingers sliding over her clit before thrusting deep inside her. Katya moaned, her body trembling as the sensation hit her like a wave. Her arms were pinned above her, her body at his mercy, and it only heightened the desire coursing through her. She'd never felt anything like this before—this complete loss of control, the sensation of being at someone else's mercy—and it both terrified and thrilled her.

Ivan's fingers moved inside her with a ruthless intensity, each thrust sending her closer to the edge. His thumb circled her clit, and Katya's breath came in short gasps, her body trembling with the overwhelming sensation. She could feel herself teetering on the brink, her body craving release, but Ivan wasn't done with her yet.

His lips brushed against her ear, his breath hot as he whispered, "Beg for it."

Katya's mind spun, her body screaming for him, but her pride held her back for a moment. She hated him for making her feel this way, hated how much she wanted him, but in that moment, all she could think about was how badly she needed him to finish what he'd started.

"Please," she whispered, her voice shaking with a mixture of humiliation and raw desire. "Please."

Ivan's lips curled into a wicked smile, his fingers thrusting harder, faster. "Louder."

Katya's breath hitched, her hands straining against his grip, her body aching for release. "Please," she moaned, louder this time, her voice trembling with need.

Satisfied with her surrender, Ivan growled in approval, his hand moving faster, pushing her closer to the edge

Katya's body trembled uncontrollably as the overwhelming pleasure built within her, her hands still pinned firmly above her head by Ivan's powerful grip. She was utterly helpless, her arms held in place, unable to move, only able to feel the relentless waves of pleasure coursing through her as his fingers worked her to the edge. Every swirl of his fingers on her clit, every thrust inside her sent her spiraling closer to the brink.

Her entire body tightened, her back arching off the wall as her orgasm hit, hard and fast. Her breath caught in her throat, her lips parting in a silent cry as the sensation ripped through her. The tight coil in her belly snapped, and for a moment, the world around her blurred into nothing but the heat of his touch and the raw, pulsing pleasure consuming her. She moaned, the sound low and needy, her body trembling beneath his grip.

Then, just as the last tremors of her orgasm faded, Ivan released her arms, and Katya immediately collapsed into his waiting embrace, her limbs heavy and weak. She barely had time to register the change before he lifted her, his hands gripping her hips as he pulled her off the floor. Her legs instinctively wrapped around his waist, and before she could catch her breath, he thrust into her in one swift, powerful motion.

The feel of him inside her was like nothing she'd ever experienced before. He filled her completely, stretching her tight and deep, his cock thick and throbbing inside her slick heat. The sensation was overwhelming—his size, the depth of his penetration—it was almost too much, yet exactly what her body craved. She gasped, her hands flying to his shoulders for balance, her fingers digging into his muscles as he began to move.

Each thrust was powerful, deliberate, driving her harder against the wall with an intensity that made her entire body tremble. She was so wet, every movement sending a fresh jolt of pleasure through her. The friction, the tightness, the way he stretched her, made her feel like she might explode at any moment.

Katya clung to him, her nails raking across his back as he drove into her again and again, his pace relentless, each thrust deeper than the last. The sounds of their bodies moving together filled the

room, the sensation of him sliding in and out of her
sending shockwaves through her core. Her breath
came in ragged gasps, her body teetering on the
edge of another climax, the pressure inside her
building with every powerful thrust.

She could feel him throbbing inside her, the sheer
force of his movements pushing her closer to the
brink. Every time he filled her, the sensation of
being stretched so tightly around him sent her
spiraling into a haze of pleasure. The tightness, the
way her body clamped down around him as he
thrust into her, made her feel like she was about to
shatter, like the pleasure was too much to contain.

Her head fell back against the wall, a moan
escaping her lips as she teetered on the edge.
Ivan's grip on her hips tightened, pulling her even
closer as he slammed into her, harder and faster.
The pressure inside her built to an almost
unbearable point, her body tightening with each
thrust, her skin slick with sweat as she clung to him
for dear life.

Every inch of her was on fire, her entire body
quaking with the intensity of his movements. The
sensation of him filling her, stretching her beyond
what she thought she could handle, was almost too
much. She could feel every inch of him, the heat of
his body, the way he claimed her with every thrust,
and it pushed her closer and closer to the edge.
She was going to explode, the pleasure coiling

tighter inside her until she couldn't hold back any longer.

And then, with one final, powerful thrust, her body shattered. Her second orgasm tore through her with a force that left her gasping, her body convulsing around him as wave after wave of pleasure crashed over her. She cried out, her nails digging into his back, her entire body trembling as he pushed her over the edge.

Ivan wasn't far behind. His body tensed, a low growl rumbling from deep in his chest as he buried himself inside her, his release coming fast and hard. He held her tight, his cock pulsing deep within her as they climaxed together, their bodies locked in the intensity of the moment.

For a moment, they stayed like that, their breaths mingling, their hearts racing in time with each other. The wall behind her still shook slightly from the force of their movements, and Katya's body trembled in his arms as the aftershocks of her orgasm slowly faded.

Finally, Ivan gently lowered her back down to the floor, her legs shaky beneath her as she leaned against the wall for support. Her breath came in shallow bursts, her mind spinning from what had just happened. She couldn't think, couldn't process the intensity of it all. She only knew that she had never felt anything like this before, and that terrified her.

Katya leaned heavily against the wall, her breath coming in ragged gasps as her body trembled from the intensity of the encounter. The air around them was thick, a lingering heat from what had just happened, their passion still radiating between them. Ivan slowly pulled out of her, lowering her back to the floor with surprising gentleness. Her legs shook beneath her, barely able to support her weight, and she clung to the wall for stability, her body still reeling from the pleasure that had consumed her so completely.

For a long moment, neither of them spoke. The only sound in the kitchen was the ragged cadence of their breathing, still heavy with the remnants of their passion. Katya could feel the sweat cooling on her skin, the way her heart pounded erratically in her chest. Her mind was a blur of conflicting emotions—desire, anger, confusion—all jumbled together into a chaotic storm she couldn't untangle. She didn't dare look at Ivan, unsure of what she'd see in his eyes.

When she finally gathered the courage to lift her gaze, she found him watching her. His chest still rose and fell with the aftermath of their intensity, but his expression was unreadable. His dark eyes, which had been filled with raw lust just moments before, now held something different, something she couldn't quite name. There was a flicker of something in them—something deeper, more complicated than just desire. It sent a chill down her

spine, and for the first time since their encounter
began, Katya felt vulnerable in a way that had
nothing to do with being physically exposed.

Ivan's hand moved almost unconsciously, brushing
against her cheek with a tenderness that seemed
so out of place compared to the roughness of his
earlier touch. His fingers lingered on her skin, a
quiet intimacy in the gesture that confused her even
more. The tender contact stirred something deep
inside her, something she wasn't ready to confront.
Katya's breath hitched, her pulse racing again as
she stared up at him, searching his face for
answers she wasn't sure she wanted.

The touch sent a wave of conflicting emotions
through her—anger at herself for giving in so easily,
frustration at how much her body craved his, and
something deeper, something that felt dangerously
close to longing. Why did he look at her like that?
Why did it feel like more than just a power play,
more than just lust? Katya's chest tightened with
the weight of the unspoken tension between them.

She couldn't stand the silence any longer, couldn't
bear the storm of emotions swirling inside her
without some kind of answer. "What does this
mean?" The words slipped out before she could
stop them, her voice barely above a whisper, but
thick with emotion. It was a question she didn't
even fully understand herself. Did this change

anything between them? Or was she still just a pawn in whatever game Ivan was playing?

For a moment, Ivan's hand lingered on her face, his thumb brushing lightly against her lips as if he was considering her question, weighing the gravity of it. His dark eyes softened, just for a second, and in that fleeting moment, Katya thought she saw something—something real, something vulnerable. It made her heart pound even harder, a flicker of hope rising unbidden inside her chest.

But just as quickly as it appeared, it vanished. Ivan's expression hardened, the softness replaced with the same cold, guarded look he always wore. "I don't know," he finally said, his voice rough, devoid of the passion that had consumed them just moments ago. His hand fell away from her face, leaving her feeling more exposed than ever. The distance between them, though small, felt like a chasm.

Katya blinked, the sting of his words cutting deeper than she had expected. She hadn't even realized how much she had wanted an answer—something concrete, something that would make sense of the chaos in her mind. But instead, he had given her nothing. She felt hollow, as if the intensity of what they had shared had drained something vital from her, leaving her raw and aching.

Without another word, Ivan turned, grabbed his clothes and walked away, his footsteps heavy on the tiled floor. Katya watched him go, still pressed against the wall, her body trembling from both the physical and emotional weight of what had just happened. She wanted to call out to him, to demand more—more answers, more explanation—but her throat was tight, her voice locked away behind the confusion swirling inside her.

As the door to the kitchen closed behind him, Katya felt a wave of shame and confusion crash over her, threatening to pull her under. What had just happened? What did it mean? She couldn't make sense of the whirlwind of emotions that tore through her—desire, anger, frustration, and something deeper, something she was terrified to name. She hated Ivan for how easily he controlled her, how effortlessly he made her want him. But at the same time, she craved more. She craved him. And that terrified her more than anything.

Katya pressed a trembling hand to her lips, still swollen and tingling from his kiss. She hated herself for it, hated how much she had wanted him, how easily she had given in. And yet, the memory of his touch, of the way he had made her feel, lingered in her mind like a dangerous whisper, pulling her deeper into a web she wasn't sure she could escape.

Slowly, she pushed herself away from the wall, her legs still shaky as she bent down to gather her discarded clothes. Her fingers trembled as she dressed, her mind racing with the implications of what had just happened. She knew she should be furious, should hate him, but every time she thought of walking away, something stopped her.

Her heart was heavy with unanswered questions, but one thing was certain—this wasn't over. Not by a long shot. Ivan was now firmly entrenched in her thoughts, in her desires, and as much as she wanted to pretend otherwise, she knew she was too far gone. The tension between them, the pull that drew them together no matter how much she fought it, was undeniable.

As Katya left the kitchen, the air still thick with the unspoken tension between them, she knew that whatever was happening between her and Ivan wasn't something she could walk away from easily. It was dangerous, consuming, and terrifying—and she wasn't sure she wanted it to stop.

Chapter 10

Katya woke up the next morning with Ivan's presence lingering in her thoughts, as if he had never left the room. No matter how hard she tried to push him out of her mind, the memory of his touch clung to her skin. The way he had dominated her, both physically and emotionally, stirred something primal inside her that she couldn't shake. Her pulse quickened at the mere thought of him—the heat of his hands, the power behind his movements. Desire burned through her, raw and overwhelming, igniting every nerve in her body. And yet, just as potent was the anger she felt toward him. Resentment seethed alongside the lust, a twisted duality she couldn't untangle.

How could she want someone who embodied everything she despised? A man who controlled her life, who had taken her freedom, who represented the very world she longed to escape? Every time she thought of the five years she was bound to serve him, her chest tightened. It wasn't just Ivan she resented; it was the betrayal that had put her in this position. She had been sold, a pawn in a game played by men more powerful than she ever wanted to be.

Her father had always been a cold and distant man, but even knowing that, she had never imagined he would betray her like this. For years, she had silently accepted his harshness, hoping that one day he might show her some measure of kindness. But instead, he had handed her over to pay off his debts, sealing her fate for the next five years.

The thought of her father sent a familiar ache through her, pulling her back to memories she had long tried to bury. Her mother had left when she was just a little girl, walking out the door one day and never coming back. Katya could still remember the hollow sound of the door closing, the way her father's face had hardened as if her mother's departure was a challenge he had to overcome, not a loss he had to mourn. From that moment on, Katya had been left to navigate life on her own, growing up under the unforgiving authority of a man who never showed her an ounce of affection.

She had yearned for someone to protect her, someone to care for her in the way her mother had, even if only briefly. But that care had never come. Instead, she had learned to fend for herself, to build walls around her heart so that her father's harshness wouldn't break her. And now, years later, she found herself in the hands of another man—one who was far more dangerous and powerful than her father ever was. Ivan's control over her life only deepened the scars left by her childhood, reopening wounds she had tried so hard to close.

As she moved through her morning routine, Katya's internal conflict intensified. She got herself dressed and brushed her hair, her hands going through the motions, but her mind was consumed by thoughts of Ivan. She told herself she should hate him. He was cruel, controlling, cold. He looked at her as if she were his property, a tool to be used at his disposal. And yet, the thought of him sent shivers through her body, and it wasn't entirely from fear. The memory of his hands on her, the way he had touched her with such fierce possessiveness, kept replaying in her mind, making it impossible to focus on anything else.

She could still feel the heat of his skin against hers, the roughness of his fingers tracing her curves, claiming her in a way that was both terrifying and exhilarating. He had awakened something inside her—something dark and undeniable—that she hadn't known existed. The men she had been with before were nothing like Ivan. They had been her age, clumsy in their touch, unsure of themselves. Ivan was different. He was older, experienced, and he knew exactly what he wanted. His dominance both repelled and attracted her in equal measure.

Her body responded to him in ways that infuriated her. She didn't want to feel this way, didn't want to crave him, but every time he was near, her resolve crumbled. She felt powerless against the pull he had on her. It was as if her body was betraying her mind, surrendering to the raw physicality of what

Ivan represented, even as her thoughts screamed at her to resist. She hated that he had this kind of power over her, and yet, there was a part of her that couldn't help but be drawn to it.

As she tidied up the playroom from the day before, her movements were automatic, but her thoughts were far away. The anger she felt toward Ivan was justified—she knew that. But there was no denying the heat that coursed through her veins every time she thought of him. She had never felt so out of control, so torn between two powerful emotions. Every time she tried to focus on the resentment, the desire crept back in, igniting a fire that refused to be extinguished.

She hated that she was in this position. She hated that she was a pawn in someone else's game. But most of all, she hated that she couldn't stop thinking about Ivan. How had she allowed herself to feel this way about a man who was so wrong for her in every possible way? He controlled her, manipulated her, made her feel small and powerless. And yet, when he looked at her, when he touched her, she felt something else—something dangerous and intoxicating.

Katya's mind spun with the contradictions she was grappling with. She was trapped, not just in Ivan's world, but in her own mind, constantly battling between what she should feel and what she couldn't help but feel. She wasn't sure how to navigate these emotions, wasn't sure how to resist the pull Ivan had on her. But as much as she tried to fight it, the truth remained—the desire she felt for him wasn't going away. And that scared her more than anything else.

Katya's thoughts continued to churn as she went about her morning tasks, her mind unable to escape the tangled web of emotions that Ivan had stirred within her. She found herself reflecting on her past relationships, or rather, the few fleeting encounters she had before her life had been so brutally altered by the debt her father had thrown her into. The men she had been with had been her age, boys really. They had been eager, uncertain, inexperienced—and none of them had left her feeling the way Ivan did.

Those previous encounters had been simple, unremarkable, lacking any real depth. They were awkward moments filled with fleeting pleasure but little else. The boys she had known hadn't known how to touch her, how to make her feel desired, how to command her body in the way that Ivan did. They hadn't possessed the raw power, the confidence, or the force that radiated off of him with every movement. Ivan was different—older, experienced, and every touch from him made her body come alive in ways she had never felt before. It both excited her and terrified her.

As she reflected on the past, the contrast between
Ivan and the boys she had once known became
glaringly clear. They had fumbled in the dark,
unsure of themselves, unsure of what she wanted.
With Ivan, there was no hesitation, no uncertainty.
He knew exactly what he wanted, and he took it.
That sheer confidence in his every action ignited
something within her that she hadn't known
existed—a hunger that seemed to grow every time
he was near. The thought of it made her stomach
churn with a mixture of guilt and something far
more dangerous: desire.

She hated that she felt this way. Ivan was
everything she despised—he was the embodiment
of the Bratva world, the very world that had trapped
her. He was cold, calculating, dangerous, and yet...
she couldn't stop thinking about him. No matter
how much she tried to convince herself that she
hated him, that she hated his control over her, there
was an undeniable pull between them, something
magnetic that made her pulse quicken whenever he
was close.

It made her feel guilty, ashamed even. How could
she be attracted to a man who represented the very
thing she wanted to escape? The Bratva was
ruthless, a world of violence, power, and control,
and Ivan was at the heart of it. She should hate him
for that alone. But the more she told herself to hate
him, the more her mind wandered back to the
intensity of their last encounter, to the way his

hands had felt on her body, the way he had made her feel something so raw, so primal.

The worst part was that it wasn't just physical. Yes, her body responded to him in ways she had never experienced before, but there was something more beneath the surface—something unspoken that lingered between them. That was where the real confusion lay. If it were only about lust, about the physical desire, it would have been easier to dismiss, easier to control. But the connection she felt with Ivan was more complicated than that. It was deeper, and that terrified her more than anything.

Katya tried to shake the thoughts from her head, but they clung to her, whispering in the back of her mind. She wanted to push him away, to keep him at arm's length, but every time he looked at her, every time he touched her, her resolve crumbled. She craved his attention, craved the intensity of what they shared, even though she knew it was dangerous. Ivan was dangerous, but that danger was part of what drew her to him. He made her feel alive in ways she had never felt before, and it frustrated her to no end.

How could she want someone so wrong for her? How could she be drawn to a man who had forced her into this situation, who controlled her every move, who could destroy her without a second thought? And yet, no matter how many times she asked herself these questions, she couldn't find an answer. The pull was too strong, too consuming.

There was something in Ivan that awakened a side of her she didn't know existed. The way he dominated every interaction, the raw power he exuded, it made her feel something she couldn't quite name. It wasn't just desire—it was something deeper, something that went beyond the physical. When Ivan touched her, it was as if the world narrowed to just the two of them, and nothing else mattered.

She could still feel the remnants of his touch, the way his hands had claimed her, the way his body had commanded hers. It was intoxicating, and even now, hours later, her skin tingled at the memory. But it wasn't just his touch that lingered—it was the way he looked at her, the way his gaze seemed to burn through her defenses, laying her bare in a way no one else ever had. That gaze haunted her, made her question everything she thought she knew about herself.

There was a dangerous edge to Ivan, a darkness that both repelled and attracted her. It made her feel things she didn't understand, things that confused her and made her question who she was. The boys she had been with before had never stirred these emotions in her. They had never made her feel this alive, this out of control. And that was what scared her the most—the lack of control.

Ivan made her feel like she was on the edge of something, something she couldn't name but desperately wanted to explore. She was constantly torn between the urge to push him away and the overwhelming need to pull him closer, to feel his hands on her again, to lose herself in the intensity of what they shared. It was a battle she fought every day, and one she wasn't sure she wanted to win.

But no matter how much she tried to resist, no matter how many times she told herself that Ivan was dangerous, that he was wrong for her, the truth remained—he had awakened something in her, something deep and powerful. And the more time she spent around him, the harder it became to deny the truth.

Katya's thoughts wandered as she stood by the window, watching the sun rise over the horizon. The house was still quiet, the children were still asleep, and the weight of everything she had been trying to push down rose to the surface. *Five years.* The words echoed in her mind like a mantra, a constant reminder that this was all temporary. She repeated the number again in her head, trying to find solace in it. Five years, and then she would be free. Free to leave Ivan, free to leave this world, free to do whatever she wanted.

But the more she thought about it, the less comfort that thought brought. Freedom. The idea of it should make her feel better, but instead, it filled her with a strange sense of dread. What would freedom even feel like when the time finally came? Where would she go? What would she do? She had no real plan beyond surviving the next five years, beyond paying off her father's debt.

Her father. Just the thought of him sent a wave of bitterness through her. She would never go back to his house—*that* much she knew for certain. The betrayal was too deep, the hurt too raw. She could never forgive him for what he had done to her. He had always been a harsh man, never kind or warm, but selling her off to pay his debt? That was the ultimate cruelty, something she would never be able to erase from her memory.

And her mother—her mother had left her long before any of this. Katya could still remember the day her mother walked out, leaving her alone with a father who barely acknowledged her existence. She had been just a little girl, clinging to the hope that her mother might come back, that maybe one day she would return and everything would be okay. But that day had never come. Her mother had disappeared from her life, and in her absence, Katya had been forced to grow up faster than she should have.

It had shaped her in ways she couldn't even explain. The absence of a mother's love had left a deep scar on her heart, one that still ached whenever she thought about it. She had always yearned for someone to take care of her, to protect her, but that had never happened. Now, all these years later, she was under the control of another man—someone far more dangerous and powerful than her father ever was. The irony of it all wasn't lost on her.

Her mind drifted to Ivan once again, her chest tightening at the thought of him. She should hate him. She *did* hate him—or at least, she told herself she did. He was controlling, cold, and unapologetic in his dominance. He embodied everything about this world that she despised. And yet, he had awakened something in her, something deep and primal that she didn't know how to deal with. She resented the way her body craved him, the way her mind constantly wandered back to the intensity of their encounters. How could she feel this way about someone who represented everything she wanted to escape?

Five years, she reminded herself again. Five years, and then she would be free. But what did freedom even mean? She had spent so long dreaming of it, imagining what her life would be like once she was free from this prison, but now that the reality of it was closer, it felt more like an unknown void. She could go anywhere, do anything, but where would she go? What would she do?

And then there were the children. Every time she looked at Kirill and Dasha, her heart ached. They had already lost so much, and seeing their quiet resilience reminded her too much of herself. They had lost their mother, and Katya knew better than anyone what that felt like. Growing up without a mother had been one of the hardest things she had ever gone through, and it had left her feeling alone and vulnerable in ways she hadn't fully understood until now.

The thought of those two precious children growing up without their mother broke her heart. She knew the pain they were carrying, even if they were too young to fully express it. She felt a fierce protectiveness toward them, an urge to shield them from the harshness of the world, from the kind of pain she knew too well. She wanted to be there for them, to help them navigate this difficult time, to offer them the kind of support she had never received as a child.

But that thought also brought with it a wave of guilt. Could she really leave them after five years? What would it do to them, after all the progress they had made? The bond they were slowly forming with her was already strong, and she could feel herself getting more attached to them every day. She had told herself not to get too close, not to let her heart get involved, but it was already too late. The way Kirill had called her "Kat" at the park, the way Dasha silently reached for her hand—it had all chipped away at the walls she had built around her heart.

The guilt gnawed at her. Could she really walk away from them after five years? Could she just abandon them the way her mother had abandoned her? The thought of leaving them felt impossible, and yet, she knew that she had to keep reminding herself that this was all temporary. She had to keep telling herself that she couldn't stay in this world, that she couldn't let herself get too attached.

But the more she tried to push those feelings away, the more they crept back into her mind. The truth was, she *was* attached. To the children. To Ivan. To the strange, complicated life she was now living. She hated it, but at the same time, she couldn't imagine what life would be like without it.

What would freedom even mean after all of this? Would she be able to leave and pretend like none of this had ever happened? Or would the ties to this world be too strong to break? The uncertainty gnawed at her, leaving her feeling more conflicted than ever.

As much as she tried to convince herself that the end goal was to leave, to be free, she couldn't shake the feeling that by the time those five years were up, she might not even want to leave. And that terrified her more than anything.

Katya stood in the children's room, carefully selecting their clothes for the day as the early morning light filtered through the curtains. The quiet hum of the house was comforting, but her mind was far from the task at hand. As she helped Dasha into her dress and buttoned up Kirill's shirt, her thoughts were spinning, trying desperately to compartmentalize everything that had happened. Every touch, every glance, every heated moment with Ivan flashed through her mind like a series of vivid snapshots she couldn't erase.

She had been trying, desperately, to shove her feelings into a box, to seal it tight, and to focus on the simple fact that she was here for one reason: to pay off her father's debt. Five years. It was just five years.

She repeated it like a mantra as she knelt to tie Kirill's shoes, her fingers trembling slightly as her mind wandered back to the raw intensity of her encounters with Ivan. No matter how much she told herself she was just going through the motions, that her role was temporary, it wasn't working.

The children moved quietly around her, still waking up, and Katya wished she could match their innocence. She wished she could let go of the emotions that clung to her like a shadow—this swirling storm of desire, resentment, confusion, and dread. Because no matter how hard she tried to focus on her duties, she couldn't escape the hold

Ivan had on her. His touch, his dominance, the way he seemed to be getting under her skin—it was all too much.

But she had to keep going, for the children, for herself. *This is temporary,* she repeated to herself, as she had done countless times before. *This is just a means to an end. Ivan is just a part of the arrangement, nothing more.* She tried to believe it, to convince herself that the intensity of their encounters was purely physical, that the heat that ignited between them didn't mean anything.

It had to be just physical. She couldn't afford for it to be anything more.

Her body's reaction to him was something she could explain away—he was a powerful, dominant man, and there was something undeniably magnetic about the way he commanded a room, about the way he commanded her. But it was only lust. It was the fire of the moment, the raw chemistry they shared. It didn't have anything to do with her heart, and she wasn't about to let it get there. She refused to.

She wasn't here to feel things. She was here to survive, to get through these five years and be free. She'd been through worse, hadn't she? She'd survived her father's cruelty, her mother's abandonment. She could survive this too.

And yet, no matter how hard she tried to push those feelings away, they kept creeping back in. The memory of Ivan's touch, the way his hands had moved over her body like he owned her—it wasn't just the physical sensation that lingered. It was the way he *looked* at her. The possessiveness in his eyes, the unspoken tension between them, it was more than just lust. She could feel it, even if she refused to acknowledge it.

Every time they were near each other, the air crackled with an intensity she couldn't escape. His gaze followed her, dark and consuming, as if he saw straight through the walls she had built around herself. And the worst part was, she couldn't stop thinking about him. She hated herself for it. She hated the way her heart raced when he was near, the way her body betrayed her with every glance, every touch.

But this wasn't supposed to be about feelings. She couldn't let it be.

I'm here to pay off a debt, she reminded herself again, as if repeating the words would make them true. *That's all this is.* But the more she tried to push those thoughts down, the more they clawed their way back to the surface.

It wasn't just Ivan who was getting under her skin. It was the children, too.

Kirill and Dasha. They had been so quiet, so closed off when she first arrived, but now... now things were different. They were starting to trust her, to open up to her, and she couldn't deny the bond that was forming between them. She had told herself not to get too attached—after all, she was going to leave in five years, and she didn't want to leave any more pieces of her heart behind when she did. But how could she not care for them?

Every time Kirill called her "Kat," every time Dasha reached for her hand without saying a word, her resolve weakened. They were just children, innocent and vulnerable, and they had already lost so much. The thought of them growing up without their mother tore at her heart, reminding her of her own childhood, of the pain of growing up without a mother's love. She knew what it felt like to be abandoned, to be left behind, and the thought of doing the same to them in five years made her chest tighten with guilt.

Could she really walk away from them when the time came? Could she really leave them after all the progress they had made, after everything they had shared? The weight of that question lingered in her mind, pressing down on her like a heavy stone. She didn't want to admit it, but she was already too attached. And the more she cared for them, the harder it would be to leave.

I have to protect myself, she thought, as if reminding herself would make it easier. She couldn't afford to let herself get too close, not to Ivan, and not to the children. She had to keep her distance, to keep her heart locked away, even though it was becoming increasingly impossible.

The more she tried to distance herself, the more she felt drawn to them. To Ivan. To the children. It was like a magnetic pull, something she couldn't control or escape, no matter how hard she tried. And that terrified her more than anything. What if she couldn't leave when the time came? What if she didn't *want* to leave?

The thought sent a shiver down her spine, her mind racing with conflicting emotions. She tried to shake them off, to remind herself of the deal she had made, but the feelings lingered, gnawing at her, leaving her feeling conflicted and vulnerable.

She had always prided herself on her ability to survive, to push through even the darkest moments. But now, standing in this quiet bedroom, surrounded by the weight of her emotions, she wasn't sure if survival was enough. There was more at stake now. More to lose.

And she wasn't sure if she was ready to face the consequences of what that meant.

Chapter 11

Ivan lay in his bed, staring at the ceiling, the early morning light filtering through the curtains. His thoughts drifted immediately to Katya. He had meant to dominate her, to control her completely, but last night had left him questioning everything. He could still feel the lingering heat of their encounter, the way her body had responded to his, the raw, fiery connection that seemed to ignite between them. It wasn't supposed to be like this.

When she had asked him what it meant—*what does this mean?*—he had been caught off guard. His response, *I don't know*, still bothered him, gnawing at the edges of his control. He could have told her it meant nothing, that she was just another woman to bend to his will. It would have been easier to claim it was a fleeting, physical indulgence. But the words had stuck in his throat because the truth was, Katya was different. And he hated that he couldn't figure out why.

She was supposed to be just another pawn, a woman forced into his world because of a debt. His life had always been about power and control, the ability to manipulate people to his advantage. He didn't let anyone close—not his enemies, not his allies, and certainly not women. His marriage had been a clear example of that. It was an arranged union, a calculated move designed to strengthen his position within the Bratva. His wife had understood the terms.

Ivan shifted in bed, his thoughts turning to his late wife. She had been a good woman—a good mother to their children—but there had never been any real connection between them. Their marriage had been devoid of passion, and their interactions were polite at best. There had been no heat, no challenge, no real emotion. She had known her role, and he had known his. Sex had been mechanical, a duty performed to produce heirs, and nothing more.

It was strange, in hindsight, how he had buried the depth of his own grief beneath the surface. His wife's death had left an undeniable void, not just for the children but for him as well. She had been his companion, the mother of his children, and his partner in navigating the complicated world of the Bratva. It wasn't love, at least not in the traditional sense, but there had been a deep respect, a shared understanding of their roles. Her loss hit him harder than he let anyone see. He had thrown himself deeper into his work, using it as a shield to avoid confronting the empty space her absence had created. The pain lingered, but he kept it hidden, ensuring the business ran smoothly, keeping the family's standing strong. Emotional detachment had always been his strength, a lesson learned early on—feelings made a man weak, vulnerable. And in his world, vulnerability was a dangerous liability.

But Katya—she was a different story entirely.

He ran a hand through his hair, frustrated. How had he lost control like this? The fiery defiance in her eyes, the way she challenged him at every turn, refusing to back down—it stirred something deep inside him that he couldn't ignore. She wasn't like the other women who had passed through his life, women who were eager to please or too afraid to resist. Katya was a storm, a force of nature that demanded attention, and it was driving him mad.

He had never craved a challenge like this before. In the past, women had been tools for release—brief moments of pleasure, easily discarded and forgotten. There had never been a need for more. But Katya... her defiance only made him want her more. He enjoyed watching her resist him, knowing that eventually, she would break. And yet, it wasn't just the thrill of breaking her down that excited him. It was the way she made him feel alive, like the fire inside him had been reignited after years of being cold and calculated.

He thought back to their last encounter, how she had tried to push him away even as her body betrayed her, yielding to his touch. He had felt her surrender in the way she kissed him back, in the way her hands had clung to him, desperate for more. But it hadn't been enough to just possess her physically. For the first time, Ivan found himself wanting more than that. He wanted to dominate her mind, her heart. He wanted her to crave him in the same way he was beginning to crave her.

This desire, this possessiveness, was new to him. It wasn't just about having control anymore—it was about something deeper, something he didn't fully understand. And that scared him more than he would ever admit.

He pushed himself up in bed, the cool sheets falling away as he sat on the edge, trying to clear his mind. He wasn't used to this—this lack of control. In every aspect of his life, he was the one who dictated the terms. His men followed his orders without question, his business dealings were executed with precision, and his enemies knew better than to challenge him. But with Katya, it felt like the rules were shifting, like she was somehow slipping through his fingers even as he tightened his grip on her.

Ivan clenched his fists, frustrated with himself. He had to get a handle on this. She was just a woman—just another debt to be paid, nothing more. Yet, even as he told himself that, he knew it was a lie. Katya was getting under his skin, burrowing deep into his thoughts in a way that no one ever had before.

He couldn't afford to let his guard down, not with her, not with anyone. Vulnerability was a weakness, and in his world, weakness could get you killed. But Katya—damn her—was making him feel things he didn't want to feel. She was making him question himself, and that was dangerous.

His thoughts returned to the way she had looked at him last night, the fire in her eyes, the way her body had responded to his every touch. It had been more than just sex. There had been an intensity between them, something raw and primal that he couldn't explain. And when she had asked him what it meant, he hadn't known how to answer.

Maybe he was afraid of the answer.

With a deep breath, Ivan stood up, shaking off the lingering thoughts of Katya. He needed to refocus. He couldn't let her distract him from what mattered—the business, his family, the Bratva. But even as he tried to push her from his mind, he knew it was pointless. Katya wasn't just another woman to dominate. She was becoming something more. And that terrified him.

As he dressed for the day, his thoughts continued to circle around her, refusing to settle. He moved through the motions of his routine, but everything felt different—charged with an energy he couldn't explain. By the time he made his way downstairs, the tension still lingered in the air.

The morning had a strange weight to it, the usual routine now accompanied by an undercurrent of something unspoken. Ivan sat at the head of the long dining room table, sipping his coffee, already anticipating the arrival of his children. His mind wandered back to the night before, the memory of Katya still fresh in his thoughts. Their encounter had left him unsettled, though he refused to fully admit why. He tried to push those thoughts aside, focusing instead on the task at hand, but it was no use. Katya had already woven herself into his thoughts, and now, it seemed, into his life.

Footsteps in the hallway broke through his thoughts, and moments later, Katya entered the room with Kirill and Dasha by her side. Her presence instantly shifted the air, a subtle tension threading between them. Their eyes met briefly, and Ivan noticed the flush that crept up Katya's cheeks before she quickly averted her gaze. There was something unspoken between them, something charged with emotions neither seemed ready to confront.

Katya busied herself with settling the children into their chairs, the routine she had taken on so naturally since arriving. Her movements were precise, quiet, as if she wanted to complete the task and leave the room without drawing too much attention to herself. But as she moved to step away, Ivan's voice cut through the quiet morning.

"You can stay and have breakfast with us this morning."

She froze, the surprise clear on her face as she hesitated for a moment. This wasn't part of the routine, wasn't what she expected. Ivan could see the uncertainty flicker across her face, and for a brief moment, he wondered if she would refuse. But after a pause, she nodded and took a seat at the table next to Dasha, her posture stiff, as if unsure of where she stood in this new dynamic.

Ivan watched her, his gaze lingering a moment longer than necessary before turning his attention to his children. Kirill and Dasha seemed unaffected by the shift in routine, though their excitement was palpable as they began talking over each other about their day at the park.

"Kat showed us the ducks!" Kirill exclaimed, his small face lighting up as he recounted the day's events. Ivan raised a brow at the familiar use of "Kat." It was the first time he had heard the children call her anything other than "Katya," and the ease with which the nickname rolled off Kirill's tongue didn't go unnoticed. It was a sign of how much they were growing attached to her.

Katya smiled softly at Kirill, the tension in her shoulders easing just a little as she listened to his animated story. "Yes, they were very hungry," she added, her voice warm but still tinged with a quietness that Ivan hadn't yet figured out.

Dasha, usually the quieter one, spoke up next, her voice small but filled with excitement. "Can we go back to the park again, Kat? I want to feed the ducks again." She glanced shyly between her father and Katya, waiting for permission.

Before Katya could respond, Kirill leaned in, teasing his sister. "Dasha wants to make all the ducks fat," he giggled, his bright laughter filling the room.

It was then that Ivan heard it—Katya's soft chuckle. It was brief, almost like she hadn't meant for it to slip out, but it was there. And for the first time since she had come into their lives, Ivan saw her guard lower, if only for a second. There was something in that moment, in the way she relaxed just a little, that made the entire room feel lighter.

"Maybe we should bring more food next time," she teased back, her smile reaching her eyes. Ivan found himself watching her, captivated by the shift in her demeanor. He had seen her smile before, but it had always been guarded, hesitant. Now, sitting at the table with his children, there was a softness to her expression that he hadn't seen.

The breakfast continued, the conversation between the children flowing easily. Ivan listened, chiming in when needed, but mostly observing the way Katya interacted with them. Dasha, who had been slow to open up to anyone since her mother's death, seemed particularly drawn to Katya now, her wide eyes watching her with a mixture of admiration and comfort. And Kirill, always the more talkative one, practically hung on every word Katya said, eager to share his stories with her.

It was an odd sensation for Ivan, watching this quiet dynamic unfold before him. He wasn't used to seeing his children this engaged, this happy during their morning meals. And while he had initially invited Katya to stay as a spur-of-the-moment decision, he couldn't deny the subtle warmth that had settled over the room. There was a connection here, something growing between them all, and it unnerved him in ways he couldn't fully explain.

Every now and then, Ivan and Katya's eyes would meet across the table. Each glance was brief, fleeting, but the tension in those moments was unmistakable. It wasn't just about what had happened between them the night before—it was something deeper, something unspoken but undeniably present. Ivan felt it in the way his chest tightened whenever their eyes locked, in the way his thoughts kept circling back to her, even when he tried to push them away.

He wasn't the only one feeling it, either. He could see the way Katya shifted in her seat, the way her gaze would dart away whenever their eyes met. She was trying to maintain her distance, her composure, but there were cracks in her armor now, and Ivan could sense it. She wasn't as guarded as before, and whether she realized it or not, she was becoming more a part of this household than she had likely intended.

The children continued to talk, their voices blending into a soothing background noise, but Ivan's focus remained on Katya. There was something about her that unsettled him—not in a bad way, but in a way that made him question everything he thought he knew about control, about dominance. He had brought her into his home to fulfill a purpose, to pay off a debt. But now, watching her laugh with his children, he wondered if that purpose was beginning to shift.

By the time breakfast ended, the air in the room felt lighter, more intimate. Ivan stood from the table, his eyes lingering on Katya as she helped Dasha out of her chair. There was a quiet understanding between them now, a growing connection that neither of them had fully acknowledged but both felt. It was unsettling and comforting all at once, and for the first time in a long time, Ivan wasn't sure if he was fully in control anymore.

After breakfast, Ivan watched as Katya led the children out of the dining room. There was something about the way she moved, the way the children followed her so willingly, that made his chest tighten. He told himself it was just control—his need to maintain order in every aspect of his life—but deep down, he knew it was more than that. It wasn't just about dominance anymore.

He wanted more than her body, more than the submission that came from her sense of obligation.

As she disappeared from view, a sense of possessiveness wrapped tighter around his thoughts, almost suffocating in its intensity. He didn't just want her to obey him—he wanted her to choose him, to need him. It was a strange and unsettling feeling, one he hadn't expected. With every passing day, he found himself craving her presence more. Her influence on the children had become undeniable, and he couldn't help but feel a mixture of pride and frustration. Pride because she was making a difference in their lives, frustration because it felt like she was slipping into his, uninvited, and unbidden.

What troubled him most was the way her defiance drew him in. Katya wasn't like the other women he had known—those who submitted easily, eager to please him because of his power. She fought him, pushed back, and he found himself wanting to know more about her. What she thought, what she wanted, what she felt. The thought of her submitting to him, not out of fear or obligation, but because she chose to, gnawed at him. It was a foreign sensation, this need for something deeper, and it only made him more possessive.

Later that day, Ivan overheard one of his men make a casual remark about Katya's beauty as they walked through the halls. The man's voice was low, almost admiring, as he commented on her eyes, the way she carried herself. The words were innocent enough, but something dark and primal stirred inside Ivan. His hands clenched into fists, a surge of jealousy washing over him so swiftly that it caught him off guard.

The idea of another man desiring Katya—imagining her in any way—made his blood boil. It wasn't just that she belonged to him by debt; it was the thought of anyone else even thinking about her in that way that made him want to snap. She was his. No one else could touch her. No one else could even look at her.

For the first time, he realized that his possessiveness had grown beyond their physical encounters. He wasn't just claiming her body—he wanted all of her. Her thoughts, her heart, her loyalty. It was an unsettling revelation, one that made him question everything he had believed about himself. He had always prided himself on his control, on the way he could separate emotions from duty, from power. But with Katya, those lines were starting to blur.

The possessiveness ran deeper than he had anticipated. He felt responsible for her now, protective in a way that went beyond their agreement. He wanted to keep her safe, wanted her to rely on him for more than just the roof over her head. But at the same time, the thought of her getting too close terrified him. She was already under his skin, and he wasn't sure how to deal with that.

As he stood in his office later that morning, overlooking the city through the large windows, Ivan tried to push those thoughts away. He had always been a man who thrived on control. Control of his business, his family, his world. Emotions, vulnerability—those were weaknesses he had learned to suppress long ago. And yet, Katya was making him feel things he didn't want to feel.

She was under his roof, bound to him by a debt, and he had made sure she knew her place. But now, she was in his thoughts, in his desires, in a way that no woman had ever been. His need for control was being tested, stretched thin by the growing connection he couldn't deny.

He hated the vulnerability she exposed in him. He hated the way he felt when he saw her with his children, the warmth she brought into their lives. It made him feel things he had buried long ago—things he had convinced himself he no longer needed.

But with Katya, it was different. She wasn't just another pawn in his game. She was becoming something more, and that terrified him.

Ivan turned away from the window, his mind heavy with the weight of his conflicting emotions. He needed to regain control, to remind himself of who he was and what he stood for. But as much as he tried, he couldn't shake the feeling that things were changing, that Katya was changing him.

And that, more than anything, filled him with a fear he hadn't felt in years.

As Ivan walked through his warehouse later that day, the weight of his emotions clung to him, unwelcome but undeniable. The corridors that had once felt like symbols of his power and control now seemed to close in on him, filled with thoughts of Katya. She wasn't just another woman to him anymore. She wasn't even just a debt to be repaid. She had become something he couldn't quite define, and that realization unsettled him deeply.

For the first time in his life, Ivan felt like he was losing control—not of his empire, not of his business dealings, but of himself. His mind kept returning to her, replaying the way she looked at him during breakfast, how she handled the children with such care, and, most dangerously, how she challenged him. She had become a constant presence in his thoughts, one he couldn't simply push aside.

He had always been in control of every part of his life. Every decision he made, every action he took, was calculated. His authority in the Bratva world was built on that very foundation—never allowing personal feelings to interfere with business or weaken his standing. Emotions had no place in his life. Vulnerability was a luxury he couldn't afford. Yet, with Katya, something was shifting. Every encounter with her left him feeling exposed in ways he hadn't felt in years.

He tried to remind himself of the facts: Katya was bound to him because of a debt. She was here to pay it off, nothing more. She had no real power in his world. He owned her, just as he owned everything else in his life. But there was something more happening between them, something that went deeper than any contract or agreement. He could feel it, even if he didn't want to acknowledge it. And it gnawed at him, threatening the tightly controlled existence he had always maintained.

Ivan's thoughts drifted back to their last encounter, her whispered question lingering in his mind: *What does this mean?* He had answered her with uncertainty—an answer he couldn't quite comprehend himself. It had been a rare moment of vulnerability, one that still rattled him. Why hadn't he dismissed her, told her it meant nothing? That's what it should have been—just another encounter, another moment of dominance. But it wasn't. There was something about her that kept drawing him back, making him feel things he didn't want to feel.

He clenched his fists as he walked, the familiar tension rising in his chest. Allowing emotions to cloud his judgment was a dangerous game, especially in the brutal world he operated in. He had built his life on power and control, both of which were essential to survival. The Bratva world was unforgiving. If anyone suspected that Katya had become a weakness for him, it could be exploited. And he knew all too well how dangerous that could be.

Yet, despite the risks, Ivan felt himself slipping. The possessiveness he had for her was growing, turning into something more than just physical desire. He had always been a man who thrived on dominance—on bending people to his will. But with Katya, it wasn't just about owning her body. He wanted more than her submission in the bedroom. He wanted her to choose him, to submit to him willingly, emotionally. And that terrified him.

He hated the way she was getting under his skin, hated the way her presence affected him. Katya was different from anyone he had ever known. She was defiant, strong-willed, and unafraid to challenge him. But instead of pushing him away, her resistance only pulled him in further. He found himself craving the fire in her eyes, the way she refused to back down. It wasn't just lust that drove him—it was something deeper, something he wasn't ready to face.

Ivan stopped by a window, staring out at the sprawling estate that had always been a symbol of his success. The power he wielded here, the control he had over every aspect of his world—it suddenly felt fragile. Vulnerability had never been something he allowed himself to feel. In his world, it was dangerous. Weakness could get a man killed. And yet, here he was, struggling to control his emotions over a woman who, by all rights, should have been nothing more than another pawn in his game.

But she wasn't. She had become more.

He ran a hand through his hair, his jaw tightening with frustration. He couldn't afford to let these feelings get the better of him. Katya was bound to him by a contract, and that was all it needed to be. He couldn't let himself forget that. And yet, every time he tried to push the feelings aside, they came back stronger, more insistent.

The jealousy that flared inside him when he heard his men comment on her beauty was proof enough. He couldn't stand the thought of anyone else looking at her, desiring her. She was his. And yet, it wasn't just about ownership anymore. He wanted her loyalty, her submission—everything. He wanted her to feel the same pull toward him that he felt toward her, but that desire for her to choose him voluntarily was dangerous. It was a weakness he didn't know how to confront.

As he stood there, his gaze fixed on the horizon, Ivan knew he was at a crossroads. He could continue as he always had—maintaining control, keeping his emotions locked away—or he could let himself give in to the growing feelings that scared him more than anything. It was a choice he wasn't ready to make, but one he knew he couldn't avoid for much longer.

The vulnerability Katya had brought to the surface made him feel exposed in ways he hadn't been in years. And that scared him more than any enemy he had ever faced.

Chapter 12

It had been a week since Katya's last encounter with Ivan, and no matter how hard she tried to focus on the children, the intensity of that night lingered in her mind. Every touch, every kiss, the way his hands had claimed her body—it was seared into her memory, refusing to fade. She hated it. She hated the way her body betrayed her, the way desire still simmered beneath her skin whenever she thought of him. Even now, as she helped Kirill button his shirt, her mind wandered back to Ivan.

She had thrown herself into her role with the children, filling her days with park visits, reading lessons, and small outings to keep herself occupied. But no matter how busy she kept, she couldn't fully escape Ivan's presence. Breakfast with him and the children had become a daily routine, an unspoken agreement that neither of them acknowledged. Each morning, she entered the dining room determined to focus only on the children, but every time their eyes met, the tension crackled in the air, thick and heavy. It was as if they were trapped in a game, both of them silently testing the other, waiting for someone to break.

She didn't want to think about Ivan, didn't want to acknowledge the pull he had over her, but it was impossible to ignore. Every look he gave her stirred something deep inside, something she didn't want to admit existed. His presence drew her in, making her feel things she had long since buried. There was a deep, undeniable desire for him that she couldn't shake, and it infuriated her. It wasn't just physical—it was something more, something she couldn't name but felt in every glance, every unspoken word between them.

As she pulled Dasha's hair into a neat braid, her mind drifted back to that night again. The way he had looked at her, the fire in his eyes as he claimed her—it was something she'd never experienced before. It wasn't just about control or dominance; there had been something deeper in the way he touched her, something that made her crave more. And that was what scared her the most.

How could she want a man like Ivan? How could she feel desire for someone who held so much power over her life, someone who represented everything she despised? Her life had been shaped by powerful, controlling men—first her father, and now Ivan. Her father had sent her here, selling her off like she was nothing more than a pawn to be traded, and Ivan had taken her, trapping her in this world for five years.

The resentment bubbled up inside her, mingling with the desire in a confusing swirl of emotions. She resented Ivan for the control he had over her, for the way he made her feel things she didn't want to feel. And yet, there was something about him that made it impossible to hate him fully. The way he looked at her during breakfast, the intensity of his gaze—it stirred emotions she didn't want to face.

As she led the children downstairs, Katya felt the weight of her past pressing down on her. Her father had never been a kind man, but she had never expected this—being sent away to pay off his debts, to be at the mercy of another powerful man. Her father's coldness had shaped her, made her strong in ways she hadn't wanted to be. And then there was her mother. She had left when Katya was just a little girl, abandoning her to face her father's harshness alone. She could still remember the day her mother left—how she had cried and begged her to stay, how her father had told her to stop being weak.

Now, with Ivan, those old wounds were reopening. The fear of being controlled, of being used and discarded, resurfaced. But Ivan wasn't her father. He was more dangerous, more powerful, and that terrified her. He wasn't just another man to dominate her life—he was something more, something she didn't know how to handle.

The children's laughter brought her back to the present, and Katya forced a smile as she watched Kirill and Dasha race ahead to the dining room. She had learned to be strong, to survive without anyone's help, but with Ivan, everything felt uncertain. She didn't want to care about him, didn't want to feel anything for him. But no matter how much she told herself to keep her distance, the pull between them was growing stronger each day.

Katya paused outside the dining room, taking a deep breath before stepping inside. As soon as she entered, she could feel Ivan's eyes on her, a brief, charged glance that sent a familiar shiver down her spine. She averted her gaze, focusing on settling the children into their seats, but the tension hung heavy in the air.

The week had passed in a blur of stolen glances and silent exchanges, and Katya knew that whatever was happening between them was far from over. The only question was how much longer she could resist the inevitable pull toward him—and how much of herself she was willing to lose in the process.

Breakfast had become a strange new routine in the household, one Katya hadn't anticipated but had grown to expect over the past week. Every morning, she brought the children into the dining room, where Ivan waited at the head of the table, sipping his coffee. The ritual felt oddly domestic, yet the tension between her and Ivan was impossible to ignore. His presence filled the room in a way that made it hard to focus on anything else, especially when their eyes met.

Each glance they exchanged was charged with an unspoken desire, a pull that Katya tried—and failed—to resist. She could feel his gaze on her, lingering longer than necessary as she settled Kirill and Dasha into their chairs. His eyes followed her movements, and though she told herself to remain indifferent, she couldn't stop the way her skin tingled under his attention.

The children, however, seemed blissfully unaware of the underlying tension. They were thriving in this new routine, excited to see their father each morning. Their eyes lit up the moment they entered the dining room, and their chatter quickly filled the space. Ivan, though still reserved, had begun to engage with them more. He asked about their day, listened attentively as they recounted their outings with Katya, and even smiled—something Katya hadn't seen before. The warmth in his expression when he looked at his children left her feeling conflicted. It was so different from the cold, calculating man she had come to know.

One morning, Kirill eagerly told Ivan about their trip to the zoo the day before. "We saw lions, Daddy! They were so big, and Kat said they could roar really loud!" he exclaimed, his small hands gesturing animatedly. Dasha nodded in agreement, her quiet smile widening at the memory.

Ivan glanced at Katya, and their eyes met briefly before he returned his attention to his son. "Did you like the lions, Kirill?" he asked, his voice softer than usual, with a hint of warmth.

Kirill nodded enthusiastically. "Yeah! And Kat let us get ice cream after!"

Ivan's gaze flicked back to Katya at the mention of her name, and she quickly looked away, focusing on her plate. It was moments like these that confused her the most—seeing him act like a caring father, but thinking of that night in the study when he'd been anything but gentle. The duality in him was disarming, and she wasn't sure how to reconcile it.

As the days passed, Ivan's interactions with the children deepened. He started asking them about their favorite parts of the day, and Katya often found herself watching in silence as he engaged with them in ways she hadn't thought possible. There were moments when she caught him smiling—a small, almost imperceptible curve of his lips—and it made her question everything she thought she knew about him.

The question seemed to catch Ivan off guard, and for a moment, he hesitated. His gaze shifted to Katya, as if silently weighing her reaction. Katya's breath caught in her throat, the unexpected nature of the request leaving her momentarily speechless.

Ivan's expression softened slightly, the hard edges of his usual demeanor fading just a little. He looked down at Dasha, then at Kirill, who was watching him with wide, hopeful eyes. After a long pause, Ivan nodded. "Maybe we can arrange that," he said, his voice quieter than usual, thoughtful. "I'm sure Kat can help make it happen."

The children's faces lit up with excitement, and Katya found herself smiling despite the tension in the room. "Of course," she said softly, her voice barely above a whisper, but loud enough for Ivan to hear.

Their mornings had settled into this rhythm—brief moments of connection, shared between the four of them, but always shadowed by the unspoken tension between Katya and Ivan. She couldn't deny that he was trying, and part of her wondered if she had been the catalyst for the change. The memory of the night she had confronted him, calling him out for being a distant father, surfaced in her mind. Maybe her words had gotten through to him after all, in ways she hadn't expected.

But with every small step Ivan took toward being a more present father, Katya couldn't shake her wariness. He was still the man who controlled her life, still the one who had the power to dictate every aspect of her existence. The man who had claimed her so forcefully, leaving her questioning her own feelings and desires.

There were mornings when she caught herself studying him, trying to understand what motivated him. His world was one of danger and dominance, far removed from anything she had ever known. Could he really change? Could he be a father who cared deeply for his children, someone who wasn't defined by the violence and control of the Bratva? Or was this simply another facet of his complex personality, another layer of control?

Katya couldn't be sure. But she couldn't deny the small flicker of hope that had begun to take root in her chest. Ivan wasn't the man she had first thought him to be—not entirely. Yes, he was dangerous and controlling, but he was also a father, a man who seemed to care about his children, even if it took a confrontation for him to show it.

As the children chattered on about their plans for the day, Katya caught Ivan's gaze once again. This time, there was something different in his eyes—something softer, more reflective. She quickly looked away, focusing on the children instead, but her heart raced in her chest.

Maybe there was more to Ivan than she had realized. Maybe, beneath the cold exterior, there was a man who could change—a man who wasn't just the controlling figure she had come to fear.

But even as she acknowledged that possibility, a sense of unease settled over her. Because if Ivan could change, then so could her feelings for him. And that was something she wasn't ready to face.

For now, she would keep her distance, focus on the children, and try to ignore the growing connection between them all. It was safer that way—safer for her heart and her sanity. But deep down, Katya knew that safety was fleeting. Because with each passing day, it became harder to separate her growing attachment to the children from her complicated feelings for their father.

Kirill and Dasha had become Katya's shadow over the past week, their bond growing stronger with each passing day. The children now clung to her in ways they hadn't before, trusting her with a vulnerability that made her heart ache. Kirill would reach for her hand without thinking, and Dasha, shy and quiet, would slip her small hand into Katya's when she was feeling uncertain. Katya found herself becoming more than just their caretaker; she had become their source of comfort, their anchor in a world that felt cold and distant. Each time she looked into their innocent eyes, she saw the reflection of her own childhood, the loss and confusion she had carried for so long.

They reminded her so much of herself—two children left to navigate a life without their mother's love, with a father who struggled to connect. She could feel their unspoken need for affection, and it stirred something deep within her, something protective. She wanted to shield them from the pain she knew all too well. It wasn't just about keeping them safe; it was about giving them a sense of normalcy, of joy, in a life overshadowed by the weight of their father's world.

To give them that escape, Katya had started taking them on more outings—small adventures to the zoo, the botanical gardens, or the park. The children lit up during these trips, their laughter filling the air as they ran through the grassy fields or pointed excitedly at the animals. Even though they were always accompanied by a driver or one of Ivan's men, these moments felt like a breath of fresh air. It was as if the heavy atmosphere of Ivan's house fell away when they stepped outside, and for a little while, Kirill and Dasha could just be children—free to explore, to laugh, to play.

Katya treasured those outings more than she could admit. Watching the children run ahead, their small hands waving in excitement as they chased after butterflies or fed ducks at the pond, gave her a sense of peace she rarely felt. In those moments, it didn't matter that her life was controlled, that she was bound by a contract. All that mattered was the happiness on Kirill and Dasha's faces, the way their eyes sparkled with joy as they experienced the world around them.

But with that joy came a gnawing guilt. She couldn't help but wonder if she was doing the right thing by allowing herself to get so close to them. She knew this bond was temporary—she had five years here, and then she would be gone. What would happen to Kirill and Dasha after that? Could she really walk away from them after becoming such an important part of their lives? The thought weighed heavily on her, twisting in her chest like a knife. She had tried to keep her distance at first, to maintain some level of detachment, but that had proven impossible. The connection she had formed with the children was real, undeniable.

Katya found herself thinking about what would happen when the time came for her to leave. The idea of walking out of their lives, of leaving them behind, was almost unbearable. She couldn't stand the thought of causing them more pain, of abandoning them the way her mother had abandoned her. The guilt gnawed at her, even as she tried to push it away, telling herself that this was all temporary. But deep down, she knew it was too late. The bond she had with Kirill and Dasha had already taken root, and it wasn't something she could easily let go of.

Despite the guilt, there was no denying the joy these children brought her. In the otherwise suffocating world of Ivan's house, they were her lifeline. They gave her purpose, a reason to keep going. Every time Dasha tugged on her hand or Kirill smiled up at her, Katya felt a warmth that she hadn't experienced in years. It was as if, in caring for them, she was healing some of the wounds she had carried for so long.

But with each smile, each shared moment, the fear of the inevitable only grew stronger.

After spending a quiet afternoon at the library with Kirill and Dasha, Katya and the children returned to the estate. The day had been fun, filled with exploring the book shelves and watching a children's puppet show. Kirill had been particularly excited about his dinosaur book, while Dasha had chosen one about animals around the world. Katya felt a rare sense of peace, these simple moments with the children grounding her in ways she didn't expect.

But as they approached the mansion, that peaceful feeling began to unravel. The closer they got to the heavy doors of the estate, the more the familiar weight of tension settled over her. She reminded herself to focus on the children, to hold on to the warmth of the day, but the imposing house ahead made it difficult to keep that contentment intact.

The moment they stepped inside, Katya sensed something was off. The air felt thick, the usual quiet of the mansion disturbed by an unsettling undercurrent. As they walked down the hall, heading toward the children's rooms, a sudden, sharp voice reached her ears. Ivan's voice—loud, furious, and unmistakably enraged.

"I don't care what it takes—fix it!" His words echoed down the corridor, filled with a cold fury Katya had never heard from him before. She froze, instinctively pulling the children a little closer, her heart pounding in her chest. She looked down at Kirill and Dasha, who were blissfully unaware of the tension, still chattering excitedly about their books.

Trying to shield them from the anger spilling through the house, she hurried them along, ushering them quickly upstairs. After settling the children with one of the maids, Katya made her way back toward Ivan's office, drawn by a mixture of curiosity and concern.

As she neared the door, she stopped just short of it, hearing the unmistakable sound of Ivan's voice, low but sharp, filled with barely contained rage. She peeked around the corner just in time to see him slam his phone down onto his desk, his hands clenched into fists, every muscle in his body tight with anger.

Before she could even step back, Ivan stormed out of his office. His jaw was set in a hard line, his eyes dark with fury, his entire presence radiating danger. For a split second, his eyes flicked to hers, but there was no recognition, no softness—just pure, unfiltered rage. His movements were sharp, every step filled with purpose as he headed for the front door, barely noticing her.

Katya stood frozen in place, her heart racing as she watched him go. She had seen Ivan angry before, but this was different. This was terrifying. It was a cold, merciless fury, and it sent a chill down her spine. The door slammed shut behind him, the sound echoing through the hallway, leaving Katya standing alone.

She drew in a shaky breath, her thoughts racing. She had always known Ivan's world was dangerous, but seeing him like this—so consumed by rage—made her realize just how deep that danger ran. Was he going to hurt someone? Or worse, was he walking into a situation that could put him in harm's way? The thought of him getting hurt sent a strange wave of fear through her, a fear she couldn't shake.

She knew she shouldn't care. She shouldn't feel this knot of worry twisting inside her, but no matter how much she told herself that Ivan was the reason she was trapped in this life, that he was dangerous, the growing attachment she felt toward him was undeniable. It wasn't just the physical attraction anymore. It was something deeper—something she wasn't ready to admit, even to herself.

That night, after putting the children to bed, Katya's mind couldn't stop replaying the moment she had seen Ivan storming out of the house. His expression had been terrifying, his features twisted with raw fury. She had never seen him like that before—so enraged, so cold. It was as if every ounce of humanity had drained from his face, leaving only the dangerous man who ruled over a world she didn't fully understand.

As she stood in the quiet of her room, staring out at the darkened night sky, Katya tried to shake the unsettling feeling that had settled over her. She had always known Ivan's life was full of danger—she had heard whispers, caught fragments of conversations that hinted at the violence and power struggles of the Bratva. But seeing him in that moment, his jaw clenched and his eyes filled with a fury she couldn't comprehend, had shaken her in a way she hadn't anticipated.

What was he capable of in that state? Was he going to hurt someone? The cold, ruthless way he had stormed out of the house made it seem inevitable. She didn't want to admit it, but a part of her was afraid—not just of what he could do to others, but what could happen to him. The thought of him being hurt, or worse, sent a strange wave of fear through her that she quickly tried to push aside.

She shouldn't care. She shouldn't feel this knot of worry tightening in her chest. After all, Ivan was the reason she was trapped in this life. He was the man who controlled every aspect of her world now, and yet, no matter how many times she told herself that he was dangerous, that he was the embodiment of everything she wanted to escape from, she couldn't shake the growing attachment she felt toward him.

It wasn't just the desire that had consumed them in their heated encounters, though that was part of it. It was something deeper, something she didn't want to admit even to herself. The way he looked at her, the way he commanded every space he entered—it did something to her, stirred something inside that she couldn't explain. She had been trying to avoid him, trying to distance herself from the feelings he evoked, but every time they crossed paths, that invisible pull between them only seemed to grow stronger.

Katya pressed her forehead against the cool glass of the window, her breath fogging up the pane as she exhaled. She hated that he was starting to matter to her. She hated the control he had over her body, but even more, she hated that he was starting to take up space in her heart.

This wasn't part of the plan. She had been sent here to pay off her father's debt, a betrayal that still weighed heavily on her soul. Her role was clear—she was supposed to endure, to survive these five years under Ivan's control, and then she would be free. But as the days passed, that freedom seemed more and more distant, like a dream she wasn't even sure she wanted anymore.

Every time she looked at the children, every time she caught a glimpse of Ivan's rare smile directed at them during breakfast, she felt herself getting pulled deeper into this world, this life. It was suffocating, but at the same time, it was starting to feel like the only reality she knew. And now, with this growing attachment to Ivan, she was scared.

Scared of losing herself to him.

She wrapped her arms around her body, trying to hold on to the remnants of her independence. Ivan was a dangerous man, and she couldn't let herself forget that. She had seen that danger in his eyes earlier, the ruthless determination that made her realize just how easily he could take a life, how effortlessly he could slip into violence. And yet, in the quiet moments between them, she had seen glimpses of something else—something human, something vulnerable.

Katya didn't know which version of Ivan scared her more.

With a soft sigh, she stepped back from the window, wrapping her fingers around the fabric of her nightgown as she turned toward the bed. Sleep would be difficult tonight. The weight of her thoughts, her conflicting emotions, was too much to bear. She lay down, staring up at the ceiling, trying to make sense of the turmoil inside her.

She thought about the children and how much they had come to rely on her. Their innocent smiles, their soft voices calling her "Kat"—those moments filled her with warmth. But they also filled her with guilt. She was getting too attached. She knew that in five years, she would have to leave them behind. Could she really walk away after becoming such an important part of their lives? The thought gnawed at her, the guilt settling in her chest like a stone.

And then there was Ivan.

She closed her eyes, trying to push the image of his enraged face from her mind. But it wouldn't go away. No matter how hard she tried, she couldn't stop thinking about him. She wondered where he was now, what he was doing, if he was safe. The fact that she even cared made her feel weak, vulnerable in ways she hadn't felt since she was a little girl.

She hated it. Hated how much space he took up in her thoughts, hated how her body still ached for his touch, even though she told herself it was wrong. But deep down, she knew the truth—she was falling for him. Slowly, reluctantly, but it was happening. And that terrified her more than anything else.

Because once she admitted that, there would be no going back.

Katya lay there in the dark, her heart heavy with the weight of her unspoken feelings. She didn't want this, didn't want to care about a man who represented everything she despised. But she couldn't deny it anymore.

Ivan was getting under her skin.

And there was nothing she could do to stop it.

Chapter 13

Katya walked quietly through the dimly lit house, the soft padding of her feet the only sound breaking the silence. After checking on the children, she had planned to retreat to her own room, ready to finally relax after another long day. The house felt still, almost peaceful in the late evening, with a cool breeze whispering through the slightly open windows. It was a rare moment of calm in a life that often felt stifling and suffocating.

Just as she turned the corner into the hallway, Katya froze. Ahead of her, Ivan emerged from the shadows, walking slowly toward his bedroom. The sight of him stopped her in her tracks.

He was not the composed and commanding figure she was used to seeing. His white shirt was stained with dirt, the fabric wrinkled and torn in places. A small but deep cut above his brow still leaked blood, the crimson streak standing out starkly against his pale skin. His knuckles were swollen, bruised and raw, a clear sign that whatever he had been doing involved violence. His usually calm, controlled aura was nowhere to be seen. Instead, he looked wild, disheveled, and utterly worn down.

Katya's breath caught in her throat. She had always known, at least intellectually, that Ivan's world was dangerous. She knew what kind of man he was, the kind of power he held. But seeing him like this, bloodied and broken, made the danger feel all too real. It was one thing to live in his house, constantly reminded of his control and dominance. But it was something entirely different to witness him like this—so visibly torn from whatever brutality he had been involved in.

She watched him for a moment, unmoving, as he walked toward her, his gaze unfocused at first. Then, as if sensing her presence, his eyes lifted and locked onto hers. Katya's heart skipped a beat. There was something different in his expression tonight, something darker than usual. His exhaustion was clear, but there was more beneath it—an anger that simmered just beneath the surface, or perhaps it was the adrenaline still running through him. Whatever it was, it sent a flicker of unease through her, a reminder that Ivan was a man whose hands were often covered in blood.

Katya stood frozen, unsure of what to do or say. She felt a strange mixture of emotions swirling inside her—fear, confusion, and something else she didn't want to acknowledge. Vulnerability. She had never seen him this vulnerable before, and it unsettled her.

Ivan's eyes narrowed slightly as he approached her, his gaze intense but unreadable. He stopped just a few feet away, close enough that she could smell the sweat and faint traces of blood on him. The air between them felt thick, charged with something unspoken.

"Don't ask," he muttered, his voice rough, almost warning her not to probe further.

Katya swallowed hard, her heart still racing from the shock of seeing him in this state. She didn't ask any questions, not because she didn't want to know, but because the look in his eyes told her that it wasn't the time. There was something in the way he held himself—rigid, like a coiled spring ready to snap—that made her realize just how close to danger he truly was.

For the first time, the full weight of Ivan's world began to settle over her. She had been living in the shadows of his life, knowing only glimpses of what went on behind closed doors, but seeing him like this—bloodied, exhausted, and barely holding himself together—made her confront the truth she had been avoiding. This was his life. And it was far more dangerous than she had ever imagined.

Despite the fear and confusion swirling inside her, Katya couldn't shake the small pang of concern that tugged at her chest. She shouldn't care. She shouldn't feel anything for him. But seeing him like this, so raw and exposed, stirred something deep within her.

Without a word, she stepped aside to let him pass, her gaze never leaving him as he moved toward his bedroom. Ivan didn't say anything more, but his eyes lingered on hers for a moment longer, as if he could sense the shift in her emotions.

Katya stood there for a moment, her heart pounding in her chest as the silence of the house pressed in around her. The image of Ivan's bloodied knuckles and the cut on his brow burned into her mind, reminding her of the reality of the world she was now a part of—a world filled with violence, blood, and danger.

And for the first time, she wasn't just afraid of that world.

She was afraid of what it was doing to her.

Despite the sharpness of his tone, Katya couldn't ignore the instinct that had flared up inside her. There was something about seeing Ivan like this—disheveled, hurt—that overrode her usual hesitation around him. She didn't speak as she quietly turned and led him into his bedroom, her heart racing. The sound of his footsteps behind her, heavy and deliberate, echoed in the silence, only adding to the tension that simmered between them. But it was a different kind of tension this time. It wasn't charged with the same intensity of their past encounters. It felt quieter, more fragile, as if the evening itself had peeled away some layer between them, revealing something neither of them was ready to face.

When they reached his room, Ivan walked past her and sat on the edge of the bed, his movements stiff, deliberate. Katya hesitated for a moment, standing at the doorway as she watched him sit there, his broad shoulders hunched slightly forward, his head tilted down. She had never seen him like this—so… human. The cold, domineering exterior he wore like armor seemed to have cracked. And the sight of it made her chest tighten in ways she didn't fully understand.

She didn't need his permission. Quietly, she moved to his bathroom and found some first aid supplies, her mind swirling with emotions she was trying desperately to keep in check. As she walked back to him, she noticed the way his chest rose and fell with deep, steady breaths, as if he were trying to calm whatever storm was still brewing inside him. She knelt down before him, her fingers brushing against his swollen, bloodied knuckles as she opened the first aid kit.

The silence stretched on, thick and palpable. Katya's hands trembled slightly as she began cleaning the dried blood from his skin, her fingers gently wiping away the dirt and grit. She was hyperaware of every movement, of every brush of her hand against his. The air between them felt charged, but not with the usual fire and intensity. It was different this time—softer, more intimate, and that unnerved her.

Ivan's eyes were on her, watching her work in silence. His expression remained guarded, but his gaze felt heavier than usual, more focused. It was as if he was seeing her, really seeing her, for the first time. And Katya felt that weight. It pressed down on her, making her heart race, her breath catch in her throat. But she didn't look up. She couldn't. Not yet.

As she dabbed at the cut on his brow, cleaning the blood from the small wound, Katya's mind began to spiral. This was his life—fighting, blood, violence. She had known, of course, that Ivan was involved in dangerous things, but seeing the physical evidence of it so close, feeling the roughness of his knuckles beneath her fingers, made it real in a way she hadn't been prepared for. She had always thought of Ivan as untouchable, powerful, and invincible in his own terrifying way. But sitting here in front of him, tending to his wounds, made her realize just how vulnerable he could be. And that realization unsettled her more than she wanted to admit.

Ivan shifted slightly, wincing as she pressed a little too hard against one of the bruises on his knuckles. "Careful," he muttered, his voice low, but there was no bite to it.

"Sorry," Katya whispered, her voice softer than she intended. Her hands stilled for a moment before she continued her work, more gently this time. The tenderness in her touch seemed foreign even to her, but she couldn't help it. Despite everything—despite the control he held over her, despite the danger he represented—she found herself caring about him in ways she shouldn't.

She wiped the last trace of blood from his skin, her hands moving slower now, reluctant to finish. She could feel the heat radiating off his body, his presence enveloping her even though he wasn't speaking. It was strange, this quiet moment between them. It wasn't like the others—there was no anger, no dominance, no resistance. Just a heavy silence that spoke of things neither of them was ready to acknowledge.

When she finally finished cleaning his wounds, Katya closed the first aid kit and sat back slightly, her heart pounding in her chest as she dared to meet his gaze. Ivan's eyes were dark, intense, but there was something softer there, something almost… reflective. She couldn't look away, even as the quiet between them stretched on, filled with all the things they weren't saying.

She found herself unable to hold back the question that had been gnawing at her mind. It was soft, almost a whisper, but it cut through the tension between them like a blade.

"Is this what your life is? Fighting, blood?"

The words were laced with something she hadn't expected—concern. She had meant to ask it with curiosity, perhaps even a hint of accusation, but instead, it came out filled with something deeper. She realized, as the question left her lips, that she didn't just want to know. She needed to understand. The gravity of Ivan's world, the reality of what it meant for him to be the man he was, had hit her harder than she anticipated. The blood, the violence—it wasn't just an abstract concept anymore. It was real, and it was dangerous. And Ivan lived in that danger every single day.

Ivan's response wasn't immediate. He didn't offer his usual sharp, dismissive tone. Instead, his gaze softened, and he looked at her with an intensity that seemed to strip away the layers he usually wore. The usual guarded, cold exterior was gone, replaced by something raw, something more human. He nodded slowly, his eyes never leaving hers.

Then, in a gesture that startled her, his thumb brushed gently across her jawline. The touch was soft, tender in a way that felt entirely foreign to the dynamic they had shared until now. It made her heart skip a beat, the warmth of his skin against hers sending a shiver down her spine. She had felt his hands on her body before—dominant, rough, claiming her—but this? This was different. This was delicate, intimate in a way that made her breath catch in her throat.

"You knew what I was when you came here," Ivan said quietly. His voice was lower, softer, and it held a weight she hadn't heard before. The usual menace was absent, replaced by something that felt more like resignation. As if he were acknowledging the brutal reality of his life, the inevitability of it. He wasn't angry, he wasn't pushing her away—he was simply stating a fact. A truth that hung in the air between them.

Katya didn't respond. She couldn't. The truth of his words sank in like a stone in her chest, heavy and immovable. Of course, she had known. She had always known. But hearing him say it like that, feeling the weight of those words as they lingered in the air, made it real in a way that was undeniable. This was his life. Violence, danger, blood—it was all part of the world he lived in, the world she had been thrust into. And now, standing so close to that reality, she could no longer pretend it didn't affect her.

The silence between them stretched, thick and heavy with unspoken thoughts. Katya's heart pounded in her chest, her hands still hovering near his, unsure of what to do next. She wanted to say something, to offer a retort or some sarcastic comment to lighten the moment, but the words wouldn't come. All she could feel was the gravity of his life pressing down on her, the realization that every time he walked out of this house, there was a very real chance he might not come back.

Her eyes flicked to his bloodied knuckles, the cut above his brow. The physical evidence of the violence he endured, the fights he was constantly engaged in. It was one thing to know about it, to be aware of the brutal world he inhabited, but it was another to see it so close. To witness the toll it took on him, the danger it posed.

"Why do you do it?" she asked before she could stop herself. Her voice was quiet, almost timid, but the question hung in the air between them. She wasn't sure what answer she expected, but she needed to know. Needed to understand why a man like Ivan chose this life, chose to be surrounded by death and destruction every day.

Ivan didn't answer right away. He sat still for a moment, his gaze dropping to the floor as if he were considering her question, weighing his response. When he finally spoke, his voice was as low as ever, but it carried an edge of vulnerability that Katya hadn't heard before.

"It's the only life I've ever known," he said simply, his eyes lifting to meet hers again. "You don't get to choose the world you're born into. But you learn to survive in it."

Katya swallowed hard, the weight of his words settling over her like a suffocating blanket. She knew that feeling all too well—the feeling of being trapped in a world you hadn't chosen, of doing whatever you had to do to survive. Her own life hadn't been easy, filled with its own kind of violence and betrayal. But Ivan's world? It was something else entirely. And now, she was a part of it, whether she liked it or not.

"You're going to get yourself killed," she whispered, more to herself than to him. But the moment the words left her lips, Ivan's eyes sharpened, the vulnerability in his expression disappearing in an instant. His gaze hardened, and for a moment, she thought she had crossed a line, said something she shouldn't have.

But then his thumb brushed against her jaw again, softer this time, his touch lingering a little longer. "Not if I can help it," he murmured, his voice low and rough, but there was something else there—something almost reassuring, as if he were trying to comfort her. Trying to tell her that he wasn't going anywhere. Not yet.

Katya's chest tightened at his words. She hated that they comforted her, hated that she was starting to care whether or not he came home every night. This was a man who had trapped her in this life, who held her under his control, and yet… the thought of him not coming back, of him being hurt or worse, sent a wave of fear through her that she didn't want to acknowledge.

She pulled back slightly, her hands falling away from his as she stood. "This isn't my world," she said quietly, more to herself than to him. "I don't belong here."

Ivan's gaze followed her, dark and unreadable. "Maybe not," he said softly, his tone unreadable. "But you're here now."

And with that, the reality of her situation, the weight of it all, pressed down on her even harder. She was here, in Ivan's world, and no matter how much she wanted to deny it, no matter how much she fought against it, a part of her was starting to feel like she was becoming a part of it too. And that terrified her more than anything.

As she stood there, the silence between them thick and heavy once more, Katya felt the pull of conflicting emotions inside her. Fear, anger, resentment… and something else. Something she wasn't ready to face.

Katya stood up, her heart still racing from the raw energy that lingered in the room after tending to Ivan's wounds. She didn't know what she had expected when she saw him bloodied and bruised, but it wasn't this—the overwhelming pull between them that seemed to grow stronger with every second they spent together. She wanted to leave, to gather her thoughts and push aside the complicated emotions swirling inside her. But as she turned to go, something stopped her. The weight of his gaze, heavy and full of something she couldn't quite name, pinned her to the spot.

Just as her hand reached the doorknob, she felt the warmth of his touch on her wrist. Ivan's grip wasn't forceful, but it was firm, commanding her attention. Her breath caught as she slowly turned back to face him, the air between them thick with an unspoken tension. Their eyes locked, and for a moment, everything else faded away. She was aware of nothing but the intensity in his gaze and the pounding of her own heart.

"Don't go," his voice was low, almost a plea, though it was wrapped in the same commanding tone she had grown used to. But there was something different about it this time. Something vulnerable.

Katya swallowed hard, her pulse quickening as Ivan pulled her gently toward him, guiding her onto his lap. She could feel the heat of his body through the fabric of his clothes, the hard planes of his chest against her as she settled into him. The tension crackled in the air between them, not just with desire but with something deeper—something neither of them wanted to name.

Their faces were so close now, their breaths mingling in the small space between them. Ivan's hand slid from her wrist to her waist, the roughness of his touch sending a shiver down her spine. But instead of being purely possessive like before, there was a gentleness in his grip that caught her off guard. She should have pulled away—should have resisted the magnetic pull between them—but she couldn't. Not this time.

Without thinking, her hand reached up, brushing a strand of hair away from his forehead, her fingers lingering against the bruised skin above his brow. Ivan's eyes softened ever so slightly, and for a moment, it felt as if the world outside his bedroom didn't exist. The danger, the violence—it all fell away, leaving just the two of them in this strange, charged bubble.

Then, slowly, as if testing the boundaries of what they were, Ivan leaned in, capturing her lips in a kiss that was startlingly tender. Katya's eyes fluttered shut as she kissed him back, her body reacting instinctively to the warmth of his mouth against hers. The kiss was slow at first, unhurried, filled with an unexpected softness that made her heart ache.

But as their lips moved together, the gentleness gave way to something more intense, more desperate. Ivan's hand slid up her back, pulling her closer until there was no space left between them. Katya's fingers found their way into his hair, tugging slightly as the kiss deepened, as if she needed to feel him—needed to anchor herself to the heat of his body, the safety of his arms, even if she knew she shouldn't.

Her worry for him, the fear that had clawed at her chest earlier, fueled the passion building between them. She had been so afraid when she saw him injured, more afraid than she wanted to admit. And now, she needed this—needed to feel him alive, warm, and strong beneath her hands. The desperation in her kiss mirrored the thoughts racing through her mind. She didn't want to care, but she did. And now, that fear was mixing with desire, creating a potent blend of emotions she couldn't control.

Ivan groaned softly against her lips, his hands roaming over her body with a mix of urgency and care. His touch was possessive, as it always was, but there was a tenderness beneath it that made Katya's breath hitch. It was as if he were holding back, as if he were afraid of hurting her, even though his desire was palpable in every movement.

The sound of fabric rustling filled the room as their hands began to roam more freely. Katya's fingers tugged at the hem of Ivan's shirt, pulling it over his head in one fluid motion. Her palms pressed against the hard muscles of his chest, feeling the warmth of his skin beneath her touch. Ivan's hands followed suit, slipping under her shirt and pulling it over her head, discarding it on the floor beside them.

For a brief moment, Ivan pulled back, his eyes raking over her bare skin, his gaze dark and heavy with desire. But there was something more in his eyes now, something that went beyond physical need. Katya saw it—felt it—and it sent a tremor through her chest. She should have been scared of what was unfolding between them, of the intensity that seemed to be growing with each passing moment. But all she felt was a strange sense of calm, as if this was inevitable, as if they had been heading toward this moment from the start.

She leaned in again, capturing his lips in another kiss, this one more urgent, more demanding. Her hands moved to his belt, fumbling slightly as she tried to undo it. Ivan's hands moved to her waist, gripping her firmly as if he couldn't bear to let her go.

They hadn't even finished undressing, but already the heat between them was unbearable. Katya could feel the hardness of him pressing against her, and the anticipation of what was to come made her pulse race even faster. But beneath the physical desire, there was something else. She wasn't just giving herself to him because of the passion. She was giving herself to him because, for the first time, she was starting to realize that Ivan—this dangerous, complicated man—was starting to mean more to her than she was ready to admit.

And that thought both terrified her and thrilled her in equal measure.

Katya's breath came in shallow gasps as Ivan removed her bra, his eyes dark with a mixture of desire and something more—a hunger that seemed to burn beneath his skin. They both moved quickly, desperately, their hands fumbling with each other's clothes as if every layer peeled away would bring them closer to something neither of them could define. She tugged his pants down, her fingers trembling slightly as she freed him, and her breath caught in her throat at the sight of him, hard and thick, the heat of his body radiating into her hands.

Ivan's hands were on her again in an instant, tugging her pants and underwear down her legs and discarding them in a heap on the floor. The intensity in his gaze deepened as he laid her back on the bed, his strong hands gripping her waist firmly, but his movements more tender than she had anticipated. There was still that commanding presence, but it was tempered by something softer, something that made her heart flutter despite the heat building between them.

He leaned over her, his lips capturing hers again in a kiss that was slower this time, more measured, as if savoring the taste of her. Katya's hands instinctively moved to his chest, her fingers running over the hard planes of muscle before one hand slipped lower, wrapping around his erection. A shudder ran through him as her hand stroked him, his cock throbbing in response to her touch. The moan that escaped her lips was quiet, almost drowned out by the sound of his ragged breathing, but the feel of him—so hard, so large in her grip—sent a thrill through her that she couldn't control.

Ivan broke the kiss and began trailing his lips down her neck, his mouth hot and insistent against her skin as he moved lower. Katya tilted her head back, her body arching beneath him as he kissed along her collarbone, his lips brushing against her in a way that sent shivers down her spine. Her hand continued to stroke him, feeling the heat of his arousal in her palm, and the sensation of him in her grasp made her ache with need.

His mouth moved lower, his lips trailing down the slope of her breast before his tongue flicked out, teasing her nipple. The sharp gasp that escaped her lips was involuntary, a reaction to the way he licked, sucked, and fondled her breasts with a precision that left her breathless. His hands roamed over her body as he worked his mouth over one nipple and then the other, alternating between gentle licks and rougher bites that sent jolts of pleasure straight to her core. Katya's moans grew louder, her back arching off the bed as his mouth moved in a rhythm that was both torturous and exhilarating.

She could feel the wetness gathering between her thighs, her body responding eagerly to every touch, every kiss. Ivan's hands slid lower, gripping her hips with possessive strength as he kissed down her abdomen, his stubble scraping deliciously against her sensitive skin. Her fingers tightened in his hair, a wordless plea for more as he continued his slow descent.

When his mouth finally reached the apex of her thighs, Katya's entire body tensed with anticipation. She felt the heat of his breath against her skin as he paused for a moment, his eyes locking with hers. There was something about the way he looked at her, as if he was claiming her with just a glance, and it made her pulse race.

Without breaking eye contact, Ivan lowered his head between her legs, his fingers sliding through her slick folds before brushing against her clit. A sharp moan escaped her as he circled the sensitive bundle of nerves with a deliberate slowness that drove her wild. The sensation was almost too much—her body felt like it was on fire, every nerve ending igniting under his touch.

His tongue followed soon after, swirling around her clit in slow, teasing motions that left her breathless. Her hands flew to his hair, gripping tightly as her hips bucked against his mouth, the need for release building in her with every flick of his tongue. Ivan growled low in his throat, the vibration sending another wave of pleasure through her as he licked and sucked at her clit with an intensity that made her entire body tremble.

He didn't stop there. His fingers thrust into her, sliding deep inside her wet entrance as he continued to work his tongue against her. The combination of his fingers and mouth was overwhelming, her body teetering on the edge of climax as she writhed beneath him, her breaths coming in shallow pants. Every thrust of his fingers pushed her closer, every swirl of his tongue sending her spiraling further into a haze of pleasure.

"Ivan… please…" Her voice was breathless, desperate as she begged for release. Her body was so close to the edge, her hips moving in rhythm with the thrust of his fingers, and she could feel herself beginning to unravel, her orgasm just out of reach.

But just as the wave was about to crash, just as she felt herself tipping over the edge, Ivan stopped. His fingers stilled inside her, and he pulled his mouth away from her clit, leaving her gasping, trembling, and aching for more.

"Not yet," he murmured, his voice low and full of command. Katya's body quivered beneath him, her heart pounding in her chest as she fought to regain her breath, her frustration palpable. She could feel the intensity of her desire still thrumming through her, her body begging for release that he had so cruelly denied.

She opened her eyes, meeting his gaze once more. There was no teasing smile, no smirk—just the raw power of his dominance, his control over her pleasure, and for the first time, she realized how much she craved it. The denial of her release only heightened her need, and as she stared up at him, her chest rising and falling with each labored breath, she knew that she would beg if he asked her to.

In that moment, Ivan had complete control over her, and Katya wasn't sure if she hated him for it or if she had never wanted anything more.

The air between them seemed to thicken, the silence broken only by their ragged breaths. Katya's pulse pounded in her ears, her body trembling from the intensity of what Ivan had just done to her. Her skin was on fire, her senses overwhelmed by his presence, his touch, his dominance. As she lay there, her eyes fluttered open, locking with Ivan's gaze. The hunger in his eyes hadn't abated; if anything, it had deepened, darkened into something more primal, more possessive.

He didn't speak as he positioned himself between her thighs, his hands gripping her hips with a strength that sent a shiver down her spine. Katya's breath caught in her throat, her body arching involuntarily toward him. She could feel the heat of his cock pressing against her entrance, teasing, but not yet entering. The tension was unbearable, every nerve in her body screaming for him, for the release she so desperately needed.

Ivan moved slowly at first, almost too slowly, the head of his cock nudging her slick entrance with a deliberate precision that made her entire body tighten in anticipation. The friction, the heat—it was too much and not enough all at once. Katya whimpered softly, her hands instinctively reaching for his arms, gripping his biceps as she tried to pull him closer, to make him give her what she needed. But he held back, his eyes still locked on hers, as if daring her to beg for it.

"Ivan… please…" she whispered, her voice barely audible, trembling with the weight of her need. She didn't want to beg, but her body was betraying her, aching for him in a way that made her feel helpless. The way he controlled her, her pleasure—it should have made her resent him, but instead, it only made her want him more.

With a low growl, Ivan finally gave in, pushing forward and burying himself deep inside her in one powerful thrust. Katya gasped, her head falling back against the bed as her body clenched around him. He filled her completely, stretching her, the sheer size of him making her feel impossibly full. The sensation of him inside her was overwhelming, sending a shockwave of pleasure through her that made her toes curl and her fingers dig into his skin.

For a moment, he didn't move, letting her body adjust to the feeling of him. Katya's breath came in short, shallow gasps as she tried to regain her composure, but it was impossible. The way he felt inside her, the way he filled her so completely, it was as if he was made to fit her perfectly. She wanted more—she needed more.

Slowly, Ivan began to move, his hips pulling back before thrusting forward again in a rhythm that was both torturous and exquisite. Each stroke was deep, deliberate, sending a pulse of pleasure through her that built with every movement. He gripped her hips tighter, pulling her closer with each thrust, his pace quickening as he plunged deeper inside her. The sound of skin meeting skin filled the room, mingling with the ragged sounds of their breathing, the primal rhythm of their bodies moving together.

"You belong to me," Ivan growled, his voice rough and commanding, his eyes burning with intensity as he looked down at her. His words sent a shudder through Katya, her body reacting before her mind could process the full weight of them. She felt it—deep down, she knew it. She belonged to him, in a way she had never belonged to anyone before. His dominance, his control over her—it was intoxicating, and she found herself surrendering to it, to him.

"Yes…" she whispered, her voice shaky but certain. "I'm yours…"

The admission slipped from her lips before she could stop it, but the moment it was out, she knew it was true. She had fought so hard to maintain control, to keep her distance from him, but now—now there was no denying the connection between them. She wanted him, needed him, in ways that went beyond the physical. It scared her, but in this moment, wrapped up in the heat of their bodies, she couldn't bring herself to care.

Ivan's thrusts grew harder, more forceful, as if her words had unlocked something inside him. His grip on her hips tightened, pulling her against him with a roughness that made her moan, her body arching to meet his every thrust. The pleasure was building, coiling tighter and tighter inside her with every movement, every stroke of his cock as it filled her, stretching her, claiming her in a way that felt all-consuming.

"Ivan…" she gasped, her voice breaking as the pleasure intensified, her body trembling beneath him. She was close, so close, her muscles tightening around him as the tension inside her reached its breaking point. She could feel the edge approaching, that sweet, dizzying drop that would send her over into oblivion.

He felt it too. His thrusts became faster, more urgent, his breathing heavy as he drove into her with a power that left her breathless. His hands moved from her hips to her thighs, spreading her wider, allowing him to sink even deeper into her with each thrust. Katya's nails raked down his back, her body writhing beneath him as the pleasure overwhelmed her, her mind spinning with the intensity of it all.

"You're mine," he growled again, his voice thick with possession as his hips slammed into hers, driving her closer and closer to the edge. "Only mine."

His words sent a jolt of heat through her, and Katya couldn't hold back any longer. With a cry, her body shattered around him, the orgasm hitting her like a tidal wave, every muscle in her body tensing and then releasing all at once. She felt herself clench around him, her inner walls tightening as the pleasure consumed her, her body wracked with shudders as she rode out the waves of ecstasy.

Ivan wasn't far behind her. His thrusts became erratic, his grip on her thighs tightening as he buried himself deep inside her one last time, his own release crashing over him with a guttural moan. She could feel him pulsing inside her, filling her completely as they both came together, their bodies trembling in the aftermath.

For a moment, they stayed like that, tangled together, their bodies still joined as they tried to catch their breath. The intensity of the moment lingered in the air, heavy and charged, but there was something else there too—something softer, more tender, that neither of them could ignore.

Katya lay beneath him, her heart pounding in her chest, her mind spinning from the aftershocks of their release. She couldn't think, couldn't process what had just happened, but as she looked up at Ivan, the raw emotion in his gaze mirrored her own.

And for the first time, she realized just how deeply she had let him in.

As they lay together, the intensity of the moment slowly gave way to a stillness that felt both comforting and unsettling. Ivan's body pressed against hers, his warmth seeping into her skin, but Katya's mind was far from calm. Her thoughts swirled in a chaotic dance of emotions she wasn't ready to face. She hadn't expected this—hadn't anticipated the flood of feelings that now surged through her.

What had started as physical, a base need for touch, for release, had shifted into something more—something dangerous. Katya felt the weight of it settle deep inside her chest, pressing down in a way that made it hard to breathe. She glanced at Ivan, his features softened in the dim light, his breathing steady now as the remnants of their shared passion lingered in the air. There was a vulnerability in him she hadn't seen before, and it mirrored something within her that terrified her.

How could this have happened?

For so long, she had clung to the resentment she felt toward him—the man who controlled her life, who held power over her every move. She had hated him for that control, for making her feel powerless, for making her feel trapped. And yet now, as she lay in his arms, that hatred felt distant, overshadowed by something new. Something she didn't want to admit to herself.

She was falling for him.

The realization hit her hard, like a punch to the gut, leaving her breathless. It wasn't just the physical attraction anymore. That had been undeniable from the start, the way her body reacted to his every touch, the way he ignited a fire inside her that no one else had before. But now, lying here, feeling the quiet thrum of his heartbeat against her, Katya knew it went deeper. It scared her.

How could she be drawn to a man who represented everything she should despise? His world was filled with violence, with power struggles, with danger lurking around every corner. She had witnessed that firsthand tonight, seen the blood on his knuckles, the raw fury in his eyes. And yet, despite all of it, despite knowing exactly what he was capable of, she felt herself falling.

She tried to rationalize it, to tell herself it was only the intensity of the situation that made her feel this way. The adrenaline, the passion—they had clouded her judgment. But deep down, Katya knew the truth. The pull between them was undeniable, magnetic, and no matter how hard she tried to fight it, it was drawing her closer to him in ways she couldn't control.

Her fingers traced the line of his jaw, the rough stubble that had brushed against her skin moments ago. There was something about Ivan that unsettled her, but not in the way she'd expected. It wasn't just his dominance, though that still held a certain power over her—one that thrilled her, even as it terrified her. It was more than that. There was a depth to him, something beneath the cold, commanding exterior, and that was what scared her most of all.

Because she wasn't just physically drawn to him anymore.

She was beginning to care for him.

Katya's throat tightened at the thought, a wave of panic rising up within her. She couldn't let this happen. She couldn't let herself fall for him, not when everything about this arrangement was temporary, not when she knew how dangerous his world was. She couldn't afford to be vulnerable, not with him, not with anyone. She had spent her whole life building walls around herself, protecting her heart, and now, in a matter of weeks, Ivan had begun tearing those walls down.

It left her feeling exposed, fragile in a way she hadn't been prepared for. And she hated it. Hated that he had this effect on her, hated that she couldn't control her own emotions when it came to him. But at the same time, there was a part of her that didn't want to fight it anymore. A part of her that longed to let go, to surrender to the connection she felt growing between them.

But what would that mean for her? For them?

Katya closed her eyes, her heart pounding in her chest. She knew this was dangerous—knew that falling for Ivan would only complicate things further. And yet, as she lay there in the quiet aftermath of their shared passion, she couldn't shake the feeling that maybe, just maybe, there was more to him than she had allowed herself to see.

Maybe there was more to both of them.

As she nestled closer against his body, she let out a soft breath, her mind still racing but her body beginning to relax. The conflict inside her raged on, but for now, in this moment, she let herself be vulnerable. Just for a little while longer. Just long enough to feel what it was like to truly let her guard down with him, to acknowledge the growing emotions she could no longer deny.

And as Ivan's arm tightened around her, pulling her closer, Katya knew she was already too far gone.

Chapter 14

Katya lay beside Ivan, her head resting lightly on his chest, listening to the steady rhythm of his breathing. The room was cloaked in silence, the remnants of their intense encounter still clinging to the air like a lingering heat. Though their bodies were entwined, the emotional distance between them felt palpable. She could sense something different in Ivan now, something she hadn't expected to see from him—a vulnerability that was slowly seeping into the space between them. He was usually so composed, so in control of every situation, but now, there was an unusual stillness about him. His breathing had slowed, and his eyes were fixed on the ceiling as though he was lost in thought, far away from the immediate reality of their shared intimacy.

The quiet between them wasn't awkward, but it was heavy. Katya could feel the tension, not from the usual charged desire that hummed between them, but from something deeper. She shifted slightly, looking up at him, waiting for him to speak, though she wasn't sure what to expect. There was a subtle shift in his demeanor, a heaviness that hadn't been there moments before, and it made her uneasy. She had seen many sides of Ivan—his raw dominance, his cold control—but this was different. He seemed…unsettled.

When he finally spoke, his voice was low and even, but there was an edge to it that made Katya's pulse quicken. "You know, I never loved her," he said, his words flat, almost devoid of emotion. It took Katya a moment to realize he was talking about his wife, the woman she had only heard whispers about. She remained quiet, sensing that this was a rare moment—one where Ivan was allowing himself to be vulnerable. She wasn't sure if she should ask questions or simply let him speak.

Ivan's eyes remained fixed on the ceiling as he continued, his tone detached, as though he were reciting someone else's story. "Our marriage wasn't about love. It was arranged. A power move. A way to solidify my position within the Bratva. She understood that from the beginning." His words were sharp, clinical, and Katya could hear the lack of sentiment in them. But she could also sense something deeper beneath the surface—something he wasn't yet revealing.

Katya listened intently, her heart aching slightly for the woman Ivan had married, for the life she must have lived with him. A life filled with power struggles, but no warmth. No love. Ivan's confession sent a ripple of emotion through her, one that was hard to pin down. She knew how cold and calculating he could be, but hearing him speak of his marriage in such a detached way made her realize just how emotionally closed off he truly was.

"She was a good mother," Ivan said, his voice softening slightly, as though that one aspect of their relationship was the only thing he held any real sentiment for. "She did her duty. Raised our children. Played her role perfectly. But we were never more than...partners." His lips twisted slightly, as if the word left a bitter taste in his mouth. "Everything I do—everything I've ever done—has always been for power. Love...that was never part of the equation."

Katya's chest tightened as she listened to him speak, her hand resting lightly on his chest. She wanted to reach out, to say something, but the weight of his words hung heavily in the air, and she felt as though any response would shatter the fragile moment. She had always known that Ivan was a man driven by power, but hearing him admit to the cold reality of his marriage made her feel a pang of sadness for him. He had built walls around his heart, walls so high that even the mother of his children had never been able to break through them.

For a brief moment, Katya wondered if that would be her fate as well. Would she, too, be nothing more than a tool in his world of control and dominance? The thought unsettled her, but at the same time, she knew she was already feeling something for him that went beyond what she had ever imagined. And perhaps, in his own way, Ivan was beginning to feel the same.

As if sensing her thoughts, Ivan's gaze finally shifted from the ceiling to her, his dark eyes locking onto hers with an intensity that sent a shiver down her spine. "I didn't care about her like I should have," he admitted, his voice quieter now, almost pained. "She was a means to an end. But that didn't mean I wanted her to die."

The confession hung in the air, heavier than anything else he had said. Katya's breath caught in her throat, her fingers tightening against his chest. She hadn't expected him to go there, to open that door. She could see the flicker of something in his eyes now, something deeper than the cold, calculating man he presented to the world. There was guilt there. And regret.

Ivan exhaled slowly, his expression hardening again, as though he was trying to wrestle control back over his emotions. "Her death wasn't an accident," he said, his tone darkening. "It was meant for me. A car bomb. A rival faction within the Bratva, trying to take me out. She got caught in the crossfire."

Katya's heart lurched in her chest. A car bomb? The thought of such violence shook her to her core. She stared at Ivan, her mind reeling. She had known his world was dangerous, but hearing him speak of it in such stark terms brought the reality crashing down on her. His wife had died because of him—because of the life he led, the choices he made.

Katya's pulse raced as she processed the weight of his words. Ivan had been living with this burden, this guilt, for years, and he had never let anyone see it. Until now. She didn't know what to say, didn't know if there was anything she could say. But in that moment, she saw Ivan for what he truly was—a man who carried the weight of his decisions, a man who had built his world on power and control, but who, deep down, was haunted by the consequences.

Her hand moved instinctively, her fingers brushing softly against his chest in a small, comforting gesture. She didn't know if it would mean anything to him, but she felt the need to reach out, to offer something in return for the vulnerability he was sharing with her. The silence between them stretched on, but it wasn't the oppressive, awkward silence of earlier. It was heavy with emotion, with the weight of Ivan's confession and the knowledge that their dynamic had shifted.

Katya could feel the conflicting emotions swirling within her—sympathy for the man lying next to her, guilt for the life his wife had led and the way she had died, and fear for what this meant for her. She had entered this arrangement knowing Ivan was dangerous, knowing the life he led was violent and ruthless. But hearing him admit that his wife had died because of a decision he made, because of the power he wielded, brought a sharp clarity to the risks she was taking simply by being in his world.

Her heart raced as she tried to process it all. The Ivan she had seen up until now had been cold, calculating, always in control. But this man lying beside her was something else entirely. He was still dangerous, yes, but there was a vulnerability to him that she hadn't expected to see, a rawness that made her feel things she didn't want to feel. She had told herself over and over that she hated him, that he was just another man who held power over her life. But now, as she looked into his eyes, she couldn't deny the pull she felt toward him—the way her heart ached for him in a way that scared her.

Ivan's gaze softened slightly as he looked at her, the tension in his body slowly easing. "I don't know why I'm telling you this," he admitted, his voice low and rough. "I've never spoken about her death to anyone. Not like this."

Katya's breath caught in her throat at his admission. She could see the struggle in his eyes, the internal battle he was waging with himself. Ivan wasn't the kind of man who shared his emotions easily, if ever. And yet, here he was, baring his soul to her in a way that made her feel both honored and terrified. It was a level of trust she hadn't expected, and she wasn't sure what to do with it.

"I'm sorry," Katya whispered, her voice barely audible. She wasn't sure if it was the right thing to say, but it was all she could manage in that moment. She wasn't apologizing for him, or for his choices, but for the pain he was clearly carrying with him, the guilt that had been weighing him down for so long.

Ivan's jaw tightened slightly, and for a moment, Katya thought he might pull away, that he might retreat back behind the emotional walls he had built around himself. But instead, he reached up, his hand resting gently on hers where it lay on his chest. His touch was surprisingly soft, and it sent a shiver through her that she couldn't ignore.

"She didn't deserve it," Ivan said quietly, his voice strained. "She wasn't supposed to be in that car. That's the part that haunts me. I made her a target, and I couldn't protect her."

The vulnerability in his words struck Katya deeply. She had always thought of Ivan as someone who didn't care about anything beyond power and control, but hearing him speak now, she realized how wrong she had been. He had cared about his wife, even if he hadn't loved her in the traditional sense. He had cared about her as the mother of his children, as someone who had been caught up in the violence of his world. And now, he was carrying the weight of her death with him every day.

Katya's chest tightened as she thought about the implications of his confession. Ivan was a man who lived his life on the edge of danger, and by extension, so were the people around him. His wife had been a casualty of that life, and now, Katya couldn't help but wonder if she would be next. The fear gnawed at her, but so did something else—something deeper, more confusing.

As she lay beside Ivan, feeling the warmth of his body against hers, she realized that she was no longer just physically drawn to him. The hatred she had once felt for his control over her life was being overshadowed by something else—something she didn't want to admit. She was starting to care for him, in ways that frightened her. The thought of losing him, of him being hurt or killed, made her heart race with an intensity she hadn't expected.

Katya closed her eyes, trying to steady her breathing, trying to make sense of the emotions swirling inside her. She had told herself from the beginning that this was just an arrangement, that she was here to pay off her father's debt and nothing more. But now, lying next to Ivan, feeling the weight of his vulnerability, she knew it was much more complicated than that.

"Ivan…" she began, her voice trembling slightly. She wasn't sure what she wanted to say, but the words were on the tip of her tongue, waiting to be spoken. But before she could continue, Ivan leaned down, brushing a soft kiss against her forehead.

"Don't," he whispered, his voice soft but firm. "Not now."

Katya swallowed hard, the lump in her throat making it difficult to speak. She didn't know what she had been about to say, but she knew it wouldn't have mattered. Ivan wasn't ready to hear it, and she wasn't ready to face the truth of her growing feelings for him.

Ivan lay still for a long moment after Katya's touch left his skin, the warmth of her hand fading but the weight of their shared intimacy lingering. His mind drifted, heavy with thoughts that had been locked away for so long. It wasn't just his wife's death that haunted him—it was the constant, gnawing fear that had settled into his bones since that fateful day.

He shifted slightly, exhaling as though the act of speaking was both necessary and painful. "After she died," he began, his voice rougher now, "I felt fear for the first time."

Katya looked at him, her eyes soft with concern, though she remained silent, allowing him to continue.

"Not for myself," Ivan clarified, his tone darkening as he stared at the ceiling, his thoughts clearly elsewhere. "I've never cared about my own safety. I've always known what kind of life I lead, and I've accepted the risks that come with it. But my children..." His voice trailed off, and for a moment, it seemed as though he might not continue. But then he did, with a rawness that startled Katya.

"I never wanted them to be part of this. To be targets because of me." Ivan clenched his jaw, the tension in his body rising. "The Bratva... my world... it's full of danger. Every single day, there's someone who would kill me just to prove they can. And by being my children, Kirill and Dasha are always at risk. Just for existing."

Katya's heart tightened at his words. She could see the pain in his expression, the guilt that weighed heavily on him. The way he spoke of his children wasn't just as a father who felt protective—it was as a man who understood the consequences of his own actions, the cost of the choices he had made. She wanted to reach out again, to offer some kind of comfort, but she could sense that he wasn't finished.

"I thought..." Ivan paused, his brow furrowing as if the words were difficult to say. "I thought if I kept them at a distance, they would be safer. That by not being close to them, by not getting too involved, they wouldn't be affected by my enemies. But I was wrong."

He exhaled sharply, the sound filled with frustration and regret. "I've been distant. Distant because I thought it was the only way to protect them. I let their mother handle everything—raising them, comforting them, being the parent they needed. And after she was gone…" Ivan's voice faltered for the briefest moment, but he pushed forward. "After she was gone, I didn't know how to fill that role. I didn't know how to be both a father and the man I need to be in my world."

Katya listened quietly, her heart aching for him in ways she hadn't anticipated. She had seen him as a ruthless man, someone who wielded power with cold efficiency, but hearing him speak now, she realized how deeply conflicted he was. His children were at the center of that conflict—his desire to protect them, but his inability to truly be there for them.

"I don't know how to keep them safe," Ivan admitted, his voice softening, laced with something that sounded dangerously close to despair. "All I know is that my world is too dangerous for them. But no matter what I do, I can't shield them from it. And that terrifies me."

The rawness of his confession hit Katya hard. She had never imagined Ivan to be a man who felt fear—real, deep fear. But here he was, admitting that the safety of his children was the one thing that kept him awake at night, that haunted him in ways nothing else could.

And then, just as she thought he might retreat back into his emotional walls, Ivan's eyes shifted to her. The intensity of his gaze sent a shiver through Katya, and for a moment, she felt exposed under his scrutiny.

"I never expected to feel this way about you," Ivan said, his tone quieter now, but filled with a weight that made Katya's pulse quicken. "You were supposed to be nothing more than a woman repaying her father's debt. But now…"

He trailed off, his brow furrowing as if the thought unsettled him, as though he was grappling with something he hadn't wanted to acknowledge.

"But now," he repeated, his gaze still locked on hers, "I feel the same fear for you."

Katya's breath caught in her throat, and she stared at him, her mind racing. She hadn't expected this—not from Ivan, not from the man who had been so dominant, so cold in his control over her life. But now, here he was, admitting that she had become more than just a pawn in his world. And that realization terrified him.

"I can't lose you," Ivan said, his voice barely above a whisper, but the intensity of his words was undeniable. "Not like I lost her."

The vulnerability in his tone sent a rush of emotion through Katya. She hadn't thought Ivan was capable of feeling this way, of admitting that he cared about her in any meaningful way. But now, as she looked into his eyes, she saw the truth—he wasn't just afraid of losing her to the dangerous world he inhabited. He was afraid of caring for her, of letting someone in after the loss of his wife.

Katya's heart pounded in her chest, a mix of fear and confusion swirling inside her. She didn't know what to say, how to respond to his confession. She had been telling herself for so long that she hated Ivan, that she despised the control he had over her life. But now, hearing him speak like this, admitting to his fear for her safety, for her life—it made everything more complicated.

"Ivan…" Katya began, her voice trembling slightly. But she couldn't finish the thought. She didn't know what to say. The emotions swirling inside her were too tangled, too messy to articulate.

Ivan shook his head slightly, as if to stop her from continuing. "You don't need to say anything," he said quietly, his hand brushing against her cheek. "I just needed you to know."

Katya closed her eyes for a moment, leaning into his touch, her heart aching with a strange combination of emotions she couldn't fully understand. She had never expected to feel this way about him—this intense, conflicted mixture of desire, fear, and something else, something she wasn't ready to name.

But as she lay there beside him, Ivan's hand still resting gently against her cheek, she realized that her feelings for him were deeper than she had ever wanted to admit. And that scared her more than anything else.

Chapter 15

Katya sat on a wooden park bench, her eyes on Kirill and Dasha as they chased each other across the grass, their laughter filling the air. But no matter how hard she tried to focus on them, her thoughts kept drifting back to Ivan. The morning sun was warm on her skin, the soft breeze stirring the strands of her hair, but the world around her felt distant, like she was watching it through a fog. The confession Ivan had made the night before—his wife's death, the car bomb that had been meant for him—replayed in her mind over and over, like a melody she couldn't shake.

For so long, Ivan had been the source of her anger, the man who held complete control over her life. She had despised the way he commanded every aspect of her existence, from the moment she stepped into his world. His dominance had been undeniable, and she had hated him for it. He was cold, calculating, and unapologetically powerful. But now, after last night, something had shifted. She couldn't stop thinking about the vulnerability he had shown her, the way he had let down his guard, even if only for a brief moment.

The weight of Ivan's life, the constant threat of violence that hung over him, suddenly felt so much more real. She had always known, in a detached way, that the Bratva world was dangerous. It was something she'd been forced to accept the moment she was thrust into this life. But hearing Ivan talk about his wife's death had made it visceral, a brutal reminder of just how fragile everything was. She had seen him injured before, but this? This was different. This wasn't just a physical threat; it was the realization that death was always lurking at the edges of his life, threatening not only him but the people he cared about. The confession had cracked something open inside her.

She wanted to be angry with him for drawing her into this world, for making her part of his violent reality. And yet, the anger she had clung to so tightly was fading, replaced by something more confusing. Sympathy. It felt strange, almost wrong, to feel sympathy for a man like Ivan. But she did. She couldn't help it.

Katya crossed her legs, her hands resting in her lap as her gaze remained fixed on the children. She could feel her emotions swirling inside her, tugging her in different directions. How could she feel for a man who represented everything she once hated? Ivan had dragged her into this life, and no matter how gentle he had been with her last night, he was still the one who held the power. He was still the man who had bought her, who had trapped her in this world. The reminder of that made her want to hate him all over again. But every time she tried to summon that hatred, the image of him laying in bed, confessing the truth about his wife, flashed in her mind.

He had been distant when he spoke about her, almost mechanical in his delivery, but there had been moments—small moments—where his mask had slipped. Moments where the pain and guilt had bled through the cracks. Katya had felt it. And in those moments, Ivan had become something more than the cold, ruthless man she had always seen him as. He had become human. And that scared her.

Her body reacted to the memory of him in ways she didn't want to admit. The way he had touched her last night, with dominance, yes, but also with an unexpected tenderness, had left her trembling. She had always been drawn to his power, to the raw masculinity he exuded, but now there was more. Now there was a connection she hadn't anticipated, and it left her feeling exposed. His touch had felt different, like she mattered to him in ways she hadn't before. And that made it impossible for her to ignore the growing feelings she had for him.

Physically, the pull he had over her was undeniable. Even now, sitting in the park with the children playing in front of her, she could feel the memory of his hands on her body, the way he had made her feel like she was completely his. Her skin tingled at the thought, her body craving him in a way that made her feel both exhilarated and ashamed. She hated that he could affect her like this, that she wanted him so badly, even when she knew how dangerous he was. But it wasn't just the physical anymore. That was the terrifying part.

The way Ivan had opened up to her last night made her feel something deeper. He had shown her a side of himself that no one else had ever seen, and it had stirred emotions inside her that she wasn't ready to face. She had always thought of herself as strong, as someone who could keep her distance from the man who controlled her life. But now? Now she wasn't so sure. She had seen a glimpse of the real Ivan, the man beneath the layers of power and control, and it made her feel special. It made her feel like maybe, just maybe, she belonged to him in more than just body.

The thought sent a shiver down her spine. Could she really belong to him? Was it possible that she was falling for him, despite everything he represented? The idea both thrilled and terrified her. Ivan's world was violent, dangerous, and filled with darkness. But the man she had seen last night was more than just the Bratva boss. He was someone who carried the weight of his family, of his past, and of his own guilt. And for some inexplicable reason, Katya found herself wanting to help him carry that weight.

She bit her lip, her mind racing as she tried to make sense of her feelings. Was it even possible to have feelings for a man like Ivan? A man who was capable of such brutality, yet had shown her a side of himself that no one else had? She didn't know. All she knew was that her heart was starting to betray her. The anger she had once clung to was slipping away, replaced by something far more dangerous.

Belonging to Ivan wasn't just about the physical anymore. It was about the way he made her feel, the way he had let her in, even if only for a brief moment. And that realization left her feeling more vulnerable than she had ever felt in her life.

As the children laughed and played in front of her, Katya sat on the park bench, her heart heavy with conflicting emotions. She didn't know what the future held for her, for Ivan, or for their complicated relationship. But one thing was clear—she couldn't ignore the pull he had over her, no matter how hard she tried.

Katya's gaze followed Kirill and Dasha as they ran across the grass, their carefree laughter filling the air, but her mind was far from the scene in front of her. The park, with its peaceful trees and bright sunlight, felt like an illusion—something outside the reality she was now living. No matter how hard she tried to ground herself in the moment, to focus on the children's happiness, her thoughts kept drifting back to Ivan.

The more she thought about him, the more she found herself torn. How could she feel so drawn to a man whose life was steeped in violence? She knew what he was capable of, had glimpsed the brutality that lurked beneath his composed exterior. The confession he'd made about his wife's death haunted her—the revelation that she had been killed by a car bomb meant for him. It was a stark reminder of the danger that surrounded Ivan at every turn, a danger that now surrounded her as well. The reality of his world weighed heavily on her, and yet, despite all of it, she couldn't ignore the pull he had on her.

She wrapped her arms around herself, as if trying to create a barrier against the thoughts flooding her mind. There had always been something intoxicating about Ivan—his power, his dominance, the way he seemed to control every aspect of her life without even trying. She hated it, resented it. And yet, she was drawn to it. The raw masculinity he exuded had always stirred something deep inside her, something she couldn't easily shake. But now, there was more to it than just physical attraction.

Last night, when Ivan had looked at her with those dark, conflicted eyes, something had shifted inside her. She had seen a vulnerability in him that she hadn't expected—a weight that he carried, one that went beyond the usual cold, calculated man she knew him to be. It wasn't just about power for him.

His confession about his wife's death had revealed a man who was burdened, not just by the responsibility of running an empire, but by the need to protect the people he cared about. It had made him seem… human.

And it was that humanity, that vulnerability, that called to her in ways she hadn't anticipated. She could feel the conflict in him, the constant struggle between the man who needed to maintain control and the man who, deep down, feared losing the people he loved. That fear had been clear when he spoke of his children, when he admitted that for the first time, he was truly afraid—not for himself, but for them. He was a man who carried the weight of the world on his shoulders, and for the first time, Katya felt as though he needed her in ways that went beyond their physical connection. He needed her to see him, to understand him, to be someone who could share the burden he carried.

But even as these thoughts ran through her mind, a part of her remained frightened. The idea of living in Ivan's world—the constant danger, the violence lurking at every corner—terrified her. She had known, intellectually, that his life was dangerous. But last night had made it real in a way she hadn't fully understood before. His wife had died because of him. Because of the choices he had made. That thought gnawed at her, sinking deep into her consciousness. Could she really stay with him, knowing that at any moment, violence could rip through their lives?

Her chest tightened at the thought. If she stayed with Ivan, she wouldn't just be putting herself at risk—she would be putting the children at risk too. Could she live with that? Could she bear the weight of always looking over her shoulder, of knowing that at any moment, everything could be torn apart? She thought of Kirill and Dasha, of their innocent faces, their laughter. They had already lost their mother. Could she stand by and watch them lose their father too? Or worse—could she live with the possibility that they might lose her as well?

These thoughts gnawed at her, making her stomach churn with anxiety. She had never wanted this life. She had never wanted to be part of this world of crime and violence. She had been sent here to pay off her father's debt, nothing more. And yet, she was sinking deeper into it with every passing day. Her connection to Ivan was growing, her feelings for him becoming more complicated, more intense. The way he made her feel, the way he had opened up to her last night, made it harder to resist the pull.

And then there was the physical aspect of it. Her body craved him, even now, sitting here in the park, far away from the intimacy of his bedroom. She could still feel his touch, the way he had dominated her, the way he had made her feel like she was his in every possible way. It was overwhelming, intoxicating, and it made it so much harder to think clearly. How could she deny that she was drawn to him? How could she pretend that she didn't want him when every part of her body screamed for his touch? But the physical pull was only part of the equation now.

What scared her most was the emotional connection that was beginning to form between them. Ivan had let her in last night in a way she hadn't expected. He had shown her a side of himself that no one else had seen, and it had made her feel something dangerous—something that went beyond mere attraction. She was beginning to care for him, not just as the man who controlled her life, but as a man who was carrying a heavy burden, a man who was just as trapped by his world as she was.

But how could she reconcile that with the violence? With the danger? Could she really live with the constant fear of losing him, of being pulled into the same fate that had claimed his wife? Could she handle the weight of being part of his world, knowing that every day could bring a new threat? These questions spun around in her mind, making her heart race with uncertainty.

Katya swallowed hard, her gaze following the children as they played. She didn't have the answers. She didn't know if she could live in Ivan's world. But one thing was becoming increasingly clear—no matter how much she tried to resist him, she was already more deeply entangled in his life than she ever wanted to admit.

Katya's heart tightened as she watched Kirill and Dasha dart across the park, their laughter filling the air with an innocence that felt so fragile in the face of everything she now knew about their father's world. The contrast between their carefree joy and the violent reality Ivan lived in was jarring. She'd come to care for them so much more than she'd ever expected, and the idea of something happening to Ivan—something that would leave these children without a father—made her chest ache in ways that scared her.

She'd tried to keep a distance, tried to remind herself that this situation was temporary, that her role here was to fulfill her father's debt, not to build a life. But every day, she found herself more and more entangled in the lives of these children, more and more tied to the family that wasn't hers. Kirill and Dasha had come to rely on her, their bond growing stronger with each passing day, and it was impossible for her to ignore the depth of their connection. They were already losing their innocence in ways they didn't understand. The least she could do was protect them from the rest of it.

The thought of something happening to Ivan, of him not coming home one day, sent a wave of fear crashing over her. She could see the scenario so vividly: Kirill and Dasha, sitting at this very park, waiting for a father who would never return. It made her sick to think about it, and she had to close her eyes for a moment to push the image away. She knew the pain of growing up without a mother—the hollow ache that never truly went away. The thought that these children could face that same emptiness without their father broke her heart in ways she hadn't prepared for.

She had watched Ivan storm out of the house just days before, his face twisted with rage, his hands bloodied when he returned. That was his world. His everyday life. She had known it before, intellectually, but now, after everything he had confessed to her, the reality was settling in. It wasn't just abstract danger anymore; it was real, it was violent, and it could shatter the lives of everyone involved, especially Kirill and Dasha.

Katya knew she was falling for these children, and the protective instincts that surged inside her were almost overwhelming. She wanted to shield them from the harshness of the world their father inhabited, to somehow carve out a safe space for them amidst the chaos. But how could she protect them from something as large and powerful as the Bratva? How could anyone?

And it wasn't just the children she found herself feeling protective of. Against all reason, against everything she'd tried to convince herself of, there was a part of her that wanted to protect Ivan too. It was foolish, she knew. Ivan didn't need protection from anyone—he was one of the most powerful, feared men she'd ever known. But still, the fear gnawed at her, growing stronger with each passing day. She couldn't stand the thought of losing him.

Her pulse quickened at the realization, the weight of her emotions pressing down on her. She was already falling for him. That much was clear now, though it terrified her to admit it. How could she let herself care for a man who lived in a world built on violence and death? A man who had enemies lurking in the shadows, waiting for a moment of weakness to strike? Every logical part of her screamed to pull back, to protect herself from the inevitable heartbreak that would follow. But she couldn't. She was already too far gone, and the thought of turning away from Ivan, from the children, felt impossible.

The children's laughter rang out again, pulling Katya from her thoughts. She looked over at them, her chest tightening as they chased each other through the grass. They were so innocent, so untouched by the darkness that surrounded their lives. But how long could that last? How long before they, too, were pulled into the violence that had taken their mother and might one day take their father? The questions weighed heavily on her, each one more suffocating than the last.

Katya knew that if anything happened to Ivan, these children would be left adrift in a world they were too young to navigate. The thought of them being alone, without the father they adored, was unbearable. She couldn't let that happen. She had to find a way to keep them safe, even if she didn't know how.

And yet, as much as she worried for Kirill and Dasha, she couldn't ignore the feelings she had for Ivan. They complicated everything, made her doubt her own judgment. She hated the world he lived in, hated the violence and the danger that clung to him like a shadow. But she couldn't deny the way he made her feel—the way his touch set her on fire, the way his vulnerability the night before had made her heart ache with something she didn't want to name.

How could she reconcile these two sides of him? The man who dominated her, who commanded her body with a single look, and the man who had laid bare his fears and vulnerabilities, showing her the weight he carried every day. The man who scared her, but who also made her feel alive in ways no one else ever had.

As the children ran back to her, breathless and grinning, Katya forced a smile, but the turmoil inside her raged on. She knew she was falling for

Ivan, and that terrified her more than anything. How could she care for a man whose world was built on bloodshed and danger? How could she open her heart to someone who might one day disappear, leaving her as empty as the children would be?

But even as these thoughts swirled inside her, Katya knew the truth. She was already in too deep, and no matter how much she tried to fight it, her heart was bound to Ivan and his children in ways she couldn't escape.

Chapter 16

Ivan sat in his warehouse office the next day, the cold steel of his desk beneath his hands as he leaned forward, his eyes fixed on nothing in particular. The cut above his eyebrow still throbbed—a sharp reminder of the fight at the docks, but the pain was nothing compared to the storm churning in his head. The memories of the night before with Katya, her touch, her presence, kept intruding on his thoughts.

He flexed his hands, his knuckles still raw from the beating he had delivered to that idiot dock worker. The man had dared to challenge him, dared to throw a punch. It had been a mistake. Ivan had nearly beaten him to death, his fists connecting with bone and muscle until the man's body had crumpled beneath him. His men had dragged him away before he could finish the job, but the damage had been done. The rage, the raw fury that had fueled him, had been momentarily satisfied, but the anger still simmered beneath his skin.

But now, sitting alone in his office, it wasn't the fight that haunted him. It wasn't the missing arms shipments or the Morozov Bratva pushing the limits of his control. It was Katya.

He couldn't stop thinking about her. Her warmth, the way she had looked at him the night before, her hands so gentle as she cleaned his wounds. She had seen him at his most vulnerable, had seen the cracks in the armor he had built around himself, and she hadn't run. She had stayed. She had cared for him. And that simple act had done more to unsettle him than any punch he had thrown.

Ivan hated vulnerability. It made him feel weak, exposed in a way that left him uneasy. In the Bratva, weakness was exploited, torn apart, and used against you. He had built his life on control, on power, on making sure no one could ever get close enough to hurt him. And yet, here he was, thinking about a woman who had somehow slipped through his defenses without him even realizing it.

Katya wasn't supposed to matter. She had come into his life to repay her father's debt, nothing more. She had been meant to serve a purpose, to be another pawn in the intricate game of power and survival he played every day. But somehow, she had become more than that. She had become someone who mattered. Someone who had wormed her way under his skin and made him feel things he hadn't felt in years.

He couldn't afford to care for her. Not in his world. Caring for someone made you vulnerable, gave your enemies leverage. It was why he had kept everyone at arm's length since his wife's death. He had learned the hard way what happened when you allowed yourself to care too much. His wife had paid the price for his position in the Bratva, and he had sworn never to make that mistake again.

But Katya was different. She had seen him as more than the cold, calculating man he presented to the world. She had looked at him with concern, not fear. And that terrified him.

The night before, after she had cleaned his wounds, they had shared more than just physical intimacy. There had been something deeper in the way they had connected, something that scared him more than any threat the Morozovs could throw at him. He had felt her concern, her care, and it had made him feel... human. He hadn't felt that in years.

But it wasn't just the tenderness that had shaken him. Beneath that vulnerability, there was a physical hunger that burned hotter than anything else. The way she had looked at him, the way her body responded to his touch—it had ignited a primal need inside him. He craved her in a way that he hadn't craved anyone before. It wasn't just about control anymore. He needed to feel her beneath him, to claim her as his own, to mark her in a way that went beyond just the physical.

He wanted to possess her, body and soul.

Ivan rubbed a hand over his face, his fingers brushing against the cut on his brow. He needed to push her away, to remind himself that she was a weakness, one he couldn't afford. But every time he thought about doing it, something stopped him. He couldn't deny the pull she had on him, both physically and emotionally. She made him feel things he had buried a long time ago—things he wasn't sure he could handle. But the desire to claim her, to make her his in every way, overwhelmed him. His body still hummed with the memory of her beneath him, the way she had moaned his name, the way her skin had felt against his.

He couldn't shake it. He needed her, wanted her, and the more he tried to push that need aside, the stronger it grew.

His thoughts shifted back to the fight at the docks. The Morozov Bratva had been testing him for weeks now, stealing arms shipments, cutting into his operations. It was clear they thought Ivan had gone soft, that losing his wife had weakened him. They were wrong. His retaliation for her death had been swift and brutal, a bloody reminder to anyone who dared cross him. But now, with the Morozovs under new leadership, they were pushing the limits again, seeing how far they could go.

Yesterday had been the tipping point. Three shipments had disappeared, and when Ivan had gone to the docks to confront his workers, one of them had been stupid enough to throw a punch. The man's blood was still fresh in Ivan's memory, his body crumpling under the force of Ivan's fists. But even as he beat the man, a part of him had felt... hollow. The violence had been cathartic, sure, but it hadn't solved the problem. It hadn't stopped the Morozovs from stealing from him, from challenging his authority.

The Morozovs had to be dealt with, and soon. Ivan had built his empire on power, on the promise that anyone who crossed him would pay with their life. The new leader of the Morozov Bratva was young, cocky, and clearly didn't understand the game he was playing. But Ivan would make sure he learned—one way or another.

And yet, even as he planned his retaliation, even as the wheels in his mind turned with strategies and tactics, his thoughts kept circling back to Katya. She was becoming a distraction, one he couldn't afford. But the more he tried to push her away, the more he found himself wanting her close. She had seen the real him, the man behind the Bratva, and instead of running, she had stayed.

Ivan stood from his desk, pacing the length of the office as his mind raced. He needed to focus, to clear his head, but Katya's presence lingered in every corner of his thoughts. She was becoming a weakness, one he couldn't shake. And in his world, weaknesses could get you killed.

But could he really push her away now? Could he go back to pretending she didn't matter, that she wasn't the one person who had managed to break through the walls he had built around himself?

Ivan's jaw tightened as he wrestled with the conflicting emotions inside him. The Morozovs needed to be dealt with. His enemies were watching, waiting for him to make a move. But as he planned his next steps, he couldn't help but feel like the stakes were higher than they had ever been.

Because now, it wasn't just his life on the line. It was Katya's too.

Ivan leaned back in his chair, the dim light of his warehouse office casting long shadows across the room. The low hum of machinery outside echoed through the walls, a reminder that while the rest of the world slept, his operations never did. But tonight, his focus wasn't on the shipments coming in and out of the docks. His mind was consumed by one thing: retaliation.

The fight at the docks had been a warning, a glimpse of the chaos that was about to unravel if he didn't act swiftly. The Morozov Bratva was pushing him, testing his boundaries in a way that hadn't happened since the early days after his wife's death. Back then, they had respected the truce he'd forged through blood and violence. But the new leader—the cocky young bastard who had taken over—was bolder, more reckless. He was eager to prove himself, and Ivan knew that allowing the

Morozovs to get away with stealing his arms shipments was only inviting more challenges.

Ivan ran his fingers over the cut on his brow, the sting bringing him back to the moment when his control had slipped. He had nearly killed the worker who dared to swing at him, and part of him wished he had finished the job. But that wasn't the solution, not now. Retaliation needed to be calculated, not fueled by blind rage. This was about more than teaching one man a lesson; this was about dismantling the Morozov Bratva piece by piece, until they were too broken to stand against him again.

The pressure on Ivan's shoulders felt heavier than it ever had before. This wasn't just about power anymore—it was about the people he cared about. His children, who had already lost their mother, relied on him. He thought of Katya, the way her presence had somehow woven its way into his life in a way he couldn't ignore. She had seen him vulnerable last night, seen the blood and the fury, but she hadn't recoiled. That scared him more than the confrontation at the docks.

If the Morozovs found out about her—if they discovered how much she meant to him—they would use her against him. He could keep her safe within his walls, but he knew how relentless his enemies were. They would exploit any weakness, and Katya and his children were becoming his biggest one.

Ivan's thoughts hardened. He couldn't allow that to happen. The retaliation needed to be swift and decisive. He would cripple their operations so thoroughly that they wouldn't have the strength to come after him or anyone close to him again. But this couldn't be like the revenge he took after his wife's death. That had been raw, fueled by rage, and though effective, it hadn't been strategic. This time, it had to be personal, precise, and devastating.

His mind worked through the possibilities, laying out the steps in meticulous detail. First, he would target the men responsible for stealing his arms shipments. They had to be dealt with quickly and brutally, making it clear that betraying him was a death sentence. There would be no second chances, no room for negotiation. It would send a message to anyone within the Morozov ranks who thought about challenging his authority again.

Next, he would strike at their financial operations. The Morozov Bratva relied on a network of alliances, shaky at best, to keep their income flowing. Ivan knew the weaknesses in their infrastructure, the delicate balance they maintained between legitimate business and illegal operations. He would dismantle it all, one piece at a time, cutting off their income streams and forcing them to rely on weaker, less reliable partnerships. Without money, they would be powerless. Without power, they would fall.

But the most important target was the new leader, Alexei Morozov. The man had been bold enough to challenge Ivan's authority, to test the limits of his patience. That couldn't go unanswered. Ivan would make an example of him, just as he had with those responsible for his wife's death. But this time, it would be different. He wouldn't kill him—not right away. Killing him would be too easy, too merciful. Instead, Ivan would break him, make him suffer the way he had suffered. He would tear down everything the Morozov leader had built, strip him of his power and leave him a hollow shell of the man he had once been.

The more Ivan thought about it, the more the plan took shape. It wasn't just about vengeance; it was about survival. The Morozovs had stolen from him for the last time, and now they would pay. Ivan could already picture it—the confusion and panic that would ripple through their ranks as he dismantled their operations, the fear that would spread as their leader struggled to maintain control. By the time Ivan was done, the Morozov Bratva would be nothing more than a memory.

The weight of the situation pressed down on him. There was no room for error. Every move had to be calculated, every strike perfectly timed. If he failed, if the Morozovs managed to retaliate before he could finish them, everything he had built could crumble. His family, his empire, even Katya—they would all be at risk. He couldn't let that happen. He wouldn't.

Ivan's thoughts drifted back to Katya again, and for a moment, the hard edge in his mind softened. She had become something unexpected in his life, something he wasn't sure he could afford, but couldn't seem to let go of. He could protect her, just as he had protected his children. But he couldn't allow her to be a weakness. If she stayed, she had to be strong enough to survive in his world, to understand the danger that came with being a part of his life.

A knock on the door pulled Ivan from his thoughts. One of his men stood at the entrance, waiting for his command.

"Is everything ready?" Ivan asked, his voice cold and steady.

The man nodded. "Yes, boss. We're waiting on your word."

Ivan stood, his decision made. "Good. Make the call. It's time to remind the Morozovs who they're dealing with."

As his man disappeared to carry out the order, Ivan felt the familiar weight of his role settle over him again. There was no room for doubt, no room for fear. The retaliation would be swift, brutal, and final. And when it was done, there would be no more testing of his limits.

Ivan would make sure of it.

Chapter 17

The morning sun filtered softly through the dining room windows, casting a warm glow over the table where Katya sat with Ivan and the children. It was a peaceful moment, one that almost felt out of place in the chaos of her mind. Kirill and Dasha, sitting on either side of her, chattered excitedly, their voices bright with energy as they recalled the story Katya had read to them the night before. Their faces were lit with enthusiasm as they pushed their drawings across the table toward Ivan, eager for his approval.

Katya smiled faintly as she watched them, though her mind was elsewhere. She couldn't help but feel the undercurrent of tension that lingered between her and Ivan, even in these quiet moments. Kirill held up a picture he had drawn of a dragon, the lines shaky but filled with the boldness of a child's imagination. Dasha, not to be outdone, presented her own drawing—a more colorful, whimsical interpretation of the same dragon, complete with wings that glittered in crayon hues.

"See, Daddy! Kat read us the story about the dragon, and this is him!" Kirill's voice was bright, his eyes flicking from the drawing to his father, waiting for a reaction.

Ivan's gaze, usually hard and unreadable, softened as he looked at his children. He took the drawings in his hands, glancing over them with a small, almost imperceptible smile. "Impressive," he said, his deep voice quieter than usual, as if trying not to disrupt the rare peace in the room. "Your dragon looks fierce, Kirill. And Dasha… yours could fly away at any moment." His words were simple, but the children beamed at his praise, their joy evident in every gesture.

Katya's heart twisted a little as she watched Ivan interact with them. There was something almost tender about the way he addressed his children, a side of him she rarely saw. It was moments like this that confused her the most. She knew what he was, the world he belonged to, the violence and control that defined his life. And yet, when he was with Kirill and Dasha, there was a warmth to him that was impossible to ignore. It made her question everything.

Her gaze shifted to Ivan, who was now looking at her. His dark eyes met hers, and for a moment, the rest of the room seemed to fade. A spark ignited between them, a silent pull that Katya had felt too many times to deny. The memories of their intimacy from nights before flashed in her mind—the way his touch had ignited her skin, the way his dominance had both frightened and excited her. She knew he was dangerous, that she should be wary of him, but in that moment, all she could feel was the raw, undeniable attraction that simmered beneath the surface.

Her pulse quickened, and she looked away, trying to focus on the children's laughter as they continued talking about their dragons. But the damage was done. The heat of Ivan's gaze lingered on her skin like a brand, impossible to ignore. She couldn't help the way he made her feel—both vulnerable and powerful in his presence. It was a dangerous combination, and yet, it was one she craved more than she wanted to admit.

As Kirill and Dasha finished showing off their drawings, Katya stood from the table, ready to usher them into the playroom. She needed to distance herself from Ivan, to shake off the growing tension that hung in the air between them. But as she gathered the plates and pushed in her chair, Ivan's voice stopped her in her tracks.

"Katya."

She froze, her breath catching in her throat, before turning to face him. His tone wasn't commanding, but it held an authority that told her this wasn't a casual remark.

"Go on ahead to the playroom," she told the children softly, brushing a hand over Kirill's hair. They obeyed, running off with their pictures in hand, leaving Katya and Ivan alone in the dining room.

Ivan stood, his broad frame casting a shadow across the table as he stepped toward her. His eyes were locked on hers, dark and intense, and for a moment, she felt a flicker of nervousness tighten in her chest.

"We're having dinner tonight," Ivan said, his voice low but firm. There was no question in his statement, no room for negotiation. "After the children are in bed."

Katya blinked, caught off guard by his directness. "Dinner?" she echoed, unsure of what to say. It wasn't a request; it was a decision, one that had already been made for her.

"Sofia will watch the children," he added, his gaze unwavering. He reached into his jacket pocket, pulling out a small wad of bills and handing it to her. "Buy a dress. Something appropriate."

The money felt heavy in her hand, not because of its physical weight, but because of the meaning behind it. Ivan wasn't asking if she wanted to go to dinner with him—he was telling her. And yet, despite the lack of choice in the matter, a strange flutter of excitement stirred in her chest.

Katya's mind raced with questions, her thoughts tumbling over one another in a whirlwind of confusion. What did this dinner mean? Was it just another way for him to exert his control over her, or was there something more? Should she say no?

Could she say no? The truth was, she didn't know if she wanted to refuse. The thought of being alone with Ivan, of feeling the weight of his gaze on her in that quiet, intimate setting, made her stomach twist in both anticipation and anxiety.

She wanted to resist, to remind herself that Ivan was a dangerous man, one who operated in a world of violence and power. But every time she thought about walking away, that spark between them pulled her back in. His touch, his dominance, the way he made her feel like she belonged to him—it was intoxicating. And now, with the prospect of this dinner looming, she couldn't help but wonder if she wanted to be claimed by him once again.

"I'll be ready," Katya said softly, her voice betraying the nerves that fluttered in her chest.

Ivan gave her a slow nod, his eyes lingering on her for a moment longer before he turned and walked away, leaving her standing alone in the dining room, clutching the money in her hand.

As soon as he was gone, Katya exhaled, her heart still racing. What had she just agreed to? She wasn't sure if she was more nervous about the dinner itself or about what it meant for her relationship with Ivan. Was this just another part of his control over her, or was there something more beneath the surface? The questions weighed heavily on her mind as she headed toward the playroom to join the children, the flutter of anticipation still swirling in her chest.

Ivan had told her to buy a dress, and as the afternoon stretched ahead of her, she couldn't shake the feeling that tonight would change something between them. What, exactly, she wasn't sure—but she couldn't deny the excitement that came with the uncertainty.

Katya had never felt this way before, and the truth was, as much as it scared her, she couldn't wait to see what would happen next.

That afternoon, with the children napping peacefully upstairs, Katya found herself standing at the edge of a decision she hadn't anticipated. Ivan's words from breakfast still lingered in her mind—"Buy a dress." Not a question, not a suggestion, but an instruction. His control over her life was undeniable, yet there was something in the way he had spoken to her that stirred an unfamiliar blend of anxiety and excitement. She had asked Sofia to keep an eye on the children and told the driver where to take her, but the knot of emotions twisting inside her only tightened as she slid into the back seat of the sleek, black car.

As the car glided through the streets, Katya's thoughts were a mess of confusion and questions. What did this dinner mean? Ivan hadn't asked her—he had told her. Could she have said no? She doubted it. The truth was, part of her didn't want to say no, but another part of her, the part that craved independence, bristled at the way he assumed she would comply. She wanted to resist, to remind herself of the danger he represented, but there was also a pull, something irresistible about the way he had commanded her presence. It was intoxicating. Terrifying. She wondered if it was foolish to want him the way she did, knowing the world he came from, the violence that surrounded him like a storm.

As the car neared the high-end boutique Sofia had instructed the driver to take her, Katya's heart beat faster. The streets outside were lined with expensive shops and people who seemed a world apart from her. The thought of walking into one of these boutiques, a place where the wealthy came to spend thousands of dollars on a single dress, made her feel like an imposter. She wasn't used to this life—luxury was foreign to her, and even though Ivan had given her the money to buy whatever she wanted, she couldn't shake the feeling of unease creeping into her chest.

But there was another feeling simmering beneath the nerves. A thrill. The idea of Ivan seeing her in a dress like the ones she imagined hung inside the boutique stirred something deep inside her, a sense of excitement that sent a shiver through her. The way he looked at her, the way his eyes always lingered on her body, made her skin prickle with desire. She tried to push the thought away, but it kept coming back—his hands on her, his lips against her skin, the way he made her feel both vulnerable and powerful at the same time.

When the driver opened the door for her, Katya stepped out, her feet carrying her toward the entrance of the boutique even as her mind warred with itself. Inside, the store was sleek and modern, filled with racks of beautiful, expensive dresses that shimmered under the soft lighting. The atmosphere was elegant, almost intimidating, and for a moment, she hesitated. She wasn't sure if she belonged here. But then she reminded herself—this was Ivan's world now. Whether she liked it or not, she had been thrust into it.

A saleswoman approached her, all polished smiles and professional charm, asking if she needed assistance. Katya politely declined, preferring to browse alone. She drifted through the racks, her fingers brushing over the soft fabrics, the delicate lace, and the intricate beading of the dresses. Each one was more beautiful than the last, but as she looked at them, her mind wandered back to Ivan. How would he react when he saw her tonight? Would he like what she chose? Would he think she looked beautiful?

The thought made her stomach flip. A part of her was frustrated by the fact that she cared so much about what he thought. Why did it matter so much to her? She had never been the type of woman who sought a man's approval, especially not one like Ivan, a man who represented everything she should despise. And yet, here she was, shopping for a dress with the sole purpose of pleasing him.

Her eyes lingered on a soft, pale dress—elegant, conservative, something she might have chosen in another life. It was beautiful, yes, but it didn't stir anything inside her. It didn't match the way she felt right now—the turmoil, the desire, the confusion that had been building inside her since Ivan had walked into her life. She wanted something more, something bold, something that would make her feel powerful.

As she moved deeper into the store, her gaze landed on a dress that made her breath catch in her throat. It was maroon, rich and dark, with a low neckline that dipped just enough to be daring. A slit ran up the thigh, exposing just the right amount of skin, and the way it was cut promised to hug every curve of her body. Katya could already picture it—the way the fabric would cling to her, the way Ivan's eyes would darken when he saw her in it. She reached out, running her fingers over the smooth fabric, and a shiver ran through her.

This was it. This was the dress.

There was a moment of hesitation as she considered what it meant to choose something like this. It was bold, almost too bold for her, but that was the point, wasn't it? She wanted to make a statement. She wanted to feel powerful, to have some sense of control in a situation where control was always just out of her reach. And if the dress made Ivan want her even more… well, that was something she couldn't deny wanting herself.

In the dressing room, Katya slipped the dress over her body, the maroon fabric sliding against her skin like silk. She caught a glimpse of herself in the mirror and froze. She barely recognized the woman staring back at her. The dress fit her like a glove, hugging her curves, the deep neckline revealing more than she was used to, but somehow, she didn't feel exposed. She felt… powerful. Sexy. Desirable. The slit up her thigh added just the right amount of edge, and the black heels she had chosen to match only heightened the effect.

Her heart raced as she imagined Ivan's reaction. She could already feel the intensity of his gaze, the way his eyes would travel over her body, hungry and possessive. A part of her wanted to be claimed by him, to feel his hands on her, his body pressing against hers. She had never felt this way before, not with anyone. The pull he had on her was undeniable, both physically and emotionally. The way he made her feel was intoxicating, and no matter how hard she tried, she couldn't shake the desire that simmered inside her whenever he was near.

Katya turned in front of the mirror, admiring the way the dress moved with her, the way it accentuated every curve. She had never worn anything like this before, never allowed herself to indulge in something so luxurious, so decadent. But tonight, she was stepping into a different world, one where she wanted to feel as powerful as the man who had pulled her into it.

As she paid for the dress and slipped back into the waiting car, Katya's mind raced with a whirlwind of emotions. What did this dinner mean? She didn't know what Ivan expected from her tonight, but she couldn't deny the excitement that fluttered in her chest. The nerves were still there, a constant hum beneath her skin, but there was something else now, too. Anticipation.

The car ride back to the house felt like a blur, her thoughts tangled between the fear of what Ivan's intentions might be and the undeniable pull she felt toward him. Every glance he gave her, every touch, had left her breathless, craving more despite the danger it represented. There was no denying that something between them had shifted, something that made her heart race in a way it never had before.

The sleek black car pulled up to the estate, and Katya stepped out, her fingers clutching the handles of the boutique bag tightly. She could feel the weight of the evening ahead pressing down on her, but as much as her mind told her to be cautious, the flutter of excitement in her chest only grew stronger. Tonight would be different. She could feel it.

Making her way through the quiet halls of the house, she passed the playroom where the children were still napping, the sound of their soft breaths barely audible through the door. A pang of guilt tugged at her heart—how could she be so consumed by her feelings for a man as dangerous as Ivan when the children needed her?

But even as the thought crossed her mind, she couldn't help but feel the draw, the deep, magnetic pull that kept her tethered to him. She reached her room, closing the door behind her with a soft click. As she set the dress down on the bed and began to unpack her purchase, the weight of the evening ahead began to settle in her chest.

Katya stood in front of the mirror, her heart pounding in her chest as she looked at her reflection. The maroon dress she had chosen earlier in the day clung to her curves in a way that made her feel both empowered and vulnerable. The deep neckline exposed just enough skin to be daring, while the slit up her thigh added an edge that made her feel bold. The black heels she wore added height, making her legs look long and elegant, completing the look that was both sexy and seductive. She barely recognized herself—the woman staring back at her was far removed from the Katya she used to be.

There was a nervous energy bubbling inside her, swirling in her stomach like butterflies, but they were sharper, more intense. Her fingers trembled slightly as she applied the finishing touches of makeup. Just enough to enhance her natural beauty, to make her eyes stand out, her lips more alluring. She didn't want to overdo it—she wanted to feel like herself, even if tonight felt like stepping into an entirely different world. The world Ivan had pulled her into, one where she was constantly torn between fear and desire, between wanting to resist and wanting to surrender.

Her gaze lingered in the mirror as she smoothed the fabric of her dress. She felt sexy, more so than she ever had before, but the anxiety lurking beneath the surface wouldn't go away. What did this night mean? Was this just another way for Ivan to control her, to remind her that her life was in his hands? Or was there something more, something deeper between them that she couldn't yet understand?

The memories of their nights together flooded her mind—the way his hands moved over her body, the way he looked at her as though he could see into her very soul. It wasn't just lust. It couldn't be.

There was a connection between them that went beyond the physical, something she hadn't expected, something she wasn't ready to admit to herself. She felt it in the way he touched her, the way he spoke to her, the way his dark, piercing eyes always found hers across a room. And now, tonight, she would be alone with him again.

Her heart raced as she thought about the last time she had been with him. The intensity of their passion, the way he made her feel so alive, so vulnerable, so desired. But beneath that desire, there was something more—a growing emotional attachment that terrified her. She wasn't supposed to care for him. He was dangerous, violent, a man whose world was built on blood and power. She should be running as far away from him as possible, yet she found herself being pulled closer to him with each passing day.

As she stepped out of the room and made her way through the quiet house, the tension only grew. The sound of her heels clicking against the floor echoed in the halls, a reminder of the path she was walking down. She couldn't stop thinking about Ivan—his power, his dominance, the way he had looked at her that morning at breakfast. The memory of his eyes locking with hers had sent a jolt through her, awakening feelings she wasn't sure she was ready to confront.

The pull he had over her wasn't just physical, though that part of it was undeniable. She craved the way his hands felt on her skin, the way his body pressed against hers, the heat and intensity of his touch. But there was more to it now. She wasn't just drawn to his body—she was starting to care about him, about the man beneath the ruthless exterior. The man who had opened up to her about his wife, who had let her see a glimpse of the vulnerability he kept hidden from the world. It scared her how much that glimpse had affected her, how much she wanted to see more of that side of him, even as she feared what it would mean for her own heart.

As she reached his study door, Katya paused, her hand hovering over the handle. She took another breath, trying to steady the tremor in her fingers. What was she walking into tonight? Was this just another power move from Ivan, a reminder of his control over her, or was there something deeper at play? The thought of it made her heart race even faster.

Finally, she opened the door and stepped inside.

The room was dimly lit, casting warm shadows across the walls. Ivan stood near his desk, his back to her at first, but the moment the door clicked shut behind her, he turned. The air between them shifted instantly. His gaze swept over her, taking in every curve, every detail of her dress. The intensity of his eyes made her feel both exposed and powerful, as if he could see right through the maroon fabric to the desire simmering just beneath her skin.

For a long moment, he didn't say anything. He simply looked at her, his dark eyes moving slowly, deliberately, as though he was savoring the sight of her. It was both thrilling and unnerving, the way his attention seemed to devour her, and despite her nerves, Katya felt a rush of heat crawl up her neck.

When Ivan finally spoke, his voice was low, filled with an unmistakable appreciation. "You look beautiful."

The words, simple as they were, sent a shiver down her spine. His tone was soft, yet there was something undeniably possessive in the way he said it, as though she belonged to him. The realization made her pulse quicken, and she couldn't help the way her body responded to his praise. She had spent so much time resenting his control, his dominance, and yet now, standing in front of him in that dress, she felt a sense of pride in how he looked at her. She felt desired, wanted in a way she had never been before.

Katya's throat was dry, and she swallowed, trying to find her voice. "Thank you," she managed, though her words felt inadequate under the weight of his gaze.

Ivan stepped forward, closing the distance between them with a slow, deliberate pace. His hand reached out, brushing a stray lock of hair behind her ear, and the brief contact sent a spark of electricity through her. His fingers lingered for a second longer than necessary, grazing her cheek before dropping to his side.

"We should go," he said, his voice still low, almost a whisper. "The reservation's waiting."

He guided her out of the study, his hand resting lightly on the small of her back. The touch was possessive but gentle, and it made her skin tingle as they walked toward the door. Each step she took beside him only heightened the tension between them, a quiet storm building with every passing second. There was an undeniable pull in the way he touched her, the way he led her with such quiet confidence, as if this night had been planned long before she'd even known about it.

The sleek black car was already waiting outside. Ivan opened the door for her, and she slid inside, the leather seat cool against her skin. As he joined her, the space in the car felt smaller, more intimate. The scent of him—dark, masculine—lingered in the air between them, and Katya found herself acutely aware of every move he made.

The car pulled away from the house, and the silence between them was thick with anticipation. Ivan's hand rested casually on the console between them at first, but as the city lights flickered past, his fingers brushed her thigh. It was a light, almost incidental touch, but it sent a wave of heat surging through her body. Katya's breath hitched, and she shifted slightly in her seat, trying to suppress the growing tension that was building inside her.

But Ivan seemed to notice everything. His hand lingered, not moving further but not pulling away either. It was as if he was testing her, waiting to see how she would react, and the awareness of his touch only made the situation more intense.

Katya's heart raced as the seconds stretched into minutes, the silence between them electric. She could feel the heat radiating off him, the quiet power that always seemed to surround him, and the realization hit her again—this man had a hold on her that went far beyond physical desire. There was something about the way he looked at her, the way he touched her, that made her feel like she was teetering on the edge of something dangerous, something she might not be able to come back from.

Her eyes flickered to his hand on her thigh, her pulse quickening with every gentle brush of his fingers. It wasn't fair, the effect he had on her. She hated the way he made her feel so out of control, yet she craved it at the same time. The tension was unbearable, and every second of his touch felt like a promise, one that neither of them had spoken aloud yet.

As the car rolled to a stop outside the restaurant, Ivan's hand finally withdrew, leaving her skin tingling in its absence. Katya exhaled slowly, trying to steady herself as Ivan stepped out and rounded the car to open her door. His hand was there again, guiding her out with the same possessive touch that sent a thrill through her.

They walked into the restaurant together, his hand never leaving her back, and Katya couldn't help but feel the weight of his presence beside her. Tonight was different. She could feel it in the air, in the way he looked at her, and in the way her body reacted to every small gesture he made.

And as much as it scared her, Katya couldn't deny that she wanted to see where this night would lead.

Chapter 18

The restaurant Ivan chose exuded sophistication and exclusivity, a place where wealth and power were expected rather than flaunted. As they stepped inside, Katya immediately noticed the way the staff reacted to Ivan's presence. The maître d' greeted him with a quiet respect, his posture straightening as he led them to a secluded table near the back of the dimly lit room. The other patrons, a mix of affluent couples and businessmen, cast discreet glances their way, acknowledging Ivan without words. His importance was clear in the way they were treated—ushered in without delay, a prime table already prepared, and the soft clink of fine glassware filling the air.

The lighting was low, casting a warm, intimate glow over their table. It felt as if the rest of the restaurant didn't exist, as if this night was designed just for them. Katya's heart raced, not just from the setting but from the man sitting across from her. Ivan looked effortlessly powerful, his dark suit perfectly tailored to his broad shoulders, and his presence filled the small space between them.

As they settled into their seats, Ivan took control of the evening immediately. Without glancing at a menu, he ordered for them both. Normally, such a move would have irritated Katya, a reminder of how little control she had in this arrangement. But tonight, it felt different. The way he spoke to the waiter, his deep voice smooth and commanding, sent a shiver down her spine. She was beginning to understand that it wasn't just about power or dominance with Ivan—it was about precision, about knowing exactly what he wanted and taking it. And tonight, it seemed, what he wanted was her.

The small talk began harmlessly enough. Ivan asked about the children, and Katya told him about their day at the park, how Kirill and Dasha had spent hours running and laughing. He listened intently, nodding at the right moments, but she could tell his mind was elsewhere. His gaze never left her face, and with every passing second, the tension between them grew.

The food arrived quickly—an array of delicate dishes that Katya barely noticed as they were set in front of her. Her appetite, once so sharp, was dulled by the knot of emotions swirling in her stomach. She picked at the plate in front of her, offering Ivan faint smiles in response to his questions, but her mind was caught in a whirlwind. Why had he brought her here? What was the purpose of this dinner?

As if sensing her hesitation, Ivan leaned back in his chair, his intense gaze softening slightly. "You seem distracted," he said, his voice low and calm, but with an undertone of curiosity.

Katya blinked, her thoughts snapping back to the present. "No, I just... I'm not used to this," she admitted, gesturing vaguely around the elegant room. "It's a lot."

Ivan tilted his head slightly, considering her words. "It's just dinner," he said, though the way he said it made it clear this was no ordinary dinner. There was something unspoken between them, something neither of them had acknowledged yet.

"I know," Katya said, but her voice faltered. She didn't know how to put into words the storm inside her, the confusion, the desire, the fear. She had spent so much time trying to keep her distance from Ivan, both emotionally and physically, but tonight, under the soft glow of the restaurant's lights, it felt impossible to hold back.

The conversation drifted again, small talk about the wine, the restaurant, but Katya could feel the weight of Ivan's gaze on her. He was waiting, watching, and it made her chest tighten with a mixture of anticipation and anxiety.

After a long pause, Ivan asked, "Tell me about your childhood." His tone was casual, but the question hit her like a blow.

Katya's breath caught in her throat. It wasn't a subject she talked about often, especially not with someone like Ivan. Her childhood was a maze of memories she tried to avoid—memories of her mother's absence, of her father's coldness. But there was something about the way Ivan asked that made her want to share. Maybe it was the intimacy of the evening, or maybe it was the way he looked at her, as if he genuinely wanted to know.

For a moment, she hesitated. Then, before she could stop herself, the words began to spill out.

"I didn't really have much of a childhood," Katya began, her voice quieter now, more tentative. "My mother left when I was young. I barely remember her, just fragments here and there. My father... he was never really the warm, loving type. I guess you could say he was more interested in work, in power, than in being a father."

She glanced down at her hands, her fingers nervously tracing the edge of her napkin. The memories of her father's coldness, the way he had distanced himself from her after her mother left, still stung after all these years. "It was lonely," she admitted, her voice soft but steady. "I always felt like I was a burden to him. He didn't know what to do with a daughter."

The words hung in the air between them, raw and vulnerable. Katya wasn't sure why she was telling Ivan all of this. She had never planned to open up to him about her past, yet here she was, revealing parts of herself she had buried long ago. She wasn't sure what to expect from him in return—dismissal, perhaps, or maybe indifference.

But Ivan surprised her.

Without a word, he reached across the table, his large hand covering hers. The warmth of his touch sent a shock through her system, a sudden burst of electricity that left her breathless. His thumb brushed lightly over her skin, a gesture so simple yet so intimate, it made her chest tighten with something she couldn't quite name.

Katya looked up at him, her eyes meeting his. For the first time that evening, she saw something in Ivan's gaze that went beyond the usual intensity. There was a softness there, a quiet understanding that caught her off guard. He wasn't just listening—he was seeing her, in a way she hadn't expected.

When Ivan finally spoke, his voice was lower, rougher than before, laced with an edge of contempt. "Your father," he said, his tone dark, "is a despicable man. Selfish. Weak." His eyes darkened as he continued, his voice now tinged with anger. "A man who wastes other people's money, who uses his own daughter to repay his debts... has no honor."

The harshness of his words took her by surprise, but there was a fierce protectiveness beneath them that stirred something in her. She felt the anger behind his words, but it wasn't directed at her—it was aimed at the man who had shaped her

childhood, the man who had left her feeling like a
burden.

"He was never a father to you," Ivan continued, his
hand tightening around hers. "A man like that
doesn't deserve the title. Family isn't something you
use or discard. It's something you protect, with
everything you have. Even with your life."

Katya's heart skipped a beat at his words. There
was a fire in Ivan's eyes now, a passion that made
her chest tighten with emotion. She had never
heard anyone speak with such conviction, and for
the first time, she realized that Ivan's world—the
one she feared—was built on a twisted but deeply
ingrained sense of loyalty and protection.

Ivan leaned in closer, his gaze piercing. "You
deserved better than him. You deserve better now."

His words hit her with a force she wasn't prepared
for. Her throat tightened, and for a moment, she
couldn't speak. No one had ever said that to her
before—not in the way Ivan had just said it, with
such certainty, as if it were a simple fact. She
hadn't expected Ivan to care about her past, about
the wounds her father had left behind, but the
intensity in his voice and the way he gripped her
hand made it clear that he did.

Katya swallowed hard, trying to steady herself.
"Maybe," she whispered. "But it doesn't matter
now."

Ivan's grip on her hand tightened slightly, his eyes never leaving hers. "It does matter," he said firmly. "It matters because it shaped you. And I think..." He paused, as if choosing his words carefully. "I think you're stronger because of it. But don't ever think you owe him anything. You owe him nothing."

His words were like a balm to the wounds she had carried for years. In that moment, Katya felt seen in a way she never had before. She had always been the girl left behind, the daughter used as a pawn in her father's games. But now, across the table from Ivan, she felt something different—something new.

Ivan wasn't just telling her what she wanted to hear. His words carried weight, as if he were making a promise. She knew how seriously Ivan took loyalty, how fiercely he protected what he saw as his. And in that moment, she realized that, in some way, he was including her in that. She wasn't just a pawn to him, a woman to be used to repay a debt. She was more.

"I protect what's mine, Katya," he said quietly, his voice softening but his tone no less intense. "With everything I have."

The warmth of his hand on hers, the quiet strength in his voice, made her heart swell. And for the first time, Katya didn't feel like she had to carry the weight of her past alone. Ivan's words, his promise of protection, wrapped around her like a shield, and she felt herself leaning into it, letting it soothe the raw edges of her emotions.

All she knew was that, in that moment, sitting across from Ivan in this quiet, intimate restaurant, she felt more connected to him than she ever had before.

And that both terrified and thrilled her.

As the evening came to a close, Ivan signaled the waiter and paid without hesitation, a silent gesture of control that Katya had come to expect. But tonight, there was something different about it. He wasn't just asserting his dominance; there was an intimacy in the way he led her out of the restaurant, his hand resting lightly on the small of her back as they stepped into the cool night air. The city buzzed around them, but for Katya, it felt as though they were in their own world, suspended in a moment that didn't belong to anyone but them.

The valet pulled Ivan's sleek car to the curb, and as he opened the door for her, their eyes met again, that same intensity sparking between them. Katya slid into the passenger seat, her pulse quickening, her breath catching as Ivan joined her in the car.

The drive home felt like a slow build, a pressure cooker of tension that hovered between them, thickening the air in the confined space of the car. The city lights outside flickered in the distance, but Katya barely registered them. Her senses were entirely focused on the man beside her—on Ivan and the way his presence seemed to dominate the car just as much as he dominated everything else in his life.

His hand rested lightly on her thigh, fingers splayed in a way that seemed casual, yet anything but. Every so often, his fingers brushed against the smooth fabric of her maroon dress, sending jolts of electricity through her skin. It was a simple touch, but the way her body responded felt anything but simple. Her heart pounded against her ribs, each thump echoing in her ears, drowning out the soft hum of the car engine.

She couldn't stop thinking about the dinner they'd just shared—the way Ivan had looked at her, the intensity in his eyes when he'd taken her hand across the table. The way he had spoken about her father with such disdain, yet still managed to make her feel seen, protected. It had been overwhelming in the best possible way, stirring feelings in her that she hadn't expected. His touch had anchored her in that moment, and now it was pulling her deeper into something she wasn't sure she could escape from.

Katya's internal struggle was growing by the second. She knew who Ivan was. She knew the kind of world he came from, the darkness that surrounded him at every turn. His life was steeped in violence and power plays, in a constant battle for control that could turn deadly at any moment. It terrified her—had terrified her since the moment she first learned of his involvement in the Bratva. And yet, despite that fear, she couldn't stop wanting him.

There was something about the way he made her feel, the way he looked at her like he owned her, body and soul. It was more than just desire—it was a connection, a tether that she couldn't sever even if she wanted to. His dominance excited her in ways she had never known before, awakened parts of her that she hadn't even realized existed. But now, after tonight, it was more than that. He had opened up to her, shown her a vulnerability that few—if any—ever saw. And that vulnerability made her feel closer to him than she'd ever been to anyone before.

As Ivan's hand drifted slightly higher up her thigh, the heat between them ignited into a slow burn. Her breath hitched in her throat, her pulse quickening as her body reacted to his touch. He was teasing her, she knew it, and yet she couldn't bring herself to pull away. She didn't want to. Every brush of his fingers against her skin sent waves of anticipation through her, coiling low in her belly.

She tried to focus on the world outside the car, on the lights and the dark streets they were driving through, but it was no use. The only thing she could think about was Ivan—how close he was, how his hand was creeping higher, inch by inch, and how much she wanted him. Her legs shifted instinctively, parting slightly beneath the weight of his touch, inviting him to explore further. Her mind whirled with thoughts—of fear, of desire, of the fact that she was falling for a man who was dangerous in every possible way. But none of it mattered, not in this moment.

As his hand moved further up her thigh, his fingers brushed the edge of her panties, teasing the sensitive skin just beneath the hem. Katya's breath caught in her throat, her lips parting as a soft gasp escaped her. She was already wet, her body betraying her desire for him. Ivan knew exactly what he was doing to her, and the realization only heightened the need building inside her.

"You like this," he growled, his voice rough and low, the sound sending a shiver down her spine.

She couldn't find the words to respond, but the moan that slipped from her lips told him everything he needed to know. His fingers dipped beneath the fabric of her panties, finding her slick and ready for him. The moment his fingers made contact with her wet folds, her hips shifted instinctively, pushing into his hand, craving more.

Ivan's fingers expertly circled her clit, rubbing in slow, deliberate strokes that made her body tremble. Katya's hand gripped the edge of the seat, her knuckles turning white as she fought to keep control of herself. But it was no use. Ivan had complete control—over her body, her mind, and the desire that was rapidly spiraling out of control.

"Don't stop," she whispered, her voice shaky, barely audible.

But Ivan wasn't done teasing her. He slipped a finger inside her, the sensation making her eyes flutter shut as a wave of pleasure washed over her. He alternated between thrusting his finger inside her and circling her clit, keeping her on the edge of release but never quite letting her fall over. It was maddening, the way he toyed with her body, bringing her so close to climax only to pull back at the last moment.

Katya's head fell back against the seat, her breath coming in short, sharp bursts as she fought to hold on. But when Ivan added a second finger, thrusting deeper, her control shattered. The pleasure was too much, too intense, and she couldn't stop herself from crying out, her body arching off the seat as she came undone in his hand.

Her hand gripped his arm tightly, her nails digging into his skin as her orgasm ripped through her, wave after wave of pleasure leaving her trembling in its wake. Ivan didn't stop, not until he had wrung every last bit of release from her, his fingers still moving inside her as her body clenched around him.

Only then did he pull his hand away, his fingers glistening with her arousal. He didn't say a word as he brought the car to a stop in the driveway of his estate, but the look in his eyes told her everything. They weren't done. Not even close.

Katya's breath was still shaky as Ivan climbed out of the car and came around to her side. He opened the door and extended his hand to her, his grip firm as he helped her out of the car. His expression was dark, filled with a hunger that sent a thrill of anticipation racing through her.

"We're not done yet," he said, his voice low and commanding, the words sending another pulse of heat through her.

Katya didn't respond, but the look in her eyes said it all. She wasn't done either.

As they walked toward the house, his hand still firmly on her back, she felt the tension building between them once again, hotter and heavier than before. And as much as her mind was still conflicted, her body already knew what it wanted.

Tonight wasn't over.

Chapter 19

Ivan's hand gripped hers as he led her through the dimly lit halls of the house, the only sound between them the soft shuffle of their footsteps and the distant ticking of a clock somewhere in the vast estate. The silence between them wasn't uncomfortable—it was charged, filled with an unspoken tension that seemed to thicken the air around them. Every step they took toward his bedroom sent a surge of anticipation through Katya's body, her skin tingling from the memory of what had just happened in the car.

She could still feel the heat of his hand on her thigh, the way his fingers had teased her until she was trembling, lost in the throes of pleasure. But it wasn't just the physical touch that lingered; it was the emotional intensity of the evening. Dinner had been more than just a meal—it had been a moment of connection, a turning point that had shifted something between them. She could still feel the weight of his hand on hers, the way he had looked at her when she opened up about her past, his quiet understanding that had shaken her more than she expected.

As they walked, her mind raced with everything that had transpired. Ivan wasn't supposed to be the man who made her feel this way. He was dangerous, controlling, a man who existed in a world she wanted no part of. And yet, every time she was with him, she felt a pull she couldn't resist. The possessiveness in his gaze, the way he claimed her body with such raw intensity, made her feel vulnerable, but also wanted—desired in a way that went beyond the physical.

She had never experienced anything like this before. Not just the raw passion, but the emotional depth that was beginning to surface between them. It scared her, how much she craved him—not just his touch, but the way he made her feel seen. She had spent years building walls around herself, walls that had been necessary to survive in her father's cold, detached world. But with Ivan, those walls were crumbling. Piece by piece, he was breaking through, and she wasn't sure if she wanted to stop him.

Katya glanced at Ivan from the corner of her eye as they ascended the staircase, his tall, imposing figure moving with a quiet confidence. His grip on her hand was firm but not harsh, and that small gesture sent another wave of heat through her. She still felt the aftershocks of her orgasm humming through her body, her pulse racing as they approached his bedroom. The anticipation was building, making her heart pound in her chest. She knew what was coming, but tonight felt different. There was a new energy between them, something that went beyond their usual encounters. It wasn't just about lust tonight; it was about connection.

Her heart fluttered as they reached the top of the stairs. Ivan paused for a moment at the door, his back to her as he reached for the handle. Katya's breath caught in her throat. There was a brief moment where time seemed to stand still, the tension thickening between them, and she wondered if he felt it too—this shift, this deepening of whatever it was that existed between them.

She wasn't sure when it had happened, but somewhere along the way, things had changed. What had started as a way for her to pay off her father's debt had transformed into something else entirely. She didn't want to admit it, but she was starting to care for him. Despite the danger, despite the darkness that clung to his world, Ivan was getting under her skin in ways she couldn't control.

Katya's breath quickened as Ivan turned the handle, pushing the door open and leading her into the bedroom. The room was dimly lit, the soft glow from the bedside lamps casting a warm, intimate light over the space. Everything felt heightened—her senses, her emotions, the anticipation building inside her like a fire she couldn't put out.

Ivan closed the door behind them, the soft click of the latch echoing in the quiet room. He still hadn't said a word, but the silence between them was filled with so much—desire, vulnerability, and something unspoken that neither of them seemed ready to acknowledge.

Her pulse quickened as he turned to face her, his dark eyes locking onto hers with an intensity that made her stomach flip. The room felt suddenly smaller, the air thicker, and all Katya could think about was the way he had looked at her tonight, the way his touch had sent sparks through her body, and the way she wanted more of him—more than she ever thought possible.

He stepped closer, his hand still holding hers, and Katya's breath hitched in her throat. Her body was humming with anticipation, her skin tingling with the memory of his touch, but it was the look in his eyes that captivated her. It was possessive, yes, but there was something else—something deeper that she couldn't quite place. Vulnerability? Perhaps. But it was enough to send her heart racing all over again.

They stood there for a moment, the space between them narrowing, and Katya could feel her resolve crumbling. She had told herself to keep her distance, to protect herself from getting too close. But standing here now, with Ivan's dark gaze locked onto hers, she knew it was already too late.

He reached up with his free hand, brushing a strand of hair away from her face, his touch sending shivers down her spine. His fingers lingered on her skin, tracing the line of her jaw, and Katya felt her knees weaken beneath the weight of his attention. Every nerve in her body was on high alert, every breath she took filled with the scent of him, the nearness of him.

"Katya," he murmured, his voice low and rough, sending a tremor through her chest.

Her name on his lips was enough to undo her completely. She closed her eyes for a moment, letting the sound of his voice wash over her, before opening them again to find him still watching her, his gaze dark with desire.

Without another word, Ivan took her hand once more and led her further into the room. He stopped in the center of the room and turned to face her, his expression unreadable but his eyes dark with desire. His gaze swept over her, lingering on her face, her body, making her feel both exposed and powerful at the same time. Katya swallowed hard, her throat dry, as she stood before him. She knew what was coming next. She could feel it in the way his eyes burned into her, could sense it in the tension that crackled between them.

As the silence stretched on, Katya's mind raced. She thought about everything that had happened that night, about the way Ivan had made her feel during dinner, the unexpected tenderness he had shown her when he touched her hand and listened to her speak about her past. She thought about the way his fingers had teased her in the car, the way her body had responded to him so easily, so completely. But more than anything, she thought about the shift that had happened between them. Tonight wasn't just another night of passion. There was something deeper here, something unspoken that neither of them had acknowledged yet.

Her heart hammered in her chest as she tried to process the flood of emotions swirling inside her. She wasn't just drawn to Ivan physically anymore—though the physical desire was undeniable. There was something more now. The way he had opened up to her, shared pieces of himself that he had never revealed before, had stirred something inside her, something she hadn't expected. She wasn't sure when it had happened, but somewhere along the way, she had started to care for him. And that terrified her.

Could she really be falling for a man like Ivan? A man whose world was steeped in violence, in power, in control? She had spent so long trying to distance herself from him, to remind herself that this was all temporary, that she was here to repay her father's debt and nothing more. But as she stood in front of him now, she realized how futile that had been. Ivan had gotten under her skin in ways she hadn't anticipated, and now, there was no turning back.

Ivan's voice, low and commanding, broke through her thoughts. "Undress."

It wasn't a question. It was an order. His tone was laced with hunger, and it sent a shiver down her spine. He sat down in a large armchair across the room, his posture relaxed but filled with authority. He leaned back, spreading his legs slightly, his eyes never leaving hers. The weight of his command settled over her, making her pulse race even faster. For a moment, she hesitated, the gravity of the moment pressing down on her. This wasn't just about undressing—it was about surrender, about giving herself over to him completely.

But then, as the silence stretched between them, Katya found herself moving. Slowly, almost deliberately, she reached for the straps of her dress, slipping them off her shoulders. The fabric fell in a soft whisper, pooling at her feet. She stood there in her bra and panties for a moment, feeling the heat of Ivan's gaze on her, feeling the intensity of his desire wash over her like a wave. It made her feel vulnerable, but at the same time, it made her feel powerful. She could see it in his eyes—the way he looked at her, the way he wanted her. It was intoxicating.

With trembling fingers, she unclasped her bra and let it fall to the floor. Then she slipped her panties down, stepping out of them until she was completely bare before him. The cool air brushed against her skin, but it was the heat in Ivan's gaze that made her body flush with warmth, her nipples harden. She stood there, exposed in every way, her heart pounding as she waited for his reaction.

Ivan's eyes raked over her body, slow and deliberate, taking in every inch of her. There was something primal in the way he looked at her, something possessive that made her breath catch in her throat. But there was also something else, something deeper, as though he was seeing more than just her body—he was seeing her, all of her.

"Turn," he said, his voice rough with desire.

Katya's pulse quickened as she obeyed, turning slowly in a full circle, letting him take in every angle, every curve. She could feel his eyes on her, could feel the intensity of his gaze as it swept over her body. When she completed the turn, facing him once more, Ivan's expression softened slightly, just enough for her to catch a glimpse of something raw and real beneath the surface.

"You're perfect," he murmured, his voice low and sincere.

The words sent a shiver down her spine, and Katya's heart swelled with a mix of arousal and emotion. She had never felt so exposed, so vulnerable, but at the same time, she had never felt more powerful. Ivan desired her, wanted her in ways she hadn't imagined, and that knowledge made her body hum with anticipation.

Her arousal built as she stood there, feeling the weight of his gaze, feeling the tension between them grow thicker with every passing second. Her breath came quicker, her skin prickling with heat, and she knew she was ready to give herself to him completely.

"What else would you like me to do?" she asked, her voice soft but steady.

Ivan's eyes darkened at her words, a faint smile tugging at the corner of his mouth. He leaned forward slightly, his posture still relaxed but filled with purpose. The faint smile on his lips told her everything she needed to know—he liked her eagerness, liked that she was offering herself to him, ready and willing to do whatever he asked.

But beneath that smile was something else, something deeper, and it made Katya's heart race even faster. Tonight wasn't just about control, wasn't just about dominance and submission. There was something more between them now, something neither of them could ignore any longer.

And Katya was ready to see where it would lead.

Ivan's smile deepened as he gazed at Katya standing there, completely exposed, vulnerable, yet somehow still powerful in her own right. When she had asked what else he wanted her to do, he hadn't answered with words. Instead, he had motioned for her to come closer, beckoning her with a look that sent a rush of desire straight through her.

Katya's pulse quickened, her body already attuned to his presence. As she moved toward him, she could feel the tension building inside her, the unspoken need that crackled between them like electricity. Each step felt weighted, her legs trembling slightly as anticipation pooled deep within her belly. When she reached him, her heart pounded in her chest, but the moment his hands touched her skin, all her nervous energy seemed to dissolve, replaced by a raw, burning need.

Leaning over him, her lips found his in a hungry kiss. It started slow at first, but quickly grew in intensity, their mouths clashing together with an urgency that neither could control. Ivan's hands were on her immediately, rough and possessive, roaming over her body as though he needed to claim every inch of her. His fingers squeezed her breasts, his thumbs brushing over her hardened nipples, making her moan into his mouth. The sensation was overwhelming—his dominance, his power, the way he touched her like she was his possession—and Katya found herself craving more.

She could feel his need for her in every touch, every movement, but there was also something else. The tenderness he had shown her earlier, the vulnerability he had allowed her to glimpse, was still there beneath the surface. It added another layer to their connection, one that made her ache for him even more.

As their kiss deepened, Katya's hands began to move, eager to strip him of the barriers between them. Her fingers trembled slightly as they tugged at his shirt, pulling it from his body and revealing the hard muscles beneath. She kissed her way down his neck, feeling the steady beat of his pulse under her lips, before trailing her mouth lower, over his collarbone and down his chest. His skin was warm beneath her touch, and the feel of him against her lips sent a rush of heat through her entire body.

Ivan leaned back in the chair, his hands sliding down to her hips as he watched her with dark, lust-filled eyes. The intensity of his gaze made her feel even more exposed, but it also fueled her desire. She wanted him—wanted to make him feel the same way he made her feel.

Her hands moved to his pants, unbuckling his belt with quick, efficient movements before unzipping them. As she freed him from the confines of his clothing, her breath caught in her throat. Ivan's cock stood thick and engorged before her, and for a brief moment, Katya hesitated, her eyes widening at the sight of him. She wasn't sure she could handle all of him. But the sound of his low, guttural moan spurred her on, and with a surge of determination, she wrapped her hand around his length, feeling the heat and hardness of him against her palm.

Katya could feel the tension building between them, the weight of his desire pressing down on her. She wanted to please him, to show him how much she craved him. Slowly, she lowered her head, taking him into her mouth. He filled her completely, stretching her lips as she took him as deep as she could manage. The taste of him, the weight of him against her tongue, made her moan softly, the sound vibrating against him as she began to move.

Ivan's hand tangled in her hair, his fingers gripping tightly but not painfully as he guided her movements. She could feel the subtle shifts in his body, the way his hips lifted slightly off the chair as she took him deeper. His breathing grew ragged, his moans louder with each stroke of her mouth, and Katya could feel the tension coiling inside him, ready to snap.

She bobbed her head, sucking and stroking him in rhythm, using her hand to work the base of his shaft while her mouth focused on the rest. His reactions spurred her on, each moan, each gasp of pleasure, urging her to go deeper, to push herself further. She wanted to see him unravel, to watch as the control he clung to so tightly slipped away, if only for a moment.

But just as Ivan's hips began to move in earnest, his body straining toward release, he pulled her away. His hand gripped her hair tightly, his breathing heavy and ragged as he held her there, inches away from him. Katya's lips parted, her chest rising and falling rapidly as she tried to catch her breath, the taste of him still lingering on her tongue. She looked up at him, her eyes wide, her body trembling with need.

Ivan's dark eyes were wild, his control hanging by a thread. He stood abruptly, towering over her, his body a wall of muscle and dominance. Without a word, he pulled her to her feet, his hands rough as they gripped her arms, and before Katya could react, he tossed her onto the bed. The force of it made her gasp, the sudden loss of control sending a thrill through her body.

She landed on the soft mattress, her heart pounding as she looked up at him. The way he loomed over her, his chest heaving, his cock still hard and glistening from her mouth, sent a wave of heat through her. He looked like a man on the edge, his restraint barely holding as he gazed down at her, his eyes filled with an intensity that made her stomach flip.

Katya's body reacted instantly, her skin tingling with anticipation as she lay there, waiting for his next move. She could see the tension in his muscles, the way his jaw clenched as he fought to maintain control. But she knew he was close to losing it, and the thought made her body ache with need.

Her chest rose and fell with shallow breaths, her legs shifting slightly as she pressed her thighs together, trying to relieve the pressure building inside her. But it wasn't enough. She needed him, needed to feel him inside her, to feel his weight pressing down on her as he claimed her body. The anticipation was unbearable, the ache between her legs growing with each passing second. She wanted him to take her, to fill her completely, to push her past the point of no return.

Ivan's gaze never left hers as he stood there, his chest rising and falling heavily with each breath. He was in control, but only just, and Katya could feel the tension in the air, thick and charged with desire. She knew what was coming next, knew that when he finally took her, it would be with a force and intensity that would leave her trembling. And she was ready for it. She craved it.

As she lay there, exposed and vulnerable on the bed, her body aching with need, Katya felt a surge of emotion. This was more than just sex, more than just lust. This was something deeper, something raw and real that she couldn't ignore. Ivan was claiming her, not just physically, but emotionally as well. And despite the fear that came with that realization, Katya knew that she wanted it. She wanted him, all of him, in every way possible.

Ivan's eyes were dark, filled with an intensity that sent a shiver down Katya's spine. She lay back on the bed, her heart racing as she watched him remove his pants and briefs. Every movement was deliberate, and as each piece of clothing fell away, her eyes roamed over his powerful body—muscles rippling beneath his skin, his tattoos winding over his torso like a dark map of the life he had lived, and the scars that marked him as a man who had seen too much. But it was his large, hard erection, standing thick and ready, that held her attention, her breath catching in her throat.

He climbed onto the bed, his body towering over hers, the sheer presence of him making her feel small and vulnerable beneath him. But there was something intoxicating about that vulnerability, the way it made her feel claimed by him, owned by him in a way that both frightened and excited her.

Their lips crashed together, the kiss rough and hungry, as though Ivan couldn't get enough of her. His hands were everywhere—fingers digging into her skin, gripping her with a possessiveness that made her head spin. She felt his cock pressing between her thighs, teasing her wet entrance, and her body instinctively arched toward him, aching for more.

When Ivan finally positioned himself at her core, the anticipation was almost unbearable. Her body was wound tight, trembling with need, and when he thrust into her roughly in one swift motion, a cry tore from her lips. He filled her completely, stretching her to the point of almost painful pleasure, and the sensation was so overwhelming she thought she might break apart from it.

"Oh god, Ivan…" she gasped, her nails digging into his back as he began to move inside her, each thrust harder and more powerful than the last. The bed creaked beneath them, the sound of their bodies colliding filling the room, but all Katya could focus on was the way Ivan made her feel—so completely consumed, so utterly his.

Ivan's grip on her waist tightened, his fingers digging into her flesh as he pounded into her relentlessly. The raw dominance in his movements, the way he controlled her body with every thrust, made Katya's head spin. But it wasn't just the roughness that had her heart racing—it was the way he looked at her, the need in his eyes, like he wanted to possess all of her.

Each thrust felt like a claim, as if Ivan was telling her with his body that she belonged to him, that she was his in every way. And the more he moved inside her, the more Katya felt herself surrendering to him—not just physically, but emotionally. She couldn't deny it anymore—this was more than just lust. She was falling for him, hard and fast, and it terrified her.

"Ivan… I—" Her words were lost in a moan as Ivan shifted his weight, his hands sliding down to her hips to reposition her on her side. He slowed for a moment, the sudden change in pace making her gasp, and then he lifted one of her legs, opening her wider for him. The new angle was different, deeper, and the sensation was so intense it sent shockwaves of pleasure rippling through her.

Ivan growled low in his throat, his lips brushing against her ear as he began thrusting into her again, this time with even more force. Katya's head fell back, her body arching against his as he drove deeper and harder, each thrust sending her spiraling closer to the edge. The pressure building inside her was almost too much, and she wasn't sure if she could take it.

Her breath came in ragged gasps, her hands gripping the sheets as Ivan pushed her higher and higher, her body tightening around him with every thrust. The pleasure was blinding, and when she finally reached the peak, her orgasm crashed over her like a tidal wave, so powerful that she thought she might shatter from it. She screamed his name, her entire body convulsing as she came, her nails raking down his back in a desperate attempt to hold onto something—anything—as the pleasure consumed her.

Ivan wasn't far behind. The moment Katya's body tightened around him, her walls pulsing with the force of her orgasm, Ivan's thrusts became erratic, his breathing rough and ragged as he lost control. His grip on her waist tightened almost painfully, and with one final, powerful thrust, he buried himself deep inside her, his body stiffening as he followed her over the edge.

"Fuck..." Ivan groaned, his voice low and hoarse as his release hit him. His hips jerked as he spilled inside her, the sensation of him filling her only prolonging Katya's pleasure, sending aftershocks of ecstasy rippling through her body. For a moment, neither of them moved, their bodies locked together as they rode out the last waves of their shared climax, the only sound in the room their heavy breathing.

Ivan collapsed on top of her, his weight pressing her into the mattress, but Katya didn't mind. In fact, she relished the feeling of his body covering hers, the warmth of his skin against hers. Her arms wrapped around his back, holding him close as her heart began to slow, her chest still rising and falling with deep, uneven breaths.

For a long moment, neither of them spoke, the silence between them filled with the aftermath of their passion. Katya's mind was a whirl of emotions, her thoughts tangled and confused. What had just happened between them felt different—more than just sex, more than just physical desire. There had been a connection, a raw, intense emotion that had pulsed between them with every touch, every thrust. She had felt it in the way Ivan had looked at her, in the way he had moved inside her, and it both thrilled and terrified her.

"Ivan…" she began softly, unsure of what to say, unsure of how to put into words the emotions swirling inside her. But before she could continue, Ivan lifted his head, his dark eyes locking onto hers with an intensity that took her breath away.

"You're mine, Katya," he said, his voice rough and possessive. "You belong to me now. Do you understand?"

His words sent a shiver down her spine, and though a part of her still fought against the idea of belonging to anyone, another part of her—one she wasn't ready to acknowledge just yet—knew that Ivan was right. She did belong to him, in ways she hadn't anticipated, in ways that went beyond the physical.

"Yes," she whispered, her voice barely audible, but the truth of it echoed inside her.

Katya felt a weight settle in her chest, an undeniable shift in their relationship. Ivan wasn't just claiming her body—he was claiming all of her, and she had given herself over to him completely.

Katya lay beside Ivan, her body still humming from the intensity of what had just happened between them. The room was quiet now, save for the sound of their breathing slowly returning to normal. The heat of his body pressed against hers, his arm draped possessively around her waist, pulling her close. She could feel his heartbeat beneath her palm, strong and steady, but inside her own chest, her heart raced with confusion and uncertainty.

His words echoed in her mind—*"You're mine, Katya. You belong to me now."* They had stirred something deep inside her, something she hadn't fully realized was there until this moment. She had given herself to him, body and soul, and yet, as she lay here in the aftermath of their passion, a part of her was terrified.

Ivan's feelings for her were clear. She could feel the shift in him, in the way he touched her, the way he looked at her. It wasn't just about control anymore. There was something deeper, something emotional that scared her more than the raw dominance he had always exerted. She was no longer just a woman paying off a debt—she was becoming something more to him. And that terrified her because she knew, deep down, that she was starting to care for him too.

Her fingers brushed against the rough skin of his arm, the scars and marks that told the story of his violent life. The life he lived, the world he inhabited, was so far removed from anything she had ever known. It was brutal, dangerous, and unforgiving.

And yet, she had found herself drawn to him, unable to resist the magnetic pull of his power, his authority. He made her feel things she had never felt before—desire, passion, even tenderness. But was that enough?

Could she truly live in his world? The question swirled in her mind, taunting her with no clear answer. Could she be the woman at his side, knowing that danger lurked around every corner? Knowing that his enemies would stop at nothing to hurt him—and maybe her, too? The thought sent a chill through her, despite the warmth of Ivan's embrace. She wasn't sure she could ever fully belong in his world of violence and power, no matter how much she might want to.

As Ivan's arm tightened around her, his grip firm but not harsh, Katya felt the weight of her internal struggle pressing down on her. She wanted to be with him, but at what cost? Was she willing to give up her sense of self, her freedom, to be with a man like Ivan? Could she ever truly belong to him—not just in body, but in heart and soul?

Her eyes fluttered closed, the exhaustion of the day and the emotional intensity of the night catching up with her. Ivan's body heat enveloped her, a comforting presence despite the storm of emotions raging inside her. She wanted to believe that this—what they had—was enough. But the doubt gnawed at her, whispering that there were no easy answers, no guarantees.

And as she lay there, feeling the steady rise and fall of Ivan's chest beneath her cheek, Katya couldn't help but wonder what the future held for them. Would she be able to embrace his world, or would the weight of it eventually crush her? Only time would tell, but for now, she let herself be held by him, clinging to the fleeting moments of peace before the conflict inside her returned with a vengeance.

For tonight, at least, she would let herself be his.

Chapter 20

The morning light filtered through the dining room windows, casting a golden glow over the table where Katya sat with Ivan and the children. The warmth of the sun was comforting, but it felt at odds with the emotional storm brewing inside her. Kirill and Dasha were laughing, excitedly recounting the details of a game they had played the day before. Their voices filled the room, echoing the sounds of childhood innocence that somehow managed to exist in the same space as Ivan's cold, controlled world.

Katya watched as Ivan leaned in, his gaze soft as he listened to the children, his face betraying none of the harshness she had come to associate with him. In moments like this, it was easy to forget the ruthless man she knew he could be. Here, he was simply a father, and a loving one at that. His strong hands, which she had seen bloodied and bruised, now rested gently on the table as he gave Kirill his full attention. Dasha showed him a drawing, her small hands holding it up with pride, and Ivan's lips quirked into a rare smile as he praised her work.

It struck Katya just how much she had underestimated Ivan when she first arrived. She had seen him only as the dangerous man who had control over her life, the man she was forced to serve to pay off her father's debt. But the more time she spent in this house, the more she realized there was a side of him she hadn't been prepared for. A side that cared deeply for his children, that could be gentle in a way that made her heart ache.

As she sat there, watching the tender interactions between Ivan and his children, Katya felt the weight of conflicting emotions pressing down on her. She had always known that Ivan was dangerous, that his world was filled with violence and power struggles, but it was moments like these that made her question everything. Could there be more to him than the ruthless Bratva leader? Was there a part of him that was capable of love, of true connection?

Her gaze lingered on Ivan, and as if sensing her attention, he glanced at her briefly, their eyes meeting across the table. There was something unreadable in his expression, a depth she couldn't quite decipher. It sent a shiver down her spine, not out of fear, but something else. Something more unsettling. In that moment, she felt vulnerable in a way she hadn't expected. Ivan had seen parts of her no one else had, and the way he looked at her now made her feel exposed—not just physically, but emotionally.

A flicker of warmth spread through her chest as she looked away, her hands tightening around the edge of her coffee cup. She tried to focus on the sounds of Kirill and Dasha's laughter, but her thoughts kept drifting back to Ivan and the strange, confusing feelings she was developing for him.

Was it possible that she was falling for him?

The idea was both terrifying and intoxicating. Ivan had power over her in more ways than one—he controlled her life, her circumstances, and increasingly, her emotions. She had told herself from the beginning that this was a temporary arrangement, a way to repay her father's debt and nothing more. But now, sitting at this table with him and his children, Katya wasn't so sure anymore. The lines between what she had once thought and what she was beginning to feel were becoming blurred.

Her thoughts drifted to the contract—the five years she was bound to Ivan. Five years seemed like a lifetime when she had first arrived. Now, with every passing day, it felt like it was slipping away too quickly, like time was moving faster than she could grasp. What would happen when those five years were up? Could she just walk away from all of this—from Ivan, from the children? Would he even let her go?

She considered her place in this strange, dangerous family dynamic. She wasn't just an outsider looking in anymore. She was part of this world, tethered to Ivan by a contract that bound her for five years. Five years to repay her father's debt—a debt that had brought her into Ivan's orbit in the first place. But what would happen when those years were up?

The thought of leaving, of walking away from Ivan and the children after all they had shared, filled her with a deep, unsettling dread. Could she really go back to a normal life after this? Would she even survive long enough to see the end of her contract? The violent reality of Ivan's world seemed to hang over her every decision, every thought, and the idea of being free from it should have been a relief. But it wasn't.

Because the truth was, she wasn't sure she *wanted* to leave anymore.

This realization terrified her more than anything else. The fear she felt wasn't just about the danger of Ivan's life or the violence that surrounded him—it was about her growing attachment to him. She could feel herself falling for him, little by little, in ways she hadn't expected. His strength, his authority, and even the way he could command a room with just a glance—it all drew her in, making it harder to keep her distance. And now, seeing this softer side of him with his children, that pull was even stronger.

But what did it mean for her? For them?

Her mind raced with questions she didn't have answers for. Would Ivan ever let her go? Could he?

And more importantly, could she walk away from him after everything they had been through? The idea of leaving him behind, of leaving the children behind, was like a heavy weight pressing down on her chest. The thought of Ivan moving on without her, of the children forgetting her, was unbearable.

She glanced over at Ivan, who was still engaged with the children, his smile warm and genuine. He caught her eye for a moment, and in that brief glance, she felt something stir inside her—a connection, a longing that frightened her. There was something between them now, something more than just the physical attraction that had always been there. It was deeper, more complicated, and that scared her most of all.

What if she stayed? What if this wasn't just about repaying her father's debt anymore? The idea of staying in Ivan's world, of becoming more than just someone bound to him by obligation, sent a rush of conflicting emotions through her. She craved his touch, his presence, but at the same time, she knew the dangers of loving a man like Ivan.

Could she survive five years in a world like his?

The uncertainty of it all hung over her like a dark cloud. The future felt murky, and for the first time, Katya realized that the biggest threat wasn't the violence or the enemies Ivan had—it was her growing feelings for him. Feelings she wasn't sure she could control.

As the children laughed and continued their stories, Ivan finally looked up and locked eyes with her again, and Katya felt her heart skip a beat. She knew she couldn't keep these feelings at bay much longer, but the question that haunted her most was this: when the time came, would she be able to walk away from him? Or had she already fallen too far to ever leave?

Katya stole a glance at Ivan again, watching him as he responded to something Dasha said with a softness in his voice that she rarely heard. He was so different in these moments, and it only made her internal conflict worse. She had seen the brutal side of him—the cold, calculating leader who didn't hesitate to use violence to protect what was his. But she had also seen the man who cared deeply for his children, the man who had shown her glimpses of vulnerability in their most intimate moments.

Her heart felt like it was being pulled in two different directions. One part of her wanted to run, to protect herself from the inevitable heartache that came with getting too close to someone like Ivan. The other part of her... well, that part of her was already too far gone. She craved his touch, his attention, and the way he made her feel like she was the only person in the world when they were together.

But it wasn't just physical. That was what scared her the most. The desire was undeniable, yes, but it was more than that. She was starting to care for him in ways she hadn't expected. Every time they were in the same room, every time his eyes lingered on her for just a moment too long, she felt herself falling deeper into his orbit. It was a dangerous game, one that left her feeling vulnerable and exposed.

Her mind told her to stay distant, to keep her walls up, but her heart was betraying her. She could feel it, every time he touched her, every time he kissed her—she was slipping. And if she wasn't careful, there would come a point where she couldn't pull herself back.

The uncertainty of their future loomed over her like a dark cloud. She couldn't shake the feeling that something was going to happen—that their fragile connection was going to break, one way or another. And when it did, she wasn't sure if she would be able to survive the fallout.

As Kirill and Dasha continued to chatter, their laughter filling the room, Katya forced a smile, but inside, her thoughts were a swirling mess of fear, desire, and uncertainty. She wasn't sure where she stood with Ivan, or even where she wanted to stand. All she knew was that she was caught in the middle of something far bigger than herself—and for the first time in her life, she wasn't sure if she could fight it.

And that terrified her more than anything.

Ivan leaned back in his chair, his gaze softening as he looked at Kirill and Dasha, their faces still alight with the joy of the game they'd been telling him about. "Go on, then," he said, his voice low but warm, "you can go play." The children, already eager to escape the confines of the dining room, jumped up from their seats with wide grins, racing toward the door.

"Bye, Daddy!" Dasha called out, her small voice sweet and full of affection as she waved at him. Kirill followed suit, giving his father a quick smile and a hasty, "See you later!" before both of them disappeared down the hall, their laughter echoing behind them.

Ivan's eyes lingered on them for a moment longer, a trace of warmth flickering across his otherwise stoic face. Then, with a slight shift in his posture, he turned his attention back to Katya.

As the children's laughter faded into the distance, their tiny footsteps pattering out of the dining room and down the hallway, Katya found herself alone with her thoughts. The air seemed to grow heavier, the playful atmosphere of breakfast replaced by a charged silence. Across from her, Ivan remained seated, his posture relaxed but his presence still commanding the room. His eyes were on her, dark and intense, as if they had never really left her the entire morning.

Katya's heart gave a small, involuntary flutter as their gazes locked once more. She had always been able to feel his power in the space between them, but now, there was something else simmering beneath the surface, something unspoken but palpable. His expression was as unreadable as ever, his face a carefully constructed mask of control and composure, but for the briefest moment, she thought she saw something in his eyes—something deeper.

A hint of vulnerability? Or was it something darker, something she couldn't quite place?

Her breath caught as the question lingered in her mind. *Does he feel it too?* This connection that had started out as something purely physical had evolved into something more complex, more tangled in emotions than she had expected. But she couldn't be sure. Ivan was impossible to read. One moment, he was dominant, untouchable, the next, he was showing her glimpses of tenderness that threw her off balance.

Did he care for her? Or was she just another piece in his carefully controlled world, a pawn in a game she didn't fully understand?

Katya couldn't help but wonder if, beneath that hard exterior, Ivan was capable of feeling the same connection she did. Could a man like him, so used to power and control, truly care for someone in the way she was starting to care for him? Or was she just another possession to him—another thing to own and control?

The uncertainty gnawed at her, and as Ivan's gaze continued to hold hers, she found herself wanting desperately to know the answer. But Ivan, as always, gave nothing away. He remained an enigma, his emotions hidden behind a wall she wasn't sure she'd ever be able to breach.

Could she even allow herself to care for a man like him? The thought lingered as the silence stretched between them, and Katya was left with the unsettling realization that she might never truly know what Ivan felt—or if she could ever truly belong in his world.

The rest of the day passed in a blur for Katya. She tried to distract herself with the usual routine—playing with the children, helping Sofia prepare their dinner—but her thoughts were consumed by a storm of conflicting emotions. She couldn't shake the feeling of dread that had settled deep in her chest. The more she thought about her future with Ivan, the more tangled everything became. She had been trying to bury the questions, the uncertainty, but by evening, it felt as though the weight of her emotions was suffocating her. She needed answers. She couldn't keep pretending everything was fine, as if her relationship with Ivan wasn't heading toward a precipice.

That night, as the house quieted and the children were tucked into bed, Katya found herself standing outside Ivan's study. Her heart pounded in her chest, a nervous energy surging through her. She hovered there for a moment, unsure if she should go through with this. Was she ready to confront him? What if his answers shattered whatever fragile connection they had built? But then the weight of all her unresolved emotions pressed down on her, pushing her to act. She couldn't live in this limbo any longer.

Taking a deep breath, she pushed the door open.

Ivan stood from his chair the moment she entered, his presence commanding the room as always. The soft glow of the lamp illuminated the hard lines of his face, but there was something in his expression that softened as he looked at her. He didn't speak right away, just watched her approach, the tension between them palpable in the air. As she stood in front of him, Katya felt her resolve wavering. How could she face him when the sight of him stirred so many conflicting emotions inside her?

Without a word, Ivan reached for her, his hand warm against her cheek as he gently brushed his thumb across her skin. His touch sent shivers through her, and before she knew it, he was leaning in to kiss her. For a brief moment, Katya melted into him, losing herself in the warmth of his lips and the strength of his body pressing against hers. It would have been so easy to give in, to let the physical connection between them drown out the emotional chaos. But the questions, the uncertainty, surged back to the surface.

She pulled back, her hand resting on his chest, stopping him before things could go any further. Her heart raced, her breath shaky as she looked up at him, the words she had been holding back now poised on the tip of her tongue.

"What happens when my five years are up?" Her voice was tight with emotion, her words tumbling out before she could second-guess herself. "Do I just walk away and pretend none of this happened? Do you let me go after everything?"

Ivan's brow furrowed slightly, his dark eyes searching hers, but he didn't immediately respond. The silence between them stretched, thick with tension, and Katya felt the vulnerability in her chest expand. She had exposed herself in a way she hadn't intended, her heart laid bare for him to either accept or dismiss.

"I need to know," she added, her voice trembling. "I need to know where we stand. Because... I don't think I can keep going like this—wondering, waiting."

The rawness in her voice surprised even her. She had never meant to be this vulnerable with Ivan, but here she was, her emotions laid bare. She hated how exposed she felt, hated that she had let herself fall this deep, but she couldn't take it back now. She needed to hear his answer, no matter how much it scared her.

The silence hung heavy between them, each second that passed twisting tighter in her chest.

Katya stood there, her heart pounding as she waited for Ivan to respond. The silence between them was suffocating, each second stretching out longer than the last. She had put herself out there, exposed her emotions in a way she hadn't intended. The question still echoed in the air, thick with tension: *What happens when my five years are up?*

Ivan's eyes, so often impossible to read, bore into hers, but his expression remained guarded. The weight of his silence felt unbearable. Katya could feel her pulse racing, the uncertainty gnawing at her. Why wasn't he saying anything? Was he trying to figure out a way to let her down gently? Or worse, did he not care enough to even consider the future?

Her chest tightened with anxiety. She wasn't just afraid of the answer—she was afraid of what his silence meant. The longer he stayed quiet, the more her heart sank. She had hoped for some kind of reassurance, some acknowledgment that what was happening between them wasn't just physical. But now, she wasn't sure if that was coming.

The memories of the last few weeks flashed through her mind—the moments they had shared, the way Ivan had touched her, not just with lust but with a tenderness that had surprised her. She thought about how he had opened up to her about his wife, about the emotional cracks he had let her glimpse. But what if she had misinterpreted all of it? What if this was just another way for him to exert control?

Her gaze dropped to the floor for a brief moment, and she pressed her palm harder against Ivan's chest, feeling the steady thrum of his heartbeat beneath her fingers. It was the only thing grounding her in this moment.

Finally, Ivan broke the silence, his voice low and guarded. "I haven't thought that far ahead," he admitted, his gaze dropping for the briefest moment before returning to hers. "All I know is that you're here now. That's what matters."

The words hit Katya like a blow. She had been waiting for something—anything—that would ease the tension inside her, that would give her hope that this was more than just a transactional relationship. But his answer felt like a half-measure, a deflection. *You're here now.* That wasn't what she wanted to hear. She didn't want to just be *someone* who was here now. She needed to be more than that.

Her throat tightened as the vulnerability she had been trying to hide started to rise to the surface.

She didn't want to sound desperate, but the raw emotion in her voice was unmistakable. "Is that all I am to you?" she asked, her voice softer now, but still filled with emotion. "Just... someone who's here now? What happens when I'm not?"

Ivan's jaw tensed, his expression hardening slightly as he processed her words. Katya's heart ached at the sight. She had pushed him, but she couldn't take the question back now. She needed to know. Her emotions, so carefully held in check all day, were beginning to unravel.

For a long moment, Ivan didn't respond, and the silence between them thickened. Katya's eyes searched his face, hoping to find something—anything—that would give her a glimpse of what he was feeling. But his expression remained unreadable.

Her pulse quickened, and she could feel the weight of her own words pressing down on her. She hadn't meant to push him like this, but she couldn't keep pretending that she didn't care. She had thought she could handle this, thought she could stay detached, but it was too late. Her feelings for him had grown too strong, and she needed to know if she was alone in that.

The air in the room felt heavy, charged with tension. Katya wanted to look away, to break the intensity of the moment, but she couldn't. She needed to know. She needed to hear him say something that would make sense of all this—of the desire, the tenderness, the connection she felt whenever they were together. But Ivan was as closed off as ever, and the uncertainty was suffocating her.

Her voice wavered as she pressed on. "Ivan, I can't... I can't keep doing this if I don't know where I stand. If I'm just someone you're keeping around because I have to be here..." She trailed off, not sure how to finish the sentence, the emotion tightening her throat. She hated feeling this vulnerable, hated that she had let him get under her skin like this.

Ivan's eyes softened slightly, and she could see a flicker of something there—something real, something human—but it was gone just as quickly as it had appeared. He reached up, his hand gently cupping her face, his thumb brushing over her cheek in a gesture so tender it made her heart ache. But even in that moment, his silence lingered.

Katya felt the tears welling up behind her eyes, but she blinked them back, refusing to let them fall. She wasn't going to break down in front of him. Not like this. But the longer he stayed silent, the more the fear gnawed at her. She had thought they were moving toward something more, something real, but now she wasn't sure.

Why won't you just say it? she wanted to scream. *Why won't you just tell me what you're feeling?*

But Ivan remained quiet, his thumb still tracing slow, soothing circles on her cheek, his expression unreadable. The tension in her chest was unbearable now, the weight of her emotions threatening to crush her.

Her voice was barely a whisper when she spoke again. "I need to know, Ivan. I need to know if I matter to you. Because I don't think I can keep doing this if I don't."

There. She had said it. The words hung in the air between them, raw and vulnerable. And now, all she could do was wait. Wait for him to give her an answer she could live with—or one that would break her heart.

Her heart pounded in her chest as Ivan's silence continued to stretch out. Time seemed to slow, each second feeling like an eternity as she stood there, exposed and waiting. She could feel the tears threatening again, but she forced them back, her eyes locked on his, searching for some sign of what he was thinking, what he was feeling.

When Ivan finally spoke again, his voice was low, almost reluctant. "Katya, you matter."

The words were simple, but they cut through her like a blade. She wanted to believe him, wanted to trust that he meant it, but the guarded tone in his voice left her uncertain. He hadn't answered her question, not really. And as much as she wanted to hold onto those words, she needed more. She needed him to say more.

But as Ivan's hand fell from her face, the silence returned, and Katya realized that he wasn't going to give her anything else.

She felt her heart sink as she stepped back, suddenly feeling a million miles away from him, despite the fact that they were standing so close.

Chapter 21

The low hum of children's laughter surrounded Katya as she sat on the bench in the museum's interactive children's area. The sound was comforting, almost melodic, as Kirill and Dasha explored the dinosaur exhibit with wide-eyed wonder. Every now and then, Kirill would call out excitedly, pointing to a massive skeletal structure or tugging Dasha along to the next interactive display. Their joy was contagious, but for Katya, it only highlighted the disquiet simmering beneath her calm exterior.

She watched the children from her seat, a faint smile tugging at the corners of her mouth, but her thoughts were far from the lightheartedness of the moment. They drifted back to the night before, to the weight of her confrontation with Ivan and the frustrating silence that had followed.

Ivan's words—or lack thereof—clung to her like an unwelcome fog. "I haven't thought that far ahead," he had said, his voice guarded, his eyes unreadable. It was as if he had wrapped himself in armor, refusing to let her in. She had wanted more, needed more than his vague response, but all she had received was a dismissal of the future, a focus on the present. And yet, she could see it in his eyes—there was something there, something Ivan hadn't said aloud, but it wasn't enough.

She wanted clarity. She wanted to know if she mattered to him beyond the boundaries of the contract binding her to his life. Every moment they spent together, their connection deepened, yet Ivan's reluctance to talk about the future had left her feeling lost, like a ship drifting without an anchor.

Katya shifted on the bench, crossing her legs and resting her arms on her knees as she tried to make sense of her own emotions. Was she just a pawn in Ivan's world? A woman who had been pulled into his orbit only to be discarded when her usefulness had run its course? The more she thought about it, the more her frustration bubbled to the surface. She had wanted answers, but the reality was, Ivan wasn't a man who gave them freely. He was a man of action, of power, of control—traits that had always intimidated her but now left her aching for more.

As much as she hated to admit it, she was starting to understand Ivan on a deeper level. He was a man who had spent his life controlling everything and everyone around him, a man who never allowed himself to be vulnerable. To open up, to speak of feelings or futures, was against his very nature. And while that realization softened some of her frustration, it didn't make the hurt any easier to bear.

Katya lowered her head, staring at her hands as her fingers absentmindedly traced the seam of her coat. Ivan had lived a life of violence and isolation, building walls around his heart to protect himself from the dangers of his world. He had been betrayed, hurt, and hardened by his experiences. Vulnerability wasn't just uncomfortable for him—it was dangerous. And yet, Katya had glimpsed something behind those walls. He had let her in, just a little. She had seen a side of him that few others had, and for that, she felt a pang of sympathy. But understanding Ivan didn't make it easier to accept his refusal to acknowledge their future.

The truth was, she was no longer just a woman repaying a debt. She had become part of Ivan's world, and whether she liked it or not, her heart was entwined with his in ways she hadn't anticipated. Every stolen glance, every brush of his hand against her skin, every moment they spent together was a reminder of the invisible chains binding her to him—not through obligation, but through emotion.

Emotion.

Katya's chest tightened as she realized just how deeply her feelings for Ivan had grown. At first, she had told herself it was just physical—an attraction born from the intensity of his power, the dominance he exuded in every action. But now? Now, it was more than that. It was the way he looked at her when he thought she wasn't paying attention, the way he interacted with his children, the rare moments of tenderness he let slip through the cracks of his tough exterior. She was falling for him, and the thought terrified her.

Could she ever escape Ivan, even if she wanted to? And more importantly, did she even want to anymore?

The weight of the question settled heavily on her shoulders. The idea of leaving Ivan, of walking away from the life she had unexpectedly become a part of, filled her with a dread she hadn't expected. Her feelings for him had grown beyond her control, and with every passing day, she found herself more and more entangled in his world—body, mind, and heart.

But staying with Ivan came with its own set of fears. His life was dangerous, violent, and unpredictable. She had known that from the start, but now it felt more real than ever. The fear wasn't just for herself; it was for the children, for the small semblance of a family she had begun to form with them. What would happen if she stayed? Could she survive in a world like his, filled with enemies lurking in the shadows, waiting for their chance to strike?

Katya's gaze drifted to the children again, watching as they laughed and played, blissfully unaware of the darkness that surrounded their lives. She envied their innocence, their ability to find joy in the simplest of things, but she also felt a fierce protectiveness rising within her. She wasn't just falling for Ivan—she was falling for the life she had begun to build with him and the children. And that thought was both beautiful and terrifying.

The noise of the museum, the children's laughter, and the bustle of families milling around felt like a stark contrast to the inner turmoil Katya was facing. She felt as though she were standing at a precipice, teetering on the edge of a decision she wasn't ready to make. Could she leave this life behind after five years? Could she walk away from Ivan and the children and pretend none of it had mattered?

As much as Katya wanted to believe she could, deep down, she knew the truth. She was already too far gone. No matter what happened, her life had changed forever. Ivan's world had become her world, and no matter how much she wanted to deny it, she wasn't sure she would ever be able to free herself from it. The fear, the uncertainty, and the intensity of her feelings all mixed together, leaving her with one undeniable truth: her heart was no longer her own.

Katya gathered the children, her hand resting on Kirill's shoulder as they made their way out of the museum. The day had been filled with excitement, the children marveling at the dinosaur exhibit and laughing their way through the interactive displays. Now, with the sun beginning to sink toward the horizon, it was time to head back home. But as they approached the black car waiting for them outside, Katya's footsteps slowed.

The driver was different.

Standing by the car door, he opened it for them with a blank expression. He was tall, broad-shouldered, and wearing dark sunglasses that hid his eyes, making it impossible for Katya to get a proper read on him. Her heart stuttered in her chest, the familiar sense of unease creeping over her.

Ivan's drivers tended to rotate, she reminded herself. It wasn't always the same person every day, and Ivan was meticulous about their safety. Still, something about this man set her on edge. The usual driver, Nick, had a quiet, steady presence she'd grown accustomed to. This man, though, felt different in a way she couldn't quite place.

"Are you new?" Katya asked, her voice calm, though her eyes searched his face for any sign of reassurance.

The man nodded curtly. "Yes, ma'am. Your regular driver is unavailable today," he replied, his tone polite but cold. There was something off about the way he answered, something in his expression that made Katya's stomach twist. She forced a small smile, but her instinct screamed that something wasn't right.

She hesitated for a split second, her hand tightening slightly on Kirill's shoulder. The children were watching her, oblivious to her inner turmoil but sensitive enough to pick up on the smallest shifts in her demeanor. She didn't want to alarm them, didn't want to show that her own nerves were fraying.

Maybe she was overthinking it. Ivan was always cautious, always in control. He wouldn't let anyone near her and the children who wasn't vetted. And yet...

Taking a deep breath, Katya forced herself to remain composed. She nodded, trying to shake off the anxiety that gnawed at the edges of her mind.

"All right, let's get home," she said softly, guiding the children toward the car.

"Everything okay, Kat?" Kirill asked, his wide eyes looking up at her with concern.

Katya managed a smile, though it felt tight on her face. "Yes, sweetheart. Everything's fine. Let's just get home."

She helped them into the backseat, her gaze lingering on the driver for a moment longer than necessary. He still hadn't removed his sunglasses, and that nagging feeling of unease refused to let go.

As the car pulled away from the museum, Katya glanced out the window, forcing herself to focus on the city passing by. But no matter how hard she tried, she couldn't shake the growing sense that something was wrong.

The familiar route back to Ivan's home should have been comforting, but as Katya looked out the window, she quickly realized they weren't going in the right direction. The streets, once bustling with activity and well-kept storefronts, soon gave way to crumbling buildings and narrow alleyways. Her stomach twisted as the unfamiliar landscape rolled past, and the unease she'd felt earlier bloomed into full-blown dread.

This wasn't the way home.

Katya leaned forward, her voice sharper than she intended as she addressed the driver. "Excuse me. Where are we going?"

The man didn't respond. He kept his eyes fixed ahead, his jaw clenched, and the speed of the car began to increase. The engine growled as they turned onto a street she didn't recognize, the buildings around them becoming more dilapidated, more foreboding.

"I said, where are we going?" Katya demanded, her heart pounding now. She could feel the panic rising in her chest, clawing at her throat, but the driver remained silent.

Fear gripped her. She turned to the children, trying to keep her voice calm, but the worry was seeping through. "Kirill, Dasha, stay quiet, okay? Everything's going to be fine."

But was it? The children's wide eyes stared back at her, filled with confusion and fear, and Katya's heart shattered at the sight. She had to stay strong, had to protect them, but how? What was happening? Had Ivan made a mistake? Or was something much darker at play?

Her mind raced, and she fumbled with her bag, her hands shaking as she pulled out her cellphone. She needed to call Ivan. He would know what to do. He always knew what to do. Her fingers trembled as she dialed his number, each ring echoing like a ticking bomb in her ear.

The car sped up again, and Katya's breath quickened, her pulse roaring in her ears as she waited for Ivan to answer. Finally, the call connected, and she opened her mouth to speak.

"Ivan, something's wrong! We're—"

Before she could finish, the driver's hand shot out, yanking the phone from her grip with brutal force. Her scream filled the car as the driver disconnected the call and threw the phone to the floorboard, her lifeline severed in an instant.

"What are you doing?" Katya cried, her voice shaking as the driver ignored her completely. "Let me go! Let us out!"

He didn't respond. His foot pressed harder on the gas pedal, the car hurtling through the desolate streets with reckless abandon. Katya's hands flew to the door, her fingers scrabbling for the handle, but it was locked and they were going too fast to jump out. The reality of the situation crashed over her like a tidal wave—she was trapped, and so were the children.

Panic set in, cold and sharp. Katya twisted in her seat, trying to comfort Kirill and Dasha, who were now clutching each other in terror. "It's okay, I'm here. I won't let anything happen to you," she whispered, but the words felt hollow, even to her.

Her thoughts spun wildly. What if Ivan hadn't heard her cry for help? What if he didn't know they were in danger? She had no idea where they were being taken, and every second that passed only heightened the fear gnawing at her insides.

She stole a glance at the driver, his face set in grim determination, and a wave of nausea swept over her. Whoever this man was, he wasn't just a new driver. He was part of something bigger, something dangerous, and Katya had no idea how to stop it.

Tears pricked her eyes, but she blinked them away. She couldn't break down now. She had to stay strong for the children, for herself. She had to believe that Ivan would find them, that he would come for her.

But the question that haunted her was whether he'd be in time.

As the car swerved down a narrow, deserted street, the dilapidated buildings growing more ominous with each turn, Katya's heart sank lower and lower. She could feel the darkness closing in, the hopelessness threatening to consume her.

"Please," she whispered under her breath, not sure if she was pleading with the driver, or with fate itself. "Please let Ivan come."

But all she could do now was hold on—and pray that he did.

The car rattled to a stop in front of a decrepit industrial building, the windows boarded up, its brick facade crumbling with age. The surrounding area was desolate—no one around, no help in sight. As soon as the engine cut off, the oppressive silence settled over them like a shroud. Katya's heart pounded in her chest, her instincts screaming at her to act, to do something. But there was nowhere to run.

The driver got out wordlessly, his movements cold and efficient, and within moments, he yanked open the back door. The children whimpered beside her, their small hands gripping hers with a desperation that mirrored her own fear. Kirill and Dasha had no idea what was happening, but their wide eyes told her they sensed the danger. She couldn't let anything happen to them. Not now. Not ever.

Without warning, the driver's rough hand closed around her arm, pulling her from the car with a force that made her stumble. She fought, her body twisting in an attempt to break free, but it was no use. He was too strong. He dragged her toward the building as if she weighed nothing, and before she could react, two more men appeared from the shadows inside the entrance.

"Let go of me!" Katya screamed, her voice hoarse with fear, but the men paid her no mind. One of them reached in and pulled the children out of the car, ignoring their terrified cries. Kirill screamed for her, and the sound tore through her like a knife.

She twisted again, trying to get to them, but her captor shoved her forward, forcing her toward the entrance of the building. The air inside was damp and cold, the smell of decay thick in the air. Dim light filtered through the high, dirty windows, casting long, eerie shadows that made everything feel even more nightmarish.

The other two men loomed closer, their faces hidden in the shadows. There was a sick amusement in their eyes, as though they were enjoying the terror radiating from Katya and the children. Her heart hammered painfully in her chest, and her mind raced, searching desperately for a way out, for anything she could do to protect the children.

But the odds were stacked against her, and she knew it. There were three of them, and they were all bigger, stronger, and armed. Still, she had to try.

The first man, the one who had driven them, released her arm just long enough to shove her inside a dimly lit room. The floor was grimy, and the only windows were set high in the walls, far out of reach. The children were shoved in behind her, their cries filling the empty space, and Katya spun around, putting herself between them and the men.

She had to stay calm. If she let fear take over, they were all doomed.

The men were talking in low voices now, their words punctuated by cruel laughter. One of them—a tall man with a scar running down the side of his face—looked her over with disdain. His eyes gleamed with malice as he muttered to the others,

"We only need the kids. Should we just kill the bitch now?"

Katya's blood turned to ice. The words seemed to echo in the air, louder and more real than anything else in the room. Every instinct in her screamed to fight, to protect Kirill and Dasha at all costs. Without thinking, she surged forward, her voice a frantic, desperate plea. "Don't you dare touch them! Leave the children alone!"

Her voice broke, but her body moved on pure instinct, positioning herself between the men and the children. Her legs trembled beneath her, but she refused to back down, refused to show how terrified she truly was. Kirill and Dasha clung to her, their little hands gripping the fabric of her shirt as they buried their faces against her back.

For a fleeting moment, she thought maybe—just maybe—her words would be enough to make them reconsider. But that hope shattered when the man with the scar stepped forward, his hand swinging toward her with vicious speed. The blow landed hard across her face, the force of it sending her sprawling to the ground. Pain exploded through her skull, blinding and disorienting, and she gasped, struggling to stay conscious.

Kirill and Dasha screamed, their cries piercing the air as they scrambled toward her. Katya blinked through the pain, her vision swimming, but she forced herself to sit up. She had to stay awake, had to stay alert for them.

The children threw themselves into her arms, their small bodies trembling with fear. Katya held them close, her arms wrapping protectively around them even as her head throbbed. She tasted blood in her mouth, and her cheek felt like it was on fire, but none of that mattered. The only thing that mattered was keeping Kirill and Dasha safe.

She pressed her lips to the tops of their heads, whispering words of comfort she didn't believe. "It's okay. It's going to be okay," she lied, her voice trembling.

The man who had hit her crouched down in front of her, his eyes gleaming with something far more dangerous than amusement now. He leaned in closer, so close that she could smell the acrid stench of cigarettes and sweat on his breath. "Nah," he murmured, his voice dripping with menace. "Let's keep her around. Feisty. Could be fun."

The suggestive tone in his voice made bile rise in Katya's throat. She recoiled from him instinctively, her arms tightening around the children as if she could shield them from everything happening around them.

The man's eyes gleamed with dark intent, and Katya's fear intensified. She knew what he meant, and the horror of it twisted in her gut, making her want to scream, to lash out. But she couldn't give him the satisfaction of seeing her panic. She couldn't show weakness, not when Kirill and Dasha were depending on her.

The man's eyes gleamed with dark intent, and Katya's fear intensified. She knew what he meant, and the horror of it twisted in her gut, making her want to scream, to lash out. But she couldn't give him the satisfaction of seeing her panic. She couldn't show weakness, not when Kirill and Dasha were depending on her.

Her breath came in shallow, rapid bursts as she clutched the children tighter against her. Her mind raced, a whirl of fear and desperation as she tried to think of a way out. The men's eyes were fixed on her, their leering gazes filled with cruel anticipation. Every muscle in her body tensed, ready to fight if it came to that, though deep down she knew she was no match for them. She had to protect the children—there was no other option.

Kirill whimpered against her, his small hands gripping the fabric of her shirt as though holding on for dear life. Dasha pressed into her side, too terrified to speak. Katya forced herself to whisper soothing words, though her voice trembled. "It's going to be okay, I promise," she murmured, brushing her fingers through Kirill's hair, trying to calm him even as her own heart pounded with terror. "Just stay close to me."

But even as she spoke the words, she wasn't sure she believed them. She could feel the weight of the men's gaze like a physical pressure on her skin, and every instinct screamed that they were far from safe. Her throat felt tight, her chest constricting with fear, but she forced herself to stay steady, to keep her breathing calm for the children's sake.

She looked around the dingy room, searching for anything—*anything*—that might help them escape. There was nothing. The windows were too high, the door was blocked by the men, and they were completely outnumbered. She felt a crushing sense of helplessness, the reality of their situation settling like a stone in her stomach.

Did Ivan hear her?

The thought flashed through her mind like a lifeline, a small sliver of hope she clung to. She had managed to scream into the phone, even if just for a moment before it had been ripped from her grasp. *Had he heard? Did he know they were in danger?*

She closed her eyes for a brief second, willing herself to stay calm. She had to believe Ivan would come for them. He had to. The man who had so thoroughly wrapped her world in his would surely move mountains to protect his children. She refused to think about the alternative—refused to believe that they would be left alone in this place, with no one coming to their rescue.

I love him.

The realization hit her with the force of a tidal wave, and it nearly took her breath away. She had been fighting it for so long, pushing back against the emotions that had been building inside her since the moment she had entered Ivan's life. But now, with danger closing in around them, there was no denying it.

She loved him and the children.

The thought terrified her, but at the same time, it gave her strength. Her fear for Ivan, for the children, outweighed any fear she had for herself. She would fight for them. She would survive for them. No matter what happened, no matter how dark things seemed, she would not let these men harm the children—or her.

Katya opened her eyes, her grip tightening on Kirill and Dasha. She could feel a shift inside herself, the fear still present but mingling with something else—a fierce determination. She wasn't just a woman repaying a debt anymore. She wasn't just a pawn in Ivan's world. She was their protector now, and she would do whatever it took to keep them safe.

The man with the scar crouched down in front of her again, his eyes gleaming with amusement as he looked her over. "Feisty little thing, aren't you?"

he said, his voice dripping with menace. "We'll have some fun with you later. But first…"

He reached for her, his hand brushing her arm, and Katya recoiled instinctively, her entire body tensing. She shifted slightly, positioning herself more firmly between him and the children, refusing to let him get any closer.

"Touch me again, and I'll kill you," she hissed, her voice low but filled with venom.

The man raised an eyebrow, clearly surprised by her defiance, but he only chuckled, standing up slowly. "Oh, I like you," he said, his tone amused. "This is going to be fun."

Katya's pulse pounded in her ears as she watched him, her mind racing. She didn't know how long she could hold out against these men, but she would fight until her last breath to protect the children. She would give Ivan enough time to find them, to save them.

She had to believe he was coming. She had to.

Katya closed her eyes for a moment, drawing in a shaky breath, trying to steady herself. This wasn't just about her anymore. This was about Kirill, Dasha, and the man she loved. She would not let these men take that away from her. She would survive this. She had to.

She whispered one final promise to herself, her heart pounding with determination: *I will protect them. I will survive. For Ivan, for the children—for us all.*

As the men continued to talk and laugh amongst themselves, Katya's resolve solidified. She wasn't just a victim. She was a fighter, and she would fight until Ivan found them.

Please, Ivan, she thought, clinging to that last thread of hope. *We need you.*

Chapter 22

Ivan stood at the head of the conference room, surrounded by his men, discussing the details of a new shipment. His mind was sharp, focused on the logistics of keeping his operations running smoothly. But then, his phone buzzed on the table beside him, the screen lighting up with Katya's name.

At first, he thought nothing of it—she often called to ask about the children or to let him know if they were going out. But the moment he answered, everything changed.

A piercing scream echoed through the speaker, followed by the panicked cries of his children in the background before the line went dead. His heart stopped, the sound of Katya's terror freezing his blood in his veins.

For a moment, the world seemed to tilt off its axis. Ivan stood frozen, his hand still gripping the phone, his mind struggling to catch up with what he had just heard. The silence in the room was deafening. His men, sensing something was wrong, had stopped talking, their eyes trained on him. But Ivan's mind was elsewhere.

In those few seconds of stunned silence, every fiber of his being was consumed with one thought: *Someone has taken them.* The woman he had started to care for—the one he had failed to express his feelings to the night before—was gone. And his children...

A tidal wave of rage surged through him, turning his momentary paralysis into a violent storm. His fist clenched around the phone so tightly that the screen cracked before he hurled it across the room, the sound of it shattering against the wall barely registering in his ears.

"Fuck!" Ivan's roar reverberated off the walls, sending a shiver through the room. His chest heaved with fury as he tried to make sense of the situation, but his mind was clouded with panic and fear for his children and Katya. This wasn't just a business threat, some petty turf war over territory or weapons. This was personal. Whoever had taken them had made the gravest mistake of their lives.

His lieutenant, Eriks, stepped forward cautiously, recognizing the shift in Ivan's demeanor. His usual calm control had been replaced by something more dangerous—an uncontained, burning rage.

"Who the fuck took them?" Ivan barked, his voice sharp and deadly. He didn't wait for an answer before spinning around to face his men. "My children, Katya…Find out who did this. Find them *now.*"

Eriks, ever the reliable second-in-command, was already moving, typing rapidly on his phone as he sent out orders to track Katya's location and find out who was responsible. But the seconds ticked by, each one feeling like a lifetime to Ivan.

His men shifted nervously, sensing the danger in the room. Ivan wasn't just angry—he was something more volatile, a man on the verge of exploding. And they knew better than to get in his way. The air in the room was thick with tension, crackling like a live wire.

Ivan began pacing, his fists clenched at his sides, his thoughts racing a mile a minute. He had always been methodical, calculated, the one who stayed calm under pressure. But this? This was different. His children, his blood, and the woman who had become more to him than he had ever intended—*they* were in danger.

The memory of Kirill's terrified scream replayed in his mind, a cruel reminder of how vulnerable his family was. *I swore I'd protect them,* he thought bitterly, his heart hammering in his chest. He had built walls around his life, around his emotions, to ensure nothing could hurt him again. But now, those walls were crumbling, and the fear gnawed at his insides, threatening to break him apart.

"Eriks," Ivan snapped, his voice laced with urgency. "Any word on her location?"

Eriks glanced up from his phone, his expression grim. "We're working on it, boss. I've got the tech team trying to track her phone, but it might take a few minutes."

"Minutes?!" Ivan's growl filled the room, and the men around him stiffened. "I don't have fucking minutes! My kids don't have minutes!" His hands clenched and unclenched as if he were ready to break something—someone—just to feel the satisfaction of control again.

"Keep it together, Ivan," Eriks said cautiously, knowing the line he was walking was thin. "We'll find them. But we need a clear head for this. We can't make mistakes."

Ivan's jaw tightened, his muscles coiled like a spring ready to snap. He knew Eriks was right—he couldn't afford to lose control now. But the rage, the helplessness, it was suffocating. The thought of his children in the hands of someone else, of Katya being hurt or worse, was enough to make him want to burn the city to the ground.

But he had to focus. He had to be smart. Ivan took a breath, trying to steady himself. His eyes flickered to the spot where his phone had shattered, the symbol of his lost connection to them, and his heart clenched. *Please, let me get to them in time.*

"I want everyone working on this," Ivan ordered, his voice calmer now but no less deadly. "Contact our sources, our informants, anyone who might know something. We need to know who's behind this, and we need to know fast."

Eriks nodded and swiftly left the room, the rest of Ivan's men following suit. Ivan was left alone, his heart pounding as the gravity of the situation bore down on him.

For the first time in years, Ivan felt truly afraid. Not for himself, but for them. For the people who had become his reason to fight. The image of Katya's face, the sound of his children's voices, haunted him as he stood there, every second ticking by like a bomb waiting to go off.

"I'll find you," he whispered under his breath, his eyes dark with resolve. "And I'll make them pay for taking you."

The fear might have been gnawing at his insides, but Ivan knew one thing for sure: whoever had dared to take what was his would regret it.

And they wouldn't live to tell the tale.

Ivan paced the room like a caged animal, his fists clenched and his mind spiraling with thoughts of vengeance. The weight of Katya's scream and his children's cries still echoed in his mind, leaving no room for anything else but pure, unbridled rage. Then, the door to his office opened, and Eriks entered, his face grim.

"Ivan," Eriks began cautiously, his eyes flicking up to meet Ivan's for only a moment before glancing away again. "We found Nick. He's dead."

The words hit Ivan like a freight train, the impact of them sinking into his chest like a brutal punch. Nick, his driver—loyal, reliable Nick—was dead. Ivan's stomach churned, not with sorrow, but with a deeper, darker sense of betrayal. His pulse pounded in his ears as the reality of the situation crashed over him. This wasn't just a kidnapping. This was an attack on his family, on everything he held dear. The betrayal was a wound that cut deep, but there was no time to dwell on it. Rage bubbled up inside him, but he shoved it down. There were more pressing matters to deal with. The loss of Nick would be avenged later, right now, he had to focus on getting Katya and his children back.

"They killed one of my men," Ivan growled, more to himself than to Eriks. "And they took what's mine."

Eriks nodded, his jaw tight with restrained anger. He was loyal to Ivan, had been for years, and the weight of this betrayal burned in him just as fiercely. But Ivan could see the steadiness in his lieutenant's eyes, the calm before the storm. "I've got a lead," Eriks said. "We managed to ping Katya's phone before the signal went dead. She's in an industrial area. A rundown part of the city."

The tension in Ivan's muscles grew tauter. He could picture the area in his mind—old factories and crumbling warehouses, a part of town where the police seldom ventured and where danger thrived. It was the perfect place for a kidnapping. No one would hear them scream. No one would care.

Ivan's hands flexed at his sides, the adrenaline in his veins pushing him into action. "What's the fastest route?" he asked, his voice sharp with urgency.

Eriks didn't hesitate. "I'll drive. It's about twenty minutes from here if we push it. I'll get the men ready."

Ivan gave a curt nod. There was no time to waste. "Do it. Gather everyone. I want our best—no mistakes."

Eriks turned on his heel and left the room without another word. Ivan stood there for a moment, the silence suffocating around him, broken only by the rapid thudding of his heart. He couldn't stop himself from thinking about what could be happening to Katya right now. The thought of her—of his children—alone in that building, at the mercy of God knows who, made his blood boil.

His fists clenched, the image of Katya's terrified face flashing in his mind. *I should have told her how I felt. I should have made her stay close to me, safe.* Regret, bitter and sharp, gnawed at him. She had come to him with questions the night before, asking about their future, and he'd brushed her off.

He had been too consumed with maintaining control, too unwilling to acknowledge what had been growing between them. Now, with her life hanging in the balance, he realized just how much she meant to him.

This wasn't just about possession or repayment anymore. Katya had become something more—something he hadn't allowed himself to admit until now. He cared for her deeply. The idea of losing her, of losing his children, was more than he could bear. But he couldn't dwell on that now. There was no room for emotion, no room for the vulnerability he had been trying so hard to suppress. He had to stay focused.

With renewed determination, Ivan moved to the weapons cabinet in the corner of the room. He pulled it open, revealing an array of guns and tactical gear. His hands moved automatically, selecting a firearm and strapping on a bulletproof vest. The weight of the gun in his hand was familiar, grounding him in a way that nothing else could. This wasn't the first time he'd gone into a dangerous situation, but it felt different. The stakes were higher than they'd ever been before.

He would not lose them. He couldn't.

His men began to gather, filing into the room with tense faces and hardened expressions. These were his most trusted soldiers, men who had been with him through the blood and violence of the

Bratva wars. There was no hesitation in their eyes, no doubt about the task ahead. They would follow Ivan into the depths of hell if necessary, and tonight, it felt like that's exactly where they were headed.

Eriks returned, his own vest strapped on and his gun holstered at his side. "We're ready when you are, boss," he said, his voice steady.

Ivan turned to face his men, his eyes burning with intensity. "This is personal," he began, his voice low and lethal. "They took my children. They took Katya." His jaw clenched at the words. "Whoever did this will pay. We're going in fast, and we're going in hard. No one leaves that building alive."

There was no need for a response. His men were already on board, the severity of the situation clear in their expressions.

Ivan's mind raced as he holstered his gun and checked the vest one last time. This wasn't just a rescue mission. This was war. The Morozov Bratva that had dared to strike at him would regret it. He would ensure that they would never forget the price of crossing him.

But underneath the layers of rage, the primal need for vengeance, was something softer, something more terrifying. The realization that this was about more than just revenge. This was about Katya—about the woman who had forced her way past his walls without him even realizing it. And about the children he had sworn to protect.

Ivan had always been a man of control, but now that control was slipping, his emotions pushing through in ways he hadn't allowed in years. He cared for her. He loved her. And that thought alone made his chest tighten in a way that had nothing to do with fear.

But love didn't make him weak. It made him more dangerous.

As he led his men out of the building and into the night, Ivan knew one thing for sure: he would bring Katya and his children back, leaving a trail of blood along the way.

As the SUV tore down the streets, Ivan's grip on the steering wheel was so tight his knuckles turned white. His jaw was clenched, and the tension in the car felt suffocating. The hum of the engine, the screech of tires as they took each turn too fast—it all blended into a background noise that Ivan barely registered. His entire focus was on what lay ahead. Each red light they passed felt like a barrier, each delay only feeding the firestorm brewing inside him.

The streets blurred, the city outside the windows becoming a distant blur of lights and shadows. Ivan didn't care about the details. All that mattered was getting to that industrial building as fast as possible. Every second they spent driving was another second that Katya and his children were in danger, and the thought clawed at him, driving his rage higher and higher until it threatened to boil over.

His heart pounded in his chest, not just from the adrenaline of the chase, but from something darker—guilt. A gnawing, relentless guilt that twisted inside him. *How did I let this happen?* The question repeated in his mind, each time sharper than the last. How had he allowed Katya and his children to be taken, ripped from his protection? *I failed them.*

He felt the weight of that failure like a physical burden on his shoulders. He had sworn to protect them. He had built his entire world on the premise of control, on ensuring that nothing ever touched what was his. Yet now, his children—his precious Kirill and Dasha—and Katya were at the mercy of men who had no qualms about violence. It made his stomach turn, and for the first time in years, fear gripped him like a vice. Real, tangible fear. Not for himself, but for them.

The guilt turned into a searing ache in his chest. He had already lost so much. His wife had been stolen from him in an instant, a car bomb meant for him that left nothing but ash and blood in its wake. That had been the first time he had felt the sting of true loss. And now, just as he had begun to rebuild something—just as he had started reconnecting with his children, just as he had begun feeling again—everything was slipping through his fingers.

His mind flashed to the image of Katya, the way she had looked at him the night before, her eyes filled with questions he hadn't answered. She had stood in his study, vulnerable, asking him about their future, and he had given her nothing. His silence had been a wall between them, and now that wall felt like the biggest mistake of his life. Why hadn't he told her how he felt? Why had he kept his emotions locked away, even when she had been brave enough to confront him?

She deserved more, he thought bitterly. Katya had opened herself up to him, had let herself feel, and he had pushed her away with half-answers and cold distance. And now, she was out there—alone, scared, and in danger. He was supposed to protect her, and instead, he had left her vulnerable. The thought of her in the hands of his enemies sent a fresh wave of fury through him, a deep, primal rage that threatened to consume him whole.

Ivan's grip on the wheel tightened even further, his mind swirling with guilt and anger. He couldn't afford to think like this. Not now. Not when every second counted. His thoughts needed to be clear, sharp. But no matter how hard he tried to push it down, the image of Katya's face kept flashing in his mind—her eyes wide with fear, her lips trembling as she screamed for him on the phone. *That's the last sound I heard from her.* His children's cries had echoed in the background, and the memory twisted like a knife in his gut.

But under all of that—the guilt, the rage—was something deeper. Something that terrified him more than the violence of the world he lived in. He was starting to realize just how much Katya meant to him. This wasn't just about the children. This wasn't just about protecting his family. It was about her. Somewhere along the way, she had become a part of him, someone he couldn't push aside as just another obligation or another piece on the chessboard of his life. Katya had embedded herself in his heart, whether he had wanted her to or not.

The truth gnawed at him, making it hard to breathe. He had never felt this way about any woman, not even his wife. What he had felt for his wife had been different—practical, calculated, built more on loyalty than emotion. But with Katya, it was raw, unrestrained. She had stirred feelings in him that he hadn't known he was capable of, feelings that made him question if he'd ever really understood love before.

Love. The word felt foreign to him, as if it didn't belong in his world. He had spent so many years burying his emotions, convincing himself that love was a weakness, something that made you vulnerable in a life where vulnerability could get you killed. But Katya had changed that. She had broken through the walls he'd built around himself, and he wasn't sure if he could ever rebuild them now.

He thought about the way she had stood in front of him the night before, demanding answers about their future. She had wanted to know if she was just another tool, another means to an end, and he hadn't been able to give her a real answer. He hadn't allowed himself to acknowledge how much she had come to mean to him. And now, he might never get the chance to tell her.

The thought alone made his chest tighten with a fear he wasn't used to. Katya wasn't just a woman repaying her father's debt anymore. She wasn't just someone who had been caught up in his world by circumstance. She was *his*. He had claimed her, body and soul, and the idea of someone else daring to lay a hand on what was his filled him with a white-hot rage. She belonged to him—no one else—and he would destroy anyone who tried to take her from him.

He had always been a man who thrived on control, on dominance. And Katya had challenged that in ways he hadn't expected. She made him feel things he didn't want to feel—things that made him question the walls he'd built around himself. But none of that changed the fact that she was *his*. She was his to protect, his to possess, and his to keep. The thought of another man—any man—touching her, hurting her, made his vision blur with fury.

No one had the right to take her from him. She was part of him now, part of his life in ways he hadn't wanted to admit. He didn't just crave her, didn't just want her body beneath his—he *needed* her. Her defiance, her strength, her vulnerability—it all belonged to him. He had marked her with his touch, claimed her with his dominance, and the idea of someone else trying to take that from him was unthinkable.

She had questioned him, challenged him, and pushed him in ways no one else had. And now, she was out there, taken from him, and the thought that he might lose her forever filled him with a dread he hadn't felt in years. But beneath that fear was something stronger—something primal. He would get her back. He would kill anyone who stood in his way, and he would make sure she knew that she was his, now and always.

Ivan clenched his jaw, the possessiveness swirling in his chest. She didn't realize it yet—how much she meant to him, how deep his feelings had grown—but she would. And when he found her, when he brought her back, he would make sure she understood that she wasn't going anywhere. She belonged to him, and he would never let her go.

His thoughts sharpened, narrowing in on the mission at hand. Whoever had dared to take what was his would regret it. They had crossed a line that couldn't be uncrossed, and Ivan would make them pay for it with blood. No one touched what was his and lived to tell about it.

The car sped through the darkened streets, the industrial building drawing nearer with every passing second. His mind sharpened, honing in on what needed to be done. This was no longer just a mission. This was personal. The men who had taken his children, who had taken Katya, would regret it. He would tear through them with a vengeance they couldn't begin to imagine. There would be no mercy. No second chances. They had taken what was his, and they would pay for it with blood.

His jaw clenched as the industrial building came into view. He could feel the primal rage inside him reaching its peak, the bloodlust surging through him like a tidal wave. But beneath that, something else stirred. The realization that Katya, Kirill, and Dasha weren't just people he was responsible for—they were his family. The family he had never thought he would have again.

With a sharp turn, the car skidded to a stop outside the building. Ivan's pulse pounded in his ears as he threw the door open, his men following suit, weapons at the ready. The industrial building loomed ahead, dark and foreboding, but Ivan's heart was set. He would rescue them. He had to.

Because losing them wasn't an option.

Chapter 23

Katya huddled in the dimly lit, cold room with Kirill and Dasha pressed tightly against her, their small bodies trembling with fear. The air was thick with the stench of damp concrete, and every sound in the dilapidated industrial building seemed to echo with a haunting resonance. The faint clinking of metal from distant rooms, the occasional creak of the building's structure—all of it kept her on edge, her senses heightened in the silence. But the worst sound, the one that kept her heart pounding and her stomach churning, came from the guard standing just feet away.

He was tall, burly, and every time his gaze swept over her, it was like a physical touch she couldn't shake off. His smirk, his leering eyes—everything about him screamed danger. He made no attempt to hide his interest, letting his gaze linger on her far too long, his lips curled in a sick, taunting smile.

"I wonder how long you'll be useful," he said, his voice laced with malice. "Might be sooner than you think that we won't need you anymore. Then, well... who knows what'll happen to you."

The words sent a violent shudder through Katya's body, but she tried not to let it show. She couldn't afford to let him see her fear. Not now, not in front of the children. Kirill was clinging to her side, his small hand gripping her shirt with desperate strength, while Dasha had her face buried in Katya's chest, her little shoulders shaking. They were terrified, and all Katya could do was hold them tighter, whispering softly to keep them calm.

"It's going to be okay, sweetheart. It's all going to be okay," she murmured, though her own heart was pounding so loud in her chest that she feared it might give her away. The weight of their fear, combined with her own, felt unbearable. She kept her eyes averted, refusing to meet the guard's lecherous gaze.

Inside, her thoughts raced like wildfire. *Did Ivan get my call?* The image of his face, his strong presence, filled her mind, and she clung to the hope that he had heard her desperate scream before the call was cut off. *Does he know we've been taken?* The uncertainty gnawed at her, tearing at the edges of her fragile resolve. She knew Ivan—he was powerful, relentless when it came to protecting what was his. But would he make it in time? Would he find them before it was too late?

Her mind whirled with fear and doubt. Every moment that passed seemed like an eternity, every second a reminder of how close they were to the edge of something dark and irreversible. She could feel it in the way the guard watched her, the way his smile grew wider with each passing minute, as if he were savoring the anticipation of what might come next.

"Better enjoy the time you've got with those kids," the guard sneered, his voice pulling her back to the present. "They won't be around forever, and neither will you."

Katya's stomach twisted violently, but she forced herself to remain calm for Kirill and Dasha's sake. *Think, Katya. Focus. Stay strong.* The urge to scream, to lash out, to fight was bubbling just beneath the surface, but she couldn't afford to act recklessly. Not with the children here. Their safety came first.

The children had stopped crying, but their wide, terrified eyes spoke volumes. Kirill's grip on her was tight enough to hurt, and Dasha's soft whimpers were barely audible, but they tore at Katya's heart. The guard's increasingly brazen comments only made things worse. His voice was like poison in the room, his words dripping with cruel intent. Every time he spoke, it was as though he was testing her, waiting for her to crack.

But Katya refused to give him the satisfaction. She focused on keeping her breathing steady, her eyes lowered to the floor. She had to keep her wits about her. The children needed her, and she needed to stay strong for them, even if inside, she was breaking apart.

Ivan will come, she told herself over and over again, as if repeating it would make it true. He has to. He'll find us. He won't let anything happen to us.

But the doubt crept in, and with it, a sense of helplessness. She had never felt so powerless before, so completely at the mercy of forces beyond her control. Katya had spent her life fighting, pushing back against the walls that confined her. But now, here in this room, with the children depending on her and a predator standing only feet away, she felt like there was nothing left to push against. Nothing but fear.

The guard's voice cut through her thoughts again. "You've got spirit, I'll give you that," he said, stepping closer, his boots heavy on the concrete floor. "But don't think for a second that it'll save you. You're just another pretty face in the wrong place. And when your time's up, sweetheart, I'll be right here to make sure you remember it."

Katya's skin crawled, but she still refused to meet his eyes. Her heart raced with adrenaline, fear, and a rising desperation that she couldn't suppress any longer. Every instinct screamed at her to protect the children, to get out, to do something—anything—to keep them safe.

But how? How could she protect them when she was completely at the mercy of these men? And what if Ivan didn't come? What if he hadn't heard her? The thought was unbearable, and yet it kept creeping in, like a shadow that wouldn't leave her alone.

The minutes stretched on, each one longer than the last. The children were exhausted, their small bodies trembling against hers as they tried to find comfort in her presence. She kept whispering soft reassurances, even as her own voice shook with uncertainty.

Please, Ivan, she thought, her heart aching with a desperate hope. *Please find us. Please come.*

She couldn't show weakness. She couldn't let them see how afraid she was. For Kirill and Dasha's sake, she had to be strong. She had to believe that Ivan was on his way, that he would tear the world apart to find them. But the gnawing fear, the icy terror that clutched at her chest, wouldn't let her rest.

The guard's eyes were still on her, his grin widening as he watched her struggle with her emotions. Katya clenched her fists, her nails digging into her palms as she fought to keep the tears at bay. She would not let him break her. She couldn't.

But as the seconds ticked by, and the room grew colder, Katya couldn't help but wonder how much longer she could hold on.

Her only hope was that Ivan had heard her scream—and that he was coming.

Gunfire erupted without warning, tearing through the oppressive silence of the building. Katya flinched, her body instinctively tensing as she wrapped herself protectively around Kirill and Dasha. The sharp, violent sounds of bullets ricocheting off walls filled the air, mingling with the muffled shouts of men engaged in combat. Her heart pounded in her chest, a wild, frantic rhythm that matched the chaos outside.

She squeezed her eyes shut, holding the children closer, whispering reassurances she wasn't even sure she believed. "It's going to be okay," she murmured, trying to keep her voice steady despite the overwhelming fear gnawing at her insides. "Just stay still. Don't move."

Her mind raced, the uncertainty clawing at her. Was Ivan out there? Was he safe? She wanted to believe he was—needed to believe it—but the sounds of violence felt too close, too real. The possibility that he could be hurt, or worse, twisted her gut in knots. Her thoughts kept jumping back to that final phone call. Had he heard her? Had he understood what was happening before the line went dead? She had to believe that he did, that he was coming for them, but doubt seeped in like poison, clouding her judgment.

The children huddled against her, trembling, their small hands clutching her shirt as if it were the only thing keeping them anchored. She could feel their fear as acutely as her own, and it tore at her. They were just kids, innocent and undeserving of the terror that surrounded them. Katya's chest tightened, the instinct to protect them at all costs roaring to life inside her.

The room itself felt colder, darker, as if the very walls were closing in. The single guard who remained kept pacing near the door, his eyes darting back and forth between Katya and the entrance, gun raised and ready. His face had lost some of its earlier arrogance, but there was still a twisted sense of satisfaction in the way he glanced at her—like he was enjoying watching her fear, feeding off her helplessness. His lewd comments had ceased with the eruption of gunfire, but the way his eyes lingered on her skin made her stomach churn.

She focused on breathing, on keeping her composure for the children, but the fear was relentless, creeping into every corner of her mind. Her thoughts bounced back to Ivan again. What if he didn't make it? What if something happened to him before he could reach them? The mere idea of him lying injured or worse outside the room sent a wave of nausea through her. She clenched her jaw, fighting back the panic. She couldn't afford to lose it now. Not in front of the children.

Each second felt like an hour. The gunfire, the shouting—it was all closing in. Her heart hammered, each beat echoing in her ears as she strained to listen for any clue, any indication that Ivan was coming for them. But it was impossible to tell. Every sound seemed to blur together into one endless cacophony of violence and chaos.

Her hands shook as she brushed a trembling strand of hair away from Dasha's face, whispering for her to keep her head down. She prayed Ivan would burst through that door any second now, that he would find them and get them out of this nightmare. But the longer the fight dragged on outside, the more that small flicker of hope wavered, threatening to extinguish completely.

Suddenly, the guard's movements became more erratic. His eyes flickered toward the door with renewed focus, his grip tightening on the gun. Katya's pulse quickened. Something was happening. She could hear the fight getting closer, the unmistakable sounds of bodies slamming into walls, the grunts of pain that came with hand-to-hand combat. Her heart lodged itself in her throat.

Every nerve in her body screamed at her to prepare, to brace for whatever was coming next. She whispered again to the children, her voice barely audible over the deafening noise. "Stay down. Don't look."

The guard cursed under his breath, adjusting his stance in front of the door, his weapon held at the ready. His grip on the gun tightened, his finger hovering near the trigger, ready to shoot at the first sign of movement. Katya could see the sweat beading on his forehead, his eyes darting between her and the door. He was nervous, but so was she. What if Ivan came through the door? What if he made it to them, just to be shot as he entered the room?

Suddenly, the door to the room burst open with a thunderous crash, the force of it slamming the heavy wood against the wall. A man came hurtling through the doorway, his body slamming against the doorframe with enough force to shake the entire room.

Without hesitation, the guard raised his gun, his face twisted in a mix of fear and aggression, and opened fire. The shots rang out in quick, brutal succession, the sound deafening in the small, enclosed space. Katya flinched, instinctively pulling the children closer, shielding them with her body as the bullets tore through the air.

The man who had burst into the room, one of the Morozov Bratva soldiers, jerked violently with each hit, his body convulsing under the impact of the gunfire. His face contorted in pain as he crumpled to the ground, a lifeless heap at the foot of the door.

The room fell into a brief, heavy silence, the only sound the ragged breathing of the guard standing over the body.

Katya's mind reeled. Relief washed over her in a sickening wave. It wasn't Ivan. The guard had shot one of his own men.

Katya's heart pounded, her relief replaced by a surge of renewed terror. Her hands tightened around the children, holding them close as the guard turned, gun raised, ready for the real fight.

As Ivan stormed into the room, the air around him seemed to shift, crackling with a deadly intensity. His eyes locked onto the guard, and the sheer fury burning in them was enough to make Katya's breath catch in her throat. There was no hesitation, no pause, just pure, unrelenting determination as Ivan launched himself at the guard, the force of his charge knocking the man back against the wall.

The guard, though shaken, quickly regained his footing, swinging his gun up to fire. But Ivan was faster, grabbing the man's wrist and slamming it hard against the wall. The gun clattered to the floor, skidding across the room. Katya watched in stunned silence as the two men grappled with each other, their movements violent and animalistic. The sound of fists meeting flesh filled the room, each blow echoing in Katya's chest.

Her heart pounded, her body frozen in place as the fight unfolded before her. Ivan was larger, stronger, but the guard fought like a man desperate to survive. The intensity of their struggle was terrifying. She clutched Kirill and Dasha closer, trying to shield them from the brutal scene in front of them, but she couldn't tear her eyes away. This was no ordinary fight—this was a battle for survival, and the stakes couldn't be higher.

Ivan growled, a sound so low and primal that it sent a shiver down Katya's spine. He was relentless, his fists hammering into the guard's body with a ferocity she had never seen before. This was the side of Ivan she had always feared—the ruthless, violent man who would do anything to protect what was his. And right now, she and the children were what he was fighting for.

But the guard wasn't going down easily. He swung wildly, catching Ivan across the jaw with a brutal punch that sent him staggering back. For a moment, fear seized Katya's heart. What if Ivan couldn't win? What if the guard overpowered him? The thought was too unbearable to entertain. Ivan couldn't lose. He wouldn't.

Her eyes flickered toward the discarded gun on the floor, just out of reach. Instinctively, she pulled the children closer, keeping them as far away from the danger as possible. The guard lunged at Ivan again, and they collided with a sickening thud, their bodies crashing against the wall. The room seemed to shrink around them, the violence suffocating in its intensity.

The guard tried to twist free, his movements frantic as he reached for something—anything—to use as a weapon. But Ivan was too strong, too focused. He slammed the man's head into the wall, the sound of bone hitting concrete reverberating through the room. The guard let out a strangled groan, his body sagging under the force of Ivan's assault.

Ivan didn't let up. He kept going, each punch harder than the last, his rage pouring out in every brutal blow. Katya watched, her breath held, as the guard's resistance weakened. His movements became sluggish, his arms dropping limply to his sides. Blood dripped from his mouth, his face a battered mess.

And still, Ivan didn't stop.

It was only when the guard slumped to the floor, barely conscious, that Ivan finally paused, his chest heaving with exertion. Katya could see the wildness in his eyes, the unchecked fury that had driven him to the brink. He looked like he was barely holding on to his humanity, like the violence had consumed him entirely.

But just as Ivan turned his gaze toward her, something else happened. Another Morozov soldier appeared at the door, his eyes wild and desperate as he rushed toward the children.

Katya's heart seized with panic. She couldn't let him take them. Not after everything they had been through. Her gaze snapped to the gun lying on the floor, and without thinking, she lunged for it.

Her fingers wrapped around the cold metal, and in one swift motion, she raised the gun and fired.

The gunshot rang out, loud and deafening in the small room. The Morozov soldier stopped mid-charge, his eyes widening in shock as the bullet struck him in the chest. He staggered back, blood blooming across his shirt, before collapsing to the floor with a dull thud.

Katya's hand trembled as she lowered the gun, her heart racing in her chest. She had just killed a man. The weight of that realization hit her like a punch to the gut, but she didn't have time to process it. All that mattered was that the children were safe.

Ivan looked up from the guard he had beaten, his eyes finding hers. For a moment, they just stared at each other, the intensity of what had just happened hanging heavily in the air. Katya could see the blood on his hands, the bruises on his face.

The sounds of fighting began to fade, the echo of gunfire and shouts diminishing until there was nothing but a heavy, oppressive silence. The tension in the air still hummed, but the immediate danger had passed. Katya remained frozen for a moment, the gun still clutched in her trembling hands. Her chest heaved with every breath, her body shaking from the adrenaline that coursed through her veins.

And then she saw Ivan.

He crossed the room in long, determined strides, his face hard and unreadable, but his eyes—those fierce, dark eyes—were filled with something deeper. Relief. Concern. Possessiveness. He pulled her and the children into his arms without a word, his hold tight and protective, as if he needed to feel them, to assure himself that they were alive and safe. Katya melted into his embrace, the weight of everything crashing down on her all at once.

The fear, the violence, the terror of losing him and the children—it all swirled together in her chest, making it hard to breathe. Her hands clung to his shirt, her fingers twisting the fabric as if letting go would mean losing him. Dasha and Kirill clung to her, their small bodies trembling in the aftermath, but Katya held them close, shielding them as best as she could.

"It's over," Ivan murmured into her hair, his voice rough, yet steady. His lips brushed the top of her head, a gesture so tender that it almost undid her completely.

Katya nodded, though the lump in her throat made it impossible to speak. Her entire body ached from the tension, and her legs felt like they might give out, but she held on. Ivan's presence, his strength, was the only thing keeping her grounded. She closed her eyes, letting herself lean into him, if only for a moment, feeling the warmth of his body against hers.

"We need to go," Ivan said, pulling back slightly but not letting her go completely. His eyes flickered over her, assessing, and Katya saw the deep concern there—the raw, unguarded emotion that he rarely showed. It was fleeting, but it was enough to reassure her that he wasn't just thinking about his children. He was thinking about her, too.

Katya's breath hitched as Ivan shifted, lifting Kirill into his arms with ease. He glanced at her, nodding for her to take Dasha. Katya quickly scooped up the little girl, her arms aching but her mind sharp with the singular goal of getting them out of there. Ivan led the way, his body tense, every muscle coiled like a spring ready to snap.

He moved with a predator's grace, his eyes scanning the dimly lit hallways as they made their way out of the building. Katya followed, her heart still racing, but the fear was beginning to ebb, replaced by a fragile hope. They were getting out. They were going to make it.

The cold night air hit them as they stepped outside, the dark sky stretching endlessly above them. For a moment, it felt surreal—like they had stepped out of one world and into another. The stark contrast between the violence inside the building and the quiet, almost peaceful night outside sent a chill through Katya. But there was no time to stop, no time to breathe.

Ivan hurried them to the car, his movements quick and precise. Katya felt the weight of Dasha in her arms, the little girl's head resting on her shoulder as she whimpered softly. Kirill clung to Ivan, his small face buried in his father's neck. The children were terrified, but they were alive.

Katya couldn't stop the tears that welled in her eyes as she helped settle Dasha into the backseat next to her brother. The flood of emotions threatened to overwhelm her, but she fought it back, knowing they weren't safe yet. She slid into the passenger seat beside Ivan, her hands trembling as she buckled herself in.

Ivan started the car without a word, his jaw tight, his eyes hard as he sped away from the building. The tires screeched against the pavement, the engine roaring as they left the site of so much fear and danger behind. Katya stared out the window, her mind still processing everything that had happened.

It was over. They were safe. But the relief she felt was tinged with exhaustion, both physical and emotional. She turned her gaze toward Ivan, watching him as he drove. His hands gripped the steering wheel tightly, his knuckles white with tension. The hardness in his expression hadn't softened, and Katya knew he was still on edge, still in fight mode.

But there was something else there, too. Beneath the cold exterior, beneath the mask of ruthless control, Katya could see the vulnerability. She could see the fear that had gripped him, the desperation that had driven him to fight so savagely to get them back. It was a side of Ivan she had never seen before—a side she hadn't known he possessed.

Her heart ached with gratitude, with a deep, overwhelming sense of affection for the man sitting beside her. She had known Ivan was a force to be reckoned with, a man who would stop at nothing to protect what was his. But now, as they drove through the darkened streets, she realized that she had become part of that. She had become part of his world, his life, in ways she hadn't fully understood until now.

"Ivan..." Her voice was soft, barely audible over the sound of the engine.

He didn't look at her, but his hand moved, reaching across the center console to grasp hers. His fingers intertwined with hers, strong and steady, and for the first time since the chaos had started, Katya felt a sense of peace.

They didn't speak as they drove, but the silence between them wasn't empty. It was filled with understanding, with the unspoken bond that had formed between them during this ordeal. Katya knew that her life had changed forever—that she had changed forever.

Ivan and his children had become her family, and she would never be the same.

As the city lights blurred past, Katya squeezed his hand, her heart swelling with the realization that, despite everything, she had found something here. Something real.

Chapter 24

As the car rolled to a stop in front of Ivan's mansion, the silence between them felt suffocating. Katya could still hear the echoes of gunfire in her mind, the chaos of the rescue pounding in her chest. The children were curled up in the backseat, their small faces pale with exhaustion and lingering fear. Kirill's head rested against the window, and Dasha had her thumb in her mouth, a sign she had retreated to the safety of her childhood habits.

Ivan was the first to move, his hand gripping the steering wheel before he released it and stepped out of the car. His movements were calculated, controlled, but Katya noticed the subtle shift in his posture—the heaviness in his shoulders that he tried to hide. She followed him out, her legs feeling shaky as she reached for Dasha, pulling the sleepy child into her arms. Ivan did the same with Kirill, his strong arms lifting his son effortlessly.

As they stepped inside the house, the contrast between the dark, cold building they'd just escaped and the warmth of their home was stark. The soft lighting in the entryway cast long shadows across the floor, but it felt strangely quiet, too quiet, after the violence they had left behind. The mansion, which always seemed impenetrable, now felt vulnerable in a way Katya hadn't expected. The weight of what had happened pressed down on her, making it hard to breathe.

Ivan's face was still set in a hard line, his jaw tight as he walked ahead of her with Kirill in his arms. But there was a slight softening in his demeanor—his protective instinct still there, but now tempered by the relief of having them home, safe. Katya watched him closely as they moved through the house, noting the tension in his body as he placed Kirill on the couch for a moment, his eyes scanning the room as if searching for threats that no longer existed.

Her mind couldn't stop replaying the images from earlier—the gunfire, the way Ivan had stormed into that room, a lethal force, and the sheer determination in his eyes when he saw her and the children huddled together. That moment when he crossed the room, killing without hesitation, his only focus on protecting them, had left a mark on her she couldn't erase. He had risked everything. He had killed for her.

And it wasn't just because she was someone repaying a debt. She saw that now. There was more.

As they stepped deeper into the house, a strange calm settled over them, but it felt fragile, as though the chaos they'd escaped was still lingering in the air. The children were too quiet, still processing everything they had witnessed, and Katya could feel her own emotions swirling just beneath the surface, too raw to address yet. She glanced around the dimly lit hallway, noticing how even the familiar surroundings now felt different. As if the night's violence had followed them here, casting a shadow over the safety they were supposed to feel.

Ivan turned to her for a moment, his eyes meeting hers, and in that gaze, Katya felt a flicker of something deeper—a connection that hadn't been there before. He didn't say anything, but the look spoke volumes. He had fought for her, and in that fight, something had changed between them. Katya felt her heart clench, a mixture of gratitude and something more, something she wasn't ready to name yet. She wasn't just grateful that he had saved them—she was in awe of him, of the way he had fought like a man possessed to protect what was his.

They moved up the stairs quietly, the tension still lingering in the air as they carried the children to their rooms. The house had never felt this heavy before, as though the walls themselves bore witness to the danger they had barely escaped.

Katya's thoughts kept circling back to Ivan—how he had seemed almost invincible earlier, a man who would stop at nothing to ensure their safety. But here, in the quiet of their home, there was something different about him. He still carried the weight of the night's events in his stance, but there was also a softness in the way he cradled Kirill against his chest. A tenderness that she hadn't seen in him before.

As they reached the children's rooms, Ivan gently laid Kirill in his bed, brushing his hair back from his forehead with a gentleness that took Katya by surprise. She stood in the doorway, watching him as he whispered something in Russian to his son, his voice low and comforting. She couldn't make out the words, but the tone was enough to make her heart ache.

This was a side of Ivan she hadn't expected to see—the tender father who would go to war for his children but could also show them love in the quiet moments like this. It stirred something deep inside her, something she hadn't been ready to confront before. Seeing him like this, so strong yet so vulnerable, made her realize just how much he had come to mean to her.

Katya placed Dasha in her bed, tucking her in with gentle hands, but her mind kept drifting back to Ivan. To the way he had fought for them, protected them, and now, the way he was looking at his children, as if they were his entire world. As if they were the only thing that mattered.

And Katya couldn't help but wonder—was she part of that world now? Did she matter to him the way they did?

The house was quiet, but Katya's mind was anything but. She felt the weight of everything they had gone through pressing down on her, but there was one thought that rose above all the others. Ivan had risked his life for her, and in doing so, he had shown her something she hadn't fully understood until now.

She wasn't just someone repaying a debt. She was part of him now, whether she was ready to admit it or not.

After the children had finally settled into a deep, exhausted sleep, the quiet of the house became almost deafening. Ivan retreated to his bedroom while Katya lingered in the hallway for a moment, her hand resting lightly on the doorframe of the children's room, as if grounding herself to something familiar in the midst of the emotional whirlwind swirling inside her. The events of the night replayed over and over in her mind, refusing to let her rest.

She moved slowly through the house, her feet taking her in the direction of her own room, but her thoughts were far from any sense of safety or comfort. She couldn't stop thinking about Ivan—about the way he had charged into that room, lethal and terrifying, to save them. The memory of him standing over the man he had beaten to death was seared into her mind. She could still hear the dull thud of his fists landing blow after blow, his face twisted in cold, ruthless fury. It should have terrified her, seeing him like that—seeing him become the very embodiment of violence. But it hadn't.

If anything, it had drawn her in.

The realization sent a shiver down her spine. What kind of person was she becoming, to feel this way? To be drawn to the raw, unbridled power that Ivan possessed, even when it came at the cost of another man's life? She had watched him destroy that guard without hesitation, without mercy, and instead of fear, what she had felt was… safety. Protection. A deep sense of certainty that, no matter what, Ivan would always fight for her, for his children, for what was his.

The house around her was so quiet now, so calm in contrast to the chaos they had just escaped. But inside her mind, the storm hadn't passed. She sank into a chair in the sitting room, her hands resting in her lap as she tried to sort through the flood of emotions.

Her gaze dropped to her hands, and a wave of nausea swept over her as she remembered the feel of the cold metal of the gun, the kickback as she pulled the trigger. She had killed a man tonight. The thought lingered, heavy and cold in her chest. It wasn't just self-defense; it was a decision, an action she had taken without a second thought to protect Kirill and Dasha. She could still see the body of the man she had shot, his lifeless eyes staring up at her from the floor.

But she didn't feel regret. Fear, yes, but not regret.

Instead, she felt pride. Pride in what she had done to protect the children, to ensure their safety when all else had fallen apart. She had stepped into Ivan's world, and she had held her own. That realization settled deep within her, solidifying the truth she had been resisting for so long: she was no longer on the outside looking in. She was part of this life now, tied to it in ways that went far beyond just paying off a debt.

Her thoughts shifted again, inevitably drawn back to Ivan. Everything always seemed to lead back to him. She could still see the hard set of his jaw as he carried Kirill out of that building, the tension in his shoulders as he fought his way through the chaos to get to her. He had been relentless, unstoppable. But the memory that stood out the most was the way he had looked at her when the dust settled—his eyes filled with something more than just possession or control.

Katya's heart clenched as she realized what that something was. She had been trying to avoid it, trying to push it away, but there was no escaping it now. She had fallen for him. Completely, irrevocably. It was more than the physical attraction that had first drawn her to him, more than the desire that had burned between them from the beginning. It was the way he loved his children, the way he would tear the world apart to keep them safe. It was the way he had fought for her tonight, risked everything for her.

She pressed her hands to her chest, trying to steady her breathing as the weight of it all crashed over her. The truth was undeniable now—she couldn't walk away from him, from this life. Not after everything they had been through together. Not after what she had seen in him tonight.

And it wasn't just about the danger or the violence, though those things still lingered at the edges of her thoughts. It was about Ivan himself. The man beneath the ruthless exterior. The father who stayed a moment longer with his children tonight, whispering softly to them. The man who had opened up to her, even if just in fleeting moments, and showed her a side of himself that few ever saw.

The idea of leaving him now, of walking away when her five years were up, felt impossible. Like tearing away a part of herself.

Katya stood, her legs shaky beneath her as she paced the room. What was she going to do? She had spent so much time trying to keep her distance, trying to convince herself that this was just temporary—that she could repay her father's debt and then go back to her old life. But that life felt like a distant memory now. And the future she had once imagined for herself? It didn't exist anymore.

Her future was here, with Ivan, with his children. She couldn't deny that now. The fear she had once felt about his world—the violence, the danger—was still there, lurking in the background, but it was overshadowed by something else. Something stronger.

Love.

It terrified her, but it was the truth. She loved him. She loved the man who had saved her tonight, the man who would do anything to protect what was his. And she knew, deep down, that she was his now. Just as much as he was hers.

Katya's heart raced as the full weight of her feelings settled over her. She couldn't walk away. Not from Ivan. Not from the life they were building together, no matter how dangerous it might be. She belonged here now, in this world, in this life.

The house had settled into a strange, eerie silence. The adrenaline that had surged through Katya during the rescue was now fading, leaving behind an ache deep in her chest. But more than the exhaustion, it was the emotional weight of everything that pressed down on her. She had killed a man to protect Ivan's children, and Ivan had risked everything to save them all. The chaos and danger still loomed in her mind, but now, standing in the hallway outside his room, her thoughts were consumed by something else.

Ivan.

His door stood closed in front of her, the wood heavy and imposing, just like the man behind it. She knew he was in there, likely wrestling with the same emotions she was. She wondered what he was thinking, if he was replaying the events of the night, feeling the same intensity she was. Her heart pounded in her chest, the sound loud in her ears as she stood frozen, staring at the door.

Katya pressed her lips together, her hand brushing against the wood of the door. She wanted to talk to him, to thank him for saving her and the children, but it wasn't just gratitude that pulled her toward him. It was something deeper, something that had been growing inside her since the day she'd entered his world. The connection between them was undeniable, and after tonight, it had only intensified. She didn't want to just talk—she needed to feel him, to be close to him in a way that words couldn't express.

Her fingers hovered near the doorknob as her mind raced. What would she say? What could she possibly say to make him understand how she felt? After everything they had been through tonight, how could she pretend that things between them were still the same? She couldn't. They weren't.

She took a deep breath, feeling the pull toward him grow stronger. It wasn't just about needing to talk. It was about needing him—his strength, his touch, his presence. She had almost lost him tonight, and that thought alone made her chest tighten with fear. She didn't want to waste another second pretending that this wasn't real, that what she felt for him wasn't consuming her whole being.

Before she could second-guess herself, Katya stepped forward and knocked softly on the door. Her hand trembled slightly, but she forced herself to remain still, waiting for a response. The silence that followed was heavy, filled with anticipation, until she finally heard his voice.

"Come in."

His voice was low, rough, and it sent a shiver down her spine. Slowly, Katya pushed open the door and stepped inside, her breath catching in her throat the moment her eyes landed on him. Ivan stood by the window, his shirt unbuttoned, revealing the tattoos that marked his skin, the ones that told the story of his life, of the battles he had fought and won. The moonlight poured in from the window, casting shadows across his strong, muscular frame, making him seem larger than life.

Her heart skipped a beat.

For a moment, neither of them said a word. The tension between them, already palpable, grew even thicker, hanging in the air like a weight that pressed down on her chest. Ivan's dark eyes met hers, the intensity in his gaze making her stomach flip. He didn't move, but the way he looked at her made her feel as though he had reached across the room and pulled her into his orbit.

Katya's mouth went dry, her mind racing with everything she wanted to say, but no words came. Instead, she stood there, feeling vulnerable, exposed in a way that went beyond anything physical. She had faced danger, faced death tonight, and yet, standing here in front of Ivan, she felt more raw and unguarded than ever before.

Ivan's eyes flickered with something she couldn't quite place. There was the familiar heat, the possessiveness that always simmered beneath the surface, but there was more than that now. Tonight had changed things between them, brought them to the edge of something deeper, something that neither of them could ignore any longer.

Katya swallowed hard, taking a step closer to him. She had spent so long trying to deny what was growing between them, telling herself that it was just physical, just a temporary connection until her debt was paid. But tonight had shattered all of that. Tonight had shown her just how much she needed him—not just as a protector, but as something more. As someone who made her feel alive in a way she had never felt before.

"I..." Katya started, but her voice faltered, the words catching in her throat.

Ivan tilted his head slightly, his gaze never leaving hers, waiting for her to continue. The intensity in his eyes was almost too much, but she didn't look away. She couldn't.

"I wanted to thank you," she finally said, her voice soft, barely above a whisper.

Ivan's expression shifted, his gaze softening just a fraction, though the intensity remained. "You don't need to thank me," he replied, his voice rough, laced with something deeper. "I protect what's mine."

There it was again—that possessiveness, that need to claim her. But this time, it wasn't just about control. There was something more in his words, something that made her heart race. She felt her pulse quicken at the way he said it, the way he made it clear that she belonged to him, and he would stop at nothing to keep her safe.

Katya took another step closer, the space between them shrinking. She could feel the pull of him, the way her body instinctively moved toward him, craving his touch, his strength. She didn't know what would happen next, but she knew one thing for certain—she couldn't resist him anymore.

Not now. Not after everything they had been through.

Ivan took a step closing the distance between them, his large frame towering over her but not in a way that made her feel small. If anything, his presence made her feel more grounded, more secure than she had in a long time. She could feel the heat of his body, the way the air between them seemed to hum with unspoken words.

"I didn't think I could feel this way," Ivan continued, his voice lowering to a near whisper. His hand reached out, brushing softly against her arm, sending a shiver down her spine. "Not after everything I've been through... not after losing so much. But you..." His words trailed off for a moment, his gaze flickering with something raw, something real. "You've changed that."

Katya's heart skipped a beat. She had spent so long wondering what she meant to him, what their connection truly was. And now, hearing these words from him, the walls she had built around her heart began to crumble. He hadn't said the word "love," but she could hear it in his voice, feel it in the way he touched her, in the way he looked at her like she was the most important thing in his world.

Ivan's hand moved up to her face, his fingers grazing her cheek, his touch gentle and careful, like he was afraid she might disappear if he wasn't. Katya felt the sincerity in his touch, in the weight of his words. It wasn't just physical—it was something more, something that had grown between them over time, through pain, through fear, through the unbreakable bond they had forged in the fires of danger.

"You're more than just someone repaying a debt," Ivan said softly, his thumb brushing across her cheekbone. "You've become a part of me. I can't imagine my life without you now."

Katya's chest tightened, emotion swelling inside her like a wave she couldn't control. The vulnerability in his voice, the way he allowed himself to be open with her—it was more than she had ever expected from him. This man, who thrived on control and power, was showing her a side of himself that no one else had ever seen. And it was for her.

But then Ivan's expression shifted, and a flicker of something darker passed through his eyes. His hand fell from her face, his gaze dropping for the briefest of moments before he spoke again.

"I'm releasing you from your father's debt."

The words hit her like a punch to the gut. Katya's breath caught in her throat, her mind reeling as she tried to process what he had just said.

"You're free," Ivan continued, his voice thick with a mix of sadness and resignation. "You can leave if you want to."

Katya opened her mouth to respond, but Ivan stepped forward, his voice softening as he spoke. "But before you say anything, I should be the one thanking you."

Her breath hitched, and she looked up at him, confused.

Ivan's eyes were intense, filled with something raw. "You killed a man today, Katya. Not for yourself, but to protect my children. You didn't hesitate. I can't put a value on that. No one can."

He reached out, brushing a lock of hair behind her ear, his touch gentle despite the weight of his words. "You showed me a strength and loyalty that most men wouldn't have. You protected them when I couldn't. A way that your father never would have. And that... that means everything to me."

His gaze locked onto hers, and Katya could see the sincerity in his eyes, the depth of emotion he was struggling to express. He wasn't just speaking of gratitude; he was acknowledging something much more profound. She had proven herself to him—not as someone paying off a debt, but as someone who had earned his trust, his respect.

"That's why I'm releasing you," Ivan continued, his voice gruff. "Not because you've paid off your father's debt. You owe me nothing, not after today. You've given me more than I ever expected. And I can't... I won't hold you to a debt your father was too weak to pay."

The sadness in his voice, the resignation in his eyes, told Katya that this was costing him more than she had ever imagined. He was giving her freedom, but with it, he was offering her something much deeper: the choice to stay, not because she was bound to him, but because she wanted to.

"You can leave if you want to," he repeated, the words quieter now, laced with an unspoken plea.

He took a step back, his jaw clenching, and for the first time, Katya saw something in Ivan she had never expected—fear. The man who had always been so strong, so unshakable, was standing in front of her, terrified of losing her. It was written all over his face, in the way his eyes darkened, in the way his hands fisted at his sides as if he was trying to keep himself from reaching out for her again.

Katya's heart pounded in her chest, tears pricking the corners of her eyes as she stared at him, unable to speak. She hadn't been prepared for this. She had thought about her future, about what would happen when her five years were up, but she had never truly imagined him offering her freedom like this—never imagined the pain it would cause him.

"I don't want you to feel trapped here," Ivan said, his voice gruff, almost broken. "You deserve more than that. And if you want to leave... I won't stop you."

His words were like a knife twisting in her heart. She could see the conflict in his eyes, the way it pained him to say these things, but he was offering her a choice. A choice she had always feared she wouldn't have.

But now that it was here, standing in front of her like a tangible thing, she realized she didn't want it. The freedom she had once craved no longer held any appeal. How could she walk away from this? From him? From everything they had been through together?

Katya stepped forward, closing the distance between them once again. She could see the tension in Ivan's body, the way he was bracing himself for the worst—for her to walk away. But that wasn't what she wanted. Not anymore.

"I'm not leaving," she said, her voice firm despite the whirlwind of emotions swirling inside her. "No matter what happens, I'm staying. I am yours now. I belong here."

Ivan's eyes locked onto hers, and in that moment, something shifted between them—something that couldn't be undone.

Chapter 25

The air in Ivan's bedroom was heavy, but not with the same tension that had gripped them during the rescue. This was something different—quieter, more profound. As Katya stood in the soft light of the room, she felt the weight of everything that had happened between them pressing down. Her heart pounded in her chest, not from fear, but from anticipation. Ivan's presence dominated the space, but this time, there was no need for control, no unspoken power struggle. This was something deeper.

Ivan pulled her close, his strong arms wrapping around her with a quiet intensity that took her breath away. It wasn't the hurried embrace of a man needing to possess, nor the calculated touch of someone in control. It was steady, grounding, as if Ivan was trying to tell her something without words. Katya leaned into him, feeling the solid warmth of his chest beneath her cheek. There was no rush in his movements, no urgency. Just the simple act of holding her, and yet it felt like everything.

For the first time, his touch didn't feel like a demand—it felt like a claim. But not the possessive claim he had always exerted over her before. This was different. It was as if Ivan, with every breath, every gentle squeeze of his arms around her, was silently telling her she belonged here. That she was his. Not just in body, but in something much deeper, something more intimate.

Katya closed her eyes, letting the moment sink in, her mind a whirlwind of emotions. This was what she had wanted—what she had feared—and now that it was here, it felt right. She wasn't standing here because of some obligation, or because she had no choice. She was standing here because she wanted to be. Because Ivan had become something more to her than she could have imagined.

As his lips brushed softly against her forehead, Katya felt a warmth spread through her body, filling every corner of her soul. This wasn't just desire, though the fire of it still burned hot between them. It was more than that. It was love—real, messy, dangerous love. A love she hadn't thought possible in a world like his. But it was there, undeniable and overwhelming.

In that moment, everything they had been through flashed in her mind—the violence, the danger, the way Ivan had fought for her, not just because she was part of a deal, but because she mattered to him. Her mind raced, trying to make sense of the shift between them. How they had gone from two people thrown together by circumstance to something more. Something real.

Ivan's hands were steady on her back, pulling her even closer as if he couldn't bear to let her go. And for the first time, Katya felt like she truly belonged in his arms, like she had found a place she hadn't known she was searching for. She opened her eyes to find him looking down at her, his dark eyes filled with an intensity she couldn't escape. But it wasn't the usual guardedness, the cold calculation she had come to expect. It was something softer, something raw.

His lips hovered just above hers for a moment, the space between them charged with a tension that made her heart race. And then, without warning, he kissed her. The kiss was gentle at first, almost tentative, as if he was testing the waters of something new. But that gentleness quickly gave way to something more urgent, more primal. His tongue teased hers, exploring her mouth with a need that sent heat rushing through her veins.

Katya felt the fire building between them, the familiar burn of desire that had always simmered just beneath the surface. But this time, it wasn't just lust driving them. It was the connection they had forged through everything they had been through together—the danger, the uncertainty, the unspoken feelings that had grown between them.

As Ivan's hands roamed over her back, pulling her closer still, Katya felt the last of her doubts melt away. She kissed him back with everything she had, letting herself fall into him completely, knowing there was no going back from this. They had crossed a line, and there was no returning to the way things had been before. And she didn't want to. Not anymore.

Katya's heart pounded in her chest, her breath coming in shallow bursts as Ivan's kiss deepened, pulling her further into the whirlwind of desire that swirled between them. The intensity of their connection crackled in the air, thick with unspoken emotions. Ivan's hands moved with purpose, his fingers grazing the hem of her dress before slowly tugging it upwards. His eyes never left hers, the dark intensity in his gaze making her feel both exposed and utterly desired.

She stood still as he peeled the fabric from her body, each inch of skin revealed sending shivers through her. Her nipples hardened under his gaze, the cool air brushing against them as her bra fell away. Ivan's hands were rough but deliberate, the callouses on his fingers brushing over her bare skin, leaving trails of heat in their wake.

Katya's hands trembled as she began to undress him in return, her fingers fumbling slightly with the buttons of his shirt, not because of nervousness, but because of the raw energy crackling between them. She could feel his body tensing beneath her touch, his desire palpable in the way his muscles tightened as she pushed the fabric from his broad shoulders. His chest was firm and sculpted, the dark tattoos etched into his skin standing out starkly against the moonlight streaming through the window.

As she unbuckled his pants, her hands brushed against the hardness of his erection, already straining against the fabric. Her breath hitched at the feel of him, so large, so ready. Ivan watched her closely, his eyes darkening with lust as she knelt slightly, pushing his pants down until he stood before her completely naked, his throbbing cock thick and rigid between them.

For a moment, they stood there, fully exposed to one another, their bare skin humming with anticipation. Katya felt vulnerable in a way she never had before, but also powerful—because of the way Ivan looked at her, like she was the only thing he had ever wanted, the only thing he needed. His gaze roamed over her body, lingering on her hardened nipples, the curve of her waist, the slickness between her thighs. The way he looked at her made her feel like she was his in every possible way.

Without a word, Ivan laid her back onto the bed, his body hovering over hers, the heat of his skin pressing down against her as he kissed her again, rougher this time. His hands moved to her breasts, his fingers squeezing them with just enough pressure to make her gasp, her body arching into him in response. His lips followed his hands, kissing a trail from her collarbone down to her chest.

Katya moaned softly as his mouth closed over one of her nipples, his tongue flicking out to tease her. She gasped, her fingers tangling in his hair as he sucked gently at first, then harder, grazing his teeth against her sensitive skin just enough to send a jolt of pleasure straight between her legs. The tension inside her was building, every nerve in her body on fire under his touch.

"You're mine," Ivan growled against her skin, his voice low and possessive. The words sent a thrill through her, making her core tighten in response. His hand slid down her stomach, brushing against her wetness, and he groaned softly as his fingers dipped between her slick folds. "All of you belongs to me," he murmured, his breath hot against her skin as his fingers found her clit, swirling it gently before sliding two fingers deep inside her.

Katya's hips rose off the bed, her body responding to the thrusts of his fingers as he moved inside her. She moaned, her hands reaching down to grasp his large, throbbing cock, stroking him slowly in time with the movements of his fingers. She felt him twitch in her hand, his hardness pulsing with every touch, and the feeling only made her wetter.

Ivan's lips returned to her breasts, teasing and sucking at her nipples as his fingers moved faster, curling inside her just enough to send her teetering on the edge of release. The combination of his hand between her legs and his mouth on her body was almost too much to bear. Katya's moans grew louder, her hips bucking against him as her body begged for more.

She was close, so close to the edge, her entire body trembling with the tension of it. Ivan's growl rumbled through his chest as he watched her, the possessiveness in his eyes making her ache for him in a way she had never known before. His fingers thrust harder, deeper, his thumb pressing against her clit in time with her stroking hand on his cock, and Katya knew she couldn't hold out much longer.

"Ivan," she gasped, her voice breathless and full of need. "Please."

Katya's breath hitched as Ivan's mouth moved lower, his lips and tongue trailing a line of fire down her stomach. Every inch he covered left her trembling, her body aching for what she knew was coming next. When his mouth finally reached the sensitive space between her thighs, she could feel the tension building to unbearable levels. The moment his tongue flicked against her clit, she gasped, her hips instinctively arching toward him. Ivan was relentless, his fingers still thrusting deep inside her while his tongue worked her with maddening precision.

Katya's fingers clenched the sheets beneath her, her body writhing in response to the onslaught of sensation. Every lick, every gentle suction of his lips on her clit sent shockwaves through her. She felt herself spiraling toward the edge, her body responding to him in ways she couldn't control. Each flick of his tongue made her arch further into him, her need building with every second.

The room felt like it was spinning, her vision blurred as the pleasure overtook her. Ivan's mouth and fingers moved in perfect rhythm, his touch driving her to the brink. Katya's moans grew louder, spilling from her lips uncontrollably. The pressure inside her built until she thought she might break apart from the intensity of it all. She couldn't think, couldn't focus on anything but the fire spreading through her body.

"Ivan," she whispered, her voice thick with need, her fingers tangling in his hair as she tried to hold on. "Please... don't stop."

Her body was shaking now, every nerve ignited by the expert way Ivan's mouth worked her. His tongue swirled over her clit, sucking gently, then harder, as his fingers curled inside her, pressing against that spot that made her see stars. Katya was helpless to do anything but give in to the mounting pleasure. Her legs trembled uncontrollably, her breath coming in shallow gasps as her body hovered on the brink of release.

Ivan's growl vibrated against her as he sensed her nearness, pushing her higher with his relentless pace.

And then it happened—his fingers hit the perfect spot, curling inside her just right, and Katya shattered. Her climax crashed over her like a tidal wave, her body convulsing as wave after wave of pleasure tore through her. She cried out his name, her voice breaking as the orgasm consumed her, her hips bucking against his mouth, her entire body trembling uncontrollably beneath him.

But Ivan wasn't finished. He continued to work her with his mouth, drawing out every last bit of her pleasure until she was breathless and trembling. His tongue moved slowly now, teasing her clit as her body slowly descended from the high. Katya lay there, her heart pounding, her body drenched in sweat, as Ivan's hands caressed her thighs, grounding her after the intensity of her release.

Her mind was hazy, her body spent, but as Ivan finally lifted his head, meeting her eyes with a gaze filled with raw hunger, she knew they weren't done yet. The night was far from over.

Ivan positioned himself between Katya's legs, his body hovering over hers as he stared down at her with an intensity that made her heart pound. She could feel the heat of his cock pressing against her entrance, the anticipation building as she waited for him to push inside. His eyes never left hers, dark and full of unspoken emotion, and the connection between them in that moment was palpable.

Slowly, deliberately, Ivan began to push into her. Katya gasped as the thick tip of him stretched her, filling her inch by inch. Her hands instinctively gripped his arms, her nails digging into his skin as her body adjusted to the overwhelming sensation of him inside her. The slick wetness of her arousal made each movement easier, but it didn't lessen the intensity of how perfectly he fit inside her, how deeply he reached.

Every inch felt like a claim, a reminder of his possessiveness, of the fact that she belonged to him in every way. He had told her that she was his, and with each slow, deliberate thrust, Ivan was proving it again. Katya's breath hitched as he filled her completely, her body arching into him as the sensation overwhelmed her.

Ivan's hands gripped her hips firmly, holding her in place as he began to move, his thrusts slow but powerful. Each time he buried himself inside her, the pleasure rippled through her, deep and undeniable. The weight of his body pressing into hers, the way he filled her so completely—it was too much and not enough all at once. Katya moaned, her head falling back against the pillows as she lost herself in the rhythm of his movements.

His moans, deep and low, vibrated through her, heightening the pleasure building inside her with every thrust. As he picked up the pace, each movement came faster, harder, and Katya's hands slid from his arms to his back, her nails digging into his skin. She clung to him, her body meeting his in perfect sync, each thrust driving her closer to the edge of pleasure.

Without breaking the rhythm, Ivan shifted his grip, sliding his hands under her hips and lifting them slightly. The change in angle made his thrusts deeper, hitting a spot inside her that sent a jolt of pleasure through her entire body. Katya cried out, her hips rising to meet his as the intensity built. The sensation was overwhelming, pushing her closer and closer to the brink.

The pressure inside her grew unbearable, the pleasure spiraling out of control. Every thrust sent her higher, her body tightening around him as she teetered on the edge of release. Katya's moans filled the room, her breath coming in short, desperate gasps as she clung to him, her nails raking down his back as she felt the pleasure reaching its peak.

Ivan's movements became frantic, his own body tensing as he thrust into her with a growing urgency. The sounds of his moans, his groans, mixed with her own, pushing them both to the edge. Katya's body convulsed around him as she finally reached her climax, her second orgasm crashing over her with an intensity that left her trembling and breathless beneath him.

Ivan followed her over the edge moments later, groaning her name as his release filled her. His body collapsed against hers, his breath ragged as they rode out the last waves of pleasure together. Katya's arms wrapped around him, holding him close as the intensity of the moment slowly faded, leaving only the quiet aftermath of their shared release.

They lay there, still entwined, their bodies slick with sweat, their hearts pounding in unison as they came down from the high together. Ivan's strong arm remained wrapped around Katya, holding her close in a way that felt different—more intimate than ever before. There was no urgency in their movements now, no need to rush or separate. For the first time, it truly felt like they weren't just together physically but emotionally bound in a way neither of them had fully realized until this moment.

The room was filled with the sound of their ragged breathing as they slowly calmed from the intensity of their lovemaking. Katya rested her head against Ivan's chest, listening to the rhythmic thud of his heartbeat beneath her ear. His hand gently caressed her back, soothing her in slow, deliberate strokes. She closed her eyes, feeling an overwhelming sense of peace despite everything they had been through—the danger, the fear, the violence. Somehow, in Ivan's arms, she felt safe.

Ivan was the first to break the silence, his voice soft, almost vulnerable in a way she had never heard before. "I didn't think I could feel this way," he began, his hand brushing through her hair with surprising tenderness. "Not after everything I've been through, everything I've lost… But you..." His voice trailed off for a moment, as if he was struggling to find the right words. "I love you, Katya. You're mine, now and always."

The words hung in the air between them, and for a moment, Katya's breath caught in her throat. She had longed to hear them, but now that he had said them, they hit her with a force she hadn't anticipated. Ivan, the man who had built walls around his heart, who thrived in a world of control and dominance, had just confessed his love to her.

Her heart swelled with emotion as his words settled into her, filling her with a warmth she hadn't known she could feel. "I'm not going anywhere," she whispered, her hand resting gently on his chest, feeling the steady beat of his heart beneath her palm. "I love you too, Ivan. I'm yours—mind, body, and soul."

It was the first time she had said the words out loud, and as they passed her lips, they felt right—more right than anything she had ever said. She wasn't afraid of his world anymore. She had faced its darkest corners and come out stronger. This was her life now, and she had chosen it, chosen him. There was no turning back.

Ivan's grip around her tightened slightly, pulling her even closer to him. The vulnerability in his eyes was gone, replaced by something deeper, something more permanent. He pressed a soft kiss to her forehead, his lips lingering there as if he never wanted to let her go. "You're mine," he whispered again, but this time, there was no possessiveness behind it. Just love.

Katya smiled against his chest, feeling the weight of everything they had been through together settle around them like a blanket. But this time, there was no fear, no uncertainty. Only love, and the quiet understanding that whatever came next, they would face it together.

In that quiet, intimate moment, Katya knew that she had found something rare—something worth fighting for. Ivan had risked everything for her, and she would do the same for him. The danger, the violence, the constant uncertainty—they didn't matter anymore. What mattered was the love they had found in each other.

As they lay there, tangled in each other's arms, Katya felt the final piece of her resistance fall away. She wasn't just part of Ivan's world now—she was part of him. And as long as they had each other, she knew they could survive anything.

Chapter 26

The sun filtered through the trees, casting a golden glow over the park as Katya walked alongside Ivan and the children. Her hand rested on her belly, a soft, protective gesture that had become second nature over the past few months. The gentle curve of her pregnancy was now visible beneath her dress, a quiet yet undeniable sign of the new life growing inside her. A wedding ring glinted on her finger, catching the sunlight as they strolled, the intricate diamond band symbolizing the life they had built together, the family they had become.

Kirill and Dasha ran ahead, their laughter echoing through the air as they chased one another through the grass. Their innocence and joy filled Katya's heart with a warmth she hadn't known she could feel. Six months had passed since the chaos of the kidnapping, since the violence and fear that had almost ripped everything apart. But now, as she looked around at her family, she felt a sense of peace settling over her—a calm that felt foreign, yet welcome.

Ivan walked beside her, his hand resting on the small of her back, a protective yet intimate gesture that had become a constant in their relationship. There was a softness in him now, a subtle shift in his demeanor that she had noticed ever since they had returned from the nightmare they had survived. Though the tension of his world still lingered, Ivan had become more present, more involved, especially with the children. Watching him now, so attentive, so focused on his family, made Katya realize how far they had come.

She had fully integrated into their lives, seamlessly stepping into the role of a mother figure for Kirill and Dasha. The bond she shared with them had deepened, a closeness that had formed not out of necessity, but out of love. In the beginning, there had been a distance between them, a natural hesitation from the children as they adjusted to her presence. But now, after all they had been through, that distance had melted away, replaced by something much stronger—trust, affection, and an unspoken understanding that they were a family.

Katya glanced down at the wedding ring on her finger, her heart swelling with the memory of the day Ivan had placed it there. It hadn't been a grand ceremony, but it had been perfect in its simplicity. Just the two of them, a small gathering of people they trusted, and a promise that they would face the future together—no matter what dangers lay ahead. She had never imagined her life would lead here, but now, standing beside Ivan with their child growing inside her, she couldn't imagine it any other way.

The wind stirred gently around them, and Katya's thoughts drifted to the ever-present reality of the Bratva world that still shadowed their lives. The danger hadn't disappeared, and she knew it never would. Ivan's world was violent, unpredictable, and filled with threats that could come at any moment. But despite that, Katya felt safe. Not because the threats were gone, but because she trusted Ivan completely. He had proven time and again that he would do whatever it took to protect her, the children, and the life they were building. That trust had become the foundation of everything they had now, solid and unwavering.

Still, the memory of the kidnapping lingered. It was a shadow that followed them, even in moments like this, when the world seemed peaceful. Katya could see it in the children sometimes, in the way they flinched at loud noises or clung to her just a little tighter in crowded places. Kirill, especially, had become more cautious, his once carefree nature tempered by the fear he had experienced that day. Dasha, too, had her moments, where she would wake from a nightmare, her small body trembling as Katya or Ivan comforted her back to sleep.

But they were healing. Slowly, but surely, the children were finding their way back to the innocence they had lost. The bodyguards, a constant presence now during their outings, had become just another part of their lives. The children were used to them—burly men in dark suits who always kept a watchful eye, ready to step in at a moment's notice. At first, the sight of them had made Katya uneasy, a constant reminder of the danger they faced. But now, she had come to accept them as part of their life. A necessary precaution in a world that would never be fully safe.

Katya caught Ivan's eye as they walked, and a soft smile passed between them. There was an unspoken connection in that glance, a shared understanding that despite everything, they had made it. They had built something real—something lasting. The love they had for each other was no longer wrapped in secrecy or fear. It was out in the open, strong and all consuming.

The transformation in Ivan was undeniable. As the months had passed since the attack on their family, Katya had watched him change in ways she never thought possible. Ivan had always been strong, distant, and often cold when it came to his emotions, especially with the children. He loved them, that much was clear, but he had struggled to show it in the ways they needed. Now, though, he was different. There was warmth in him that hadn't been there before, a softer side that he let them see, and it filled Katya with a sense of pride.

She knew that her presence, her love, had played a part in breaking down the emotional walls Ivan had built around himself for so long. Katya would often find herself smiling when she caught glimpses of him with Kirill, helping him with his schoolwork at the dining room table. Ivan would lean over, his brow furrowed in concentration as he explained a math problem, his large hands dwarfed by the pencil he held delicately. Kirill's eyes would light up when he finally understood, and Ivan would give him a small, approving nod. It was a quiet moment, but in those moments, Katya saw the man beneath the Bratva leader—the father who wanted to be there for his children in every way he could.

Dasha, too, had grown closer to Ivan. The little girl adored him, always seeking his attention and approval. Katya would watch from the doorway as Ivan tucked Dasha in at night, his large hand brushing gently over her hair as she snuggled into her blankets. He would speak to her softly in Russian, telling her stories from his childhood, and Dasha's eyes would flutter closed as his deep, soothing voice lulled her to sleep. It was a side of Ivan that only his family ever saw, and Katya felt honored to be part of that inner circle, to witness the love he was finally allowing himself to show.

But while their home had become a sanctuary of sorts, a place of peace and love, the world outside it was still as dangerous as ever. Ivan was at war with the Morozov Bratva, the men who had dared to attack his family, and his retaliation had been swift and brutal. Katya knew that Ivan would never change that part of himself. He was a leader in the Bratva, a man who commanded respect through fear and power. The violence that came with his life was something she had learned to accept, even if it still scared her at times.

The war between Ivan and the Morozov Bratva had escalated in the months following the kidnapping. Ivan had been relentless, crushing their operations and leaving a trail of destruction in his wake. He didn't just want revenge—he wanted to annihilate anyone who had been involved in the attack on his family. Katya had seen the intensity in his eyes when he spoke of the Morozovs, the fury that simmered beneath his calm exterior. He was a man who would do anything to protect what was his, and that included her and the children.

Katya had accepted that part of Ivan a long time ago. She understood that his world was one of violence and power, and while it frightened her, it also made her feel safe in a way she had never known before. She knew that no matter what happened, Ivan would protect them. He had proven it time and again, and now, as his war with the Morozovs raged on, she trusted him completely.

But more than just trusting Ivan, Katya had found her own place in this world. She was no longer just an outsider looking in, no longer the woman repaying her father's debt. She had become part of the Bratva family in a way she hadn't expected. The other men respected her, not just because of her relationship with Ivan, but because they saw the strength she had shown during the kidnapping. She had killed a man to protect Ivan's children, and that act had cemented her place in their world. Katya wasn't afraid anymore. She had faced the worst, and she had survived.

Her life with Ivan was different now—darker in some ways, but also more fulfilling than anything she had ever known. She felt stronger, more confident, more in control of her own destiny. The fear that had once gripped her when she thought about Ivan's world had faded, replaced by a fierce determination to stand by his side no matter what. She wasn't a victim of circumstance anymore. She was a partner, someone who understood the stakes and was willing to face them head-on.

Ivan had changed, yes, but so had she. And together, they were building something powerful—something that couldn't be broken, no matter what the outside world threw at them.

As she walked beside him, her hand resting in his, Katya knew that their journey was far from over. The dangers of Ivan's world would always be there, lurking in the shadows, but for the first time in her life, she felt ready to face them. She wasn't alone anymore. She had Ivan, and together, they would face whatever came next.

Katya glanced at Ivan, his strong profile set against the soft afternoon light, and felt a surge of love so strong it almost overwhelmed her. This was her family, her life. And despite the violence, despite the challenges, she wouldn't trade it for anything in the world.

As they reached a bench near the edge of the park, Ivan motioned for the children to come over. Kirill and Dasha came running back, their faces flushed with excitement from playing. Ivan picked up Dasha, holding her in his arms, while Kirill stood beside Katya, leaning into her as she rested a hand on his shoulder. They were a family now. Not perfect, not without challenges, but a family nonetheless.

Katya's hand moved instinctively to her belly again, feeling the slight flutter of movement from the baby growing inside her. A new life. A new beginning. And with Ivan by her side, she knew they could face anything. The world might still be dangerous, but together, they were strong.

This was her life now—a life she had once feared, but now embraced with everything she had. Ivan, the children, their unborn child—this was her family. And she would protect them with the same fierce love and loyalty that Ivan had shown her. They had come so far, and as she looked at the people she loved most in the world, she knew there was no turning back.

They were together, and that was all that mattered.

I hope you enjoyed
Indebted to the Bratva.
Scan the QR code below
and share your love with a
review!

Look For The New Book In

The Volkov Bratva Series

Coming Soon!

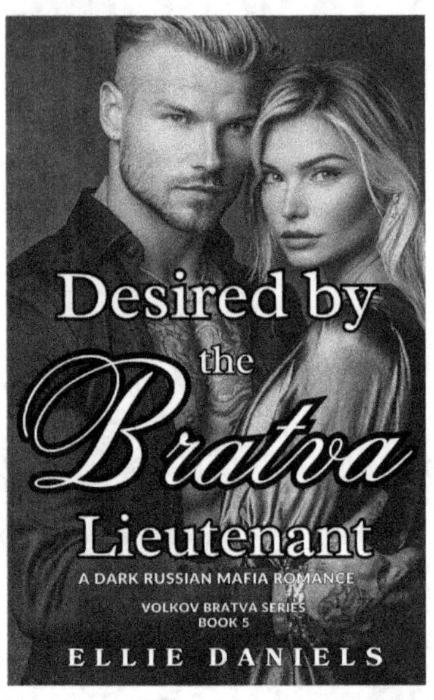

When a brilliant young lawyer is assigned to the Volkov family, she finds herself caught in a deadly game of power and desire. Eriks, the dangerous and irresistible Bratva lieutenant, won't take no for an answer—and the more she resists, the more obsessed he becomes. In a world where danger lurks in every shadow, can she fight the temptation, or will she surrender to the dark allure of the Bratva?

About the Author

Ellie Daniels is a Colorado author who ignites passion and desire through her captivating erotic romance novels and sizzling short stories. When she's not crafting worlds of desire and intimacy, Ellie enjoys quiet moments at home with her loving husband, their devoted chihuahua, and four playful cats. A sensualist at heart, she believes in the transformative power of passion and connection. Cherishing close relationships, Ellie finds inspiration in the complexities of love.

www.ingramcontent.com/pod-product-compliance
Lightning Source LLC
Chambersburg PA
CBHW060857140726
47996CB00001B/13